THE SINGING FIRE

A NOVEL

Lilian Nattel

SCRIBNER

NEW YORK   LONDON   TORONTO   SYDNEY

SCRIBNER
1230 Avenue of the Americas
New York, NY 10020

SCRIBNER and design are trademarks of Macmillan Library Reference USA, Inc., used under license by Simon & Schuster, the publisher of this work.

For information about special discounts for bulk purchases,
please contact Simon & Schuster Special Sales:
1-800-456-6798 or business@simonandschuster.com

Designed by Colin Joh
Text set in Adobe Garamond

Manufactured in the United States of America

1   3   5   7   9   10   8   6   4   2

Library of Congress Cataloging-in-Publication Data
Nattel, Lilian [date]
The singing fire : a novel / Lilian Nattel.
p.   cm.
PS3564.A8734S56   2004
813'.54—dc22   2003057344

ISBN 0-7432-4966-6   OCLC 52559223

For my husband, Allan, whose actions speak of love, whose presence brings in light, whose observations show that there is always a new way to look at things

For love is as strong as death . . . ; its flashes are flashes of fire, the very flame of God. A flood of water cannot quench love, nor rivers overflow it . . .

—The Song of Songs 8:6–7

THE
SINGING
FIRE

PROLOGUE

Longing

1886

They met in a place of smoky bricks and smoky fogs and a million pigeons nesting by a million chimneys. Sea winds blew the fog from the docks to the depot, from the railroad tracks to the high road, from there to the lane, working into all the hidden alleys as narrow as needles. In the mud of the alley, cobblestones separated so donkeys and barrows could enter, brick walls leaned back to make room for stalls, and up high hung clothes that trembled in the air. Everything born and everything made found its way over the river to London. And here they met, the two mothers, the one we remember and the one we forget. The river brought them, the docks received them, the streets took them in.

It was in Whitechapel with the wind sweeping up the high road past the hospital and the convent and the bell foundry tolling bells. Carts and carriages jammed the wide road, steam came from cookshops and drizzle from the heavens. In the wind, street matrons held on to their hats, for every woman wore one, even if it was just a battered sailor hat, and she used her nails to fight instead of hatpins. It was time to retrieve the Sunday boots from the pawnshop, for wage packets were in hand, and shopkeepers stood in doorways shouting their wares above the sound of wheels and wind and the rattle of trains, their windows bright in the gray-green rain. The wind raged past new warehouses six stories high, holding all the goods of the Empire for the West End, it swept past the Jerusalem Music Palace with its twenty-seven thousand crystals in the gaslit chandelier, past the gin palace of daz-zling color, past the club, the assembly room, the shooting gallery, past all the old houses, built after the Great Fire, now crumbling from stone and brick into the ash of the street. The wind saw the nuns and the Sal-vation Army Band, with its brass instruments and its bold uniforms, and everywhere the placards and posters in Yiddish: "Milk fresh from the cow!" "Cheapest and best funerals!" "New melodrama starring the Great Eagle, Jacob Adler!"

This was the high road of the ghetto, the one square mile where Yiddish was spoken, the irritating pimple on the backside of London, the subject of parliamentary debate, the hundred thousand newcomers among the millions, ready to take fog as their mother's milk here in the East End, where all the noisy, dirty, and stinking industries were exiled from the city.

The Jewish streets stretched up from Whitechapel Road, pushing into the twisting alleys, pushing back the pimps and the prostitutes and the thieves whose stronghold was just above in Dorset Street. Smack in the middle was the Jews' Free School, to the right was the steam bath, to the left the rag market. The dairyman from Ilford was carting his milk cans full of vodka to sell. If you liked to gamble, down below was Shmolnik's coffee house, and if you were hungry, you could have the best fish and chips, invented up here by a Dutch Jew in the Lane.

It was Saturday night in the Lane, meaning Petticoat Lane and all its contiguous streets. Among the tailors, the corset sellers, the letter writers, the cigar and boot makers, naphtha lamps flared in the dark-ness. People spoke Yiddish, they spoke English, they spoke in the lan-guage of the street, where their lives took place. "Hi! Hi! See the strong man! See the singing dwarf! See the contortionist! Only a penny!" In the dusk there were crowds of buyers and sellers, and between the stalls, one man juggled fire and another swallowed it. The fortune-teller's bird picked out cards with its beak and every card told a fortune. Signs advertised marvels. Oilcloth guaranteed to last twenty years. Magic firelight that a little child could use. Medicine sure to cure the ills of all five million cells in the human body. Here you could buy used goods of every kind except for one thing. Even in the rain there was a queue for it, people eating supper and talking and waiting. And what did they want that they couldn't get secondhand? A ticket to the Yiddish theater of course.

No one in the world loved theater more than Londoners, and among them none more than the Jews. When they came to the free land, the old made a match with the new, and a butcher from home who changed his name to Smith built the Yiddish theater. And what a theater! It had a parterre and a balcony, curtains with pulleys, chandeliers, trapdoors in the stage for every sort of magical effect discussed by the people waiting in the rain to buy balcony tickets. The great Jacob Adler was playing the lead tonight, and even the beigel seller, whose husband gambled her meager earnings, had found the pennies for tickets to the theater.

There were other important people waiting in the queue, a bootmaker who wrote poems, a presser who wrote bad plays, a tailor who told bad jokes, and his wife, who was pregnant and dreaming of the baby. All around them was tobacco smoke and the talk of the street, of work and no work, the horse that won, the husband that ran away, the children's boots given out by the school. Someone spat and someone hissed while ticket holders for the good seats went inside, among them an old man and his grandson, a journalist who had no idea that his future wife was on her way from Minsk. For in the Court of Heaven, there is a golden throne and a golden desk where God puts strange matters into a golden book. And so it was written: the young woman from Minsk and the tailor's wife. Only King Solomon the Wise could judge between them.

It was all very well for the Holy One above to make such plans in heaven. But earth is for people, and the mother of a people has to go with them. She can't be left behind with nothing but her shroud crumbling into dust. And so she rose from the graveyard—maybe it was in Minsk or Pinsk or Plotsk—and came with the boats to Irongate Stairs. And though her grandchildren would speak a different mother tongue and have customs unknowable to her, they would also rise from the graveyard for the sake of their children, so that they would not be abandoned in their exile. The human heart, knowing it will die alone, needs to belong to others so it can live; those others who are somehow like us—and in being like us raise us out of the uncountable billions that rise and fall, rise and fall, unremarkable as ants, as cells, as the hands clapping when the curtain rises, torchlights burning at the foot of the stage.

ACT I

Here I take from your hand the deep bowl of staggering, the cup of my anger; you shall not drink it again. I will put it in the hands of the tormentors who commanded your soul, "Get down, that we may walk over you" so that you made your back like the ground, like a street for passersby.

—Isaiah 51:22–23

CHAPTER 1

The Sea Sounds Closer

LONDON, 1875

St. Katharine's Dock

The girl was sitting on the step of a shop that sold parrots, their English accent better than hers. She had her bag by her feet on the wet ground, her hands folded in her lap while the Tower of London rose gray and crumbly above dockhands moving cargo. Around them milled men in aprons and caps, owners in silk hats, horses pulling carts, cats eating rats, and snarling dogs fighting over treacle leaked from a burst cask. The girl was seventeen years old and alone, so she prayed to God, Help me please, because that is what a person does when there is no one else.

To her surprise, someone answered.

"Hello there!" A portly man pushed aside the Chinese sailor who was leaving the shop with a bird in a cage. It took a moment for her to realize that she understood him. "Can I help you?" the man asked in Yiddish. He wore a bowler and a sack coat like the foremen on the dock.

"I'm just not sure which way to go. It's so foggy," she said as she stood up.

"Anyone can see that you're a newcomer, so how could you know? That's why I'm here. I'm from the Newcomers' Assistance Committee. My name is Mr. Blink. It used to be Blinick. Do you have any family waiting for you? A friend?"

"I came by myself." She tried to sound as self-possessed as her oldest sister. There were five older sisters in Poland, all of them either intelligent or married and some of them both.

"Well—don't worry," Mr. Blink said. "I'll take care of everything. What's your name, my girl, and where are you from?"

"Plotsk. I'm Nehama Korzen."

"Such a coincidence!" He beamed. What a friendly face he had. It was all pouches, smaller ones under his eyes and bigger ones under his cheeks and an extra chin that told her this was a man who ate meat every day, as much as he liked. "I'm a Plotsker, myself. I don't know any Korzens. Too bad. But a *landsmann* is as good as relations, right? You just come with me. First thing we'll go to the city office to pay the entrance fee."

"I didn't know about any fee. How much is it?" she asked, putting her hand over her waist, where she'd sewn a hidden pocket with all the money she had. It had seemed like so much at home. But what was a ruble worth in London?

Mr. Blink stopped abruptly. "You mean no one told you? My dear child, this is terrible. How could they send you off like that—completely unprepared?"

"Nobody sent me. It was my own idea."

"And you didn't know. What a shame. A real pity."

"A Jew doesn't give up a *landsmann* to the authorities, does he? Please, don't do that," she said.

"You see that man standing there?" Mr. Blink pointed at someone holding a torch as he led his horse through the fog. "A policeman. But if you're with me, he won't pay any attention to you."

"What will I do? I can't go home."

"Maybe I can do something." He put his hand on her elbow. "I might be able to draw on the committee's loan fund."

"Oh, would you?" A black snow was falling on her. It smelled of burnt tobacco. She covered her nose with her hand.

"A promise I can't give, but I'll do my best," he said.

"I'd be so grateful. And a job?"

"There's always something."

"I'm a hard worker." She could picture the tickets to London in her mother's hand. She'd send for all of them, mother and father, her five sisters with their families. They wouldn't think that she was so stupid anymore.

"But first you come home with me," Mr. Blink said. "You have a good meal and a good sleep and things will look better. Tomorrow, I'll make the proper inquiries."

In the beginning, she hadn't thought to run away. She was working with her father, sewing in the sleeves of a satin gown. He was a custom tailor, and she was the last of his daughters to work in his shop. She was singing and sewing and daydreaming about her future, which would include a house of her own and, even more important, some heroic act that would surprise everyone. She cut the thread. "Father," she said.

"Mmm?" He worked carefully, his glasses low on his nose, a religious man in a worn caftan who was bothered by the impieties of younger men but would say nothing, showing disapproval just in his glance and the dismissal of a waving hand.

"I hear that in London a Jew can stand for Parliament," she said. "Isn't that something?" He agreed that it was something. "It's the free land. Nobody has to do anything he doesn't want."

"But in Poland a Jew can own his grave," Father said. "You want something more?" Nehama laughed but Father didn't as he added, "Your home is your home. Nothing else is the same."

The back door was open to the courtyard surrounded by small houses that were old and run-down. In them lived Nehama's married sisters. She was always surrounded by sisters. She couldn't open her mouth to sneeze without one of them saying, Bless you. Where's your handkerchief? Why aren't you wearing woolens? Where's your head? The other sisters were all fair, like Father. Only she and Mama were dark. She'd been named for her grandmother because she was born just after Grandma Nehama died. Nehama means "consolation," but her mother had been inconsolable. She was depressed for a year, ignoring all her fair-haired children, who pinched and slapped the baby when no one was looking. It was their duty to curb the *yetzer-hara,* the evil inclination, because she was the youngest and Mother let her get away with murder. They should have pinched harder. Nehama still had a strong *yetzer-hara.*

"If I was young, I'd go to London in a minute," Mama said. The shop was small, the back door propped open with a stone. In the courtyard the sisters' laundry hung like angels in the smoke from the nearby feather factory.

"Then you'd let me go?" Nehama asked.

"Who's talking about going? I only meant in theory," Mama said. Her hair was still dark, her hands scrubbed raw after baking so she wouldn't stain the fine cloth when she came to sew.

"But in theory a boat ticket costs less than a dowry," Nehama said.

"Don't be silly. Sending away a child, that's for desperate people." Mama shook her head. While she sewed she sighed, as if it was hard to breathe in the smoky air that blew in from the feather factory.

"But I'd send for you. I'd send for everybody!"

"You and who else?" Hinda called from the other room. She was the prettiest of the sisters. "You'd better keep the price of the ticket for your dowry. You'll need it because no one's marrying you for your beauty."

"So who needs beauty if you know business?" Rivka said. She was the oldest sister and had a business importing cotton. "I can't keep the store closed more than an hour to take inventory. What are you waiting for, Nehama?"

"Go, go. I'll finish here," Mama said.

Nehama crossed the courtyard with her oldest sister to the small house where the store took up the front room. Rivka planned to have a real shop soon, with two stories and heavy shutters that locked out thieves and rioters.

"Do you think I'm ugly?" Nehama asked, seating herself at the table to write up the accounts.

"Ugly? I wouldn't say that. Your hair is too curly, but it matters more that it's dark." Rivka lifted a bale of fabric onto the counter, unrolling it and checking for holes. She wore a kerchief over her hair but wasn't too pious not to let a few golden strands fall across her forehead. "Too bad you don't have our coloring. I mean mine and Father's. Jewish boys go crazy for fair hair. But your eyes are nice. Very blue. And you wouldn't be so dark if you ate eggs."

"I hate eggs." Nehama erased a sum with a rubber. She added every column twice, and each time it came to something different.

"You hate everything good for you."

"Not everything. I'd like a shop. I could run it."

"There's no money for you to have a shop. You have to be practical about what you can do."

Nehama kept a list of things she might do. Page one: businesses. Importing cotton, wheat, eggs, oranges. Selling corsets, rope, kerosene, wooden barrels. Page two: occupations. There wouldn't be so many for a woman, but never mind. She wrote them in large letters to fill up the page, all her pent-up energy making the penciled letters as dark as black ink. "Why doesn't anyone listen to me? I could be a teacher like Leah and Shayna-Pearl."

"You want to talk ugly? Leah's scarred from the smallpox. It's a mercy from God she became a teacher. And Shayna-Pearl is so bad-tempered no one could stand her for a week. Thank God that there was enough money for them to go to school. But now, unfortunately— well, when it's the youngest's turn there just isn't much left. You never liked to face reality, but there comes a time when you have no choice."

"You could send me to school, Rivka." It wasn't fair. Nehama added up the accounts herself. She knew what was going in and going out.

"And don't I have my own children to consider? Someone has to tell you how the world works, and I can see it's up to me. Make your-self into an attractive girl, Nehama, and your dowry will stretch fur-ther. I mean attractive in temper, not just in looks. You should eat eggs because they're good for you and never mind if you like them. That's what makes a nice girl."

"Fine. If I can't do anything I want here, then I'll go somewhere else." Along the river she'd seen the large boats that carried everything a person might dream about. She could be on such a boat, the force of her desires driving the steam engine. A life that she made herself, one that was worth remembering at the end of it. "Maybe I'll go to Lon-don. Girls don't need dowries there."

"I never heard anything so stupid. You don't know what you want."

"How am I supposed to know? Every time I take a step, I have a sis-ter telling me when to lift my foot and when to put it down."

"Thank God, or who knows where you'd end up. Just because Mama makes you a dress in the latest fashion, you think you're a special salami. Let me tell you, Nehama, someday you have to find out that you're just plain beans and you give everyone gas." Rivka slapped a roll of cotton onto the counter. "You see this? It would make a serviceable dress for everyday. The dirt won't show on it. If you want I'll give it to you at cost, Nehameleh, and you can save a couple of yards if you make it up yourself without any fancy-shmancy business. A mother that sees you in this will realize that you know what's what and she'll think of giving her son to you."

"I don't like it," Nehama said. "It looks like an old woman's."

"All right. Insult me. That's what I should expect. Just remember when you end up depending on handouts for a piece of bread that if you weren't so stubborn, it could have been avoided."

Rivka went back to her bales of fabric in a huff, and Nehama added up the columns of numbers once again, hoping that with God's help the sums would stay the same.

On *Shobbos* they all sat together in the women's gallery of the synagogue, Nehama, her mother, and all her sisters. It was a modern synagogue with an open balcony, where the women could look straight down at the Holy Torah as it was paraded in its crown of silver and its gown of velvet. Her next older sister, Bronya, was breathing noisily. Seven months pregnant and still she did business every market day, charging a few pennies to weigh goods on the scale she brought to the market square in a wheelbarrow. Her husband was a carpenter, not a bad trade, but he stank of onions. How could Bronya stand him? "Your turn next, Nehama," she said.

"Not me. I'm helping Father. He can't afford to marry me off."

"I hear the matchmaker's been sniffing around." Hinda shifted her baby from one breast to the other. "I ought to give her some tips about you."

"There's a fine young man on the next street to ours," Bronya said. "You can smell him coming. Aah—dead animal skins. But a tanner can still be very pious. And just think how you can help him by collecting cow shit for tanning."

"Such language! Don't tease your sister," Mama said. "You know how sensitive she is to odors."

Down below among the men, the Holy Torah, which has no odor, was unrolled all the way to the beginning. The reader chanted: "And the earth was chaos and void. On the face of the deep, in the darkness, there was a great wind from God sweeping over the face of the waters . . ."

She'd show them all. The time for thinking was over.

Nehama secretly bought the ticket the day that one of her sisters pointed out the tanner and another told her to keep her ideas to herself when the matchmaker came. She didn't consider everything she was leaving until she stood on the boat, looking back at the docks, where no one waved good-bye. The spray from the river and the rain from the heavens splashed her face, diluting her tears the way London merchants diluted milk with water and mixed flour with sawdust. And in the blink of an eye, the Vistula River, queen of Poland, flowing between green banks of willow trees, became the Thames, empress of the world, slapping the base of the Tower of London, where queens were beheaded. On the gray waters of a nation that disdained spices and ate boiled beef, steaming ships came in with the west wind, carrying perfume and elephant tusks and Sardinian sailors with great gold earrings.

Thrawl Street

So this was an English house. There was an iron stove instead of a tile oven, a painting of dogs in red jackets playing cards, and a large menorah with nine silver cups for oil. The menorah was on the top shelf of an open wooden cabinet, beside it a set of leather volumes in Hebrew. Nehama couldn't read the titles, but she could write her initials in the dust.

Mr. Blink worked very hard. All through his meal, men came to call, and for their sake he interrupted his dinner, inspecting goods and making payment from his cashbox. Nehama was uneasy though there wasn't any reason. After all, what kind of shopkeeper back home didn't deal with gentiles? They brought all sorts of small things: silk handkerchiefs, a gold chain, a silver spoon, a pocket watch, ivory buttons. One of the visitors smelled of the river, and one of them smelled of the sewers, and the one that smelled of freshly turned earth brought a wedding ring set with red stones. Nehama wiped the gravy from her plate with a piece of soft bread. It didn't occur to her that it might not be kosher.

She spent the night on a cot in the kitchen. When she woke up the next morning, Mr. Blink's housekeeper gave her some breakfast, sweating heavily as she put the bowl of porridge on the table, and Nehama surreptitiously covered her nose with her hand. The housekeeper sniffed and muttered, pointing to the floor, but if she expected Nehama to wash it, then she was much mistaken. In truth, God alone knew what she was saying, and it was a relief when she went out.

For a while, Nehama sat at the table, too excited to eat. People said that she had her grandmother's eyes, and hadn't she come by boat from someplace small to a bigger world just like her grandmother, who grew up in a small village? It was a shock, Grandma Nehama's first view of the town with the cathedral rising high on the hill. She was young and coming to marry a man with a baby because her family couldn't afford anything better than to make her a second wife. Standing on the boat and smelling the docks of Plotsk, she almost changed her mind, but what could she go back to? So she married the man. His daughter was a skinny baby that was fading away, and of all her children this one was her favorite because she had brought it back to life. When the daughter grew up and had five girls, it was Grandma Nehama who took care of them. It's easier to fall in love with a skinny baby than with a hairy man, she always said.

Nehama stood at the window, wiping away the dust with her sleeve so that she could look out on a street of old and crumbling houses not very different from the *heim*. It wasn't so frightening. As soon as she got her entrance papers, she could go down and walk in the street like a free person who has no sisters. She wasn't sure what she'd do next, but it would be something marvelous and she'd send for her family. Then she, the youngest sister, would be first.

If she was really listening, she might have heard a grandmother's voice telling her: *You want to know about London? If only you'd listen to me,* shaynela. *I know what's what. Believe you me. In Plotsk you had seven thousand gentiles. Here there are five million. You think Plotsk is an ancient town. After all, kings are buried in its cathedral. But that's nothing. Whitechapel Road was a Roman highway. You think in Plotsk people are poor? Then open your eyes. When these people don't have work, potatoes and onions are a luxury to think on while they boil a crust of bread with salt. Thieves stole the lead from these old roofs, and the water pours through. You want water? You should have it in a lucky hour. Here the water company turns on the tap for just ten minutes a day, please God. And if you just walk a little further on, you'll come to the bank where the money of the world pours without end and everyone in this street is holding out his hands, hoping to catch some. If he has to knock a person over the head to get his, that's good too. Be careful,* shaynela.

Barrows clattered in the street as she ran down the stairs to Mr. Blink's pawnshop. He was presiding over his shelves, taking a pair of Sunday boots from a tired wife and giving her some coins in exchange. Waiting by the counter was a man wearing a uniform. He had a thick mustache and a dark mole on the bridge of his nose, and though he was too scrawny to be impressive, it was never a good thing to be in the vicinity of an official. Mr. Blink would deal with him. Perhaps he already had. She didn't think otherwise, for there'd always been someone to take care of things at home in the courtyard surrounded by small houses.

"Good morning, Mr. Blink," she said. "Have you arranged for my papers already?"

He turned toward her, his face covered with stubble like a hedgehog's skin, and there was no friendliness in his eyes today. "Are you crazy? Didn't my housekeeper tell you to stay upstairs, out of the way?"

"I'm sorry," she stuttered. "I didn't understand her. I thought she wanted me to wash the floor."

"Well, you've made a mess of things, that I can tell you. This man here is a police officer."

"Perhaps I can give him something and he'll forget it," Nehama said, trying not to cry. "Is there a place I can exchange my money?"

"It's too late for that," Mr. Blink said. "You'll have to go with him, and I'll do my best for you from this side."

"Don't let him take me."

Mr. Blink was shaking his head sadly. She should have tried harder to understand the housekeeper. Her sisters were right. She never listened.

"I told you that I'll do what I can. I'm sorry, my dear. Very sorry." He stood with his arms crossed, eyes filled with disappointment as the policeman grabbed her by the arm and dragged her out to the police wagon.

Whitechapel Road

They rode through the great street where carcasses swung huge and bloody, music came from every other door, and steam hung out of cookshops above the carts and carriages and hansom cabs. Business was several layers thick: stores with their glass fronts reflected passersby, on the pavement stalls were heaped high, costermongers stopped with their barrows while men called customers to see the wares inside. The high road smelled of the meat market at one end and the hay market at the other, and Nehama couldn't hear her own thoughts for the sound of tolling bells and a marching band. It was just as well, as all her thoughts were grim.

"Mr. Blink will fix everything," she said helplessly. No one could understand her. No one but Mr. Blink, who spoke Yiddish like a brother.

"You sound like all them other girls of his," the policeman replied in his garbled language. "Foreigners every one. But it's no concern of mine. I get my quid from him regular to bring you in. Right, here you go." He was leading her toward a building that seemed too important for a newcomer's papers. It was huge and rotund, surrounded by gardens of rhododendron bushes, standing over the street of old gabled houses like a sultan on an elephant. Nehama recognized the word "London" on the archway. The second word, "Hospital," must mean something like City Authority. Beside the hospital was a mountain of rubbish, and on the stinking mountain women were digging for whatever they might find to sell.

Nehama went through the doors. What else could she do with the policeman gripping her arm? The entrance was so clean it made her nostrils hurt. Women hooded in white like the sultan's harem glided here and there. What did they do in the eternal light of gas jets, these women with their knowing looks? One of them led her to an office, where she was motioned to sit in a cane chair. Behind the shining desk an official took notes. His jacket was well fitted; a gentleman, then. Standing beside the desk was a young man whose coat fit even better, and on the wall behind him was the portrait of a short, fat woman in a crown.

"Now you might see what I've been telling you," the older man said. "This is how we stop venereal infection from spreading. Lectures are not the same as a firsthand look." He wore spectacles while he wrote, removing them to study Nehama. He looked tired, as officials often do. "Constable?"

"I caught her soliciting, sir."

"Mr. Blink," Nehama said, nodding firmly to let them know that she had a connection in London, who would straighten everything out as soon as he could.

"It were a captain of the navy she approached," the policeman said. "She seen me and run."

"Thank you, Constable." The official turned to the young man. "The Contagious Diseases Act allows the police to pick up anyone they might have reason to suspect of prostitution. We'll have the examination next. If the patient shows symptoms we'll keep her here for treatment."

"And if not?"

"She's released, of course. Though heaven knows we may see her here again before long."

The official rose from his chair and came around to Nehama, moving her head to the left and right, lifting her chin as he examined her. Did she look innocent enough? "Nurse, please," he said, opening the door.

At his call for someone, Nehama nearly fainted, thinking that it was a guard coming to take her to prison. But it was only one of the women in white robes, who took her by the arm as they walked along a corridor with many doors, following behind the official with his tired, reedy voice and the gentleman who walked bowlegged, as if he'd rather be on a horse.

"I expect to join my father in his practice after my training's complete," the young man said. "I don't believe he sees many of this sort in Harley Street."

"Quite so. I've been bitten by more than one. A few less hysterical ladies for me to examine would be welcome." The older man sighed. "I'd be relieved if the Contagious Diseases Act was amended. There's been some discussion of applying it only to women meeting sailors at the docks and those in towns where soldiers are billeted."

"If I may differ, sir. All men have appetites, and good men are diseased. Even my father sees them, and with all due respect, any girl on these streets is likely to offer her favors for her supper. That is casual prostitution, and she won't seek treatment on her own, I assure you."

"Quite so. I can't argue with that. In here."

He opened the door, and Nehama was more confused than ever. This wasn't any prison cell. There was a cabinet in the room. A table with straps. A trolley with instruments.

"Up you go," the nurse said as she turned up the lamp hanging above the table.

Nehama looked at the oak cabinet, with its vials and jars and mortar and pestle for grinding powders. This official now checking her ears and pulling on her jaw with his hand that smelled of spirits, was he a doctor? She wasn't ill, but that was all to the good. They would write a certificate of health and Mr. Blink could bring it to the officials. Then she would get her entrance papers. Perhaps there would even be a discount and she would be able to repay Mr. Blink very soon.

"One ought to be careful of foreigners, if I may say so, sir," the white lady said.

"I'm not sick," Nehama said in Yiddish. "You see that, don't you?"

"Throat's clear," the older doctor answered, pushing Nehama back as if she were to lie down. "Open the dress, Nurse."

Nehama shook her head as the white lady touched her buttons. What kind of girl did they think she was? Looking in her mouth was one thing, this quite another. The lady pushed her hands aside, and Nehama jumped off the table. Enough was enough. "I'm telling you. I'm fine. Show me where to wait for Mr. Blink." The policeman knew Mr. Blink. He could send a message. Nehama made a writing motion with her hands.

"You see what I mean, sir? Turn on you in an instant, they can." The lady took hold of Nehama's shoulders.

The official doctor grabbed Nehama firmly by the arm. She tried to shake him off. "Please, sir. Send a message with the policeman."

They were lifting her back onto the table under the light as hot as the sun. The older man held her down while the lady buckled the straps over her arms. What did they think to do to her? What would they dare? She kicked the table, the doctor, the woman in white, the young gentleman between the legs, and he gasped. The doctor slapped her. "That's enough!"

She paused in shock, as they meant her to. And it was then that they strapped her legs apart. They pushed up her dress. They pulled away her underthings. She screamed and pulled on the leather straps, arching her back and screaming again. Her chest was bare and her legs open and the air touched the curly hairs that no one but her sisters and her mother had seen. And the strangers watched her. The one with graying hair to his collar and the long jaw like a horse was touching her—here and here and here—while she screamed, pee dripping down her leg.

"Quiet her, Nurse," the doctor said, and the lady tied a gag around Nehama's mouth. She fell quiet. She turned her head to one side, looking at the cabinet with the glass front between scrolled panels, and she memorized the colors of the jars while someone put an instrument to her naked chest. Her nipples rose in the cold. Someone pulled her legs up and forced her knees further apart. The pressure between her legs hurt. She was undone.

"This girl is clear of venereal illness. You can see that her hymen is intact. She may be released."

"I'm sorry that I wasn't able to observe the untreated disease, sir," the younger man said.

"We'll have another patient soon enough."

The white lady removed the straps. She pushed Nehama, sobbing, to the door. Outside the hospital the constable was waiting. She didn't resist as he made her step up into the police wagon to take her to prison. Her sisters would never have allowed it. They would have known whom to bribe. But here anything was allowed.

Dorset Street

The sky was gray and ready to burst when the police wagon stopped, not in front of a prison but at a tavern with a sign swinging on one rusty bolt. A cornucopia was painted on the sign, and out of it fell fruits of some sort, the colors and shapes so worn they weren't identifiable. The sign hung over a doorway, and there Mr. Blink was waiting. Somehow he'd known where to come for her, and at last everything would be fixed. Beside him stood a young woman smoking a short pipe. She looked about the same age as Nehama's next older sister, maybe twenty-one or twenty-two. Her hair was dark and her skin pale as a doll's, her nose long, her lips wide, and when she smiled Nehama could see she had all her teeth. She was short and stocky, a body for pulling plows and surviving famines.

"Where were you for so long?" Mr. Blink asked angrily.

"I was in a hospital," she said, and then told him the whole story because someone must comfort her. The young woman with the pipe was nodding and smirking as if she understood Yiddish and didn't think much of it. Mr. Blink was waving his hand to say, Get to the point. Patrons of the tavern came in and out, looking like drunks do anywhere, wounded and stinking. One of them knocked Mr. Blink's bowler hat into the gutter, and he picked it up, rubbing away the dust on the brim, while Nehama cried out, "Why did they do that to me?"

Mr. Blink studied her without saying a word. Nehama put her hand to her hair, fallen out of its pins and hanging loose around her shoulders. Mr. Blink's voice was sad, his eyes empty of any emotion. "So you're no longer a good girl."

"I'm not?" She hadn't thought—well, something had happened but she'd hoped that perhaps it wasn't really the thing and now it seemed that her sisters were right, she was stupid, stupid not to know.

"You know what I mean," Mr. Blink said. "It's too late to do anything about it."

"What will happen to me now? God in heaven." The rain fell, drenching her as Mr. Blink stepped back into the shelter of the doorway.

This was her punishment. Before she stepped on the boat she had made herself a thief, and then God had made her— She wouldn't think of the word. To buy the ticket, she had sneaked into her sisters' rooms and taken from each of them a piece of finery to sell. A pair of earrings, a blouse, a silk kerchief. From the middle sister, Shayna-Pearl, she'd taken nothing. Not because she was afraid of Shayna-Pearl's temper but because her sister only had books and Nehama wouldn't sell a book. She'd left a note that said her dowry should be given to her sisters so that they could replace what she'd taken. But Bronya's earrings were the only thing her husband had ever given her. Repayment doesn't exonerate a sin, does it?

"I told you to stay in my rooms above the shop. And you didn't listen. May God forgive you. Now. Well, now . . . What shall we do with you? To the loan committee, I can't go. Not under the circumstances. But still the entrance fee must be paid. There's only one thing to do. The fee will be paid by someone I know, and you'll work for him to pay it back."

The young woman with the pipe rolled her eyes. She wore a brightly colored, badly made dress. "Should I take her now?" she asked in Yiddish. Another *landsmann*. Who knew there were so many Jews in London?

"This is Fayge," Mr. Blink said. "Here they call her Fay. She'll take you to the Squire, and if you can't be a good girl, then at least you can work hard. Remember that you're only here because he paid for you, and he can turn you over to the authorities any time he likes." He walked away just like that. In a big city, people come and go, her grandmother used to say.

Nehama followed the other girl inside, her skirt dripping on the floor. The tavern was long and narrow, and at the far end the Squire sat at a table near the map of London 1809 and a door marked PRIVAT. If only there wasn't so much noise, she might have heard her grandmother trying to talk to her.

You see him? He's called the Squire because he wears a watch with a chain, but he's just a man who used to be a sailor. He's a gentile, of course, are Jews fishermen? But now he makes his business with girls. A good drama he likes, and he can buy the best seat. In the theater he wears a long scarf and an old wool cap. A man in a silk hat is nothing to him. The magistrate doesn't worry him either. But listen to me, my girl. He's afraid of the wind. I'm telling you this so you should know that even a man like him is afraid of something. You don't have to look at the floor. Look at him and see what he is. Then turn around and go away. Right now and not a minute later. Do you hear me, Nehameleh?

But Nehama heard only the noise of the pub as she followed the stocky young woman with her solid walk to the Squire, who was knitting a scarf the color of the Spanish sky.

"That's the Squire's friend, a smuggler," Fay whispered.

The smuggler was a small man, even for these streets, where men didn't grow big, and he wore a Russian greatcoat, the collar around his ears. As he read his newspaper aloud, he took great bites of bangers and mash and swallows of beer, speaking up so the Squire could hear him above the accordion and the click of draughts and the toss of an iron ring at the hook on the back wall.

"There were a row in Angel Alley what put two in the London Hospital. A drowned child found in the Thames. And an ointment from India what cures bad eyes."

"I could do with that," the Squire said. "I smashed my spectacles yesterday. Go on."

"Ships stalled in the channel. An east wind. And one ship lost."

"Bloody wind. Naught you can do about it. Even the best knife won't save a man from drowning in it." The Squire took the watch from his pocket, rubbing the gold back against a piece of silk to shine it.

"This is Mr. Blink's new girl," Fay said.

So this was the man who was going to save her from the authorities because she wasn't fit for the Newcomers' Assistance Committee. The Squire looked her up and down as if he'd be glad to take his price out of her skin. Maybe he'd sell her to a factory. There were terrible factories in Plotsk, where girls breathed fumes all day long and coughed up black tar. "Tell him that I can sew," she said to Fay. At least sewing wouldn't kill her.

"It's not sewing he wants," Fay said in Yiddish.

The Squire nodded as if he understood. "You tell her she cost me ten pounds."

"What kind of work do I have to do?" Nehama asked. She looked directly at the Squire. Her grandmother used to say that if you don't use your eyes while you're taking the train from Pinsk to Minsk, your pockets will be picked clean and you'll have no one to blame but yourself. His face was hard and his lips were soft. He smelled like poison. Later Nehama would find out that he made a special grease to keep his hands and lips from chapping.

MINSK, 1875

Moskovskaya Street

The Rosenbergs lived in a stone house with a wrought-iron fence in front and an apple tree in back. The house was three stories, the garden behind it small and private. A doctor lived next door, and sometimes he had musical evenings, the sound of the piano and violin drifting into the garden, where the ghost of the first Mrs. Rosenberg sat in the apple tree. There were now three living Rosenbergs left in the house: the second wife, the husband, and their daughter.

The first Mrs. Rosenberg had been a mousy woman who took to her bed after Father pointed out her many failings. When she died, he fetched his distant cousin, a widow from a fine family, to be his second wife and take care of his home and children. She wasn't supposed to get pregnant. He already had his sons.

The girl was too beautiful, more like a *shiksa* than a Jew, so why should anyone think she was his child at all? In fact there was no evidence. Mr. Rosenberg was a notary and liked the word *evidence*. It made him feel more like a lawyer. Or even a judge. He'd have been one if he'd been born a generation later, when the czar was more liberal toward Jews and let a few into higher schooling. But as it was, all he was authorized to judge were the bricks made in his factory on the outskirts of Minsk, a town of little distinction.

The apple tree was still heavy with fruit, though it was late in the season. Under the care of the first Mrs. Rosenberg, the tree in the garden bloomed early and bore fruit into the fall. Emilia sat on the bench under it, thinking of how she would live with Mother when they ran away. The ghost of the first wife could come, too. Emilia didn't mind sharing a garden with the dead. In the garden with its brick wall covered by ivy, it didn't matter if Emilia was a bit cold in her fall coat. A thrush was singing, a squirrel chittering, the ghost rustling the branches of the apple tree, all perfectly peaceful while Emilia cut out a string of paper dolls.

"Look!" she called up to the ghost of the first wife, unfolding the paper dolls. She knew the paper dolls were simple, but she was only nine years old. Next year she'd be able to make paper-cuts of roses and trees like Mama. The ghost of the first wife nodded in approval. She never spoke. Probably the dead couldn't speak because they didn't have real bodies. But they listened all the time, and really, as long as a ghost could nod or shake her head, she was just as pleasant as half the guests that Father invited for dinner. He never came into the garden. The only door was through the kitchen, and he wouldn't lower himself to be seen there.

"I don't think Father will be mad tonight, do you?" Emilia asked the first wife, folding the paper for another set of dolls. She'd make boy dolls this time. Maybe she'd show Father. She would say these were her half brothers. She carefully traced the tall hats, thinking that Father would be in a good mood and he would smile as she unfolded the paper dolls.

The ghost of the first wife came down from the tree and sat beside her on the grass as if she'd like to put her arm around Emilia. But there wasn't any need for that. Emilia was a lucky girl, being both pretty and clever. Mama always said so. Mama said that Emilia would not make the same mistakes she had. "When Father sees the boy paper dolls, he'll kiss my cheek and give me a coin," Emilia said to the first wife. "Don't you think so?"

The ghost of the first Mrs. Rosenberg shook her head. She was making a wreath out of fallen leaves. Gold leaves and red, and flowers that blew over the wall for the first wife's use.

"Maybe you're right," Emilia said. "Kisses are for babies." Perhaps he would be in a good mood and not throw the soup today. Yesterday they'd had beet borscht. When the soup hit the wall, it had left a red stain. The maid had scrubbed and scrubbed, Mama too. But there was still a pink mark, and Father was angry that his hard-earned money would have to be thrown out on painters. From now on there would be only chicken soup in the house, he said. Mama loathed cooked chicken. It looked too much like a living thing.

Her mother opened the kitchen door. She was dressed for cooking, with an oversize apron from collar to hem. The cooking wasn't going well. Emilia knew it because Mama's cheeks were red and she was wearing the cameo brooch. Mama always wore the cameo when she was feeling wobbly. "What are you doing, Emilia?"

"Cutting paper dolls." Mama made beautiful paper-cuts, scenes of trees and flowers and sea animals riding waves. Father said that she should stick with playing the piano—paper-cuts were usually made by men to mark the eastern wall for prayer or decorate windows for festivals—but Father didn't refuse to hang them, because Mama's paper-cuts were so admired by his friends. "Well, come inside and have your lesson," Mama said. "The German Bible is still on your desk, waiting for you to get past Adam."

The house was large. It had guest rooms and a library, where Father met with editors and other intelligent people, but Mama taught Emilia her lessons at a desk in the kitchen. Under the calendar on the left wall, there was a pine cabinet full of books and next to it a sewing chest without a single needle or spool of thread but everything you'd need for cutting beautiful scenes out of paper: the board, the small knife, paper and ink of many hues, stencils of trees, roses, eagles, lions.

"Mama, isn't the brisket done?" Emilia asked as she came into the kitchen. The maid was peeling potatoes, and something smelled burnt.

Her mother poked at the meat with a silver fork as if it might rise up out of the pot and accuse her of anti-Semitism. "Maybe I should pour in a little more water. It will make gravy. Go on. Read."

"But if Father doesn't like it . . ."

"Don't look so worried. Let me ask you—can he be any worse than a Russian officer?" Mama's voice was tense, but she smiled as she pushed Emilia to her desk.

The pages of the book lying open on her desk were stained with smudged pencil notes. Better a story from Mother. "Tell me about the Russians," Emilia said.

There were two tables in the kitchen—the big one beside the window for preparing meat dishes and the small one for dairy opposite, next to the cabinet of books. Mother waited until the maid came back from the cellar with the carrots. Freida liked a story, too. When they were both settled at the table by the window, peeling and cutting carrots for the *tzimmes,* she began. "It was in the year of the Polish rebellion. We hid the rebels in the woods around our village, and my husband—my first husband, *alleva sholom*—gave them boots and coats. It was winter, and you could see the footprints of horses in the snow when the Russian soldiers came."

"And then what happened?" Emilia asked, though she knew the answer. She was watching the shapes the curtains made as they fluttered against the open window. The curtains were yellow and sheer, like candle flames lighting her mother's face.

"When the Russians came to our village, they didn't know who was doing what, but they blew up my first husband's mill just the same. The officers came to our house, and I was sure they intended to kill us all. So I invited them in."

"Why didn't you run away? That's what I would do," Emilia said.

"No, you listen to me. It's better to open a door yourself than have it smashed to pieces. What can you do afterward with a broken door? I brought out the crystal goblets, and I served them wine until they were drunk. Then I played the piano for them and they cried sentimental tears. Because of that, they only stole everything we had and no one was shot."

"But you lost everything, Mama." Emilia had heard the story many times. How Mama's first husband, the miller, died of a broken heart soon after the mill was destroyed.

"Not everything. I'm telling you—out of this you came. When I finished mourning, I married your father. How would I know that a woman who could charm Russian officers couldn't charm him? He's a stone, your father. A hammer. After the wedding night, he told me that he didn't want another man's child in his house. That was my son by the miller. So I left him with someone—what else could I do? He was fourteen years old. But still, I saved whatever I could, a penny here and a penny there, and I sent it to him. I want you to know that a mother never forgets her child."

"Yes, Mama," Emilia said. But she didn't believe it for a minute. She didn't even know the name of this half brother.

Emilia had her dinner with the maid in the kitchen. On special occasions and the Sabbath, she ate in the dining room, but when she was older she'd have to eat there all the time with her parents and half brothers and their wives. For now she could sit with Freida and wave at the ghost of the first wife, and after Father returned to the factory, she snuck into his study to read.

The study was the nicest room in the house. It had two windows facing south and west, so that it was as bright and warm as could be. Father's desk was in the corner, and Emilia didn't go near it, not daring to take the chance of accidentally messing it up. On the desk were spread many newspapers, which Father used to glean facts obscured by the czar's censors. Cabinets lined the opposite two walls, and under the south-facing window, Emilia sat on the thick carpet with a book in her lap. Today she was reading *Travels in Italy and the Levantine*. Emilia always read with a purpose. There were certain facts she wished to corroborate, as Father said.

Emilia was so engrossed in *Travels in Italy and the Levantine* that she forgot to pay attention to the sounds outside the study. She was thinking that she'd take Mama to Italy. In Italy the sky was warm and blue, according to the painting on Mama's wall, and here it was again in the colored plates in Father's book. No one could be sick in such a place.

Father had many books. He was a cultured man. He preferred Russian to any other language. It was just yesterday that he'd said so before throwing the soup. He asked why Mama insisted on teaching her daughter German. He read only Russian. No other language was worth reading, but perhaps his wife thought he was an ignoramus compared with some others he might name. Then he threw the soup. Emilia was in the kitchen, but she heard the tureen smash against the wall. She didn't eat any more dinner after that. Freida took away her plate and brought her a piece of cake. Emilia wasn't hungry, but she had a bite of it so that later she could remember the taste and imagine she was eating cake in the cabin of a beautiful ship sailing away, and Father was left all alone to feel great remorse.

Because Emilia forgot to pay attention to anything but the book and her plans, she didn't notice her father standing in the doorway. He was not a tall man, in fact he stood several inches shorter than her mother, his face ruddy from brick dust, his beard thick and dark and long like Tolstoy's. He wore a frock coat and trousers, though he kept every religious law, because this was the modern age. "What are you doing?" he asked. His voice was loud. It had to rise above the machines in his factory.

Emilia dropped the book, and as luck would have it a page crumpled under it. She sat very still, hoping that Father would forget her while he picked up the book and brought it to his desk, where he carefully smoothed out the page, closed the book, and put another on top of it to iron out the unfortunate crease. Emilia crouched on the carpet, eyes lowered to her father's boots, wiped clean of brick dust. They were his nice boots, the leather smooth and shining. The boots came toward her. A hand pulled her up by the ear.

"What do you have to say for yourself?"

"I was reading, Father." Why couldn't he just smack her and have done with it? Surely her ear would come off her head.

"These books are not yours, I believe."

"No, Father."

"You do not understand, I see, the difference between what belongs to you and what belongs to others." He let go of her ear. It was hot as she rubbed it. "You will bring me something of yours."

"I don't have anything." After she sailed away on the boat, he would realize that he'd lost his only daughter, and then he'd wish that he could beg her forgiveness.

"Nothing? I see clothes on your back. Shoes on your feet. Surely these are not mine. Bring me your Sabbath dress. Hannah!" he called Mother. "Hannah!"

There always had to be a witness. That was the law, Father said.

Mama helped Emilia take down the dress hanging high in the wardrobe, all the while shaking her head as if she couldn't believe the fecklessness of her daughter. "How could you be so foolish?" she asked. "When are you going to learn what's what in life? You want to read something, then take the book and hide it, for God's sake."

Soon Mama and Emilia stood side by side in the study, Emilia's hand hiding in Mama's so that the trembling of her fingers wasn't visible. Newspapers, paperweight, pens fell onto the soft carpet as Father swept them off his desk. The book that he'd so carefully placed there also fell and a dozen pages crumpled, but he paid no attention. He laid the dress on his desk. He pulled it flat, an arm, the other arm, the sound of a slight tearing as threads parted. Then he took scissors from a drawer and cut carefully. A torn collar, a ripped cuff. The corner of a pocket hanging loosely. "Here." He threw the dress at her. A button smacked her on the cheek. "Idiot! You'll wear this for Sabbath dinners. When the dress is too small, you may have another, and perhaps you'll remember the laws of property." Then he shouted some more at Mama, and she took to her bed.

Emilia ran out to the garden and threw herself down. One evening Father had said she looked charming in her Sabbath dress, and she'd give anything to hear him say it again. She cried herself to sleep, autumn leaves blowing across her legs as she dreamed of Italy. She would live in a villa. There she would paint beautiful paintings of green hills and grazing goats. The ghost of the first wife sat with her while she dreamed.

LONDON, 1875

Dorset Street

Dorset Street meant not only the street itself but the warren of courts and alleys off it, where fog settled from October to March, swallowing the pitiful lamps and dousing the meager fires of old cottages and gray doss-houses. Every few doors there was a public house with its magical sign—the Unicorn, the Black Lion, the Green Dragon, the Horn and Plenty. Here gin was plentiful and women smoked short-stemmed pipes, but shoes were a privilege pawned for rent.

In one of these courts, the Squire had a house where the girls slept in small rooms upstairs and guests came into the parlor below. Now he sat there in a carved armchair, eyeing Nehama. "We'll call you Nell," he said. There was a table beside him, with a bowl of apples and pears on it. Several girls were sitting on the sofas, mending their stockings, as Nehama crossed her arms over her breasts, looking up at the porcelain shepherdesses on the shelf above the mirror so she wouldn't see her naked reflection. The wallpaper had a pattern of peacocks on it.

"A funny-looking snatch she's got," the Squire said with a grimace. "Never seen one like that before."

Nehama couldn't help but follow his eyes and look down, wondering if there was something wrong with her. The other girls laughed. They all had bright dresses with many ruffles.

"The Squire will get you one of these," Fay said, pulling at her skirt. "A girl in the trade needs the clothes for it."

Nehama clenched her teeth so they wouldn't chatter. It was the Squire's pleasure and his right to look at her. He'd paid for it. That was what Fay had explained to her while they walked from the pub to the house. Nehama should have run away. If she were smart, if she were good, if she were any one of her sisters, she'd have run. But she hadn't understood what was actually meant until she stood here naked, with Madam Harding giving a satisfied nod and Fay translating, She says the Squire got his money's worth, no one's had you yet. And Nehama didn't know whom she hated more, Mr. Blink for giving her up or herself for being given.

The Squire bit into a pear. "You think it works right, Madam Harding?" he asked the older woman who stood next to the mirror.

"The only way to know is to try it out." The windows rattled. The wind was blowing hard.

"Right. I will. Just give her the broom first. Fay, tell her to lie down."

"You got to lie down," Fay said in Yiddish.

"What—on the floor?" Nehama asked. "I need a drink of water first. I'm terribly thirsty." She glanced at the door, but even if it wasn't locked, she wouldn't run out naked. Could she let anyone see her like this?

The old prostitute, called Madam Harding, pushed her to the floor, her hands on Nehama's breasts. It was the second touch of violation, the first having been Madam Harding's fingers between her legs, and Nehama wondered why her muscles had frozen. She didn't kick or scream while the tallest of the girls took her on one side, the palest girl on the other. She only called out, "Why don't you help me?" and her *landsmann* Fay answered, "I had my turn, too." Nehama turned her gaze to the wallpaper with its peacocks. She couldn't be lying on the floor like this; she was there in the wallpaper among the exotic birds and fear was just a peacock's tail staring with many eyes.

When the beating began, she heard the peacocks scream, and then she was unaware of the girls and their rancid breath as they bent over her. It was the linden tree she smelled, the one in her family's courtyard, and the smoke from the feather factory, and mud when you pick up the washed linens that have fallen into it. She didn't see the girl looking down at her with eyelashes so pale she seemed to have none, and she didn't feel the other girl kneading her arm and leg in the rhythm of the broom handle. For when the soles of her feet were welted and numb, the handle was used on the inside of her, like a butter churn. She hardly noticed when the Squire followed it.

Later Nehama went to sleep. The youngest of the prostitutes, a girl named Sally, gave her laudanum to relieve the pain, and when Nehama cried over and over, Don't look at me, Sally told her not to worry, for she was wearing a thick cotton nightgown and no one could see her. It was a good lie.

As the weeks passed, Nehama often dreamed that she was sleeping with her sisters in the old bed with the iron posts, an arm around her, an elbow in her ribs, a hand on her hair, only to wake up with the youngest prostitute lying beside her. "I was cold," Sally would say. The other girls didn't like Sally. "Tell me something, Nell. About your sisters."

And Nehama would try in her new English, fitting the pieces of language together like a puzzle that would show her a picture of something true. But if she said, "Mine sister learn me to read," Sally would shake her head.

"Not that one. Tell me how they thrashed you for telling tales. How they called you a disease."

"The pest," Nehama would correct her.

"The pestilence," Sally would add with a smile. She was called the Spanish girl because of her dark eyes and dark lashes and staccato walk as if she were dancing the flamenco, but she'd never been outside of London. She was two years younger than Nehama, and at fifteen no bigger than a child. She was small-boned and small-breasted and four feet five. She'd done well as a virgin, passing it off for months.

Sally was disliked because she was a Papist. This she explained to Nehama one day in the quiet hour after the girls had slept and before the trade started up. Sally was sitting on the floor, brushing the hair of a wig. Her own hair fell out in handfuls, so she kept it short, and when she was working she wore the wig.

Nehama sat on the bed. The room was so small that the bed touched one wall and Sally's feet the other. There was a window that looked into an alley, and though it was boarded up, air came through the cracks. Above the window, Nehama had pinned a theater poster that she'd found in the street, blown off a wooden post.

"The others hate me because they're going to hell and I'm not,"

Sally said, brushing and braiding the wig. "Should I curl the hair like yours, Nell?"

"Straight hair is better," Nehama said. She was looking at her knees through the yellow gauze of her nightgown. Her knees looked the same as always. That was the strange thing.

"I want to look like her. That elegant, she is." Sally pointed her brush at the poster for *Colleen Bawn,* with its illustration of a young woman drowning in a cave, her locks floating on the water and a white gown billowing around her. "See the shaking waters, the rolling surf and watery effects," the poster read. Sally sneezed. Her feet were raw with chilblains. "I'm sorry you're going to hell like the other girls. Why don't you get baptized in the true church? It isn't hard."

"I'm a Jew," Nehama said. "Like Fay."

"So? You can be baptized. Then you confess and the priest absolves you."

"What do you mean *absolves*?"

"When you're ready to die, you have the priest take off all your sins. You dress nice like her in the poster, and you're buried like a beauty." Sally was playing with a locket on a gold chain.

"My sins are too many." But it wasn't sins she counted night after night, it was shillings and pounds, calculating her debt to the Squire. She must pay him off. No other thought could take precedence. "Who gave you that locket?"

"Nobody. I rolled the captain of the ship."

"But you're so small. How did you take it?" Nehama asked. "That must be worth something."

"Size is nothing. Didn't you never roll no one?"

Nehama shook her head. The last customer had been a big man. Nehama had heard herself gasp as he worked his way inside her. But she wasn't really there. No, she was somewhere else, figuring sums. So much for rent. So much for food. Not enough left for what she owed on the dress and the entrance fee.

"What do I do?" Nehama asked.

"It's easy. I'll show you." Sally had shown her everything. How to douse a sponge in vinegar and put it in so she wouldn't get pregnant. How to stretch her money by eating cheap shellfish in season. How to be first when a gentleman came slumming. But she couldn't show

Nehama how to drink till she didn't care anymore because Nehama threw up first and, as Sally said, it was a waste of good gin.

"Don't sit there like a ninny. Get on top of me." Sally lay down on the bed.

"Like this?" Nehama kneeled with one leg on either side of Sally, who was lying flat as a child in a casket.

"No, you're too dainty. Be a great bloke what's had his drink." Sally pulled Nehama forward. "That's right. Now you wiggle. Don't be shy. Come on." Sally laughed. They were so close that Nehama could see the skin under smudges of rouge wiped away by the pillow. "Just when he's most busy and he wouldn't notice a fire, you put your hand in his pocket."

"Not there." Nehama pushed the other girl's hand from the inside of her thigh.

Sally dangled the locket. "You don't need to be a master gonoph."

"Let me try," Nehama said, pushing Sally over as she took her turn lying down. Sally sat on her, as light as a baby, moving the locket quickly from one hand to the other.

"Hi! Give it back now," Sally shouted when Nehama snatched it out of the air. "That's mine."

"Fine. Here it is." But as the old prostitute walked by the doorway, paused, and returned, Sally put her hands behind her back, looking at Nehama with frightened eyes.

"What's this!" Madam Harding held out her hand. Her hair was dyed black, and the dye had left a line along her temple. "Trying to keep something back. You know what we thinks of that sort of thing."

"Not me," Sally said, picking up her wig and brushing it furiously. "It were her. She took it from the sailor, and I was just looking at it."

"I should know it's the sly Jewess." The old prostitute slapped Nehama so hard her nose bled.

"What?" Nehama pinched her nose. There was blood on her fingers, a stain on her sleeve where it dripped.

"Don't say another word to me with your sharp Jew tongue. It'll cost you to have that blood cleaned off. Add it to your debt."

Nehama glanced at Sally. Her shoulders were hunched, her eyes panicky. Nehama's sisters had sometimes taken the blame for her, but they were golden and strong. She was dark and her thoughts were dark as the wind blew night in from the sea, though she was as strong as any of them. "A bit of blood isn't any worse than what else is on this," she said.

"Never mind your lip or I'll tell the Squire you ruined it altogether. Take that off and the laundress will have it."

Nehama smiled. "A blessing on you," she said in Yiddish. "May the cholera eat out your intestines."

The night of the Sardinian sailors, Nehama lost her sense of smell. Madam Harding played the piano as usual, and Nehama sang because the other girls had voices made hoarse by smoking tobacco and opium. Sometimes they asked her to sing a foreign song, but she would only shake her head and begin with "It's a cold haily night of rain," and everyone clapped to the beat as if they were friends in a music hall.

There were a dozen sailors, so each of the girls had two at a time, for which the Squire could charge triple the price. They ate and drank in the parlor with the girls on their laps, while the mirror turned them into twenty-four men and their drunkenness into forty-eight as the old prostitute brought out bottle after bottle, and Madam's playing knocked flat the statue of Diana the huntress that stood on top of the piano. The lamps were made of lion glass, each one with a frosted lion reclining after his feed.

Nehama had the bald sailor and the one with two gold earrings. She fed them bites of sausage, first one, then the other, and in the mirror framed with gilt she was perched on a knee, laughing as well as the other girls. And just as quick as they did, she offered her breasts to a mouth, expecting it to bite and pull as usual, but instead the lips and tongue were soft. And when her sailors put up a bet of three sovereigns, she said, You're on. Pulling up her gown, she spread her ass for the bald one and licked up the one with earrings right there in the parlor with the velvet sofa. She did it in front of everyone; she saw them watching her. The gold coins sparkled. The statue of Diana the huntress wobbled on top of the piano as Madam played. The one she licked didn't stink as she thought he would. The surprise of it made her quiver, and as she dug herself deeper into the one behind her, she lost her sense of smell. God took it away and abandoned her to the evil inclination. This was her real ruin, and she knew she could never see her mother again. How was she to understand that it was the strength of her life asserting itself?

The difference between hell and earth is that, even in the midst of misery, the body can find some pleasure to keep it alive.

Her sisters used to tell her that when Grandma Nehama was eighteen, a marriage was arranged for her. Before she left home, she visited her parents' grave to ask their blessing, and then she traveled by boat with her aunt. At last someone would belong to her—even if it was just a widower with a young child. But on her wedding day, when she met her husband, she was not as taken with him as she expected. He had hair growing in his ears, and the speech he gave for the bride was full of warnings about the shortness of life, as if she didn't already know it. But the baby daughter, who was nine months old, was something else altogether. She was tiny and dark and sad, and Grandma Nehama fell in love with her.

There was a wet nurse for the baby, and Grandma Nehama saw with her own eyes that milk without love wasn't putting enough weight on the baby. And why should it? Didn't she remember getting thinner while she was mourning, no matter how much the neighbors urged her to eat? So when the baby's eyes were full of sorrow, Grandma Nehama gave it her own milkless breast to suck, and she did not sing to it "Sleep my child, may heaven guard you," for this baby had already seen the angel of death. Instead she sang about the wind. It became her particular lullaby, this old song that went "Dark burns the fire in its agony. And the wind, the wind, the raging wind . . ." She sang from morning till night, and whether it was the sucking or the songs, no one could say, but eventually Grandma Nehama's breasts ran to milk as thick as cream, and on it the baby grew plump.

After the night's work was done, Nehama lay awake in Sally's bed, the younger girl's arms around her while she listened to the wind as if it were a song she'd forgotten and might remember if only she listened hard enough.

MINSK, 1876

Moskovskaya Street

Winter came to Minsk, and snow rose in great drifts reflecting street-lamps while sleighs carried men of substance home from their factories and offices. In the evenings they took their fur-cloaked wives to the theater, where the choice of the season was Italian opera, the Italians being hot-blooded as everyone knew, hoping that some heat would waft from the stage to the audience. Whoever could afford to burn coal kept their cellars full, and their stoves blew smoke at the wind as it knocked bricks from chimneys. But in the garden on Moskovskaya Street, the ghost of the first wife didn't feel the cold. She sat high in the apple tree, shaking the branches as if it were imperative to get someone out of the warm house into her garden.

Emilia sat in her mother's dressing room, glancing now and then at the window while she read Russian poetry aloud to please Father, who could hear it from his room. She wished that she looked like Mama, but she was nothing like either of her parents. Mama said it was a family trait to take after an aunt or uncle or great-grandfather, each generation following a circuitous path through its descendants. Emilia was golden-haired and gray-eyed like one of her aunts. She hadn't met any of them—the daughters of a rich man are sent far and wide when they marry for the family's honor.

"They say your cousins look like me," Mama said, putting down the letter from her sister while Freida twisted her hair into intricate knots. She picked up the silver-backed mirror. "A little more curl here, if you please."

"Emilia!" Father called. "What are you doing in your mother's room?"

She turned to the Russian verses again, but it was too late. As sure as the moon is jealous of the sun, he was coming out of his dressing room, buttoning his high collar. "Are you telling the child stories?" he asked.

"Only about deportment at dinner."

"She'll be eating in the kitchen," Father said.

"Yes, but she won't be a child forever."

"Just don't give her any of your ideas." He wasn't looking at Emilia, his eyes were all for Mama. On the wall above her dressing table, there was a painting with a hawk hovering high above the goats, as if considering which one would make its dinner. "Who do you think the child looks like?" he asked, switching from Russian to Yiddish. The despised mother tongue was suitable for such discussions.

"My older sister. Exactly her," Mama said, as if she hadn't answered the same way a thousand times before. She began to rise from her chair but sat down when he shook his head. Father preferred her to be seated. She was taller than he, but his suit was cut by the tailor who clothed the count.

"I believe the child looks a lot like the editor of the *Minsker Journal*," Father said. "He used to be our guest much too often, I think." Sometimes it was an editor. Sometimes their old lawyer. Or a physician. They had to have a different doctor every year. Emilia's neck began to itch. Soon her feet would itch, too, but she didn't dare scratch.

"Don't be ridiculous," Mama said. Why did she have to argue? It only made Father worse. The apple tree beat harder at the window. It was the first Mrs. Rosenberg, but Father took no more notice of her now than when she was alive.

"So I'm ridiculous." Father's voice got quieter.

"You know what I mean," Mama said nervously. The maid edged toward the door. "What have your guests to do with me?"

"So I'm asking myself." He picked up Mama's mirror as if to see her true face in it. Emilia tried not to breathe. He seemed to have forgotten her.

"I'm busy with the house," Mama said. "Such a large house needs more than one servant. If you gave me a bigger allowance, I might have a minute free to go out, but as it is . . ."

"So now I'm an idiot and a miser, too. Very good. But blind, I'm not. I saw the way you looked at the lawyer. And he's old enough to be your uncle. It's disgusting." Emilia wasn't sure what was disgusting about it, but even so she knew enough to be ashamed.

Father turned the mirror over. A gift from Mama's older sister, the one she said that Emilia resembled, it was engraved with all the sisters' names.

"He was just bringing papers for you to sign," Mama said. She didn't sound ashamed.

"An excuse, you always have. Do you practice it in front of the mirror?" His voice was hardly more than a whisper, his mouth twisting as he broke off the handle with a loud snap, throwing it into her lap. And though Emilia held herself very still, Mama flinched. Then Father took the letter opener from her table and scratched the names on the silver back of the mirror. He had broken everything her sisters sent her. She didn't have a single picture of them left. "Never forget, my wife, that I can send you both packing," he said. In the painting above Mama's dressing table, the hawk was very small above the green hills. There was a villa with white columns. That was where they'd go when Father sent them packing.

"Your daughter has done nothing to deserve such an insult. And let me tell you, neither have I." But it wasn't true or else Father wouldn't be looking at Mama like that. He turned his eyes to Emilia, examining her like a spot of blood in an egg, spoiling it, making it unkosher, and eggs were so expensive. She couldn't help but reach a hand to surreptitiously scratch her neck. Shame and fear were such itchy feelings, and hatred the itchiest of all.

Mama stood up, the ivory handle falling to the floor. "Freida," she called. "Come back and help me off with this dress, please. I'm feeling faint. Mr. Rosenberg will have to greet the guests himself."

"Sit down," he said. And she did, as always.

"My dear husband . . ."

The words went on, but Emilia wasn't listening anymore. She was looking at the style of Mama's new dress with the mother-of-pearl buttons, imagining that she was grown up and had just such a dress herself. When she was grown up, there would be admiration in every man's eyes. After Emilia and Mama ran away to their Italian villa, they'd hold salons, Mama playing the piano and Emilia dressed in a white gown embroidered with rosebuds. She'd greet the guests, extending her gloved hand just so, and she would tell her admirers that she was named after the Polish heroine Emilia Plater, who had disguised herself as a man to lead a cavalry troop against the Russians.

Father and Mama went down for dinner, his steps firm and quick, hers slower as she held on to the oak banister. Emilia reached behind Mama's dressing table to take the book from its hiding place. *One Hundred Steamships and Clippers.* She was copying the illustration of a two-thousand-ton steamship with a clipper bow, one funnel, three masts, and room for fifty-four first-class passengers. Later she'd paint the drawing with watercolors and name the ship *La Bella.* Painting, like playing the piano, was an accomplishment that wives should have. Maybe Father would even allow her to pin the drawing on her bedroom wall. No one else would know that behind one of the first-class portholes, the one she'd paint with yellow curtains, were Emilia and her mother.

Outside the window the first Mrs. Rosenberg would be watching from the apple tree. She shouldn't be left behind in an empty garden. Emilia pushed aside the curtains, throwing open the window to tell Mrs. Rosenberg that she was welcome to come live with them in the villa among the grazing goats.

The moon was a crescent in the sky, visible between the branches of the apple tree as if Mrs. Rosenberg held it in her dark lap. Emilia didn't bless the moon. She hadn't learned how. Her mother was too modern to teach her the women's prayers. But Emilia didn't need to empty her heart before heaven as long as she could speak to Mrs. Rosenberg, who shook the branches of the apple tree in answer. She knew what it was like to live in the house in Moskovskaya Street, and had left the only way she could.

Sometimes a person has to make the best of an unpleasant decision.

More snow was falling. But it would quickly disappear as the roots of the first Mrs. Rosenberg's apple tree dug down into the warm deep of the earth.

LONDON, 1876

The Horn and Plenty

The streets were cold and wet, and the Sunday boots were pawned, yet in the Horn and Plenty, women stood at the bar and ate while men played draughts at the tables. They lived for the pub, the naphtha lamps, the warm stove, the posters of music hall singers, the barmaid in her orange and yellow dress, the games and the songs as cheerful as in a place where you might expect to live past the age of thirty. A woman needed a place to talk, leaning on the counter while she gave a finger of gin to her baby. The one with the long face was telling how her bloke had put a shilling on a horse, and when the horse won, they'd stand everyone for a drink. She was a casual prostitute, on the turf just now and then. The rest of the time she worked for the Squire, who was her uncle, following his whores to make sure they came back.

Nehama was writing numbers on the back of a Christian tract while she stood at the bar with Fay and Sally and the woman who promised to stand them a drink, whose name was Lizzie. She had thin hair falling over her face, and she wore a white apron in the old-fashioned style. Nehama had a proper whore's dress, bright and shiny and ruffled. And proper East End boots that let in water at the seams. In her pocket she had a letter from her mother:

"My Nehameleh, you should stay well and not have any sickness from the damp. It is a bitter thing for a mother to lose her child and I will never understand what you did. How could you leave us all? Only a mother can know such pain. My eyes are so swollen, they look like bees. So you should know, I did what you asked though Father didn't want I should give away your dowry. I split it among your sisters, and it was worse than throwing dirt on a grave. They all forgive you except Bronya as you know she holds a grudge and Shayna-Pearl because even though you didn't take anything from her, she expected to make a teacher of you though God in heaven knows you should be married and living under your mother's roof. Remember to wear your woolens, it's so damp this time of year. God forbid you should take sick. Your mother."

Once a month Nehama wrote her mother the sorts of lies that could be expected. At night she forgot the cold while she worked the trade, and afterward she kept warm by sleeping with Sally from dawn till noon, arms around each other in the small bed they shared. Whenever she thought of throwing herself in the river, she reminded herself that the younger girl needed her. Everyone must have a reason for living. If you couldn't hold your gin, then there had to be something else.

"It's a long shot," Lizzie was saying. "That's the only kind worth putting anything on." Her baby was asleep, its mouth open. "If our horse places, then I'll have me a house with a garden, I will."

"Not me," Sally said. When she wasn't working, she wore a brimmed bonnet that half hid her face. "What would I want with a garden? I'll have a wig made from real human hair. And a dollhouse with ten rooms and three staircases, and that's not all because I'd have a little desk, too."

"Why do you want a desk?" Fay asked. "You can't write."

"For the drawers," Sally said, taking a swallow of gin. She had to stand on a box to reach the counter. "For the secret drawers."

The barmaid put a jug on the counter for a thickset man who used to be a stonecutter and still wore the leather cap, though no one had wanted stone cut by hand for years. "What about you, Nell?" she asked. "If your horse places."

Nehama looked up from her calculations. "If I had a winning horse," she said, "I'd go to the seaside. I'd take us all to the theater on the pier, and we'd have silk fans to flap like this." She picked up the Christian tract and fanned herself like a lady. She was making an extra bit from rolling men, and she figured she could buy her freedom in—she multiplied and divided like her oldest sister had taught her—seventeen months. "If only I didn't have to pay for the entrance fee," she muttered. "You know what it's like, Fay. A stone around your neck."

"What are you talking?" Fay asked.

"The entrance fee for foreigners to get their papers to stay in London." Nehama went over the numbers again, hoping she'd made a mistake.

"There's no entrance fee. Why do you think they call it the free land?"

"I mean the ten pounds the Squire paid for me," Nehama said.

Fay laughed, all her good teeth showing and a couple of the bad ones. She wore a black straw hat that flapped as she laughed. "Oh, that's rich. It went to Mr. Blink." She waved her hand, and the barmaid poured another glass of gin. "It's a finder's fee, that's all. He's good at finding, he is."

"No entrance fee," Nehama repeated. Then there wasn't any Newcomers' Committee and Mr. Blink had tricked her from the start. She'd been the fool. A bloody fool, and for that the world requires a usurious rate of interest.

"What difference does it make?" Fay asked. "You have to make it up just the same and pay for your lovely dress, too."

"I'm not hungry." Her hands were cold and her belly hot. She pushed her plate of sheep's trotters toward Sally. "Here, you have the rest."

"And me?" Fay lit her short pipe. "I'm a mother's child, too. What's the matter with you? Doesn't a *landsmann* come first?"

Nehama didn't answer. The Squire was waiting, and she had to make her way to the back of the pub between the rough-hewn tables of men drinking and playing draughts while they boasted of how much they'd got from coshing and rolling. The Squire smiled. He always smiled when he was annoyed.

"Well?" he asked. His table was round, just big enough for three to sit and talk while they drank, heads close together. He was knitting another scarf, this one of gold and silver. The other one had been found on a customs agent, ankles and wrists tied together, his jaw broken.

She handed the Squire a pile of money, and he let the coins drop through his fingers, clattering on the table. One fell onto the floor. He didn't move to pick it up. He was drinking with his old friend who smuggled tobacco and the customs agent they were bribing, the smuggler wearing his greatcoat and the customs agent his uniform. The two men were eyeing her as if they could get her cheap, being the ponce's friends. It was the same word in Yiddish and in English: *ponce*. Where did it come from first?

"That's all?" the Squire asked.

Nehama nodded. She'd given Sally half her take this morning. The younger girl's cough had kept her from earning what would be expected.

"It's not enough," the Squire said.

There were two kinds of criminals, liars and thieves. Mr. Blink was one and she was the other, so she shrugged, and then she spoke in a voice that didn't seem to belong to her but said cheerfully, "There's not many customers about. It's too cold."

"How much do you owe me now?" the Squire asked. There was another crack in the glass that covered the map of London on the wall, but the door marked PRIVAT was just the same. He sometimes took a girl there for rough pleasure after time was called and the pub emptied. "You're the best of my girls, Nell." The Squire looked at her fondly. There was so little fondness in this street.

"This is everything," she said, and hated herself because she wondered if his lips were as soft as they seemed. His hands were never chapped, nor his lips. He made up some kind of grease for his skin that he'd learned about in his sailing days.

"Are you quite all right, then?" he asked. The customs agent stoked his pipe. "Perhaps you want a doctor."

She flinched. How did he know that she still had bad dreams about the examination in the hospital? "I'm very well, thank you," she said.

"I ought to bring you to the infirmary. You might have a disease." The Squire drummed his fingers on the table. Nehama couldn't keep her eyes off his hands. Whenever he slapped her, he moved so fast she couldn't steel herself for it. He lifted his hand, and when she winced, he stroked her cheek.

"I've ordered warm weather from Him upstairs," she said. "Sunny as Spain it's going to be, and the customers will queue up for miles. You think I should warn the girls to get ready?"

The Squire laughed. "Right. I'll want more than this tomorrow." He scooped up the coins. "Or I'll have the rest in trade." He hardly ever took his own whores to bed. People said he was so rough, he couldn't make any money from them afterward. His hand was warm, the skin smooth, his eyes fixed on hers, his face like wood pitted by water, and Nehama wished that she could part from her body.

It must have been near her eighteenth birthday. She wasn't sure because she was born on the full moon, and the nights were too foggy to see the sky. But she'd be eighteen soon, and she was pregnant. The sponge doused in vinegar had failed, and the Squire would get her an abortion as soon as he found out. If she died, he'd be furious. But if she lived she'd owe him the money for the abortion plus interest. And she wanted the baby. She'd never wanted anything more.

Her sisters had told her about the time that a neighbor's boy was *khapped*. Snatched away to serve in the draft and make up the kidnappers' quota of new recruits. *Khapping* was a common tragedy when Mama was a young wife with a couple of babies and the czar passed a law that Jewish children must serve for ten years before they began the regular army draft. Mama was sewing the trimming on a gown when the neighbor came running in from the courtyard and Grandma Nehama listened to the story, a baby in each arm. It was a tragedy, but what could anyone do? A bribe they didn't have. Grandma Nehama found out where the kidnappers were staying, and out she went, taking with her a hatchet. Her daughter and son-in-law pleaded with her. Murder wasn't going to solve a thing. She would die too, there would be more *khappers,* and the boy would be lost anyway. Mama cried till she didn't have any breath left. You think I'm going to let a Jewish child be taken away? Grandma Nehama asked. You think there aren't enough graves already? It was spring, and her skirts were muddy when she arrived at the place where the kidnappers were staying, and for some reason, the mud smelled of wine. Maybe because it was just after Purim, and when people got tipsy to celebrate the holiday, they weren't too steady with a bottle. Grandma Nehama gave the innkeeper a few *groschen* to keep the *khappers* drunk. Then she went upstairs with her hatchet and she chopped off the boy's smallest two toes from his right foot. He was seven years old. Back to his mother he went, and he grew up to be nothing special, just a man who limped and made custom shoes for people with unusual feet. His wife visited Grandma Nehama's grave at every festival. She was the best friend of Nehama's oldest sister and told her what was said to the boy that night. Put up your foot. Remember that as long as you can preserve life, there's hope.

Whitechapel Road

It was a Saturday night, and the street was lit by a few flickering lamps, the courts and alleys off it by none. But those that knew this place could see that the clump of shadows on the stairs was women talking, hands folded under their aprons. That small patch of darkness in the passage was a baby sleeping, and the grayness over there by the archway was only boys tossing stones. The faint rustling was rats. The shadows that lay too still in pools of deeper darkness was somebody else's business and you ought mind your own. Nehama had learned to see well in the night, and she made her way easily, walking with Sally to the high road, where everything was bright.

In Whitechapel Road the darkness was layered with torches and the stalls with everything edible. There were gin palaces and public houses, clubs and shooting galleries, music halls and preachers saving souls, and every store that sold books or bread or hats was open till midnight. Nehama fed Sally hot pies and cider until she looked like a healthy girl. They watched the stilt walkers dance, and the puppet

Punch beat up his wife, Judy, and the contortionist put his legs around his neck as he walked on his hands, jumping out of the way of the donkey pulling a barrow of cabbages. And their laughter made them happy girls clapping along with the crowd. Then Nehama took Sally into a pub she knew that was in an alley off the high road. One that was quiet and dimly lit and as old as the first king. The men that came here didn't sing or play darts. Their wage packets were thick, and they meant to spend it all.

Nehama slid next to a man who had a glass and a bottle that was nearly empty. "Have you ever had two girls, mister?" she asked in a voice as hushed as the darkness. "And one never been with a man?"

The man slowly turned to look at Sally. "How old are you, girl?" he asked.

Sally only smiled. "She's my little sister, mister," Nehama said.

The man drank the rest of his bottle. "How much?"

"I daresay more than you've got."

"That what you think?" He grabbed her arm. But she just smiled. And Sally smiled, and her cheeks were the red of a Spanish child.

"It's all right, sister," Sally said in her high voice.

And the man never knew how well she picked his pocket clean while they lay with him in the back room of the pub.

By morning, Sally had picked the pockets of five men. She was very pleased with her work in the high road. "The Squire's going to be fond of me today," she said as they were walking back.

"I'm not giving mine to him." The wind was whistling through the cracks in the dawn, and it was singing her grandmother's song.

"You're having me on, Nell."

"Keep your share, but don't say you got it with me. I'm putting it aside for something."

She wouldn't have the baby in Dorset Street. It would be by the sea in a nice boardinghouse where she'd have a room to herself. After the baby was born, she'd carry it outside to the good sea air, walking along the pier and listening to the music of minstrels and bands. At the end of the pier would be the theater where she'd see the new plays, nursing the baby to sleep. Her baby would have fair hair like her sisters, and when the golden curls touched its shoulders, the baby would be dressed in a white cap and a white dress and she would have a picture taken of her baby sitting on a donkey. The photograph would be sent home, and everyone would see the beauty of her child.

Dock Street

Nehama hid the money from that night. The railway station was just a fifteen-minute walk straight down from Dorset Street, and she didn't see anyone follow her as she took a roundabout route through alleys and courts. She hadn't even said good-bye to Sally but slipped away in the afternoon, when everyone was just rising from sleep. Now she waited alone on the track while the red locomotives came in puffing smoke under the iron ribs and glass roof of the train station, looking here and there for someone who might have followed her, but she didn't see anyone she knew. There were so many people standing on the platform, holding third-class tickets. There was nothing to worry about. No reason for her hands to sweat. She was just another person who'd got soaked on the way to the train station. The woman next to her was asking, "Is this the train for Brighton, then?" Nehama could feel the heat of the train as it rushed into the station. She was nodding, about to say, "Are you having a holiday?" when she saw Lizzie standing over there by the clock tower, her thin hair falling over her face. And then the Squire was pushing between two men carrying fighting cocks in a crate. In front of her the train had stopped, around her the crowd was waiting for the doors to open, there was nowhere for her to go when he grabbed her arm.

He walked with her behind a pile of rubbish in the train yard, holding her tightly against him, so tightly that she stumbled like a drunk and nobody took notice. The rain had stopped and the fog come up. It hid the river and the Tower, it softened the rattle of trains. But the Squire was larger than the fog and the whistle of his walking stick louder than church bells as they reached the back of the rubbish heap. She didn't see the first blow; the stick swung behind her legs, knocking the breath out of her as she fell against a broken wheelbarrow, covering her head with her arms and curling her legs as she tumbled into the mud. He struck again, and she screamed loud to please him so that he wouldn't kill her as she fought for breath. She couldn't faint, she had to think of the baby.

"I'm sorry," she gasped, half sitting, her back against the rubbish heap. In the distance ordinary people were boarding the train. Porters pushed carts loaded with trunks. "I won't do it again."

"I don't give chances. Not to them as runs away. It's a matter of what's mine," he said, lifting the walking stick. It was made of black-thorn, a cane for warding off vicious dogs. The top was curved, the stick burred with thorns. "Did I pay for you? Was you worth it?"

"Yes," she said, arms crossed over her belly. "I mean no. Don't hurt me."

"And why not? This is mine," he said, bringing the stick down. "And this and this." The stick followed her as she rolled from side to side, taking everything it could find. She gave it her back, she gave it her bottom and her legs, but the baby she hid under her cloak, under her arms, inside her skin.

"Please don't kill me," she begged. She was lying on her side, cheek in the mud. It was a thick mud, a gray clay mud. "Please."

The Squire leaned on the cane, wiping his face of sweat. He wore a plaid waistcoat and a green scarf around his neck. Behind him a train blew steam as it left the station.

Her body was burning; she could feel every bruise, and the only place she didn't hurt was her belly. "It was a mistake. I was just out walking," she whimpered. "Lizzie saw me just walking."

"Then you won't walk so far again." He tapped her arm with the stick. It was wet with mud and blood. "You'll remember?" he asked, squatting beside her. "Give me your hand on it." She reached out a hand, and he held it for a moment, looking at her closely as if she were naked and he was noticing the oddness of her private parts.

"I'll remember," she whispered, kissing his hand as if she loved it.

Then he took out his knife. Gravel bit her cheek. The clock tower chimed as he lifted her dress. "I'll make sure of it," he said, and the knife was dull in the dull light.

He was getting rid of the baby, that was it, and then she would bleed to death. Her eyes were blurred with mud. She wanted to see the clock tower so she'd know the time that her life ended. Never mind. What did it matter? She'd follow her child into the other world so it wouldn't be there alone.

But it was only her thigh that he stroked, saying, "Here's the mark to remind you of what you owe. You forget and you're dead." Only now, when the Squire cut into the flesh of her thigh, could she run from her body, hiding up there with the unseen moon, and there she stayed, listening to her grandmother sing: "The wind, the wind, the raging wind . . ."

Dorset Street

The ceiling slanted down toward Nehama as she slept and woke, unsure of the time. Fingers of light and dark came in through the cracks with the whistling wind as she listened to the sounds of the lodging house. Mice in the walls. Feet on the stairs. The squeaking of beds on old floors. Shouting. A thump. A song. Coughing. That was Sally, sitting on the floor, resting her head and arms on the bed. Nehama was naked. Even her thin nightgown had been taken away so she wouldn't leave the room. She thought it was Sally who'd covered her with the blanket. In the stupor of her waking and sleeping, it felt like a soft blanket. Soft and thick. The beating hadn't got rid of the baby. Anything was believable.

"Are you awake?" Sally asked. "There's something for you to eat."

Nehama shook her head. She only wanted to talk about the seaside. The promenades. The donkey rides. The colored sand and shells and pebbles to arrange in a box with seaweed. The theater at the end of the pier. "When my horse places, we'll go to Brighton," she said.

"Then I'll want a chair for the beach," Sally said. Her short hair stood around her head in thin puffs.

"We'll hire two. And have a bag of cherries." Nehama touched a wisp of her dark hair. The baby's would be fair. There would be a cap trimmed with lace to protect it from the sun.

"A drop of white satin for me." Sally didn't care how thin a gown she wore. It could be as transparent as glass. But as long as there was the feel of cloth against her skin, she believed that her body wasn't visible, and she was sure that the priest would give her absolution before her death because no man had seen her naked.

"Not me. I'll drink chocolate made with cream and whipped egg."

"We'll swim in a bathing machine."

"For hours," Nehama said. But the blanket was starting to scratch her. It was made of rough, cheap wool, and her eyes watered, the tears mixed with mud.

The air was mild, the sun shining palely, and Nehama could hear bells—maybe a school bell or a church bell. She sat hunched in the doorway of the Horn and Plenty, watching the sign swing on one bolt as if about to fall but never falling. No one paid her any mind. A dead wife could lie on a table for a week for want of money to bury her, and there were plenty of men and women smoking a fag or nursing a wound, crouched in the doorways of doss-houses.

The baby was coming out of Nehama like a foggy drizzle. What luck, the other girls would say. The rags she'd stuffed into her under-things were soaked. It must be four o'clock. The muffin man was ring-ing his bell, a tray of muffins on his head. The sad-looking costermonger with his barrow of old vegetables bought a muffin for tea. So did the knife grinder, and also the little tailor that mended whores' dresses, stepping high as if he might avoid the muck of sewage and blown-about rubbish.

Sally opened the door. "The Squire's placing his bets. I'm to stay with you till he's done." She took a drink from her bottle of laudanum. Soon her eyes would glaze. "You're looking awful white."

"So what?" Nehama was losing the baby and with it every desire. Eating was too much effort. Sleeping impossible. Her friends would have to watch out for themselves. Sally held out the bottle of lau-danum, but Nehama shook her head. She needed nothing.

Sally pulled her bonnet forward. "The sun's in my eyes. And I'm getting awfully sleepy." She sat down on the step. "Someone might beg a copper off a cove and go to the infirmary and I wouldn't know noth-ing." Her voice was very soft and tired.

"Someone might." Nehama didn't move. The Horn and Plenty stood at the corner of Dorset Street and Bell Lane. Within a block there were Jewish shops. It was as close as that, her old life. But she was some-one else now, a bit of cabbage leaf left on the ground at midnight when the Saturday night market packed up and the lamps went dark.

"There's not much left in this bottle. I'll have another drop, I think." Sally leaned back against the door and closed her eyes.

"I'm too tired to move."

"You're sick." Sally opened her eyes, momentarily wakeful. "Get on or I'll call the Squire."

"All right, already." Nehama pulled herself to her feet. If she died in a Jewish street, maybe someone would say the prayer for the dead. Sally didn't say good-bye as she slumped in the doorway, holding tight the nearly empty bottle of laudanum.

Frying Pan Alley

Buyers and sellers pressed close together, with wares spread on the ground in front and stalls behind, one leaning up against the next. The market stretched along Petticoat Lane to the surrounding streets, Goulston and Wentworth, and the smallest passageways like Frying Pan Alley. People thronged among bright awnings and painted tables, admiring the jugglers and fingering nearly new coats, looking at masks and pastries, for it was the eve of Purim and there was a queue at the green coffee stall. It had four tin cans mounted with brass plates, separate compartments for bread, sandwiches, and cake, and only a penny for a warm cup of coffee mixed with chicory.

"FRIED FISH! 'TATERS HOT! BUY MY PRETTY MEAT!"

"ALL THE NEW SONGS ONLY A PENNY!"

"Excuse me." A fat woman wearing a kerchief and a dark red shawl looked at Nehama nervously, her hand over her pocket, and Nehama, with her face burning, bumped the old cow as she walked by to push her into the gutter the way a girl from Dorset Street should, though the pain in her belly made her dizzy.

"TONIGHT IS PURIM, BROTHERS. GET YOUR MASKS!"

"HAMMENTASHEN FRESH!"

She had to sit down. In the shadows of a narrow alley, no one would notice her. Past the school. Past the stall that sold toffee and monkey-nuts to children. Past the girls dancing around the organ-grinder. To sit on a stoop and enter a dream where nothing mattered as blood seeped through her dress.

Her sisters used to tell her what Grandma Nehama said about the good inclination and the evil inclination. Everyone has both the *yetzer-hara* and the *yetzer-hatov*. The rabbis explain that the *yetzer-hara,* the evil inclination, is necessary for a man to build a house or make a family. But Grandma Nehama said that when a woman has a child, she puts her good inclination into it and that their mother had given them everything, you could see it in their golden hair. But you, her sisters would say to Nehama, are dark. Your hair is dark and your skin is dark; Mama gave away everything good to us. There wasn't anything left for you. Thank God our grandmother isn't here to see you filled with the evil inclination.

They said this on the day the two middle sisters found her standing on the doorstep of a tavern and they smacked her so she'd remember. The song she heard that day was a Polish drinking song, and it was the same melody as the last hymn sung in the synagogue on Sabbath mornings. Hymns and drinking songs often share the same tunes. But a woman's voice was not to be heard in the synagogue as the sound of it might inflame the evil inclination of men, which when harnessed properly begat children in houses but when allowed to run free—well, the results were all around.

Grandma Nehama cooked and cleaned, hauled the water, hung the laundry, and kept the accounts, which she taught the oldest sister. When any of the men on the street began a business venture, their wives came to Grandma Nehama so she could calculate what interest would be on a loan of capital to buy a barrow and a stock of lemons, or a machine and some leather, or a counter and shelves with goods to put on them. You have to sell this much, she would say, just to pay the interest, and don't forget on top of that you need to make enough money to buy food for the children. She did her figuring on brown wrapping paper, standing next to the tile oven, where it was warm. Then she would say whether it was a good idea or not. Mr. Pollack, who lent money when no one else would, didn't like Grandma Nehama. She was depressing his business. A handsome man with brains enough not to threaten her, he came to see her about it, offering her a percentage. She considered it for a week. The evil inclination and the good inclination fought hard, and she got a chill because the instinct for self-preservation, the *yetzer-hara,* was weakened. But when she rose up from her sickbed, she started the Women's Singing Society. On Thursday evenings there was no sewing in the workshop. Women came to sing and drink tea, and if each of them put a few *groschen* in a jar like the men did in their friendly societies that doled out sick benefits and gave out loans, then it was no one else's affair.

Of course those were in the days when she was living. A grandmother's spirit can't lift a feather in this world. But she can see what's going on. And if you could hear her, she'd be whispering prayers in a graveyard:

Holy souls, I greet you. May our sins not be judged harshly, for we are all dust and ashes and we have no strength to contend with the fiery angel, the evil inclination. So I bow before the King of kings, the Holy One, and ask for mercy for this child. Let it be a time of compassion. The wind from the east is blowing so hard that the river will overflow with the mama-loshen. *For the sake of our mothers, turn the wind and bring them safely into the channel.*

The full moon was climbing secretly into the sky. Later it would look down on the small Jewish corner of London, where people would wear masks and eat pastries and watch skits that made them laugh. And they'd drink until they couldn't tell the difference between the good uncle of the Jewish queen and her enemy, the minister who'd issued the king's decree to kill all the Jews on Purim. But you never know how things will turn out. On that day, he'd met his downfall. And a hundred generations later, Nehama was born on Purim. She'd made her first appearance just as the moon came into a black sky. And if a grandmother's spirit had watched her then, why shouldn't it watch now? The sky stretches from Plotsk to London, after all. And the moon is just as full.

CHAPTER 2

At the Threshold

LONDON, 1876

Frying Pan Alley

Nehama saw it all dimly, the children dancing around the organ-grinder, the stall of holiday pastries and the stall of feathered masks, the jacket seller reaching up with his pole to unhook a used jacket and hand it down to the prospective customer. It was all she could do not to faint.

"You bleeding," a voice said in a heavy accent. "*Gotteniu.* Just look."

"A genius you are," Nehama said in a similar accent as she turned her head slightly. A young woman stood just outside the door to the house.

"You're from the *heim!*" She looked at Nehama's ruffled dress, stippled with blood. "Where do you live?" She spoke in a crude Yiddish, the cadence of water carriers and cart drivers.

"Don't worry. It's not your business." Nehama answered in the *mama-loshen* without thinking, as if the pain of the miscarriage had made her forget that the mother tongue didn't belong to her anymore.

"Maybe you have someone I could fetch for you?"

"Oh yes. My grandma, *alleva sholom.* And while you're at the grave, be so kind as to ask my grandpa what he does with his balls while he studies Torah with the saints in heaven."

"Oh, you're so funny. I'm killing myself laughing. Too bad you're bleeding your death."

"Forget it." Nehama tried to get up so she could walk out of the alley and away from the school that was ringing its bell. She stumbled, crumpling half on the stoop and half off it.

"Dear God in heaven, thank you very much," the young woman said, pulling Nehama up. "Why did I have to come outside just this minute? God forbid she should die here on the step. Not to mention that I always had too much of the good inclination, God help me. Up you get, Miss Comedienne."

Nehama had no strength left to resist the hand on her elbow, leading her inside and up a flight of stairs to a room with flaking walls and a window stained with yellow fog. She bit her lip to keep herself from fainting as she sat on the pot the young woman gave her, leaning her head against the other girl's knees until the rest of the baby came out. The young woman helped her to the bed, then emptied the pot out the window onto the roof of the shack in the backyard, its contents joining fish bones and a broken bowl and boots too old to pawn.

Against the wall, there was a dresser with a few dishes, some cups, a board, bread. A shawl and a coat hung on hooks. Above the fireplace, a cheap blue china vase stood on the mantel, the sort that old clothes men gave as a premium when they paid a penny for a used shirt.

"I'm Minnie," the young woman said. "In the home I was Malkah, but now I want an English name. And you?"

"Better you should call me Nehama. I'm not so fond of English names."

"All right, Nehama. This dress is finished. Let me take it off. I'll get rid of it, and here, you put on my old one. You don't have to thank me."

"I'm not thanking you. I just want to go." If only she could sit up, but she was still so dizzy.

"You're not going somewhere with my dress. Just lie down and don't die while my back is turned."

Nehama meant to close her eyes for only a minute, but she woke up on the straw pallet not sure of where she was. A paraffin lamp was burning on the dresser and a candle on the table. The red-haired young woman and her husband were arguing. It must be about me, Nehama thought groggily.

"You see this bread? I bought it from someone that looked exactly like Shmuel the baker back home," the man was saying. He was short, with a round chin, a skimpy beard.

"There was no baker named Shmuel. Unless you mean Shmuel with the hump, maybe?" Minnie was about the same age as Nehama. Eighteen, nineteen. It was the coarseness of her voice that made Nehama feel she could stay here for a little while.

"I mean the husband of Pearl. If she kept her mouth shut, you never saw such a beauty," the husband said. Water dripped from a leak in the ceiling onto his cap.

"No, no. He was married to Hanna-Rivka. She was something to look at." Minnie's sleeves were rolled up, her freckled arms plump. "You don't remember anything." She turned. "Let her be the judge. Tell me, my friend—who's right?"

"Our guest from the *heim*!" he said. "Come here and join us." It must have been the dress that was fooling him. The high-necked brown dress she'd borrowed from his wife, and the Yiddish as if Nehama were some girl awaiting her betrothal. If he only realized that she was a *dybbuk*. A ghost that haunts the living.

"I just, I . . ." Nehama stammered.

"You should sit with us. Have something to eat," he said. "We'll tell each other stories about where we're from. Isn't that what newcomers always do?"

Nehama came to the table made from crates and boards stamped EAST INDIA COMPANY. Minnie poured her a cup of weak tea. In the shops used tea leaves were well mixed with new ones before they were sold in a twist of brown paper.

"Does it matter what used to be?" Minnie asked. "Only that we're strangers here, together. This is my husband, Lazar. He's a presser in a tailoring workshop." She cut a slice of black bread, spreading it thick with butter.

Lazar took off his boot. A nail was sticking up, and he banged it back in with a piece of wood. Outside the organ-grinder was playing, and he hummed along. "Before we were strangers. Now we're *landsmann*."

How Nehama hated that word. *Landsmann*. It meant a pimp standing at the docks or a whore that fetched a broom. "We're still strangers," she said.

"Watch what you're doing." Nehama's hand was trembling, and Minnie took the cup from her. "You're spilling tea on our fine table. Look at this. No milk. Go to the dairy, Lazar. What is a room without milk? I'm not going to drink my tea with lemon like a *greener*. Go already."

When she was alone with Nehama, she leaned forward and said, "All right. Now we can talk. Tell me what's what." She was smiling. Nehama didn't. The high collar on the brown dress was choking her. The cheap wool scratched her skin. She was hungry for winkles and sheep's trotters and the loud hum of the Horn and Plenty that made her forget she was a ghost. "I have to go," she said. "I don't belong here, and you know it yourself. You saw what was going on."

Minnie cleared away the dishes, putting them on the dresser. "What do I know? That you were irregular. A dress was stained. It's not a pestilence, it can happen to anyone. One month you bleed like a slaughtered chicken and the next—nothing. It's the nature of girls. When I got it, I bled for two weeks. I was white as a sheet. Later it gets better, my mother says."

"I doubt it." The room was making Nehama sick. She couldn't stand the tin candlesticks on the mantel near the vase. Or the box in the corner, labeled in Yiddish, "For Passover." A ghost ought to stay among the dead. If it comes too close to the living world, it might get trapped there, yearning for the body it can never have again. She couldn't sit one more minute with this woman, who might be one of her sisters saying, We should have slapped you harder. "I'll leave tonight," Nehama said.

"And why should you? Before you came, we had trouble making the rent. Now we can have a lodger."

"With what will I pay you rent?"

"Tell me what you can do."

Nehama was so tired. She just couldn't stand on her feet tonight. "If your husband brings me some finishing from the workshop, I'll do hems. Or buttonholes. Tomorrow you can find a real lodger. There's no shortage."

"Listen to me. You can't run away naked, and I'm not rich enough to spare that dress you're wearing. Stay with us until Passover and give me what you get from sewing the buttonholes. Then we'll call it even."

"You still don't understand, do you? The dress I was wearing when you found me . . ."

"The dress? Oh, you mean that *shmata*. The rag I threw out." Minnie's eyes were as green as marshgrass. "What a mess. I can't remember what it looked like. Can you?"

And the odd thing was that Nehama couldn't. Did it have two ruffles or three? Was the skirt green? Or maybe it was blue and the sleeves green. "All right. Just until Passover."

"Good. When Lazar comes back, we'll go to the Lane. It's Purim in London. We have to drink until we don't remember the difference between the name of a good man and an evil one. Am I right?"

Nehama met Minnie's knowing eyes with her own. "I'm not putting a foot outside until I can go far away. I don't dare."

Minnie sat and thought for a while, drinking her tea with lemon after all because you make do with what you have at hand. "You know, women often die from too much bleeding down there. Like my own cousin, she should rest in peace. If someone died in my room, I'd put an advertisement in the *East London Telegraph*. It would be a religious obligation to give a relative the chance to bury someone properly before I gave up the corpse for a pauper's burial."

For a minute, Nehama had some hope. No one would look for a dead whore. "But I can't afford an advertisement," she said. "And I don't want any debts."

"Debt? Who's talking debt? I'm only saying what I would do if a person died in my room. You're absolutely right. Today you don't go to the Lane. You stay here and don't put a foot out the door. In a few days, we'll see."

"Only tonight," Nehama said.

"Tonight, tomorrow. You show me how to sew a hem. I drive Lazar crazy with my ten thumbs. But first I'll do your hair in the new style. Curls are in fashion now. If I had a coal stove, I'd heat up rags and do mine, but what does it matter anyway? Those curls never last. You'll see what a beauty you are when I'm finished with you. Who taught you to sew?"

"My father," Nehama murmured. "In the *heim* he's a custom tailor."

"Oh, you have *yikhus*." Minnie laughed, and Nehama smiled a little because *yikhus* meant a lineage of rabbis and great scholars and businessmen so fine they never saw a peasant, nothing like her family, but among the working people a custom tailor was the cream, someone with skilled hands who fitted gowns and coats on people of quality and so absorbed something of their honor.

"And you?" Nehama asked.

"My family has *yikhus,* too. A horse and a cart, that was our *yikhus*. And my uncle was a porter who carried hundredweights. The plainest of the plain. Do you know this song?" As Minnie took the pins from Nehama's hair and began to brush it, she sang something in Yiddish.

Nehama shook her head. "I never heard it."

"I'm trying to fix your hair. Stay still and I'll teach you the song. It's as good as anything in a music hall." The stroking of the brush and the hands in her hair, turning and pinning, made Nehama sleepy, and for the first time, in her half dream, she thought there might be a place somewhere between depravity and a courtyard full of watchful sisters. A place where it might be all right to have a friend who wasn't surprised and wasn't shocked and who sang in a low, quiet voice:

> In the police station I sit in anguish
> They just want to torture me.
> For them it's all a good laugh
> And I should entertain them.
>
> How is it possible to sing anymore
> When troubles are pressing?
> Oh, the strength is leaving me
> For thirst and for hunger.
>
> You, God in heaven, you understand
> What kind of men have arrested me.
> Send down from heaven a fire
> And burn up the whole station.
>
> Send me home, dear God,
> To delight in a fresh life.

And on cruel men and cutthroats
I'll never look again.

Nehama hadn't heard any songs like this from her sisters. The melody was something new, too, and she couldn't stop herself from joining in, though the scar on her thigh was aching. If you looked from a distance, you'd see two girls side by side at a rough table, their hair pinned up like their mothers', one dark and one ginger. If you could hear well, you'd know that someone else was joining in, too, for even in the next world a new song is welcome.

The Lane

Nehama stayed and sewed, amazed that the desire for life made her eat and sleep even when she woke up to the sound of a baby crying and there was no baby there. She slept on a straw pallet, dreaming about Sally and the Squire and the Horn and Plenty. When she awoke, her eyes on the cheap blue vase above the fireplace, she listened to the creak of a bed, the sound of newspaper pushed into boots to block the holes, the bang of a kettle on a tripod in the fireplace, the Yiddish conversation of morning. "Get up. Have tea. The bedbugs bit me all night." A month passed, and the full moon brought Passover. She ate the sweet mixture of nuts and apples and the bitter herbs on *motzos,* she sang the old familiar songs, strange in her mouth.

The end of Passover came with a break in the drizzle, the sun shining on wet pavement. In the Lane a crowd listened to the street doctor holding a vial of green fire, and another crowd watched a little rat in a monk's hood walk across a wire toward the hand holding a morsel of food. The salesman of used clothes flung a sample of his trousers, which landed on a stall of paste jewelry. The news vendor spread the weekly across his table, embellishing accounts of stranglings and stabbings with his deep voice and the flourish of his hands in pantomime of foul deeds. The throng pushed and shifted, the boot makers, the drunks, the match girls scarred by phosphorus, the beggars and the boys selling lemons. The one-man band marched beside the streetcar striped green and red, and all the while the bell foundry tolled its bells, practicing for the future.

"WHO'LL BUY A HAT FOR TWO BOB, WORTH FIVE, SO HELP ME GOD!"

"THIS WAY FOR THE SINGING DWARF!"

Nehama felt herself more akin to the gentile girls wearing straw hats than to these strangers with their unfamiliar accents. "You're telling me these are Jews?" she asked Minnie.

"Not from the *heim,* but still Jews of a kind. Dutch and German," Minnie said. "You have to talk English with them. They don't speak the *mama-loshen.*" Jews from Poland had been arriving in a slow trickle for twenty years. After all, a flood begins with the rising of the river, but Yiddish wasn't often heard in these streets, yet. "The Dutch sell fish."

"I don't like them," Nehama said.

"Never mind. I'm not making you a wedding. Come with me. Let's get you a hat and show these *yekehs* how to bargain. Try this one with the blue feather."

"Perfect for you," the seller said. "With this hat you could visit the queen. And a special price for you today." He had a foreign face. Nothing Polish in it. A girl arriving at the docks would never believe that he was a *landsmann.*

"I don't want the hat," Nehama said. She wanted no finery. There were girls on either side of her, pushing in to look at the hat. Let them have it.

"I fancy this one," Minnie said, picking out a hat with a bunch of cherries dangling from it.

"Even better. Suits you exactly right, miss," the seller said.

Minnie tried it on, tilting her head this way and that, and ignoring the big woman who squeezed beside her to reach for the hats. "Maybe I'll take it. How much?"

"Two bob."

"Sixpence," Nehama said. The sun was warming her back. It was the first time she'd felt warm in months. Why shouldn't she pretend for a minute that she was in the market square in Plotsk? She was only eighteen, and at home she'd have had a new dress for Passover.

"This hat is practically new. And with cherries. Are you trying to kill me?"

"Ten. And not another penny," she said. Someone was playing a tune on musical glasses set up in a small barrow.

"Give me a shilling and I'll throw in a red bow for your hair. Such fine dark hair as you have. Red's just the color," the seller said.

"Done." The hat on Minnie's head, the red bow on Nehama's curls. At home, red ribbons were worn to keep away the evil eye.

"'TATERS! WARM YER HANDS AND FILL YER BELLY FOR A PENNY!"

"GIVE A PENNY FOR A LAME WIDOW WITH TEN CHILDREN!"

"A good bargain," Minnie said to Nehama, walking arm in arm past the man swallowing fire. "But now I have a problem. An old hat walking with a new hat doesn't go. So you'll help me get a new hat for Lazar, right?"

"Can you afford it?" Nehama asked.

"Look—it's only a bob. A week's rent from a lodger. What's that? Nothing. Less than nothing."

Nehama shook her head. "If it was me, I'd put it away, and in a few years, I could send for my family. Then I'd start saving for a shop."

"You couldn't," Minnie said. "There's too much to buy in London. You'd never manage it."

"I could," Nehama said. "If I made up my mind."

"Talk is cheap," Minnie said. She almost looked pretty, her eyes shining with mischief under the hat with cherries. "You show me what you can do."

"Maybe I will." Nehama touched her new red bow. A person had her hands full with the real evils of the world without thinking about eyes gazing from the sky.

"FISH HEADS! HAVE THAT FISH HEAD, MISTER. LOOK AT THE SMILE HE'S GOT ON HIM! HE DIED HAPPY KNOWING YOU'D HAVE HIM FOR THE THIRD MEAL ON THE SABBATH. MAKE YOU SMART, HE WILL."

Every Passover the story of the Exodus from Egypt is retold, but there is always another chapter to the history of a people. After the Jews stopped running for their lives, they started to complain. Every day, sand. Every day, manna to eat. It came from God, but always the same—white, plain. In Egypt they'd had onions and garlic and meat, and a person always had a job. Sure, it was no pleasure to be a slave, but is it such a joy to walk in the desert day after day? They complained and they rebelled, and in the end, God in heaven made them wander in the desert for forty years until a new generation came that was used to the sand. For them it was all normal. The sand. The freedom. In every person's heart there is both the old generation and the new, struggling together.

After Passover, Nehama continued to wake in the night from dreams of a baby in a white cap trimmed with lace. The baby had Sally's face. Worse, sometimes it was the Squire's. Nehama awoke sweating, and occasionally she cried out. Her grandmother cried out, too. They were in exile together.

MINSK, 1882

Moskovskaya Street

The flowers in the garden were brown and mummified, and in the countryside the peasants were cutting golden rye with scythes as sharp as the angel of death's, though not quite as sharp as their new czar's. The "little father" had been ruling for a year, and the streets of Minsk were crowded with refugees. They came from towns where Jewish professionals and students had been allowed to live among the proud Russians as long as they were not too visible, but now that the court's eyesight had become keener, it revoked all permits to live outside the Pale of Settlement, where Jews were grudgingly tolerated as they must live somewhere, one supposed. As many of the refugees were housed as the Jewish community could accommodate, but still there were many that slept in the street. Their faces had no expression; they didn't look anyone in the eye as they begged.

Emilia Rosenberg wasn't allowed out into the streets. A girl of sixteen had to be carefully watched. The brick walls of her garden were high, and the only door was the one that led into the kitchen, where the maid was disguising Mother's dry brisket with carrots and potatoes. In the garden, the branches of the tree bent low, as if the ghost of the first Mrs. Rosenberg was reading the newspaper Emilia left on the bench when she went inside. There was to be a dinner with guests, and admiration was better than any lady's tonic made with opium. If everyone else found her charming, then why should her father's opinion be of any consequence?

The dining room table was covered with an embroidered cloth and set with wine goblets, brandy snifters, shot glasses for vodka, and silverware of many sizes. At the head of the table, Father said the blessings over wine and bread. Next to him were Emilia's brothers and their wives. She sat with her mother at the other end of the table, in exile with the Sabbath guests. They were refugees, a brother and sister who'd been evicted from their village in the *vilda riechus*—the wild odors of the countryside—and a young man expelled from the university under the new laws that restricted Jews. His name was Mr. Levy, and the president of the Jewish Council had asked Father, as a favor, to hire him as a tutor for Emilia.

The sideboard was crowded with the silver samovar, soup tureens, and platters of fish, chicken, and brisket. Above it was one of Mama's paper-cuts, a scene of the first garden, with its Tree of Knowledge and the snake. Steam from the chicken soup curled in front of it, and the snake smiled as it smelled the scent of meat. Emilia nibbled on a piece of *challah* sprinkled with salt, eyeing Mr. Levy. She was wearing her new autumn gown, which brought out the gray of her eyes and the gold of her hair. It was just too bad that her swanlike neck was concealed by a high collar. But Mama had insisted.

"I used to envy you young people," Father said. "We never had your chances. But now it's all come to nothing—the professions are closed to Jews just like they used to be. And even a trade to put something in your mouth, you don't have. So tell me what you learned at the university, Mr. Levy."

Her brothers were eating silently as usual, their wives discussing winter cloaks. With fur collars or without this year?

"What I studied is of no consequence, sir, since I had to leave." Mr. Levy didn't seem to care that he was using the wrong fork. He had no beard, only a mustache as black and independent as a cat's tail.

"Character is everything, my young man," Father said. "I own a factory, and I hire the workers because their nature is to be a hammer and mine the hand that holds it. As the song says, 'A pretty girl is plucked, an ugly one left on the branch.'"

Mother was talking to the brother and sister from the countryside, telling them about the time she'd charmed the Russian officers and saved her first family from death. She waved her hand in an elegant gesture. Only Emilia would know that, under the lacy cuff, her wrist had white scars. One day when Emilia had come in from the garden, she'd seen Mother's wrist running like meat set to drain. There's been an accident, Mama had said. Emilia had bound her wrist in a strip of her apron and run next door to fetch the doctor. Since then, Mama said she didn't like to go out much. When your charm fails, you feel the cold terribly, and so she wore her heaviest cloak to the opera. What would she do when winter came?

The maid dug a serving fork into the overcooked chicken, putting a wing on Mr. Levy's plate. "Pardon the dryness," Father said. "Mrs. Rosenberg considers herself too good for the wifely arts."

Mother kept on talking to the guests as if she didn't hear a word Father said. She'd lent her ruby earrings to Emilia because they matched the silk roses on her new gown.

"I'm afraid that Miss Rosenberg takes after her mother."

"But someone's true nature isn't easily revealed." It was foolish of Mr. Levy to disagree with Father. A guest should just enjoy the good wine and keep his opinions to himself.

"On the contrary," Father said. The gaslit chandelier cast blue shadows over his plate. "A man of experience can see a person's nature in a glance. And no amount of good influence can change it."

Emilia thought about her sleeves. She really ought to have sleeves off the shoulder. She had nice shoulders—maybe for spring.

"You see my wife," Father said. "And daughter—"

"I beg to disagree, sir," Mr. Levy interrupted. "Unless you know a person's thoughts, you don't know him."

He was looking at Emilia as if he had some business with her. But he had no right to gaze at her so boldly, as if he could picture her dreaming about an Italian villa where she walked in a loose white gown, barefoot, the grass soft, a paintbrush in her hand, a canvas on the easel. As if he saw the table for making paper-cuts and her mother walking toward it from the villa, holding a tray of fruit for their lunch. There was no brick wall. You could see for miles.

"Am I right, Miss Rosenberg?" he asked.

"I'm sure I don't know." She could have any number of admirers sitting in her father's parlor. She didn't need Mr. Levy and his eyes digging into hers. Mother would at least agree to a winter cloak with a fur collar.

"What you need to know," Father said, refilling his wineglass, "is what a person does behind your back. Let's say you have a wife. A beautiful wife. Other people might also like to admire her beauty. Can you be sure of her when you're not there? Beauty, my friend, conceals slyness."

Emilia's brothers were not too beautiful, nor were their wives. They motioned to the maid to bring more food while Emilia wished herself young enough to hide behind the damask curtains.

"My daughter is clever as well as beautiful," Father said. A stranger might think it was a compliment.

Mother fell silent. She put her hand on Emilia's. "I expect to be a wife and mother like any other girl," Emilia said. "Mother taught me what I need to know."

"I'm sure she did," Father said dryly.

The guests looked from Father to Mother. The brothers drank more wine, eyes glazing. Their wives suddenly asked to be excused from the table. Father waved them away.

"May I be excused, too?" Emilia asked.

"I don't know," Father said slowly. "Tell me what you've done and then I might be the judge."

"I mean from the table, please."

"Ah. I see." Father sat back quietly for a moment. Then he leaned forward. "Why did you call in the doctor?"

"It was nothing, Father. I—"

"Does your mother enjoy his company very often?" He tapped the table with his spoon.

"It was only once, Father. For myself. I wasn't well."

"And yet you look the picture of health to me. I must have my eyes checked." He threw down the spoon. It was just a spoon. No reason to be afraid. But Emilia's hand was wet and her mother's hand was cold.

"I was having female troubles," Emilia said. She'd asked the doctor that lived next door to come in and have another look at Mother's arthritic hands. Sometimes they hurt so much she couldn't play the piano or draw the pictures for her paper-cuts, and then she had no reason to get out of bed. Emilia was afraid of another accident with a knife. "I wasn't well, Father."

"Your mother's child. *My* daughter would not be a liar." He rubbed his thumb on the rim of his wineglass.

"May I be excused, Father?" She could feel the guests looking at her. But she didn't blush. She'd stopped blushing long ago.

"You think I don't know what's going on under my nose?" Father snapped. He was often irritable on Sabbath eve, contemplating a whole day without a cigar or cigarette. But this time he didn't throw the wineglass at the wall. He didn't sweep the platter of potatoes onto the floor. He only said, "Stupid girl. Yes, please leave the table." And he called to the maid. "Freida. I believe we're ready for dessert, now. Enough philosophy, gentlemen. What do you think of the news—is it good for the Jews?"

Throwing a shawl over her shoulders, Emilia took a plate of bread and jam from the kitchen pantry and carried it out to the garden. Mama didn't swallow a mouthful when she was upset, and as a consequence she was altogether too thin. She didn't realize that you have to push every bad thought away or it will eat you up. And Emilia had no intention of wasting away. The consumptive look wasn't well regarded by matchmakers. She didn't care what Father said. Everyone else agreed that she was as lovely as the loveliest gentile girl. Someone was bound to want her.

It was the smell of a cigar that made her quickly brush the crumbs from her skirt, tucking the plate under her bench. "Who is it?" she asked.

"Mr. Levy," a low voice said.

"Shouldn't you be in the parlor with my father and brothers?"

"I can't smoke there." Mr. Levy leaned against the apple tree. The darkness was mild in the shelter of the brick wall and the low clouds above.

"It's still *Shobbos* out here," Emilia said.

"I won't consult the calendar if you won't. I thought you might like to know that your father hired me."

"But I don't need a tutor." Certainly not one that was going to stare at her at every meal.

"Well, it's no great pleasure for me either, you know."

"Then go somewhere else."

"If I could," he said. On the other side of the garden, cats were yowling, tangled in a heated exchange.

"Well, I'm sure the world is large enough." She shrugged.

"Certainly. For those with means. But for me . . . Apparently it's my fate to be stuck nowhere doing nothing. You don't know what it's like."

The ghost of the first Mrs. Rosenberg rustled the branches. "Anyone that lives here knows what you mean," Emilia said.

"Well, don't worry. Somehow we'll pass the time together until you marry. I could study while you embroider or whatever it is your mother taught you." He sighed. It wasn't fair that a man so full of himself should make her catch her breath with his sigh. It was the mustache. So cheeky.

Emilia clasped her hands around her knees. The ghost was laughing in the tree. "My mother isn't fond of embroidery."

"Then I could read you the Romantic poets. Girls like that sort of thing." The ghost laughed so hard that apples fell and bounced on the ground. It wasn't at all ladylike. But the dead have no manners.

"If you're going to be my tutor, you'll have to learn a thing or two. I won't be bored by anyone less than a husband. Do you read German?" she asked.

"No, I'm afraid. Only English and French."

"I prefer German philosophy. Perhaps I should read it to you." A branch was creaking. The wind was blowing dead leaves.

Mr. Levy stood up straight. "You speak German?"

"Fluently. My mother taught me history, geography, philosophy, and literature in three languages. I speak four."

"I'm a donkey's ass," Mr. Levy said, looking at her again as if he saw deeply and liked what he saw very much. The creaking branch snapped. "If you'll pardon the vulgarity." As the branch fell, it slapped his face. "What the . . ."

"Are you hurt?" Emilia asked.

"It's nothing. A few scratches."

"Stay here. I'll go inside and get something from the maid to dress it." As she opened the kitchen door, Emilia wondered whether his cheek would be smooth or rough with stubble. Over her shoulder she could see the red point of his cigar under the tree, and the ghost of the first Mrs. Rosenberg dancing on top of the brick wall.

LONDON, 1882

Frying Pan Alley

The grandmothers came. The west wind swept them into the channel, the mist of the river took them up. The newcomers jumped over Commercial Street, the old divide between Jew and gentile, moving up and down and to the right along roads that turned blue on reformers' maps as Yiddish signs were hung outside shops. Rents went up. In the backyards were workshops, chicken coops, foundries. There were Yiddish newsstands and Yiddish plays. Coffee houses opened where you could gamble in Yiddish. There were all kinds of chances and they wanted all of them. They had great hopes for their children, who were stringy as roosters, the boys almost as tough as the girls minding babies while waiting a turn to jump rope.

If you could hear a grandmother's voice, she'd tell you why they came: *To argue about stuffed fish. You think that's crazy? Then listen to me. Some cook it sweet, and the ones that cook with pepper think they're better than the others. But in the* heim, *believe me, you would be grateful for anything. People that have plenty don't leave home for the pleasure of living eight to a room in a house of prostitutes and criminals. A house? A ruin. Rats tear the paper off windows that have no glass. But in the street at least there's a* heimisheh geshmeck, *a taste of pickles and smoked fish. Beer! Gin! Feh—what's that! Someone should have a little schnapps. You write to them, Nehameleh. Just like I'm saying. Tell them how fine it is here. You think for this they'll leave their home and their business?*

But Nehama was sure that her family belonged here. She was saving part of every wage packet, and all that she'd done would be forgiven because it would have been for this: to bring her family to the free land. First Mother and Father, then sisters with their husbands and children. Enough of them to fill a house, a row of houses. She'd teach them all English and save them from lies. She wrote letters home, and her family wrote back with holiday wishes several times a year. If you held the thin paper to the light, words flew into the yellow candle flame. Whenever she wanted to jump away from the sewing machine, whenever the night called her, she thought of them and the roll of savings under a loose board.

In the sixth year of her freedom, Nehama wrote: "Dear *Tatteh* and *Mama,* may you live to be a hundred and twenty, *kein ein ahora*. I heard there are pogroms. The new czar hates the Jews. How is it in Plotsk? Will you come? I can send for you now. . . ."

While she waited for their answer, the west wind was blowing fog toward the Tower. It was unlike anything in the *heim*. One day the fog was brown, another green as a bottle. It was black, it was yellow, it was white as candles. At last the letter arrived.

"My dearest daughter, may no evil befall you. Don't worry. We're all right. Three of your sisters are pregnant, *kein ein ahora*. Your mother sees well only from one eye, all the less to see the troubles of these days. But thank God in heaven, there were no pogroms here. Of course home is home. The family, the house, the shop. Everything is here. . . ." And in a large scrawl at the end in her mother's hand, "Just stay well."

Not coming? She couldn't believe it. Nehama read the letter again. And no one was asking her to go home anymore. She held the letter until the sweat from her hands smeared the ink. She fell asleep holding it, and for the first time she heard her grandmother's voice as a whisper in her dreams: *Nehameleh, just use your head. God gave men 613 commandments. To women the Holy One gave only 3. And why? Because a woman knows what to do. Her mother tells her what's what and that's how she knows. If she has no mother, then she should listen to her grandmother. Am I right?* The sound of it surprised her, but when she woke up, it was forgotten.

She was lodging with Minnie and Lazar and working as a plain sewer in a tailor's workshop. The only reason she wasn't a "best" by now was that women never were. The workshop was like a thousand others where all the cheap clothes of London were made by newcomers. It was in a small back room with a low ceiling, sewing machines on the table where four workers and the boss squeezed side by side, with just enough room between the table and the fireplace for a pressing table. The walls were peeling, the window looked out on a yard where chickens were slaughtered, the glass plastered with dirty feathers.

"You should be glad that you can't smell it," Minnie said to Nehama as she soaped seams. The window shook in the autumn wind. Lazar was pressing jackets with a coal iron, his cheeks red from the rising steam. At his feet one of the boss's children played with broken buttons.

"Forget it," Nehama shouted above the click-clack of her machine. Minnie's face was drawn. They were all tired, working fourteen hours a day, and her eyes were tearing at the pain in her back. But fall and spring you worked until you fell. These were the busy seasons. Come the cold of winter or the sweat of summer, you'd have no wages. Only time and hunger. "Let's sing," Nehama said. "Something from that play we saw. You know the one I mean, *The Tailor's Fate*. It goes like this. 'Grab a little drink,'" she sang, "'as long as you're among the living. Once you're in the next world, no one's going to give you any. There's no yesterday and no tomorrow . . .'" The best machinist whistled along with her, though his eyes stayed on the cheap wool he was ballooning together under the hiss of gas jets.

He'd just been hired, a new hand in the workshop. He wore a checked jacket, a hat pushed back, and boots with one sole flapping. When he glanced in Nehama's direction, she looked away, wondering how he could walk with a light step when his feet must be wet and raw. He wasn't a big man, not much taller than she was. A narrow face, a short black beard, eyes that had an interest in everything as if anything could be laughed over except, perhaps, a young woman from the *heim* you'd like to talk with.

"So what's going on here?" the boss asked.

"Didn't you see *The Tailor's Fate*?" Nehama asked.

"My fate won't be worth a farthing if this order isn't finished." He was a thin man with the bad temper of someone who's hungry but won't let himself eat. He slept on a bench in his workshop and coughed up wool fibers.

"Your life's not worth much even with ten orders," Nehama said. There was the sound of a clattering pot in the next room, where the boss's wife was nursing one of the twins while she cooked.

"No lip from you," he answered. "There's a dozen hands wanting work in the pig market." He put out his cigarette and lit another.

"But skilled hands, not so many." Nehama laughed. "Didn't your grandmother tell you the old saying, Mr. Shiller: 'Sing while you work, win at cards'?"

He pinched her cheek. "What should I do with you? A plain sewer that's as good as a best I want. But your friend, Minnie, is another story. Her wages is charity. What do I need it for? So watch yourself, Nehama Korzen. Or out she goes."

"So?" Nehama said while Minnie shushed her. A pot fell, the babies screamed, Mrs. Shiller was crying. "Come on. I'll teach you one of my grandmother's songs."

"I'm warning you," he said.

Nehama leaned forward, her sewing machine silent as she took her foot off the treadle and stared at him. She put her hands on top of the sewing machine, her chin on her hands, and she continued to stare, her eyes on the gap between his yellow teeth, until he ran out of threats. Mr. Shiller then got very busy, sorting through the pile of jacket pieces cut in the factory as if the world was held in place by fifty-two sleeves and twenty-six backs. And when she began to sing, cigarette ash fell from his cigarette onto the floor.

Nehama pumped her sewing machine again, lifting her eyes to meet the curious gaze of the new hand. "It takes more than a wage to make me someone's dog," she said.

After work he followed her into the glaze of darkness outside. His name was Nathan, and as he opened his mouth to speak, he coughed, searching his damaged boots for inspiration.

"What do you want?" she asked. Nathan cleared his throat, glancing at the stalls with secondhand goods.

"Soon I'm going to the Jewish Board of Guardians." He took his hands out of torn pockets to push his hat back even further, smiling at her as if it was a joke they shared, this shyness of his, and he said, "For a loan. I'm going to buy a sewing machine."

"You think you'll get it?" They pushed by the seller of a nearly new left shoe and the buyer of an ounce of sugar. Shops were open till midnight, the shopkeepers standing outside calling to them: "Fresh." "New." "Cheap." "Beautiful." "Delicious."

"Every penny," he said, matching his steps to hers, though he didn't try to take her arm. And lucky for him or she'd have pushed him into the gutter. "Giving money away, they're against. It's hard to imagine, but the English Jews don't believe in charity. It makes them look bad in front of the gentiles, who say that charity turns people into paupers. But a pauper isn't just a poor man."

"No—then what?" she asked, looking at his eyes in the light from a dress shop.

"He's a poor man that expects something from the richer." Nathan winked. "But a loan is something else. I pay him interest. I give him collateral. Well, what can I say? There's a profit—it's business. And Londoners believe in business more than in God." He laughed, and she laughed with him, surprised that she could like a strange man. But then he asked her, "Where are you from?"

And she realized that he was just like anyone. It begins with that: Where are you from? Why, I'm from there, too. What a coincidence. And her face felt like ice. "A small town. Nowhere special," she said.

"Of course. We're all from someplace worse—or we'd stay there, right? My father asked me not to change my name, but I can't make up my mind. Tell me, am I a good son or not?" He was looking at her as if she could tell him what he was and it would be true.

But how could she like a man she couldn't smell? Maybe he stank of onions. Maybe something nicer, like cigars. How could she tell? She'd smelled nothing for years, not the sweat of newcomers or the rubbish on the landing outside her room or the burnt wick of a candle winking out. A world without odor, a half world without flavor.

"Let me walk with you," he said, breathing hard as if they were running, though a person could make his way only slowly in the night-time crowd just released from work.

"Do I own the street? Walk where you want." She stopped to get some hot chestnuts from a cart, and he stopped with her. "Where are you from?"

"A wild field," he said. "My father had a small flour mill in the middle of the countryside. I used to fish for trout in the stream. We had to travel two days to the nearest town with a synagogue for holidays." Jews that lived among the peasants didn't have an easy time. They were neither here nor there, and when they came to a synagogue, they were told to stand at the back as if they'd brought a disease with them. But his voice was untroubled.

"Yes," she said, holding out the sack of chestnuts. "I remember the holidays at home."

"I didn't go to school," he said. The warmth of his body was pushing away the cold night air. "I taught myself, and I have to tell you, a prodigy I wasn't."

"My sisters taught me," she said. The Lane was narrowing into Sandys Row, the crowd thinning, the stalls giving way to old military shops, the wind brushing her with its memory of the sea.

"I heard a joke and I have to tell someone. Do you want to hear it?"

"Is it any good?" she asked.

"No, it's a terrible joke. After all, we just met. I have to save the good ones."

"Tell me." And she laughed at the joke though it was very bad because the sound of his voice was pleasant and the desire to know whether he smelled of fish or wet wool was a dark pain making love to everything she knew.

Nathan walked Nehama home every evening with a bad joke for all occasions, even the High Holy Days. Already half the Yiddish-speaking men and most of the women had stopped going to synagogue on the Sabbath. Of course they lit Sabbath candles and kept kosher. To reformers they seemed very pious. But in the Days of Awe, when a person ought to tremble before God, there was more than one man around the corner from the synagogue, taking a break with a cigarette, Nathan among them.

While inside, the ram's horn sounded. The people stood shoulder to shoulder in the heat of their sins and their strivings as they had since the wind swept light into darkness, before towers or bridges or factory smoke, before girls longed to run away. And in the women's section, with her eyes closed, Nehama Korzen could be anywhere, was everywhere, crying out with them all: "We begin as dust and we end as dust. At the hazard of our life we earn our bread. As a fragile vessel. As a shadow that passes. As a dream that flies away . . ."

She was standing next to Minnie, who beat her chest carefully so as not to damage her new holiday blouse. As soon as the confession was over, Minnie leaned against the back wall. "I want a hat like hers." She pointed to the woman sitting in front of them. "Not one feather but two. Pink like my sleeves." Minnie was pregnant. Just enough to need the waist of her skirt let out.

"Really." Nehama was thinking of a time when her own waist had thickened. And when it thinned again, she could imagine that it had never been any different.

Minnie yawned with the tiredness of carrying two souls. "You should have a new hat, too."

Nehama was bareheaded, like all the unmarried women and girls.

"I don't want another hat," she said. Her body was hers and she was full of her own strength.

"But you do. It doesn't matter if you're married or not. Every girl in London wears a nice hat. You should have one with an ostrich feather like this." Minnie made a swooping gesture with her freckled hand. "Just think of it, Nehama. A purple ostrich feather."

"I like blue," Nehama said. So why should she wonder what the child she'd lost might have been?

"Oh—it's always blue with you. But never mind. It suits you—let it be blue."

"A hat with a blue ostrich feather. Very nice," Nehama said, her voice faint. But not because Nathan had got the loan for his sewing machine and was talking about having his own workshop with a wife who would be his, too. No, she was sweating only because her new skirt was warm for the fall weather and the synagogue was packed, the women of Frying Pan Alley standing at the back, far from the railing, where physicians' wives could look down on the Holy Torah and their husbands in silk hats bowing to it.

"Nehama—you're not listening," Minnie said, fanning Nehama with her hand. "I said you need some air. Let's go already. I confessed enough for both of us."

"From your mouth to God's ear." Nehama put her arm through Minnie's as they pushed through the praying crowd of women. "But I hope you shouted. I hear the Holy One is very deaf on one side."

Nehama and Minnie walked home, holding on to each other in the fierce wind. Stalls turned over, tiles were knocked from roofs, and when Nehama saw a man in a scarf, she looked for someplace to run, but it was all right. The Squire would never be out in such a wind. It shook out all her pins until her hair lay around her back and shoulders like a dark shawl.

At home her married sisters had been shorn on their wedding days. But Nehama wouldn't cut her hair to get married. If Nathan wanted her, he'd have to get her hairpins for a wedding present. And she would stand under the wedding canopy without a sister to lift her veil when it was time to take a sip of wine. The wind would lift her veil, the raging wind, a grandmother's voice, her friend's freckled hand.

MINSK, 1886

Moskovskaya Street

Emilia sat in the garden as she had so many times while the ghost of the first Mrs. Rosenberg scattered apple blossoms and brought the fruit into a perfect roundness. It was just before her twentieth birthday, and she was reading with her tutor, Mr. Levy, in the last light before darkness fell. There was a foot of space between them. She could measure every inch by the quickness of her breathing as she listened to him turn the pages of his book. She couldn't help but give him a quick sidelong glance.

He looked back at her and smiled. He'd taken to wearing high boots and a loose white shirt like a Russian. "I'd make you a good husband," he said.

"You have a high opinion of yourself," she answered. He'd been her tutor off and on for four years, teaching her to read English and French while she taught him German. Sometimes he went away for months and returned with no explanation. She suspected that he was an anarchist, but it didn't matter. All he could offer her was well-worn books, and she would have a husband that could take her to Italy. Mr. Levy was a friend, and as a friend all that one could want. "A man as clever as you doesn't need a pretty wife," she said.

"Then you'll do, won't you?"

"Oh, get back to your book." Emilia pouted as if she were insulted, knowing that she must be even prettier in the soft dusk. There was great pleasure in being pretty for a friend.

She shifted a little closer to him. Mr. Levy smelled of ink.

"Yes?" he asked.

"If I were to think of being your wife, I'd have to know where you're always going off to. Otherwise one could only imagine what kind of man I might be getting." She tapped his arm with the edge of her book.

He put his hand on hers. "One that would take care of you," he said.

She didn't pull away. They'd held hands before. Twice. He knew her as her husband never would. "You couldn't take care of a mouse, Mr. Levy."

"I don't wish to marry a mouse, Miss Rosenberg."

The second time they'd held hands was on the day that Mother was leaving to visit her sisters. On the threshold of the house, she touched her chest, gasped, and fell down the stairs. Mr. Levy held Emilia's hand while she waited for the doctor's pronouncement. As it turned out, Mother didn't have a bad heart. The doctor said it was hysteria, and the train ticket was returned.

"How can I trust you?" Emilia asked.

"That is what a wife does," he answered.

The first time Mr. Levy had held Emilia's hands was the evening they all went to the opera. Father had rented a box for his guests, who came with their wives dressed in their nicest gowns. But Mother was the most beautiful, even if she was thin.

Between Act I and Act II, there was talk of the pogroms and sending their grown children away from Russia. Between Act II and Act III, the sons' prospects and the daughters' dowries were considered. In the meantime, the young sons were outside smoking cigars as if they'd been smoking all their lives, and the young daughters discussed what they simply would not accept in a proposed husband. No one bald. No one whose work involved bad-smelling chemicals. No one with a first wife. That was Emilia's contribution. She didn't expect Father to overhear her. He was engrossed in conversation at the other end of the box. Mother didn't turn around. She was leaning against the railing, looking down at the stage.

"I have a hypothetical question," Father said in the tone that generally made his guests consider the lateness of the hour. But the box seats were very good, with royal velvet upholstery and royal velvet curtains, so no one moved. He examined the end of his cigar. "What do you do, for instance—let's just say as a hypothetical example—if a girl is a *mamzer*? A bastard." He didn't mean an illegitimate child. In Jewish law there was no such concept. A *mamzer* was a child born of an adulterous union. "Maybe no one else suspects," Father continued. "But if you do? Well, according to religious law, she can only marry another *mamzer*. So tell me. Do you say nothing? After all, no one else knows. But if someone finds out later . . . It's wrong. Very wrong. I'm just saying. For example."

There was a time that her mother would have turned and faced him, but when a person lives with a battering ram, she loses some agility. Mother threw up into the velvet curtains. Everyone rushed to help her, and later Father paid for the damage. No one gave Emilia a glance as she ran outside to the carriage. Mr. Levy found her there, sitting as still as if she were already dead. Only when he held her hands did she start to shake. And after that evening Mother never left the house, though she tried when her sisters begged her to visit them.

But now everything was normal again. Father was at the theater, Mother in bed with a headache, the maid gone to see her cousin. Mr. Levy and Emilia were alone in the shade of the high brick wall. The apples were budding; the wall was rich with ivy. She could feel the wind on her cheeks, and she knew that her spring gown brought out the fine color of her skin. Underneath the dress, her corset was laced tight against her waist and breasts, ending just under her nipples at the top and at the bottom pointing down from her belly.

She could tell that Mr. Levy was going to kiss her. The change in his posture, in his breathing. A good girl would stand up and walk away. Or at least a girl that was chaperoned. But the ghost of Mrs. Rosenberg withdrew from the garden, and there was only the warm spring wind touching Emilia here and there. She would never be like her mother. When she was married, she would always be on guard, charming her husband. It was her vocation, the work of a wife, but until she was a wife her dreams, the nighttime dreams of a young woman, didn't have to involve husbands.

They were just like this. A garden, the smell of ink, a friend who could be charmed or not since nothing depended on it. Who would think that such a small thing could be so inviting? As they kissed, his hand found its way down from the nape of her neck, over a bare shoulder, along the line of her bodice. Low-cut gowns were the fashion this spring, but Mother had made her put a little insert of silk there. Under his fingers the silk pressed against the mound of her breasts; her nipples touched the hard edge of the corset. Her tongue touched the edge of her lip.

Any other day, she would have jumped up from the bench. She would have walked around the garden and chattered about anything, concentrating on the new earrings she was promised for her birthday. But Father had rented the box at the opera again. How could Mother go when she fainted at the thought of leaving the house? There would have to be a hostess, and it could only be Emilia. When Father accused her of being a *mamzer*, there would be no one to distract the company with a sudden, violent illness.

She wouldn't think of it. No, there was only the garden, Mr. Levy, his lips and his fingers, her breathing so fast it made her dizzy, her body as liquid as in a dream. The sun fell below ground. The sky was pink, it was blue, it was black. He found button after button on her new spring gown and the strings of her new corset and admired her new silk underwear embroidered with lilies, which were yet not so wonderful as her naked skin under his lips.

Two months later the summer sun warmed branches heavy with apples. Emilia thought she was dying. She'd been sick for weeks; she was getting weaker. So tired she had to have naps like a child. And there was no one to tell, no one to hold her as she passed from this world to the next. Father was angrier than ever, Mother sleepier.

Emilia sat under the tree, pretending to read the newspaper as Mother came into the garden. It was warm; Mother wore a blue silk dress with elbow sleeves. Emilia could see the white scar on her wrist flicker as she crossed her arms. For someone that walked around in a daze most of the time, she seemed wonderfully alert.

"I want you to tell me what's going on," Mother said.

Emilia didn't think she meant the news, but even so she said, "There's an article about the London Jews. They're warning people to stay away. Too many refugees are going there."

"Don't change the subject, my daughter."

"I didn't know there was a subject," Emilia said. "Can't we talk later? I'd like to finish the article, please." Her voice was too shrill. Even Mother would hear something in it. And all Emilia wanted was to enjoy the sun without intrusion.

"The maid told me. She found the shawl. How could you hide such a thing from me?" Mother was actually shaking a finger at her.

Emilia's shoulders tensed. "What are you talking about?"

"Don't lie to me." Sunbeams fell through the tree onto Mother's face, staining it with light and dark. "You know I mean the shawl you hid in the cupboard with the Passover dishes."

A couple of times Emilia had been surprised in the garden by a wave of nausea. She'd used an old shawl to wipe up the mess at the foot of the apple tree. "I'm sorry. I should have thrown it out." If her mother knew how sick she was, she'd realize what a small matter this was. But these days Mother never noticed anything except how cold she was, how her head ached, how there must be something stronger than the powders from the chemist.

"You think I haven't heard you throwing up in the mornings? I had two children myself. I know how it begins." Mother's face was hard. It had been a long time since they'd read together in the kitchen. "You're pregnant, my daughter."

"What?" Emilia asked. It couldn't be. She wasn't married. She was deathly ill and she deserved sympathy. Clear soup. Plumped pillows.

"How could you do it?"

"I don't know what you mean," Emilia said. Was that it? Not a lingering illness, just in trouble like a simple shopgirl. A person can feel very hot and stupid when she's ambushed by shame like an uncouth enemy.

"How long since you had your monthly? You don't remember. Well, it's not only a shame on you, my daughter. But the whole family." Mother shook her head. "How long did you think you could keep this to yourself?"

"It's my business," Emilia said. It would be better to be dying.

"I don't know what your father will say. What you've done to me . . ."

"Oh, it will be just the same as always." It wasn't her fault. They'd left her alone in the garden. Only an idiot would leave a girl alone with a young man. "You'll take your powders and sleep, Mother. You wouldn't notice a pogrom."

"How dare you! I'll—"

"What can you do to me? Really. I think you made up that story about the Russian officers. Charming them—how is it possible? More likely you took to your bed like you always do. Where were you when I was alone in the garden? Just think of that." Her voice was as hard as her mother's face.

Mother paled. "What did you say?"

"Nothing. I just meant—"

"I heard what you meant." Her mother sat down heavily on the bench, looking at her as if she wasn't even worth slapping.

They sat together, the weak mother and the strong daughter. The mother wondered how she'd become so weak, and the daughter how much longer she could bear to be strong. They sat for a long time, listening to the bees in the rosebushes. When Mother took her hands away from her face, her jaw was set. "Something has to be done. We'll get you married."

She sounded like any other mother. Like one that made arrangements and carried many keys. "But how?" Emilia asked, like any daughter hoping that her mother wouldn't turn her back on her, counting on her to figure a way out. "Mr. Levy's gone away again."

"Then we'll have to find him."

"If we ask after him, Father will wonder."

"We can't have that. It would be the worst thing. All right." Mother picked up the newspaper and tapped it against her palm. "Then someone else."

"Who?"

"I'll speak to the matchmaker. We won't have just anyone." Mother glanced at the newspaper as if she might find someone there.

"He should own a villa," Emilia said dreamily.

"That would be nice." Mother's voice cracked, but she smiled a little. Grasshoppers sang in the sun. "I always thought I might live with you after you were married," she added quietly, putting a hand on Emilia's cheek.

Emilia let her head rest on her mother's shoulder as if she were a little girl again, struggling with a page of hard words.

"I'll send for the matchmaker this afternoon." Mother stroked Emilia's cheek. "It won't be the first time that a baby was born less than nine months after a wedding."

"Oh." A gust of wind blew dirt into Emilia's eyes. She blinked, trying still to imagine the villa.

"Too particular you shouldn't be, but we can't settle for a butcher or a tailor either, God forbid. People would be suspicious. Our family runs to big babies. That's what we'll say."

"No one will believe it, anyway." Emilia bit her lip. "Who's going to marry me in such a rush?" A man that would like to throw it in her face, that's who. "Someone that wants a slave, Mama. You know what it's like. There must be another way. Please . . ."

"There's no other way. Do you think you're the only one your father's going to throw out of the house?"

Her eyes filled with tears. She turned away so her mother wouldn't see.

Mama looked at the brick wall as if she would take it apart with her hands if she could. "Maybe we'll think of something else."

The ghost of the first wife was sitting on top of the wall, her back to them as if she were tired of the garden.

The plans were made at the dairy table in the kitchen while the maid shelled peas in a large bowl and Mother cut fantastic creatures out of gold paper. And when the table was littered with unicorns, sphinxes, and winged horses, the story was complete. They would travel as two widows, mother and daughter, whose husbands had been killed in a pogrom. The unborn child was to be named after its lost father. A pity on him. The maid was entrusted with Mother's jewelry, which she would sell to pay for their passage. They had to go where two more Jewish refugees were nothing worth noting; Mother remembered the article that Emilia had been reading in the garden. London would be damp and Mother's hands would cramp, but it couldn't be helped. At least Emilia had some English, and while they packed, she taught her mother a few words.

Mother laughed and grew a year younger every day closer to their escape. Emilia was absentminded, remembering Mr. Levy sitting with her at the table, making her hold her tongue between her teeth, hissing like a lisping snake: "Thhh . . . This. That. This. That." And she imagined that they were married, living in the villa. The child was born; it was a boy. He drank milk from the goats.

A week later, Emilia stood at the front gate, fiddling with the latch. Behind the house, the apples in the tree were turning red as the ghost of the first Mrs. Rosenberg rose up from the garden.

"We have to go," Emilia said. The trunk had been taken to the ship earlier in the morning, and Freida was now fastening the brooch on Mother's summer cloak. It was the last piece of her jewelry.

"Just another minute." Mother clung to the maid.

"The carriage is waiting," Emilia said. It was in the road, just outside the gate, the driver holding the horse's head and having a smoke while he sweated in his wool cap.

"I just need a drink of water." Mother wiped her eyes as she sat down on the front step. "I'm a bit dizzy. Would you get it for me, Freida?"

"Hurry," Emilia said. She couldn't stand the waiting. The thing in her belly was making her queasy again. "You have the tickets, Mama?"

She nodded. "We'll be two widows, an old one and a young one," her mother said with a peculiar smile, as if she were telling a tall tale that no one would believe.

"Let me have them." Emilia held out her hand nervously. The blue tickets were for the train, the green for the first-class cabin. She slipped them into her gloves.

Mother fanned herself with her hand as she looked at the open gate. "Do you find it very hot?"

"Not so hot," Emilia said. It was a cool day for August, and cloudy. Mother was squinting as if the light was too strong.

"Listen to me," Mother said urgently, looking past her as if she were talking to someone else.

"We'll talk later. Once we're on board the train," Emilia said, following her mother's gaze. The ghost of the first Mrs. Rosenberg stood by the gate, but how could she be here, outside the garden, on the other side of the wall?

"Do you remember the story of Tamar in the Bible?" Mama asked as the ghost of the first wife came to the steps and sat down beside her. Emilia frowned and pointed back to the garden, but the first wife was looking only at Mother.

"She was a woman from among the Canaanites who married into the Hebrews," Mother said. "As tall and beautiful as a queen. She faced the father of her child in the Jewish court and forced him to acknowledge it."

"Mama . . ." Emilia kneeled in front of her, rubbing her hands to remind her that she was here among the living and they had first-class tickets.

"The great King David is descended from Tamar on his grandfather's side," Mama said to the first wife as if this were just the time for conversations with the dead. "And on his grandmother's side there was Ruth."

"The train leaves in an hour." Emilia pulled on her mother's arm.

Mama was looking intently at the ghost of the first wife. "Ruth left her mother's house for a strange country with strange customs and took them on as her own. She had golden eyes just like my son. For her merit, I'm asking you, stay with my girl. Promise me. You have to promise."

When the first Mrs. Rosenberg nodded, Mother closed her eyes, rolled down the steps, and lay in a heap at the bottom, her brooch fallen onto the stones.

The maid stood in the doorway, holding the glass of water.

"We have to fetch the doctor," Emilia said, patting her mother's cheeks. The skin was cool and slick as wet stones, her mother's breathing shallow.

"Wait here," the maid said. "I'll run next door."

Emilia picked up her mother's brooch, holding it in her hand as she looked at Mother's face, so lovely without any pain, like the cameo. "I thought you'd go this time, Mama. Because you were going with me," she said. "I was that foolish."

When the doctor came, he'd bring his assistant to carry her mother inside. He'd give instructions about powders and compresses, and then her father would arrive and he would break things in his suspicious rage, ordering Emilia to get rid of the pieces. It would be the same tomorrow and the next day and forever.

The driver had finished his cigarette. "If you're not going, I'll get another fare," he called through the front gate.

Emilia hesitated, the cameo brooch still in her hand. The train wouldn't wait. The ship would sail across the sea with an empty cabin. She couldn't let her mother do this to her, no matter how helplessly Mama lay on the ground, a smudge of dirt on her cheek, one arm flung back. Emilia stood up, made sure that the tickets were tucked safely into her gloves, and forced herself to walk to the gate. When she was seated inside the carriage, she leaned out the window as the driver took up the reins, waving frantically good-bye as if her mother might wake up and bless her going.

The driver flicked the whip at his horse's rump, but before it could take a step, the ghost of the first Mrs. Rosenberg slipped into the seat beside Emilia. The dead can still make promises to the living. They can keep them if the living will allow it.

LONDON, 1886

Prince's Street

It was Saturday night and the Sabbath was over, naphtha lamps flared, shutters snapped open, barrows were hauled over cobblestones, stalls set up, awnings unfurled, sacks thrown onto curbstones. It was the people's night, wage packets in hand despite the summer drizzle, music coming from every corner, "Hi! Hi!" shouted from doorways with wet banners proclaiming the escape artist, the strongman, the contortionist just on the other side of a threshold, only a penny.

It was Nehama's favorite time of the week, and her favorite place was here in the queue outside the theater, where Jews ate fried fish and chocolate, their children hopping from one foot to the other. All around them was tobacco smoke and the talk of the street, of work and no work, the horse that won, the husband that ran away, a jacket nearly new and such a bargain, the brawl upstairs, a broken nose, a war somewhere and whether it could come here, the editorial about keeping Jews out of England. Everyone was excited, and she heard Yiddish words that she'd never learned at home. The words turned blue in the rain and red with the flare of a match; they would carry her inside and upstairs and continue all through the play while the audience ate and drank and children gasped at marvels.

Nathan was telling a joke. It wasn't such a good joke, but though her hands were cold and her cheeks stung, she laughed till her sides ached. So did Minnie and Lazar and the neighbor from upstairs who liked a drink, and the rough-stuff cutter who made up poems about boot factories. Minnie's oldest was playing tag with the little boys while ticket holders for the good seats went inside, folding umbrellas made by the people in line. Someone spat, someone hissed. Inside the box office, the ticket seller finished his supper and smoked a cigarette. Then he opened the window and shouted, "Balcony seats! Have your money ready. No deals."

The Yiddish theater was in Prince's Street, a real theater, not just a shaky platform in a coffee house. It was built by Mr. Smith, the butcher, with an orchestra pit, a parterre and a gallery, a curtain that went up and down on pulleys, and plaster grapes above the chandeliers. It played every night but Friday, and could have played then, too, if the religious court hadn't threatened to pull Mr. Smith's certification of kashrut. He was a *landsmann* of Nehama's, but as she said, there was a whole congregation of Plotskers up in the balcony and not one of them got a penny off their ticket.

Nathan was whistling as they went upstairs. Here and there in the balcony were "patriots," who had roses or maybe a bottle of wine for their favorite actors. Nehama held tight to the railing as she climbed the slippery steps. "I wouldn't know it was summer except that the busy season is over. I'm that wet and cold. Your coat is soaked. Stop dripping on me," she said, scanning the balcony. "There they are." She slid into her seat next to Minnie and Lazar and their two children. They all lived in the same house in Frying Pan Alley, where Nathan had his workshop in the back room. Lazar was his presser and Minnie a general hand.

"You call this dripping? I call it a storm." Nathan shook out his coat.

"Move a little," Nehama said. "Your elbow's sticking into me."

"Where—should I jump up and hang from the chandelier?"

"Your coat is taking up half a seat." She rolled it up and put it on the floor between them. "Did you fix my sewing machine? The treadle keeps sticking. I told you."

"Tomorrow, I'll oil it."

"You think machine oil is the cure for death?" She shook her head. "I'm afraid we need a new sewing machine, Nathan."

He shrugged. "Maybe I'll be lucky at cards." He played cards once a week during the busy season. When he had no time for cards, he placed a bet on a horse. Never more than a shilling or two, but why throw it away? A lodger would be glad to pay a shilling a week for a place to sleep on their floor.

"Your luck is why we still have the old one," she said.

He crossed his arms. Only two things he insisted on: running the workshop as if he were boss of the world, and his two bob a week for cards. "You want me to give up betting?"

"When the Messiah comes. Give me an orange." She was just start-ing to show and already she could feel the baby fluttering inside her. She was sure their child would look like Nathan. She hoped so.

"All right. Here you go, Nehameleh." He took out his knife to cut it in sections the way she liked it, with the peel still attached. On Sab-bath afternoons when they made love, he traced the scar on her thigh as if it didn't ruin the smoothness of her leg. The scar was shaped like a crescent moon, but Nathan wasn't afraid of the night.

She would have a new song to sing to her child and a new story to tell it.

In the pit, the orchestra put down its supper: bread smeared with garlic and chicken fat, ginger beer to wash it down. Near them sat the wealthier Jews of Whitechapel, just as in the synagogue they sat close to the platform where the Torah scroll was chanted. Mr. Smith gave his signal: torches were lit at the foot of the stage and the orchestra began to play. The patrons of expensive seats shushed loudly from within wreaths of cigar smoke that ascended to the balcony as a man walked onstage between the shadows. This was the great Jacob Adler, who enjoyed the swooning of every Jewish girl in the East End. He wore a gray wig and a long, threadbare shirt. Under it his legs were terribly skinny. Even bowed.

"But he isn't handsome at all," Minnie whispered.

"It's the makeup," Nehama said.

"Well, I wish he'd put on a little less," Minnie huffed. She was holding her baby in one arm and flowers in the other. "For sixpence, I want a hero that doesn't hurt the eyes." She gave her flowers to Lazar.

Onstage the beggar was picking through rags. He was supposed to be in Odessa, but he could have been in Minsk or Pinsk or Plotsk or London, muttering to himself as he put his bits and pieces into a bas-ket, then taking them out again. Is it yours? he asked, looking up at the audience with confused eyes as he scratched under his arm. If you're telling me no—then it must be mine.

In the *heim,* beggars brought home for *Shobbos* were called guests. Some of them were just poor and some of them were crazy, but it was an obligation to sit and eat with them and not cause any embarrassment. Here in London, they were all guests, poor and sometimes crazy.

Onstage the ragpicker found a child crying among the rags. He looked around. Is she yours? he asked. Yours? Or maybe yours. Poor little thing, the audience whispered. But who wants nobody's child? Then you must be mine, the ragpicker said, lining his basket with a thousand pigeon feathers. And he put the baby in the basket.

Grandma Nehama used to bring home a different guest every *Shobbos,* each one stranger than the one before. There was the man who had a dog, though Jews never had dogs, and it did everything the beggar did, waved hello with a paw, barked all through the grace after meals, and peed on the floor. Then there was the man who spat when he talked. He'd traveled around the world and came with his wife, who said she was the queen of beggars.

Nehama brought her eyes back to the stage. The ragpicker's daughter was growing up. So beautiful, the audience sighed. And see how she loves her father. Does it matter how odd he is? A father is a father. Am I right?

The strangest guest to visit Grandma Nehama had a beard so long he rolled it up and tied it with string so it wouldn't get away. He claimed to have a daughter somewhere and asked for money to put toward her dowry. Grandma didn't believe him, but when you give charity it's not right to question. So she put whatever she had into the knotted handkerchief he held out. Mama was maybe six or seven at the time. There were already a handful of younger half brothers and sisters, and she was jealous of them.

The beggar, with his beard rolled up and wearing his seven layers of clothes, asked Grandma, "Tell me, do you have any problems?"

She laughed. Did the beggar think he was a rabbi? But she just said, "You know I do. My daughter runs away whenever my back is turned. This one here, my oldest, the evil eye shouldn't notice her."

"Come here to me," the beggar told Mama, banging his stick on the floor. She couldn't help but stand in front of him, trembling. "So tell me, little girl, what are you afraid of?"

"You smell bad," she said. Her mother shushed her.

The beggar nodded. "You know, you're right." Then he put his dirty hand on her head and said the traditional blessing, "May God make you like the four Matriarchs . . ."

When he left, a note was found beside the straw pallet where he'd slept: "Blessed are you and blessed is your family. Elijah the prophet was here." Was it true? Grandma didn't know.

But Mama never ran away again. Because of the blessing, when she grew up and was married, she never lost a pregnancy. Nehama was counting on the beggar's blessing to protect her baby, too. The first one she miscarried didn't count. That was in another life. This baby was her husband's, her beloved's—though she would never use such a word out loud—and she awaited their child, her heart heavy with joy.

Onstage the ragpicker's girl was in court. Such a good girl, so fine, and yet she was falsely accused of murder. How could it be? The ragpicker cried at the sight of her in chains while the audience groaned.

Nehama and her neighbors didn't take in beggars for Sabbath dinner. Instead they had lodgers sleeping on the floor or they wouldn't make the rent and then they'd all be out on the street. It was only here in the theater that they could be blessed.

The stage was dark except for a flickering light, now on the hands of the unseen magistrate, now on the bowed head of the girl. The situation was hopeless. Only a very odd beggar, one that wasn't quite right in the mind, would think otherwise. But the beggar of Odessa still had a voice. And what a voice—one in a million. It was, after all, not just anyone but the great eagle, Jacob Adler, who rose to his feet in the court. Who cried out against injustice. Against corruption. Against his daughter's pain and the injuries of the poor, the lost, the defeated. Of course the audience knew it was the actor and not a beggar who spoke for them all. The magistrate was another actor, moved to fake tears by the speech. He unlocked the chains of the beautiful daughter, played by an actress who was having an affair with Adler.

It didn't matter. The voice of the people had risen up from the grave and come over the sea; it had come here to the cloud of smoke under the plaster ceiling; it spoke through the cloud in a mother's voice to mothers and a tailor's voice to tailors. It said everything that the heart would say if it weren't shattered. Onstage the beautiful girl went free; in the balcony all the daughters and sons believed that they might go free, too. Passover could still come to them in London, for each generation has its story and is commanded to speak as if its scars are a snake that sees in the dark.

The audience rose to its feet, and Lazar threw flowers down from the balcony.

It was then that Nehama felt a familiar pain in her belly. She grabbed Minnie's arm.

Whitechapel Road

A grandmother's spirit wouldn't be surprised to find the London Hospital between a theater and a dustheap where women collected pails of bone and ash and anything else they could dig out to sell. Nor would she be surprised that patients were in no rush to leave the hospital. *Where else can a woman rest? Not a hand lifted to her. No broken glass. The doctor speaks in a whisper. At first a person wonders if she's alive or dead. Is this her hand with no dirt on it? And a nice bed she has, all to herself. A tray with a cup of tea. The room so clean that even a fly drags itself outside to die on the dustheap. While she rests, she forgets to be afraid for everyone. Who can blame her? People say that after the world was made, God went back to heaven. But a piece of the Holy One stayed behind to bear the exile with us, and She, the Shekhina, cries with us. Let me tell you, by now she must be drowning in tears. Maybe she needs to have a rest in the hospital, too.*

There were twelve beds in the ward and twelve windows that cast rectangular shadows like doors in the wall opposite. If you opened such a door, there might be another world. One without mistakes. One without sin.

Nathan was standing beside the bed, rolling and unrolling his cap. Minnie sat on a stool. "You'll have another baby," she said, speaking in a hush like all the visitors, awed by the constant swish of mops and buckets of carbolic acid.

"The doctor said there won't be any more." Nehama glanced at the children visiting the woman next to her.

"So what does he know—how many pregnancies has he had?"

Nehama didn't answer. She wasn't made right. There was no getting away from it. Her husband's child had run away from her womb. It had been like this for several days—whenever she tried to speak to Minnie or Nathan, they insisted on talking nonsense.

"Do you remember what the dress looked like?" she asked. "The one I was wearing when we met. I think the skirt was green with a ruffle." It was important to remember. If only she could ask Sally.

"That was ten years ago." Minnie's face was wet with summer sweat. "What does it matter?"

"Were the sleeves yellow? No, also green . . ." And Sally was in Dorset Street, drinking laudanum or sleeping. Maybe she had a new wig. A nice wig with real hair.

"I got a new sewing machine for you," Nathan interrupted. "On good terms, too. You'll see how a jacket can practically sew itself."

"I'll make another dress." Nehama turned her head to stare out the window. "Then I won't owe anyone a thing."

"I've been thinking," Nathan said. "Maybe it's all for the best. My mother died after one of her pregnancies. The midwife said her insides gave out. This could be a blessing, Nehameleh."

She looked at him with such hatred that he stepped back. "Wait!" she called, her eyes blurring.

"Sha, it's all right," he said. "I'm not going anywhere."

"Would you tell me a joke?" she asked in a tired voice. "The one about the priest and the Jew." At the far end of the ward, a student nurse was stripping a bed.

Nathan sat down, his face serious. "There was a priest who caught a Jew, a convert to the church, eating meat on Friday . . ." His hand was cold and his mouth trembled.

The nurse in her white habit glided from bed to bed. On Nehama's left, a woman was dying from a botched abortion. On the other side, a mother of seven prayed that she'd lose this baby, for if it was born, she'd be too weak to work for her children's supper and too hungry to make any milk.

Nehama watched the shadows on the wall. She could see a beggar standing in one of the doorways there. It must be the crazy ragpicker who spoke before the magistrate in the theater, beckoning now as if he meant to give her a blessing. She should go and ask him to defend her in the Court of Heaven. Yes, that was what she would do. Just like this, it was so easy. And when the magistrate let her go free, she would find her lost babies. But what was this blocking her way? A cool fog, a damp wind that made her shiver. Someone was singing to her:

> *The house is in shadow, the street is in gloom*
> *Dark burns the fire in its agony*
> *And the wind, the wind, the raging wind*
> *It can't yet be seen, it can't yet be known.*

Go away, Nehama whispered. *Sing with me,* someone answered. The dead should stay in the world to come, she thought. But a cloud was passing over the sun, the shadowy doors closed, leaving her in this world with the white wall and the wind rattling glass. Outside the hospital, women were climbing up and down the mountain of rubbish as if it were a ladder between heaven and earth.

CHAPTER 3

On Your Knees

1886

St. Katharine's Dock to Frying Pan Alley

The dreams began after Nehama left the hospital. Girls without faces came off the boat, they were greeted by *landsmann*, they lost babies. Night after night, she felt the spray of dirty water, she smelled tea and perfume, the stink of the river, the stink of the dockworkers, and when she awoke, smelling nothing, she was afraid to lie down again. She'd grown so tired that she had almost injured herself on the sewing machine. This morning she was walking to the Lane for fish for *Shobbos* but her feet had taken her here instead. She stood in the doorway of a shop, sheltered from the crowd and the black ash falling from the Queen's Pipes as she wondered what to do. A cage hung in front of the shop door, and in it a bedraggled parrot was having a drink from its small bowl of gin while Nehama bit her nails to the quick, drops of blood salty on her lip. It had been more than ten years since she'd been here. Everything looked the same and yet different, because now she understood what was said and what wasn't.

A few feet away men shouted, "Take me," pushing and punching, desperate to get to the front of the crowd of dockhands while the fore-man called for the day's laborers. Five pennies an hour. Two hundred and fifty tons to unload. Blocks of indigo powder, flower essences shipped in fat, marble from Italy, osprey plumes, tea, tusks of ivory. It was a warm, slippery day and any of them might fall and be crushed. Dreaming was all very well when you were safe in your bed, but on the docks you'd better have your wits about you.

Someone else was watching for girls traveling alone. A representative of the Society for the Protection of Hebrew Girls held a lace-edged handkerchief against her nose, keeping away from the Irishmen and their grappling hooks. Instead she stood by a man in a black frock coat and silk hat, talking to him as if she had no idea who he was. If Nehama still lived in Dorset Street, she'd have spat. The pimp was nicknamed the Hat because he'd won it from a gentleman along with the gentleman's girl, which gave him his start in the trade. If a person came off the boat, who would she turn to—the lady who spoke only English and looked with distaste at the passengers, or the gentleman who called out in a familiar language, his face full of concern?

He was moving toward a girl wearing a cameo brooch and carrying a leather case, new and expensive. A girl like that, wearing more on her back than Nehama made in a month, could surely take care of herself.

"Where did you come from?" the man in the silk hat asked in Yiddish.

The girl was walking toward him. With her uncertain, trusting face. Her hands sweating on the handle of her case. And under her dress, thighs that had no scar yet in the shape of the new moon. So it would begin.

Nehama wasn't some kind of saint to give up her life for a stranger. What if he recognized her? What if he told the Squire? She cursed under her breath as she pulled her shawl over her head, half hiding her face. Her feet were carrying her willy-nilly toward the pimp. Her heart was beating so hard it would surely burst and then she would find herself in the next world with her grandmother. Better to stay in this world and go to the theater after *Shobbos*.

Emilia looked this way and that, but since she was not a block of perfume or a tusk of ivory, nobody was rushing to unload her from the ship. There was a mist on the river that smelled like a dead horse as it fluttered across the Tower and the great masts of ships. While other passengers ran to meet their relatives, Emilia tried not to inhale. She was pretending to belong to someone. Perhaps that man in the silk hat, who also seemed to be alone. He smiled at her encouragingly. London was not as cold a city as people said. She smiled back tentatively. The sky was busy with the smoke of factories, the dock with the shouts of foremen directing crates into the upper stories of warehouses, the hydraulic lifts rising high like iron giants.

"Where did you come from?" the man in the silk hat called above the noise of the equipment. He spoke a rather nice Yiddish.

"Minsk," she said, moving closer so she wouldn't have to shout.

"How wonderful." Well, she didn't know what was so wonderful about Minsk, but he looked friendly and there was a pleasant odor about him. At least some people bathed. "I'm also a—" But before he could finish what he had to say, a woman, hurrying along, collided with him, and he turned toward her angrily.

She looked about ten years older than Emilia, attractive in a Jewish sort of way. Dark hair and dark skin and startling blue eyes. Wearing a plain dress, not very clean. In a red shawl like other Jewish women meeting the ship. Evidently a popular color among people whose relatives traveled in steerage.

The man in the silk hat pushed the woman away, and she nearly stumbled.

"Oh, excuse me, sir. A pickpocket has cleaned you out," she said. Her voice trembled, and she had her shawl over her head as if she was a religious woman overcome by modesty.

"A gonoph? Me?" He was feeling his pockets, peering over the woman's shoulder along the docks.

"There he is—over there. You might catch him." The woman pointed, he ran off, and she grabbed Emilia's bag. "Cousin, I'm sorry I'm late. How you must have worried."

She must be mixed up. After all, when people emigrate, families can be split up for years. How are you supposed to recognize someone?

"You must have me confused with someone else," Emilia said, answering in Yiddish as she tried to snatch her case back, but the woman pulled her closer.

"Shh. Listen to me; I'm not your cousin," she said. "But him, he's not your *landsmann* either. Where are you from?"

"Why is everyone so curious?" Emilia asked. "But if you must know, it's Minsk."

"Well, keep it to yourself or every shark you meet will claim to be a Minsker. I think you should know that man over there is a pimp."

"A what?"

"You heard me." A pimp—was it true? He looked so kind. And this woman with eyes like the sky of ancient Israel and her hair throwing off hairpins in the wind from the river, what was she? "There hasn't been very much work. If a man is fat, he's living off someone else, you can be sure of it. And you are?"

"My name is Emilia," she said.

"That's an unusual name for a Jewish girl."

"Well, it's mine. Emilia . . . Levy. I'm Mrs. Levy."

"So all right, Mrs. Levy. Do you have somebody here? A relative, a friend. I can put you in a hansom cab."

Emilia shook her head. "No one." The woman was looking at her as if she were a new sort of insect. A girl on her own. Like a grub that eats cabbages. It has to be picked off and disposed of. "Don't I have to register with the authorities or something?" Emilia asked brusquely.

"Aah," the woman in the red shawl said, her face clearing. "That's exactly why I'm here. To tell you there's no such thing."

A crowd of sailors and their women were tumbling out of a tavern. The woman pulled Emilia aside into a doorway where a parrot swung inside a cage. "No Jewish Council? Nothing?" Emilia asked.

"There is a Jewish Board of Guardians. They'd find a place for you. Yes, that's where you should go. I'll take you. And they'll put you in a house where you can be the lady's maid or something like that. Maybe a governess. I'm sure you'd make a nice governess."

"No," Emilia said. "They wouldn't want me in a month or two." She put her hand on her belly. "My poor husband . . ."

The other woman's eyes flashed with pain—why should Emilia's troubles matter to her?—but she just shrugged as she said, "It's not my business if you have a baby coming. Tell me where you want to go."

"I should get a room. I have a trunk," Emilia said. The little purse of money under her skirt wouldn't last forever. But she had to have a place to sleep.

"A trunk." The woman sighed. The parrot squawked. "Well, if you have nowhere else to go, you can lodge with me. I'm Nehama Katzellen. My husband is a tailor."

"You have a room to let?" Emilia asked. Oh, please do. She was so tired, and the frozen heart that had got her this far was starting to hurt as if it were waking up all pins and needles.

"Just a bench. Better than the floor," Mrs. Katzellen said. The parrot looked from one to the other, eyes bright as those of a matchmaker meeting with prospective in-laws.

"How much?" Emilia asked.

"A shilling a week," Mrs. Katzellen said. "A room will cost you six."

Emilia wondered how many shillings a purse full of rubles would buy. "All right," she said. The parrot drank from its little bowl and began to sing a sailor's song.

"Come with me and hold up your skirt," Mrs. Katzellen said.

They walked through corrugated streets where wheels pushed mud and dung into sticky dunes the color of babies' stools. Women lifted their skirts; children stamped on the ridges. Emilia's eyelashes were wet. It must have been the damp from the river. It would be terrible for her mother's hands. So it was all for the best that she'd come alone and her mother would realize it herself. Surely, she would.

Ravens cawed, their wings clipped to keep them at the Tower. Above them chimneys scraped the sky with burnt coal while Nehama led her new lodger through busy streets, thinking that she could slip into the crowd if someone tried to grab her. She was listening for the sound of thick boots hitting the ground with a pimp's stride and a voice calling, "Hi! You there!" But all she heard was the light click-click of her new lodger's footsteps, the clash of a pawnbroker's bells, someone calling "cat's and dog's meat," the thud of a coffin sliding into a hearse, and her own heart beating out an old Yiddish street song: *And so it turned out, when the pimp took her hand, she became as still as the walls.*

Nehama gasped for breath, a stitch in her side as she caught sight of the first Yiddish sign outside a store: "Smoked fish on special." And over there was a bill posted on a wall, "Fireworks! Complete Orchestra! The Great Jacob Adler Plays Tonight!" Soon there were more bills and more signs in the *mama-loshen*, and she was pushing her way into a crowd of women in red shawls. No one could find her here. Not in Frying Pan Alley, a street like a heart that expands and contracts, taking in countless stalls and barrows and at the end of the day squeezing them out so that the walls meet and even darkness can't reach down to touch the ground. She let the shawl slip from her head. Right behind her was the new lodger, Mrs. Levy, golden-haired and brilliant in her finery; no baby would run away from such housing.

Frying Pan Alley

The ghost of the first Mrs. Rosenberg seemed perfectly comfortable in Frying Pan Alley, which was more than Emilia could say for herself. Perhaps the dead are more adaptable because they don't have to contend with a wardrobe. In Emilia's trunk there were evening dresses, day dresses, and tea gowns, but not a single ghetto dress—something shapeless, colorless, and slightly higher than the ankle to sweep above the ridges of rubbish and horse dung in the East End streets where Yiddish was the official language. It was called the Ghetto by streetcar drivers, journalists, parliamentarians, and reformers, and Emilia sometimes laughed in the middle of the day, thinking that she had left the Pale of Settlement imposed by the czar only to find herself in the Ghetto. *Plus ça change, plus c'est la même,* she would say. The more things change, the more they stay the same.

The difference between the rich and the poor was in the number of buttons they had on their gowns. The poor couldn't afford a maid to do them up in back. It was Nehama who helped her dress in the morning while the husband pulled trousers on over his *langeh gatkes,* the long underwear darned in rough ridges like scars. He told bad jokes, his wife scooped a fly out of the pitcher and poured the milk into his teacup. She had everything and nothing. A home, a husband, a place in the world, all of it secondhand like the shabby goods in the rag market. And she would offer Emilia the same fly-spoiled milk as if Emilia could swallow a drop.

There was a stain on the elbow of Emilia's sleeve as she bent over the trunk. It was used as a bench in the workshop; at night a straw pallet was thrown on it and there she slept. She scratched a bite on her wrist.

"You have to squeeze bedbugs like this," Nehama said, pinching her thumb and forefinger together. They were both in the back room, the trunk on one side of the table with its two dark sewing machines, Nehama sitting opposite. Behind her the pressing table was against the wall.

"I'd rather be bitten. It smells horrid." The stench didn't seem to bother Nehama. Nothing ever bothered her. She was as steady as a rock, as impervious to delicate feeling.

"You'll get used to it. Listen to me. If you take that dress out of the trunk, it's going to be covered with soot," Nehama said.

"I have to put things in order." Every morning Emilia took out the contents of the trunk and put them back in again. Refolding the silk gowns on the worktable made her forget that there was no water to bathe and she was starting to stink.

"It's worth something, what you have in that trunk." Nehama was looking at the gowns with a competent eye, the sort of eye that would not blink as it added tiny sums to arrive at the penny left over from a wage packet.

"Thank you." Emilia placed a gown of gold brocade into the trunk.

"I'm not giving you a compliment. Listen to me. A widow that has a child coming needs money. But if you dirty everything, what good will it be?"

"As good to me as your room is to you." Emilia dropped the lid of her trunk, digging the key into the lock and snapping it to the right.

"I can't argue with that—you're sleeping on the trunk." Nehama knotted the thread with a quick flick of her fingers, a hint of derision in her voice.

How could a rock know what Emilia felt?

She'd worn the same dress all week. When she walked, and she had to walk in the street—the rooms held the heat like a baker's oven—her gown fell in sad, ragged folds, the hem dragging in the sewage that dribbled through the gutter. People jostled her, they shouted at her to buy things. She'd never handled a *kopeck,* and now she had a purse of money. It was all she had, and they wanted it, they pressed her for it, they begged her for it, and she felt herself weakening, doling out a handful of coppers, feeling a flush of pleasure as she chose this or that until she looked in her hand and saw the object that had glittered in a barrow now dim and cracked and useless.

"Look. I can make you a dress and you can save what you have in the trunk. You want it or not?" Nehama asked.

Emilia sat on the trunk, leaning her stained elbows on the worktable. "How much would you charge?"

"Just pay for the material," Nehama said. Her head was bent, her eyes on the buttonholes of the jacket, the thick needle quickly drawing thread in and out. "You see the sewing machines are quiet, and Nathan went to Soho to look for work. It's the slack season. I have time."

"I don't want a gift. No, you must have a little something for your trouble. Let's see what I have for you." She unlocked the trunk again, looking for the sort of trinket that would appeal to someone in Frying Pan Alley. "Maybe this?" It was a beaded purse, a present from Freida. Mother had packed it so the maid's feelings wouldn't be hurt.

Nehama reached down and picked up the book that lay on top of Emilia's dressing case. "What is this?"

"It's the German Bible. My mother and I used to read it together."

"Why not the *Taitch Chumash*? Let me guess. In your house Yiddish was for the maid and the greengrocer. Maybe even the tailor that made your gown." Nehama fingered the end of Emilia's sleeve. "It's not bad, this dress."

"It was made by the best tailor in Minsk," Emilia said.

"My father was a tailor. He made better. And he spoke Yiddish, too." Nehama put the book back into the trunk, and although it was the scorned German Bible, she laid it down carefully, her hands lingering for a moment over the book as if reluctant to move away from the touch of it.

Emilia studied her, but all she could see was the same woman as before, poorly dressed and poorly bathed. Even so, she asked, "What book would you like?"

"Something in English. About economics," Nehama said. "Do you have anything like that?"

"I don't," Emilia said. "I brought only a few books."

"Well, what do you have?"

"This book is in English. *Fairy Tales and Stories*."

"That's what you want to give me? A whole world there is and you want me to read grandmothers' stories?" Nehama tapped the table with her thimble.

"It's how I learned to read English," Emilia said. "You'd be surprised what you can learn from a grandmother's story. Would you take this for the dress?"

The dusty light from the window could hardly illuminate the eye of a needle as Nehama threaded it. She shook her head. "If you don't give me anything, that's all right. It's charity. But if I'm not going to have a good deed written in the Book of Life, then I'll want proper payment." She smiled at Emilia as if they shared a joke, and even if it wasn't clear what the joke was, a person ought to laugh anyway to have some pleasure. "One book isn't enough. I'll have three."

"Two," Emilia said. "Two and you make me a coat as well."

Nehama laughed. "Two and no coat."

"Agreed." Outside donkeys brayed, barrows rumbled, children threw stones.

Nehama turned back to her jackets and her buttonholes. "You should come with us to the theater. My grandmother used to say that there are two kinds of souls. There is the soul in a song, and the soul in tears. If you have both of them, you are blessed and the Holy One will hear your prayers."

"Personally, I think God is tired of prayers," Emilia said, expecting to shock her landlady, for everyone knows that impoverished Jews are rich in piety.

But Nehama smiled as if this was the joke they shared, and she said, "So many prayers. They're like the cries of the street vendors. Cheap, fresh, beautiful prayers. Who can buy them all? Tell me, Mrs. Levy, am I right?" Nehama looked at her with those bright blue eyes and Emilia wondered if she'd seen her come from the Lane with that broken clock yesterday, hiding it in the yard where a little girl was lifting her skirt to pee.

In the evening while her landlord and landlady were at the theater with their neighbors, Emilia sat in the front room, writing a letter blotted and pierced wherever her pen lost its footing on the rough surface of the table. She wrote by the light of a paraffin lamp, shadows hiding every feature of the narrow room. This was her favorite time of day, the noise of the street smothered in darkness.

My Dearest Mother,

The voyage was uneventful and I have settled in lodgings. I hope that Father's temper has improved and that you have recovered from your untimely spell of "illness."

My landlady and her husband have gone to the theater. Of course I did not join them. What use do I have for the Jargon? They have two rooms. I sleep in the back, which is a tailoring establishment. But do not think that I have any fear at all. My surroundings are certainly temporary. I have locked my trunk and put the key on a ribbon around my neck. My landlady shall make me a dress suitable for the ghetto, and I will save my things for a setting appropriate to them.

I am supposed to be an orphan. A girl traveling alone must be an orphan. If you write to me, pretend that you were the faithful family servant like our Freida and sign yourself "Mrs. Plater."

Do not be concerned with the shakiness of my handwriting. I am quite well, it is only the table that makes my hand unsteady.

Ever your daughter,

Emilia

Frying Pan Alley

The busy season began with a small order. Nathan was in the back room finishing it, Lazar doing the last of the pressing. Soon there would be no time for reading except on the Sabbath, so Nehama sat at the table in the front room, the English book in front of her, whispering the foreign words under her breath and breaking her teeth on them. In the rooms upstairs, Pious Pearl was drunk and yelling at her sons; men argued at cards in the FPA Workmen's Club. Outside in the street an old woman was selling lavender. A barrow clattered across the cobblestones.

Emilia was also reading at the table. She had a newspaper, turning pages in the time it took Nehama to move from one paragraph to the next. Her belly was protruding in the shapeless dress Nehama had made. She could have sewn it with some style, but she couldn't bear to see the golden Mrs. Levy with her baby growing under a beautiful gown. Did God have to give so much to this woman that there was nothing left for another? "How can you read with all that racket?" Mrs. Levy asked in her educated accent.

"This is hardly noisy," Nehama said. Minnie's son was pretending to be a streetcar, whistling and hooting as he drove from the workshop to the cookstove. The baby was sitting on his back, squealing, her hands gripping her brother's hair. "You should hear how it is when the busy season really gets started."

"So tell me what's so interesting in that book," Minnie asked as she stirred the soup. She still had only one room upstairs with no stove, just a fireplace, and as Nehama had two rooms with a stove but wasn't any hand at using it, Minnie cooked down here and the two families ate together.

"It's about a woman that loses her child," Nehama said, glancing at the newspaper. Was Emilia reading the article or studying the advertisement beside it for a slim line of corsets guaranteed to gather in the most rotund belly? "Her child is a little boy about your Sammy's age."

"*Thpoo, thpoo, thpoo.*" Minnie spat, blowing away the evil eye. "And?"

"And she's so upset, she forgets she still has two daughters." Nehama looked over Emilia's shoulder as she turned the page. There were toys advertised here, trains with miniature steam engines and dolls dressed more elegantly than living children. She could sew dresses just like these if she had a child with a doll. But she couldn't get pregnant again, though in her sleep she dreamed about the babies she'd lost as if they were growing up, and in such sleep her grief was softened. Then she'd wake up, listening to her lodger turn in her sleep, and Nehama kept her eyes closed over the envy pouring from them.

She reread the paragraph that described a mother's crazed sorrow so exactly. She could read it again and again as often as she wished. She didn't need a sister to tell her the story or an actor to play it for her on the stage because she had a theater here in her hands; the curtain rose when she opened her eyes and fell when she closed the book. It was amazing. Her middle sister had dozens of such books. Rich people had thousands, and lucky for them that they needn't work or surely they would starve, their eyes eating only words.

"It's a silly story," Minnie said. "A person can't forget her child."

"That's what my mother used to tell me," Emilia said. "But I don't think it's true."

"Your mother, she should rest in peace," Nehama said, looking at Emilia sharply.

"Yes, *alleva sholom*," the young woman murmured, shifting uncomfortably. The shallow wooden seat was hard for a pregnant girl. But why did she look flustered, her eyes recoiling from Nehama's?

Nehama flipped through the pages of her book. "Here's another story. It's called 'The Jewish Maiden.' Who would think there would be a story about a Jewish girl in a book?"

Minnie looked at the illustration. "And very pretty, too."

"Wait till you read it." Emilia rubbed her belly. Nehama could remember touching her own belly the same thoughtful way, wondering who grew inside. "If you find a Jew in a story," Emilia said, "you can be sure that he's greedy and sly and ends up hanging on the gallows. A Jewish girl is always pure and beautiful and dies a real Christian."

"So what good is the book—do you see your own life there? Better to go to the Yiddish theater," Minnie said, cutting potatoes into the pot of soup. "There you'll see something you won't forget."

"Yiddish isn't a language."

"Then tell me, what are we speaking?" Nehama asked. Any stupid girl could have a baby, while Nehama worked from morning till night and found herself making nothing.

"Yiddish is a jargon. You have to speak it among people who don't know anything else." Emilia looked from one to the other, her voice filled with righteousness. "Well, a language must have a literature. Where are the great Yiddish writers, then?"

"The same place as Goldfaden, who made the Yiddish theater just ten years ago." Nehama had her own opinions, and they were just as good as this young woman's. "Don't think you know everything. I'm a little older than you, and when I left home there wasn't a single play in Yiddish. Now there's melodrama and history and new songs every week. No one sees more plays than the Jews. Nathan reads the Yiddish papers that come from the *heim*, and each one has a new story in it. You'll see, we'll have our own great writers before you look around."

Emilia tucked a stray lock of golden hair behind her ear. "Do you think it's possible to catch up with three hundred years of literature?" She took a sip of tea, grimaced, and added more sugar as if sugar cost nothing.

"I only know that a person yearns for his own language. Why should you think of yourself as Russian?" Nehama asked. "Someone that tries to borrow another's soul ends up with nothing to guide him in life."

"So you think my soul is such a superior guide?" Emilia asked bitterly. "To bring me here of all places. I was raised to be someone else."

"You think you're the only one?" Nehama took a page of the newspaper, folding it to make a book cover, but as she wrapped the book in it, the cover split down the back.

Emilia shook her head and reached for the book. She measured it against a doubled sheet of newspaper, turning over the edges to make a slipcover. "My mother showed me how to do this." She paused. "My mother—she should rest in peace—told me everything, but I don't know what I should believe."

"Things didn't turn out the way you thought," Nehama said. She poured another cup of tea for them both. When there is no other comfort, there can at least be tea.

Emilia turned her head to look at the stove, where steam billowed from the pot of soup as Minnie tasted it. "My mother told me that she was married in a village near Plotsk. That would make us practically *landsmann*. Who knows if she was telling the truth? It's just a story like the ones in that book." She shrugged. "But if you sit beside me, I can help you with some of the words."

From the other room Nathan was calling, "I want your help, Nehama."

"It's just a small order," she called back. "What do you need me for?"

He came to the front room, frowning in the way he did during the busy season. Heaven forbid someone should tell a joke in the workshop. Nathan was a boss, and you might think he ran the business for God, as if sewing cheap jackets made the earth turn around the sun. "Lazar has nothing to press. He has wages coming to him. Should I pay him to clean his ears?"

"So let him go home. Next week we'll have a big order and we'll all be working fourteen hours a day."

"I don't know about next week," Nathan said. When he frowned, his lips thinned, his jaw clenched. A thread fell from his beard. "I only know about today. We can finish the order tonight and get another tomorrow. Am I by myself here or do I have a wife?"

"All right. Don't shout. I'll be there in a minute." Nehama put the book carefully on a shelf.

Petticoat Lane

When the busy season came, there were wage packets to spend and in the Lane sunlight glinted on second-, third-, and fourth-hand treasures: chipped china shepherdesses, shaving boxes, stuffed birds, bracelets, bootjacks, dominoes, hatpins, chessboards, earrings, butchers' steel, saws, accordions, rusted pistols, mango boas, pins set in pink paper a yard long. Steam rose from baked potatoes and fried fish, and it was as delicious as truffles to people that ate out of a twist of newspaper in the street. Everywhere jackets and dresses hung on rails above the crowd like spirits taking in the excitement while sellers reached up with their metal poles to bring down the perfect fit.

"COATS LIKE NEW! LADIES' DRESSES!"

"CORSETS MADE FROM THE BONES OF THE LEVIATHAN!"

Nehama was looking through the bookseller's barrow. When she came home with a purchase, Nathan would tease her again. Another book? Who knew I married a scholar? Thank God my father is in the *heim* and doesn't know he ought to provide board for you. She made her choice by the feel of the cover. *Pride and Prejudice* it was called, and the bookseller assured her it was the finest quality. Nehama's middle sister had books like this. Of course the leather binding was worn and there was a page or two missing, but that was nothing to complain about—weren't there still several hundred perfectly good pages?

"COWCUMBERS. LOVELY COWCUMBERS!"

"FINE WARNUTS, ALL CRACKED!"

Pious Pearl the beigel lady sat on a crate like an empress surrounded by her sacks of beigels. She wore a shawl over her head because bonnets were for the rich, and at her feet there was a zinc pail with coke embers to keep her warm. "A blessing on you, missus. You should live till a hundred and twenty. And what's wrong with you, mister, that you don't buy nothing of an old woman? May all your limbs wither. May your teeth rot."

"And how about a blessing for me?" Nehama asked.

"Maybe yes, maybe no. You'll take . . ."

"A dozen," Nehama said.

"Hmm." Pious Pearl rubbed some vodka on a sore tooth. Then she took a drink. If it didn't help on the outside, maybe it would on the inside. The neighbors were scandalized: a Jew drinking—and a woman, yet? But Nehama liked her.

"A copper fer a man what's blind and lame . . ."

"See the strong man, only a penny!"

"What do you have in there?" Pious Pearl asked as she put the beigels into Nehama's basket.

"A book for my new lodger. She wants to read out loud while we sew."

"Whose idea is that?"

"Mine," Nehama said.

"It's not a bad thing to have someone read while you work. All the cigar makers do it. But a book with a leather cover? You're getting too fine, Nehama. Watch out or you'll find yourself growing upside down like an onion, with your head in the dirt and your feet in the air." She turned to the next customer. "Beigels! Beigels! A blessing on you, mister."

"FISH ALL ALIVE. FRESH FOR *SHOBBOS*!"

"SMOKED FISH. BETTER THAN FRESH!"

Nehama's grandmother used to shop like this in the old market in Plotsk, taking with her the oldest sister and teaching her how to figure sums in her head so she could make a good bargain. Rivka used to keep track of the money that the Women's Singing Society had in the bank, for it wasn't long before the glass jar became full. In a little book, she recorded how much was given out for a loan or when someone's husband became sick or, God forbid, for a burial. Hinda, the second sister, baked with Mama every Thursday so that the women could have honey cake with their tea. The women never sang "bai-bai-bai-bai" like religious men in their ecstatic trances. They sang about the bad and the good things in life, and everything was revealed in their singing. Even the house burning, even the police station, the bad street, and the lost child, even playing at love in the cemetery. There's no "bai-bai-bai" for women, Grandma Nehama used to say. Not even after the grave. But that's no reason not to sing. She was the one who saved money for the middle sisters to go to school. They tried to teach Grandma Nehama to read Russian—there were no books yet in Yiddish—but it was too hard and she gave up. If only I was thirty years younger, she'd say. This was the story the sisters would tell Nehama while they hung their laundry in the courtyard. There was no singing society after you were born, they said. Mama was in mourning and she wouldn't have it.

Nehama was humming as she pushed her way past the fruit stall and waved to Minnie, who was struggling with the baby in one arm and her little son pulling at her sleeve for a copper to get a baked potato. "Finally I found you," she said to Nehama. "It's so crowded today someone must be giving out money. Look, isn't this a beautiful fish?"

Nehama unwrapped a corner of the newspaper to poke at it. "How much?"

"Not too much considering that this is the best." In the tightly wound mass of Minnie's hair, a comb with paste jewels caught the sun. "Here, let me put the fish in your basket. What's this? Not another book."

"It was very cheap," Nehama said, catching Minnie's son by the shirt as he tried to dart away after some glittering thing.

"So all of a sudden you're wanting to be a *shayner*?" She meant one of the fine people. Lawyers and owners of factories. People who didn't use their own hands like the *proster*, the plain working people. "I'm worried about you, Nehama. You have a lodger from who knows where and you look at her like you have to beg a piece of bread from her. You listen to me. You have nothing to be ashamed of in front of her."

"Who's ashamed?" Nehama asked nonchalantly. Let Minnie watch someone else. A free person's shame should be private. "Is it a sin to read a book? Show me where it's written."

"I'm not talking about books. I want to know why you think so much of her. A *shayner* sticks her nose where it doesn't belong and only trouble comes from it. You remember the lady visitor who came to the house yesterday? The Jewish Board of Guardians sent her. She told me that my children are dirty and they'll get sick if they don't have baths. Let her send her maid with a tub and some water. As if I don't care about my babies." Minnie put a copper into the outstretched hand of a beggar.

"I don't think anything of Mrs. Levy." Nehama stopped at a stall, fingering the hat with feathers and flowers so Minnie wouldn't see the sadness in her eyes. "She pays the rent and for free I can learn something."

"From her? Listen to me. I have my own door and a husband that isn't just a name. For a widow and an orphan she's not very sad, your Mrs. Levy. Do you really believe anything she says?"

"Not for a minute. But God doesn't care if she lies. She's having a baby, just the same."

"Aah. I knew it. Just remember the old saying: In front of a man whose father was hanged, don't talk about hanging a picture. You shouldn't have a lodger who's pregnant. Let her board somewhere else."

"What do you think would happen if I sent her away? Anything, I'm telling you. She's too young. She doesn't deserve it. Tell me, does she?" Nehama shielded her eyes from the sun so that she could see her friend's face.

"I don't know what she deserves, but she's a *shayner*. She can pay for whatever she wants in life. Even the angel of death can be paid off."

"If she doesn't lose everything first. I'm only doing for her what you did for me."

"I didn't do anything," Minnie said. "We were girls together. But I'll tell you what I need now. A new hat. And when will I get it? Don't ask. Right now I want some bones for soup. Come on." She put her arm through Nehama's, and they went to look at bones.

"LADIES AND GENTLEMEN, LOOK AT THIS VIAL OF BLOOD. THIS IS WHAT HAPPENS TO YOUR HEART WHEN IT IS EXPOSED TO THE FOGS OF LONDON. BUT ALL IS NOT LOST, MY FRIENDS. THERE IS A REMEDY, IMPORTED FROM THE ORIENT . . ."

Frying Pan Alley

It was a cold autumn, the coldest in years, and people were saying that the river might freeze. Even ghosts were staying indoors. Pubs did a brisk business, so you might see a Jewish ghost or two there among the bright colors and warm lamps. But mostly they kept to the tailoring workshops among their *landsmann,* where it was crowded enough to stay warm though yellow fog snuck through the cracks and the sound of coughing was all the song you could hear. The ghost of the first Mrs. Rosenberg was perched on the stove among the coals heating for the pressing iron. Emilia sat on the stool provided for her in the workshop. She didn't mind reading aloud. It passed the time. "*Pride and Prejudice.* Chapter fifty-seven," she said.

Between the pile of finished jackets and the piles of pieces, Nehama was sweating under the gas jets, Minnie beside her and Nathan working opposite. Emilia kept a wary eye on him, the landlord. In a small room like this one, a person didn't have much room to duck if something got thrown. If Nathan hadn't yet, he must be saving up his temper. Even her father had once gone three months without throwing anything.

Emilia's stool was jammed between the sewing table on one side and the pressing table on the other, and it was a wonder that she wasn't scorched when Lazar passed by with coals for his iron. At the pressing table, his iron hissed as he pressed a temporary shape into the cheap jackets. There was also a learner helping out, a middle-aged man named Itzik, newly arrived and hoping to send for his family later. He mopped his brow with his cap, the crown of his head covered by a black *yarmulkeh* and several long hairs combed over the bald parts. A word of English he didn't speak, and while Emilia read aloud he kept asking in Yiddish, "What? What?"

"Shh, Itzik. We're at the part where the girl's sister has run off and no one knows what's become of her," Nehama said. "The uncle is talking. Let me listen and I'll tell you."

Emilia read in a deep voice meant to be the uncle's: "'It appears to me so very unlikely that any young man should form such a design against a girl who is by no means unprotected or friendless . . .'"

"That's just it," Minnie interrupted in Yiddish for their new hand's benefit. "A person without a friend is grass for the cow."

"I don't know from cows," Itzik said. "But sewing for nothing isn't a life for a human being. That I can tell you."

"You're a learner." Nathan frowned. "You want to learn somewhere else, be my guest. But if you're in my workshop then you keep quiet and work."

"Never mind that. I want to hear how the story comes out," Nehama said. "Go on."

Emilia sneezed and blew her nose, then tucked her handkerchief into her sleeve. "'Well, then,'" she continued reading, "'supposing them to be in London, they may be there, though for the purpose of concealment, for no more exceptionable purpose. It is not likely that money should be very abundant on either side; and it might strike them that they could be more economically though less expeditiously, married in London than in Scotland—'"

"Is something happening in London?" Itzik asked.

"Of course, London," Nehama said. "Is there somewhere that the evil inclination is stronger?"

It was always like this when Emilia read, more interruptions than story. The fog must sweep away any sense of politeness. "Now it's the older sister who's answering," she informed them, "the sensible one."

"The older sister is always the sensible one," Nehama said, rolling her eyes.

"What? What?" Itzik asked.

Emilia blew her nose again. It was red and raw and most unattractive. She glanced at her landlord, scowling as he counted the number of finished jackets.

"Go on," Nehama insisted.

"'Why all the secrecy?'" she read. "'Why any fear of detection? Why must their marriage be private? Oh no, no, this is not likely. His most particular friend, you see by Jane's account, was persuaded of his never intending to marry her—'"

"Jane?" Itzik asked.

"Another sister," Nehama said.

"Is there no end to sisters?" Itzik shook his head.

"Never," Nehama answered.

"Listen to me. This should be a play," Lazar said. "I'd call it *The Anti-Semite*."

"But there's no anti-Semite in the story," Minnie said. "Not even any Jews."

"Ah, you have to know how to dramatize literature," Lazar said, turning the jacket over and pressing down the seams. "In the play, they would all be Jews. Except for the handsome captain that lured the sister away. But the mother in the book . . ." He shook his head. "Who could imagine someone so ridiculous? No, in my play she'll know what to do. A Jewish mother always knows."

"My husband, the Shakespeare," Minnie said. "Then you need a ghost for your play."

"All right, I'll give you a ghost. But we have to have a stepmother. A wicked stepmother." Lazar quickly lifted his iron as the smell of burning wool rose up. Crestfallen, he put the ruined jacket aside.

"Watch what you're doing! Five bob burnt up. You think a tailor pisses gold?" Nathan took the book from Emilia's hand and slapped it on the table beside his machine. "Enough already. No one says another word until the order is finished."

Emilia sat very still, because when your landlord is angry, it's best not to be noticed.

But after a few minutes of needles whirring and no conversation, Nehama spoke up as if he hadn't said anything at all. "Why should the stepmother be wicked?" she asked.

"Didn't you hear me say 'no talking'?" Nathan shouted. "You think I meant the walls?"

"If the walls can operate a sewing machine, then you tell them to be quiet," Nehama said.

Why did she have to argue? It only aggravated the situation. Now it would come. The accusations, a slap, a thrown pair of scissors. Emilia blinked, her eyes filling with tears. It was from the heat, only the heat.

"A wall is for shouting at," Nehama said. "Not a wife. You think I'm a wall, Nathan? Tell me right now."

He threw a jacket across the table. "What am I supposed to do with this? The sleeve is crooked. You think we make slop here? This is a stock shop. I promised the wholesaler the order tomorrow."

"Fine, Mr. Boss. Everyone stays until the order is finished. But if you want me, too, then just remember that a grave is quiet, not a person." She gave her husband a little smile as she ripped out the sleeve of the jacket.

Nathan caught her eye; he shrugged. "Wives! One is more than enough for me, let me tell you."

That was it? A shrug? Emilia turned to the ghost of the first wife for an explanation, but she just stood in the doorway, watching while Emilia's heart beat faster and faster.

"Just listen," Nehama said as she started up her sewing machine. "If you want me to see your play, Lazar, the stepmother should be the heroine. You think it's easy to be a second wife?"

"All right," Lazar said. "A ghost and a nice stepmother. Anything else? Tell me now, because later I'm not adding one thing."

"Mrs. Levy—what do you say?" Nehama asked.

Emilia glanced at Nathan, but he was just putting another spool of thread in his machine. Treadles were pumping, needles flying up and down, the iron thumping as Lazar flung jacket after jacket onto the pile. "The second wife is hard done by," Emilia said to Nehama, as if they were writing the play together and could make it any way they liked. "She can't bear her husband's cruelty."

"No, that's not how it goes," Nehama said.

"What do you mean, no?"

Nehama pumped faster. A hem on one side. A hem on the other. "The husband is all right. He's good to her. But there's a child."

"Well, yes. A child left behind. The child of the first husband," Emilia said. The stove must be overheating. Her face was flushed.

"From the first wife," Nehama said. "And the baby's life is saved by the stepmother, who nurses her and loves her most among all her children. And when the child grows up and becomes a mother herself, she has daughters—"

"How many generations do you think I can squeeze into one little play?" Lazar asked. But the women were looking at each other as if they didn't hear him, for together they were making a play that would tell the most important story.

"Only one daughter," Emilia said. "Who can't bear it anymore."

"Not another minute," Nehama conceded. "She has to make a life for herself. Even if it isn't easy."

"Why does it have to be so hard? It isn't fair," Emilia said. And Nehama was nodding as if she knew it, too. But how could anyone here understand?

"Aah. I see what's going on," Minnie said. "You need me to straighten this out, my friends. You're thinking of a husband for our Mrs. Levy." She clapped her hands. "And I have just the thing in mind. A tanner of sheepskins. I see him all the time, he buys the dog *dreck* for tanning from the widow that lives in the cellar across the way. Or if you don't mind children, there's the pawnbroker. It's a miracle that he has enough room for all of them above the shop. Where are you going, Mrs. Levy? Don't go after her, Nehama. You can't see anything out there, it's no use . . ."

In the alley Emilia couldn't tell one side of the street from the other as she tried to get a breath of air and see some kind of future in the yellow fog. It smothered the clamor of the street, the noise of barrows, and the testing of bells in the foundry, so faint that they sounded indistinguishable from the landlady calling her name. So how could she know that they were separated by just a few steps?

Goulston Street

With winter came the slack season, and the washhouse in Goulston Street was full of women scrubbing their linen, sheltered from the cold. Tables, tubs, sinks, and mangles for wringing out the washing were on one side of the room. On the other were the kettles of laundry boiling on stoves with great black pipes sending the mother tongue up into the sky so the grandmothers of a hundred generations could hear it.

The women's faces were red from the steam and their arms red from harsh soap as they paddled their linen. Water went down through the drain in the cement floor, down to hidden pipes that carried away the angry sewage. There was always some sewage in the water they used to make tea, and from time to time, it was drunk with a bit of cholera for flavor.

There were two women working the tub on the next table, like sisters pushing back strands of damp hair with the same knobbly fingers. In the dim winter light that came through the washhouse windows, all the women bent over their tubs looked similar. But Nehama could hear the difference in their voices. The one that whistled when she spoke, always out of breath. The one that talked very fast, trying to say everything before she was stopped. A woman whose voice was loud and long like a train coming into the station.

"Be careful," Emilia said as Nehama took the boiled sheets from the kettle to the tub. She'd come to the washhouse to get warm. "I heard of a woman in Minsk that was scalded to death doing that."

It had been four months since she'd arrived. Nehama didn't know anything more about her, and it would be no one else's business if only she wasn't keeping Nehama awake at night with her sobs. "You know, I don't believe in mixing in with other people's business," Nehama said as she pounded the sheets with a paddle.

"Really?" Emilia asked. Nehama looked at her sharply. There was nothing but innocence in those wide eyes as gray as rocks. Of course, you can't actually read a rock.

"You should at least visit the pawnbroker. Everyone knows he's looking for a wife to be a mother for his children, and he would provide well for you."

"I'm thinking about it," Emilia said.

Nehama stirred the sheets with wooden tongs. "Thinking isn't a living." Whenever she had a minute here or there, she tried to read a bit on her own. To her surprise, in this way she'd finished several books.

"I'm sure you know all about living."

"I know something," Nehama said as she added blueing to the wash. "I know that when the baby comes you're not going to be able to do anything on your own and you'll have to go home if you don't want to marry again." Nehama pounded the sheets harder, ignoring the pain in her arms.

"That's impossible. Have you forgotten?" Emilia's voice mixed with the sound of water and beaten laundry. "I'm a widow and an orphan."

"Yes, sure. Even a beggar can come up with a better story." Nehama gave Emilia her favorite stare. And she stared right back. An eye for an eye. Her coat wouldn't button over her belly, and she was holding it closed. Under the coat a small heart was beating, and it didn't ask whether the mother was thinking of its arrival. "Tell me another old wives' tale," Nehama said bitterly.

"If you like." Emilia didn't drop her eyes. Such gall; if it were gold, she'd be rich.

Nehama crossed her arms, letting the pain ease away. "So?"

"There was a princess. Everyone except the king exclaimed over her loveliness. For some reason he was offended by it. In fact, he used to say that she wasn't really a princess at all. The king liked to throw things. Soup, wine, glasses, a letter opener. The queen couldn't stand it, and she tried to take her own life. Is this a better story?"

"I saw something like it in a play," Nehama said, thinking of the sort of king that enjoys watching the queen's frightened face. "Go on."

"The only thing to do was leave the palace."

"To get away from such a king, a person would have to leave the country," Nehama said, recognizing a true story when she heard it.

"Of course, but unfortunately our princess had a little accident first."

"With a prince?" Nehama asked. She leaned on the tub, forgetting the washhouse. The concrete walls were gone. She didn't see the attendant sitting on her stool and taking pennies at the door.

"Worse—with a messenger who had to travel about."

"That would make it hard to find him," Nehama said.

"Oh, the princess found him. No one thought she would, but she asked the old servant to help her. And you know how servants are. They all talk to each other."

"Well, you know how masters are. They forget that servants have ears and a brain in between them. Where was he?"

"In town. He had a small room, the kind you'd expect of a messenger. Just a bed and a table. It smelled like dirt and vodka. After he poured her a cup of tea, she told him everything. And he said . . . He asked if she was sure it was his."

"Of course it was his." In the young woman's eyes, Nehama could see a stone breaking, and yet she didn't look away. "Was he such a bargain she should go looking for him? He must be drunk all year and sober on Purim."

"So she said no."

"But it was a lie," Nehama said. She didn't let go of the girl's eyes. A person's story is more delicate than a prayer.

"If he had to ask . . . Well, what was the use? He'd never believe anything else. Better to be a princess on her own than a queen putting a knife to her wrist. Men are too cruel. She already had the boat ticket." Emilia's fingers were trembling, and she clutched them tighter over her belly. "So what do you think of my old wives' tale?" she asked. "It has a moral like all good stories. You still think I should go see the pawnbroker?"

"It's very interesting. But you know, there's always two kinds of stories. Let me tell you one." Nehama's sisters used to say that to each other. She hadn't known then what they meant. "There was a girl."

"A princess," Emilia said.

"No, just a girl. She was the youngest of six."

"In fairy tales the youngest is always the favorite," Emilia said.

"Well, you're right. But being the favorite doesn't mean that money grows on trees." Nehama had yet another book in her pocket; was she really reading it, the youngest sister, careless and stupid? "Let me tell you. By the time it was the girl's turn, there wasn't anything to do for her but marry her off to someone she couldn't bear."

"So she ran away." Emilia wiped her fingers on a handkerchief, returning her attention to Nehama with a skeptical gaze. How can you surprise me? it seemed to ask. I've read a hundred books.

But in the washhouse, Nehama was the older sister, and she had a story to tell. "Listen to me. Running away doesn't come free. She had to steal what she needed. But never mind. In the end she married someone else. It was Guy Fawkes Day, and the firecrackers banged like guns."

"Did she love him?" Emilia asked. "It wouldn't change anything, of course, but did she?"

"A funny thing. Until then she didn't know." How nervous she'd been when Nathan entered her. She was afraid she was going to laugh and once she started she'd never stop. Nathan thought he was hurting her. Imagine! "When the groom went to sleep," Nehama continued, "the bride cried to herself because she wanted him to go away."

"So she didn't care for him," Emilia said.

"No—because she did." Just like that, amid the shouts of "Remember, remember, the fifth of November," the window lighting up with firelight, she knew she loved him.

"But now they were married, and a man that wants nothing but you before the wedding wants something else entirely afterward," Emilia said.

"*Shh*. Let me tell you about it."

"So? I'm listening."

"There was something about her," Nehama said slowly. "Well, if her husband knew, he'd leave. And she'd always be waiting for him to find out, so scared that she couldn't stand it. Better he should go right away."

The morning after the wedding, Minnie had come in to take away the sheets for washing, and what a production she'd made from the drop of blood she found there. Nehama herself hadn't been surprised. She'd felt as if she'd been rubbed with sandpaper, and she was irritable with everyone, wishing she could wipe away Minnie's smug little smile as she shooed her out.

"So what did the girl do?" Emilia asked, as if it really mattered to her.

"Well, she talked with her new husband. She said to him that she'd made a mistake. She hadn't told him about the scar on her leg." Nathan was sitting on the unclothed bed, cross-legged like a tailor in the *heim*. "So she leaned against the table and lifted her skirt to show him. On the table were their wedding presents. A kettle. A box of tea. Good tea. There weren't any used leaves in it. And a frying pan." Everything was fried in the East End. The faster you cooked, the less coal you needed, and coal cost money.

"What did he think of it?" Emilia asked, meeting Nehama's unfaltering gaze.

"At first he stared at her like she was crazy, but looking at her bare leg, he didn't seem to mind." Nathan hopped off the edge of the bed to get a better look. His hand was on her leg. "Then the girl asked him if he wanted to know how it happened. And he said that there weren't any secrets between a husband and a wife. Except when there were. He thought that was a good joke, and he laughed."

"He wouldn't laugh if he knew." Emilia fingered the cameo brooch on her coat. She wore it all the time, touching it with pink fingers that had gotten grayer over the months, an edge of dirt and grease under the fingernails.

"The girl tried to explain how things used to be. Someone arrives from home, spoiled and knowing nothing. Who's going to tell her what's what? Nobody speaks the *mama-loshen* except for a few criminals that would sell you to anyone." Nehama shook her head. "Well, she's going to find out for herself how things are, and she won't be spoiled anymore."

"And then?"

"The girl couldn't say another word. Her throat closed up. So he had to speak. And he asked, 'Could you get a loaf of good rye bread in London back then?' When the girl just shook her head, he said, 'Ah, it was really an uncivilized country. But look, then I came—well, me and a few others. You don't need to explain any more than that.'"

"Tell me, how did she get the scar?" Emilia asked.

"There are cruel kings here, too. The streets are full of them." The young woman was looking at her as if she could see everything now.

"I'm sorry," Emilia said softly, but Nehama couldn't endure the sympathy in her eyes.

She turned back to her laundry. The water had cooled. "Not everyone is a king, and not everyone is cruel."

"You can be fooled," Emilia said.

"Only for a while. Listen to me. A husband can be all right. Better than all right." Nehama lifted the sheets out of the tub.

After she showed Nathan the scar, he'd held her in his arms, tenderly stroking her long hair. It wasn't cut. He'd agreed that a woman in the free land didn't need to wear a wig, and there on the table was his wedding present: a box full of hairpins and an ivory comb. And while his arms were around her, Nehama had decided that this was worth anything.

Now she carried the sheets to the mangle, pushing them through the double rollers as she turned the handle. The mangle was green and gold and carved with angels. Who would think such a thing could be made for a washhouse in the middle of the meanest part of London? Next door in the costermongers' stables, the donkeys were braying. When darkness fell, in a thousand dirty windows, eight candles would be lit to remember the miracle of light while in the street children playing kick the can would bring back the sun by booting it into the sky.

1887

Whitechapel Road

Mr. Shmolnik was not merely a pawnbroker but also the proprietor of the coffee house next door. All the Jewish gambling establishments were "coffee" houses. After all, a person has to drink something warm and have a little bite between card games. Upstairs from the shop, he had a flat, where Emilia sat at the kitchen table while Mr. Shmolnik's mother, who also happened to be the matchmaker, made tea. She was a small, dry figure of a person, her skirts swishing across the floor as she put more coal in the stove. It was the first of January, the year of the queen's jubilee.

For the occasion of examining a prospective daughter-in-law, Mrs. Shmolnik wore pearls, a High Holy Days kerchief made of silk, and what were surely her nicest earrings. Emilia was wearing her ghetto dress. Its ugliness suited her. If she was at home and married, she wouldn't step outside the house with a shape like this.

Dear Mother, she imagined writing, I have news. I am engaged. My trunk will provide the dowry, and I shall have as many ghetto dresses as a person might want.

"In the *heim,* my son was an innkeeper," Mrs. Shmolnik said. She seated herself opposite Emilia. "Even now, look what he has. Three rooms and not a single lodger!"

There was fresh honey cake, cherry preserves, and tea with lemon served in glass cups. An insect crossed the table to share their meal, and Mrs. Shmolnik, with no reference at all to the virtue of hospitality, smashed it and flicked the remains to the floor. "Very nice," Emilia murmured. The window was clean, and light waddled freely about, illuminating the iron stove, the dresser with a brass samovar and chipped plates on it, and, pinned to the wall, a lithograph of the Twelve Tribes of Israel.

Mrs. Shmolnik followed her gaze. "Only sixpence," she said proudly.

"A bargain." Emilia shifted her weight, but it is impossible to get comfortable if you are eight months pregnant and seated on a shallow wooden chair. Her ankles were swollen, and her feet simply could not bear to carry her back downstairs. She would have to stay forever in this room with the hideous lithograph for company.

"A young woman like you has lots of strength, thank God. Looking after the shop and children, you'll need it." Mrs. Shmolnik was evidently enjoying the cake, her lack of front teeth hardly any hindrance at all. "Of course a woman wants to be busy."

"How many children?" Emilia asked faintly. Her hands were folded on the table. Perhaps it was all a dream. Her head seemed to be on the mildewed ceiling, and she couldn't feel her belly at all.

"Five children from the first wife and three from the second. I won't mince words with you, Mrs. Levy. My son is a good prospect. The best. If I had another choice, I wouldn't look at you twice—a pregnant widow from God knows where. But a third wife isn't so easy to find. Still, I won't say yes if it makes my son's life harder. Troubles he already has enough in this world. He needs a wife for his children."

Emilia looked at the immense shadow she cast. Such a shadow, she supposed, could be the mother of countless children. "What are they like?" she asked.

"A blessing, every one of them," Mrs. Shmolnik said. She put a piece of sugar in her mouth. "The eldest is fourteen, apprenticed to a printer. The middle children are in the Jews' Free School, and the babies are downstairs. I'm an honest person, Mrs. Levy. There's no tricks with me. I would like my son to see you, and you can see the shop."

"Thank you kindly," Emilia said, wondering how on earth Mrs. Shmolnik would maneuver her back down the narrow staircase. But a strong hand gripped her arm, and when they reached the bottom, Mrs. Shmolnik pushed open the door to the shop.

"Avram," Mrs. Shmolnik called. "I have someone for you to meet."

The shop was tiny and smelled of feet, for it was customary among the gentiles to bring a man's Sunday boots to pawn on Monday, redeeming them at the week's end. You could find anything on the shelves of Mr. Shmolnik's small shop, and by a miracle he always found a place for one more item. A sewing machine. Sheets. A wedding band. An artificial foot. Everything. On the door there was a sign that said "Closed for an hour," and outside a line of tired women carrying bundles waited for their salvation.

Mr. Shmolnik was an unremarkable, brownish-looking man. His hair, eyes, beard were the color of mud-smeared cobblestones with a round cobblestone in the middle of his face for a nose. He stood behind the counter, sorting linens.

"This is Mrs. Levy," his mother said.

"*Sholom aleichem.*" His voice was raspy, his fingers stained yellow.

"*Aleichem sholom,*" Emilia replied in the customary manner.

"The coffee house is just through that door." He pointed. "But my best goods are right here." He bent down to pick up first one child, then another, seating them on the counter. "You see?" The girls looked to be around two years old, black-haired and black-eyed, cheeks too red, dresses too big, a sour smell coming from them. "This is Sureleh, and this is Malkeleh. Twins were too much for my second wife, *alleva sholom*. She never laid eyes on them."

"Avram, what a thing to say! *Thpoo, thpoo, thpoo.*" Mrs. Shmolnik blew away the evil eye; it shouldn't get any ideas from her son standing awkwardly, looking and not looking at Emilia. It wasn't his fault that his breath smelled of bad teeth.

One of the twins was playing with a large object, banging it on the counter, while the other cried, "Mine! Mine!" pushing her sister. The grandmother gave them each a slap, and Mr. Shmolnik shook a finger. "Malkeleh, enough," he said. "I have one for you, too." From a shelf behind the counter, he took the prosthetic foot. "Here, take it, my pretty."

"You see what lovely children?" Mrs. Shmolnik asked loudly. "From my son, you'll have children as good as these."

"*Sha,* Mama," her son said. "Mrs. Levy, I'm grateful you'd consider. Believe me, I know how it is to lose your beloved."

"Two of them," Emilia couldn't help saying.

"My luck hasn't been good." He turned away and wiped his muddy eyes.

"Never mind," Mrs. Shmolnik said. "A person can't mourn forever. Well, children, the shop has to reopen. You send us a reply soon, Mrs. Levy. Don't wait too long." She looked at Emilia's expansive middle. "I'll make you a nice betrothal."

In the hansom cab, Emilia closed her eyes to the street of pawnbrokers and newspaper vendors calling, "Stabbing most foul! On Thursday last . . ."

Dear Mother, she imagined writing, What was your plan? The purse is getting thin and soon I must marry Mr. Shmolnik. My hair will be cut and I shall sport a wig like a religious woman must after her wedding day. And when the wig makes my head itch, I shall scratch like they do, digging under the wig as it tilts to one side in a drunken tremor.

Prince's Street

On the eighteenth of January, in the balcony of the theater in Prince's Street, the audience waited for the play to begin on Jewish time, an hour or so late. The pawnbroker, Mr. Shmolnik, wearing a new hat, sat with his children in the front row of the balcony. In the row behind him was a rough-stuff cutter in the boot trade, the smell of glue sealed into the seams of his gray skin. Every Thursday evening he led a literary circle in a room at the Jews' Free School, and in his pocket he had a poem dedicated to Dina, the daughter of the High Priest of ancient Israel, or rather to the actress playing her. He'd read it aloud while waiting in the queue, and Minnie had cried. He sat in the same row of seats as Nehama and Nathan, Minnie and Lazar and their children, Pious Pearl the beigel lady, her numerous sons with their watery eyes, and her husband, who'd bet his wage packet on horses but had somehow managed to hold on to enough of his stake to buy the sixpenny tickets for the balcony. They were all eating their supper, and if the children got impatient, they'd crack nuts and throw the shells onto the hats of people seated below the gallery.

They'd all come to see *Bar Kokhba: The Last Days of Jerusalem*. Nobody could say how the play would turn out, even if someone had seen it a hundred times, for scenes were rewritten to taste, and even so the actors were quite independent of their lines. As it is written: the Jews are a stiff-necked people. There was the time when the actor playing the Roman commander refused to be the villain of the piece and declared Jerusalem a free state. But however the play turned out, everyone knew that there would be a grand finale, an amazing spectacle promised before the end.

Beside the pawnbroker and his children, a Hebrew teacher was holding a bouquet of roses. He'd come from the West End, where some of the Jewish newcomers were forming a colony among the prostitutes in Soho. He was missing three fingers on one hand and was peeling his orange rather awkwardly. Everyone had oranges. That was the smell of the theater: oranges and cigars.

"Who are the flowers for?" the boot maker asked.

"For Jacob Adler. He's playing the leader, Bar Kokhba."

"But it was all Bar Kokhba's fault that the rebellion failed," the boot maker said, as agitated as if he personally was being led off in chains.

The teacher offered him a piece of orange. "Wait till you see Adler. He makes a wonderful Bar Kokhba. So determined," he said, as if he didn't think it strange at all that a man should be enraged by imaginary deeds.

The heel cutter waved his bitter cigarette as he protested, "But Adler can barely sing a note. He should never have been cast in this role."

"And you're an expert?" the teacher said. "You! A boot maker!"

"So you have something against boot makers?" He took a bite from his onion sandwich.

"Well, you know. Some trades shrink the brain. Give one a *yokisher kop*," the teacher said, meaning a gentile head. He used the Cockney slang, turning *goy* backward. It was a terrible insult.

So the boot maker replied in kind, "Then teaching must turn out cripples."

The teacher pushed the boot maker's shoulder as he said, "Crippled in the head, you tailors and boot makers."

Now someone shouted from behind them, "You want tailors, you have tailors." And someone else was answering, "Don't lump me with you. A Polish tailor is a thief."

The boot maker's lip was split. The teacher had blood on the hand that was missing fingers. But wait—Mr. Smith, the owner of the theater, was signaling frantically: the orchestra began to play, the torches were lit. The women were shushing the men. In this play, everyone spoke in verse. Not for anything would such a drama in the *mamaloshen* be missed; it gave dignity to their language. Dignity for sixpence: it would be cheap at twice the price! The curtain was rising.

While they waited for the spectacle, the audience cheered the Hebrew rebels and booed the troops of mighty Rome, who were dressed remarkably like Cossacks. Rome was faltering and mustered its troops from far and near, even recalling them from Britain to fight the proud Hebrews in the Holy Land. The audience gloried in the strength of its ancestors as the great Jacob Adler sang the famous solo of the leader Bar Kokhba. They hissed as the Jewish traitor went over to the Roman side, capturing Dina, the leader's beloved, attempting first to seduce and then to ravish her.

In the balcony, matches flared like a hundred red eyes. Smoke threaded upward from cheap cigarettes while Nehama waited for the heroine's tragic end. It was the same in all the versions of the play: her fate didn't change. And why was that? she'd like to know. Already from the few books she'd read, she'd learned of half a dozen heroic types. There was the Frenchman who escaped from his miserable convict's life to rise up to the position of mayor. Later he risked his life to save his daughter's lover from the guns of insurrection—that was another sort of heroism. A third was the cleverness of women in the books about making a good marriage. Yet her favorite type came from the last book she'd read, about the girl who wasn't beautiful or good but rebellious. She never compromised herself, not for love and not for God, and always she looked for a way to live. Why must the Jewish heroine throw herself off the tower?

Minnie was weeping. Nehama wept, too. It shouldn't be like this. Onstage, Dina stood on top of the tower, exhorting the people to continue their fight. Then—rather than give herself up to the Romans and to shame—she jumped from the tower and died her tragic death. The rebels in their terrible grief and rage set the tower on fire. A green fire it was, like flames from the other world. And the spark rising up, up to the curtains was cold. Anyone would know it. An effect of stagecraft. Only their imagination made it a fire.

But the grandmothers who'd risen from the grave knew how strong imagination could be, strong enough to carry them over the sea with their children.

"Fire!" someone called.

"Where?"

"There. Don't you see it?"

"The orchestra's still playing."

"It's all right. Just part of the act."

"Don't sit like a bump. Can't you feel the heat?"

"Go back to your seats!" Jacob Adler shouted from the stage as the audience stood up. "There's no fire. No danger. Please." He waved to the musicians in the orchestra pit. "Louder." The actors playing the Hebrew rebels sang. They danced faster and wilder to get the audience's attention.

There was silence in the gallery. "It's all right," someone said. The audience shifted as if people might be convinced that the alarm was false and remain in their seats.

It was just Bengal fire. A chemical. Something used a dozen times. And Nathan was telling everyone to wait a minute. Half the dangers in the world can be avoided just by waiting. But Lazar was pushing Pious Pearl aside, and Minnie was trying to crawl over the seats, pulling her son after her. The smoke from a hundred bitter cigarettes was thickening into a fog.

"Don't listen to Adler! He wants to get to the door first, himself."

"Where's the exit?"

"Move. Move already!"

"Fire! Fire!"

"Dear God, my children. Take Mama's hand. Hurry."

The audience was rising; panic swept through them in a wind of contagion carried on their breath. A trembling on your right, a curse on your left. The actors were still singing and dancing and pleading with the crowd. But the play was out of their control. It had shifted to the parterre and the gallery, and it was their turn to weep.

"Help me," Minnie said, trying to hold her baby in one arm, her son in the other.

Nehama took the baby as she pushed her friend back down. "It's all right. Just sit and wait."

"Go to hell," Minnie said, climbing down over the Hebrew teacher, who was still clutching his flowers. "Give me the baby!"

"How can you hold them both?" Nehama asked, and her last sight of Minnie was a look of hatred as the crowd engulfed her.

Frying Pan Alley

The house was quiet, all sound gone with the grandmothers to the theater, and only fog walked in the street. Emilia sat by the stove to get the last bit of warmth while she wrote to her mother. There was no more coal. On the stove she had a candle. It was as much light as she could afford, but it was very bright, and as the wax pooled, she rolled it in her hands. There were shadows behind her, nothing but shadows and the ghost of the first wife sitting on the bed.

She was writing a letter slowly, warming her fingers in the melting candle wax.

Dear Mother,

I cannot do it. I cannot stomach Mr. Shmolnik, and I dare not think what will happen to me.

Her dress was torn. It wasn't very modest, but she looked down indifferently at the rip in her skirt. Nehama would never go around with a ripped skirt. She would mend it invisibly, not caring how worn the fabric was or how cheap. Emilia crumpled the letter and took out another sheet of paper. If Nehama were at home she'd make a face over wasting paper which could be turned to good use. A patch for a window crack or a sole for a shoe or even a feather in a hat if someone used her wits. But Emilia was here all alone, so she didn't have to see any disapproving glances. She was glad to be alone. Really, she was.

Dear Mother,

I feel most peculiar. There is a wrenching pain in my abdomen—it must be indigestion. The food I eat is rather more greasy than I have been accustomed to.

She had to marry. How else could she manage? That was what her landlady would say. Emilia gazed at the debris of ash and feathers and bones swept into the corner. She ought to give her child a name and a room just like this, so small that if one sneezed, the spit landed on the wall, for if one lived in a room like this, one would not carry a handkerchief. The ghost of the first wife didn't have a handkerchief either. The dead and the poor must understand each other, and if Emilia followed their lead, she'd turn into one of them. But she had a trunk full of gowns that would fit her again. That was the difference. If only she could open the trunk and convince herself of that.

Walking slowly to the other room, one hand on the wall to support herself, the other holding the stub of her candle, she coughed as fog seeped through the crack in the window. The workroom smelled of wool and gas jets and onions. Emilia kneeled in front of her trunk, fumbling with the key. Her eyes were running, she couldn't manage the lock. All she could do was put her head down on the trunk and wait for someone living to find her in her hiding place.

Prince's Street

No one ever knew for sure how the gaslights went out just then. But in the darkness, the audience heard the rustling of wings. And the *yetzer-hara*, the evil inclination, the primal instinct, rose up from every soul and became a single soul, the soul of the crowd needing to save itself. It thrashed and struggled, stepping on its own flesh to break free from the hot darkness. There were side doors, but who thought of them? This was a soul running from flames, a soul that believed in a single exit at the front, where tickets were taken and a sign read "Amazing Spectacle!" People fell as the crowd from the main floor climbed up toward the front door and the crowd from the gallery climbed down, jammed against each other, unable to get out, like twins stuck in the birth canal, killing themselves and their mother.

Nehama held her free arm over the baby's head so it wouldn't smother. Under her feet someone was dying and there wasn't a thing she could do about it. Was it a man or a woman—who could say? There was only a softness and the crowd trampling as Nehama was carried along, trying not to vomit as she felt herself walking on the wood floor again. If you could call it walking when your face was pressed against the cheap rough cloth of someone's back, and your feet moved an inch forward. A man bent to help a boy fallen on the staircase, groaning as someone pushed them both down. At any moment she could drop and die beneath a hundred feet, but she had no right. Not as long as she was holding Minnie's baby. She could not deny her longing to live even when it meant walking over someone. This instinct for self-preservation, which the rabbis called the *yetzer-hara*, this was her treasure now. It would save her friend's child. So she pushed and she listened to the roar of the blind crowd. Which way? It was too dark to see. But if they were running from the sound of crackling flames, then she had to hear something else. The gasping breath of terrified mothers. A cracking beam. A cracking bone. For among the terrible sounds there might be a clue to the way out. And then, quieter than the baby whimpering in her arms, she heard the voice of her dreams:

Children, children. There's always another way. Use your head. Is there a small door? A side door? Always—I promise you. Why don't you hear me?

Why don't you listen? Dear God above, for this I left my grave? My children are dying. My children are killing each other. How can you bear it?

If the grandmother's spirit could have heard the Holy One's answer, she would have caught the sound of weeping. But even she didn't listen, believing that God was far away in the distant heights.

Nehama made her way to the side door, using her elbows and her knees in the accusing darkness. Beside her someone was praying to make sure that if he died it would be with the holiest of prayers on his lips. Was it someone she knew? The pawnbroker, perhaps. It didn't matter. She must not compromise herself, not for love and not for God, and she jabbed the man with her elbow, she stepped on his feet to make her way past him. If she had to be a sister to kings and squires to save this child, she would do it. She would even listen to her step-grandmother cry.

Outside, people wandered in a daze while gentile neighbors brought them tea and blankets, their breath steaming in the cold air. There were four hundred people in the single narrow block in front of the theater and more arriving every few minutes. Nehama looked among them for Nathan and Minnie, Pious Pearl and Lazar, the pawnbroker, the baker Grodzinski and the boot maker who was president of the workingmen's literary circle, but all she could see were the same faces over and over, all of them familiar, none of them known, until someone stopped her and made her drink some tea. The air was cold and she was hot; she was the fire burning down the theater, and the flames would eat her alive. And even when Nathan found her, that wasn't enough to quench the fire, not even with his tears on her face and hands.

He huddled on the ground beside her, and their heads touched while his shaking fingers stroked her hand.

"Never, I'm telling you, Nathan. I'll never walk through that door again." They were sitting with their backs against the wall of a warehouse opposite the theater. The baby was sucking on her fingers.

"It's all right," he said.

"No, it's not. I have to go in there and look for Minnie. Maybe she's lying with . . ." Nehama couldn't finish the sentence. Inside the theater the dead were laid out.

"Wait," Nathan said. "Finish your tea. Then we'll go."

The tea lasted a long time, long enough for a dockworker to bring them blankets and a missionary a Bible. Nehama threw the Bible at a lantern, turning the spot of light into the darkness it should be.

"Nehama?" a voice called. "Nehama! Answer me if you're alive. . . ." The crowd opened and closed like the mouth of a great fish, and out of it fell Lazar and Minnie, her hair as red as roses in the dim light of the kerosene lanterns. Her son was in his father's arms as she fell on Nehama, kissing her and the baby as if they were both her children.

"Hersh the boot maker," Minnie whispered. "From down the street. I heard that he fell. It could have been my baby. What would I have done?"

"Don't think of it. We're all right," Nehama said. A person who has a double portion of the *yetzer-hara* is very strong. It is her duty to protect the weak. Only then did she feel the cold and begin to shiver, holding on tight to her husband and the friends who were sister and brother to her, and the children with their soft, high voices, crawling over her.

All night, the Jews of Whitechapel came through Prince's Street, asking after friends, neighbors, cousins, brothers, people they weren't speaking to yesterday, people whose names they didn't know but wished they'd found out when they could.

They came in the thousands. They wore caftans, they wore kicksies, they wore red shawls and nursed babies, they held hands, they walked with crossed arms wearing the black ribbon of anarchists, they carried their prayer shawls to say morning prayers, they carried baskets of buttered bread and pickled herring.

At dawn, the police rode in on horses. "Clear out. Clear out. Now then, mister. Don't raise a fuss. We can't have us a riot."

In the reading room of the theater, empty chairs were pushed against the walls to make space for the tables in the center of the room. Seventeen bodies were laid out. Two of the dead had been pregnant. One was a mother of eight children. Another her youngest son. The boot maker from Frying Pan Alley lay on a table, his poem still in his pocket, and next to him was an old man from Goulston Street, who'd saved a boy from being trampled. The boy was with his father in the Prince's Street synagogue, saying *kaddish,* the mourner's prayer, for the old man, whose name they didn't know. Sir Samuel Montagu, M.P. for Whitechapel, came personally in his carriage to express his condolences.

After the inquest, five hearses carried the bodies to the cemetery between the lines of old women on Brick Lane. At the top of Brick Lane was the mission that had once been a Huguenot chapel and would someday be a synagogue. Above the door was a sundial inscribed *Umbra Sumus*. We are shadows. Beyond was the Old Nichol, the worst five blocks in London, but none of the Nichol gang dared come near. The old women were keening, and they would have ripped out the eyes of anyone who disturbed the mourners.

Every house in Whitechapel sat *shivah*. For a week the blinds were drawn, and black crepe was draped over the fronts of synagogues.

After the great fire of 1666, London was rebuilt with glorious cathedrals. But no property was lost in Whitechapel. Only people can die in an imaginary fire. And the voice of the people. And their lives made large enough to show them their meaning. These can die.

CHAPTER 4

Keener the Greatness

1887

Frying Pan Alley

It isn't true that a mother is born with her child. It may happen sometimes by an act of grace, but most often a mother is made as she strug-
gles with her need for sleep and freedom of movement, over and over
choosing to hold and feed and wrap a loudly wailing, soft-skinned
being that produces marvelously pungent odors.

The baby lay in an orange crate beside the bed. Emilia fed it, she
wasn't sure how often, because someone put the baby in her arms and
someone brought the baby's mouth to her breast. She didn't feel the
suckling. All sensation had left her, and she blessed God, for after the
labor she never wanted to feel anything again. It was night; she lay in
the bed with Nehama, her landlord banished to a bench in the back
room, knowing that the January dawn wouldn't come until the morning was well under way. She felt a great satisfaction at knowing something. A fact. Surely a person aware of the facts can rise from her bed. If
only her limbs weren't so heavy and her head so light. It made her want
to lie here forever, feeling the shadows of day and night on her closed
eyelids.

Emilia was holding on to a postcard. Someone had tried to take it
from her, and she believed that she had scratched that person, though
she wasn't entirely sure. It was important, this postcard. It held crucial

information. The postcard had arrived on the day after the baby had come, and Emilia had clutched it ever since.

> My dear Emilia,
>   A mother always hopes that her daughter will make herself a satisfactory marriage. A girl lives for such a short time before making her choice and then has many, many years to abide by it afterward. I know that your mother would have wished to be with you. A mother's wishes, however, are not always respected in heaven and sometimes God decrees something else. My love is with you,
> Ever your servant . . .

It was signed "Mrs. Plater," after the young woman who led the Polish cavalry against the Russians.

Emilia had several such postcards from her mother. The others were in her trunk, but this one she couldn't put away until she'd figured out its hidden meaning, and first she had to swing her feet to the floor, getting herself out of bed carefully, slowly. No one must awaken. She crouched in front of the orange crate where the baby lay, waiting to feel like the child's mother as she reached down to stroke the small hand. There should be a rush of love, a sense of duty, but she was so cold. If only there was more coal.

The baby had lived inside her; now it was here and there was no home for it. There ought to have been a home for her child. A home and pretty dresses and a rocking horse for when it was bigger. A rocking horse, a piano, then a French governess. She'd never thought her child would live in the Jews' Orphan Asylum in Norwood. But there was no other choice, and anyway the country air was said to be very good. In the morning she'd do it. She'd take the baby there and leave something for it to remember her by. Go to the asylum and give up the baby to the fat matron in her black dress and lace shawl, contemptuously asking why and what and so on. Whatever would one say to such a person?

Nehama would know. She ought to take the baby there. Emilia stroked the tiny hand. How soft it was, though it didn't feel like anything of hers. The hand was any hand. That was what she would have to remind herself. The tears on her face were just tears of tiredness as she stood up and lit a candle stub. Her fingers were stiff because she was still weak, ripping a corner off the newspaper and writing with great effort, "Nehama, please take her."

Emilia dropped the note into the orange crate, lifted her shawl from the nail in the door, and took her purse from the mantelpiece. She left the house quietly and ran into the street. She had to run, because if she stayed, she would be a person in endless mourning, unable to bathe or comb her hair. She must not delay; her life had momentarily thrown her off, but it had come back for her. This was the secret message from her mother. She didn't know that she still wore her nightgown as she ran in stocking feet shredded by cobblestones. The ghost of the first Mrs. Rosenberg flew behind, wishing that it was time for her to speak.

It wasn't unusual for children to be born in one family and raised by another. Parents were lost in accidents, illness, prison, and debt, and if they managed to survive, they might not be able to feed all the children they had. They considered a son or daughter lucky if it could go to childless relations who were better off. There was no legal procedure. The child just went to someone and was raised there. Sometimes people without children wanted one that wasn't any relation at all. The prospective parents went to the Jews' Free School, perhaps, or the orphan asylum, asking the headmaster or matron to recommend a child to them. Usually they didn't want infants. It didn't pay to take babies when a third of them wouldn't reach the age of five. Better to see if it lived and how it turned out.

Rain pounded against the window while Minnie nursed the week-old infant. She was sitting on Nehama's bed, her own baby crawling on the floor. Nehama stood by the window, looking again at the note. "Please take her," she said for the hundredth time. "That's what it says. But what does it mean?"

"I don't know." Minnie moved the baby away from her breast, its face scrunched in sleep. "And I don't care. You have to do something, Nehama."

Whenever Minnie nursed the baby, Nehama's breasts ached as if she were full of milk, and she couldn't sit still. "Sha, sha," she murmured now, taking the baby. She had sewn a gown from the softest flannel and embroidered it with red thread to keep away the evil eye. How small the baby was in it. How warm. She fit right here, between the crook of Nehama's arm and her hand under the head. She opened her eyes for a moment, then closed them again. Her eyes were dark, and Nehama wondered what color they would be.

"It happens all the time, a baby and no means to take care of it," Minnie said. "But only a *shayner* like that Mrs. Levy expects someone else to make arrangements. What can you do? There's the baby. So you just listen to me. The trunk's still in the back room. You sell what's inside and give the money to the orphans' asylum. They'll put it away for her, and when she's ready to leave, she'll have something to start with."

"No, I'm telling you what the note means. That I should keep the baby as mine." The thought had come to her slowly as the days passed. She'd been bathing and dressing and holding the baby while Emilia slept endless hours; her absence was just another sort of sleep. The thought was merely waiting to make itself known. There was no other possibility. Nehama's arms were full with the baby to hold in them.

"What about Nathan?" Minnie went to the stove. She had some good bones for soup.

"He's only the boss in the busy season," Nehama said. Last night she'd asked him while they were lying in bed, What if by a miracle we got a child? And he'd answered, A baby that's no relation, it's betting on a dark horse. She'd turned away from him, her back rigid, neither of them sleeping until the moon set and the day arose slowly, sluggish in the cold of winter. Then he said quietly, If my wife gets a baby and she didn't risk her life having it, am I going to decide for God?

"Did you think about everything—what if she comes back?" Minnie asked.

"Let her. Then she'll see what's what. You don't give away a jewel and then expect it to be returned."

"It happens plenty," Minnie said, salting the soup. "The lady of the house thinks she doesn't want the bracelet and gives it to the wet nurse. It's just mother-of-pearl, nothing fancy. But then it comes back into fashion and she wants it."

"A bracelet, maybe. But not a child. Mrs. Levy is too fine. She can manage on her own only if she's free. That's why she left the note for me." Nehama hesitated, hating her dry breasts for making her ask. "I could pay you to nurse the baby —"

"It's a mistake, I'm telling you," Minnie interrupted, casting a quick glance at Nehama. "But don't insult me. I make too much milk for one child anyway."

The wind rattled the glass pane, a window bag keeping out the draft while Nehama rocked the baby, swaying just the way she'd seen mothers in the alley sway their many children. The baby opened her eyes, locking on to Nehama's as if they'd known each other from the days of King Solomon.

The story went that there were two mothers who came to King Solomon the Wise. The women lived in the same house. In fact, they were prostitutes and the house was a common lodging house. They gave birth within three days of each other, but one of the infants died while the mother slept. No one else knew whose baby was whose, and each of the mothers said the living baby belonged to her. King Solomon was asked to judge between them.

For weeks Nehama waited for Mrs. Levy to return. Every knock on the door made her more afraid than she'd ever been.

Berwick Street

A room in Soho might be rented by a woman in a nightgown. It was hardly more peculiar than most of the spectacles that met the sour gaze of landladies there: Frenchmen, prostitutes, and Jews trying to follow their betters to the West End, creating their own little ghetto among the prostitutes that worked the theater district. The shopkeepers' signs in Berwick Street were in Yiddish, and the market smelled just like the East End, but here Jews bought gallery tickets to the English theater. They felt themselves to be more cultured than the Jews of Petticoat Lane, more worldly even if they were just as poor. Wasn't it a short walk to see all the nice things in shops that they couldn't afford? And the water company that served the shops of Regent Street also provided for Berwick Street. A person could actually turn a tap in the yard and have water pour from it. The ghost of the first wife saw it herself.

The organ-grinder cranked out "The Marseillaise" while Emilia waited for her breasts to dry, sitting by the window and watching the prostitutes go in and out of the pub across the street. Every time she wondered about her child, she pushed the thought from her mind, turning her head from side to side, her breath quickening as she looked out the window for something else to occupy her. With practice, she could stop the thought almost before it arose. Her mother used to say that a woman should put her eyes on the most pleasant thing in her view; this would save her sanity. In Emilia's room there was a bed, a table, and a wardrobe with a cracked mirror. She didn't give the mirror a glance, attending instead to the colors outside her window. It was hardly London at all. The French children wore pink and blue hats, their coats as red as the red sky. The organ-grinder's buttons were gold, multiplying the pale winter light into a dozen suns. The unemployed men marching from the East End to the West to riot carried banners painted in red and black, and on Purim the Jews wore masks and robes of many colors. They performed in the street, half in English and half in Yiddish, with a real woman playing the Jewish queen as she triumphed over the evil minister who ordered the death of the Jews in ancient Persia. Her hair hung down in ripples of night, no kerchief covered it, and religious men called to their sons to come inside, away from the seductions of the red sky and the immodest woman.

When Emilia's body returned to an approximation of its former shape, she sent a boy to fetch her trunk and bring it to the post office in Soho. There it stayed for a month in case there were inquiries, but the man who was sent to fetch it was told that no one had come to ask any questions. It was the beginning of spring, French wives were setting geraniums in their window boxes, when two men carried the trunk up to Emilia's room, just past the market in Berwick Street.

In the street there was a parade with violins and trumpets, and the rough women standing outside the Hound and Hare were adding their comments to the general commotion. While the ghost of the first wife watched the parade, Emilia was having a bath, her eyes closed so that she could lie peacefully in the zinc tub and enjoy the hot water, for which she'd paid extra. When finally the water turned cold, there was no choice but to dry herself off and open the trunk. Her fingers were stiff as she put on one of her old dresses, calling out to her landlady to come and help her with the middle buttons.

Emilia faced the cracked mirror, inspecting her feet, her ankles, her hips, waist, shoulders, face. She had a more fashionable shape than before, the shoulders rounder, the chest plumper. It could serve her well and the gown even better, declaring that she didn't belong to Soho. Her mother used to say that mud can easily swallow a woman and the world not be any different for her absence.

The violinists and trumpeters were playing "God Save the Queen" as they led the procession to the newly dedicated Synagogue of Soho. The ghost of the first Mrs. Rosenberg leaned on the windowsill, watching the fog come off the trumpets and the sky come down to bless the men in their prayer shawls. The men danced with the Torah scroll and the women with its shadow. The men were singing wedding songs, for it is written that the Holy One is the bridegroom and Israel his bride. The women were silent as they were among men whose piety forbade them to hear the siren tones of a woman's singing voice.

Under the wedding canopy, everything is beautiful. Only later does the bride ask why her husband doesn't speak to her and why he comes to her too late.

Here and there a Jewish boy broke out of the parade to make eyes at the prostitutes standing in the doorway of the Hound and Hare.

Frying Pan Alley

Naturally a ghost gets to talking with other ghosts. So I tell her, Mrs. Rosenberg, you want to know why I came? For my grandchildren. And is London so different from where I was? Every day I thank God for the fog. It's very heimish, *damp and dark just like the grave I left at home. But now that summer is here, it's too hot. Believe me, it's a fire, and not a false alarm like what happened in the Prince's Street theater. Just yesterday every presser was a playwright and every seamstress an actress. Today they're afraid to be in a crowd. The theater is closed. Do they think panic is a plague like cholera? Between you and me, maybe they're right.*

Now there's been another tragedy. Not, God forbid, with my Nehameleh, but she can't sleep and at night she thinks of all the tragedies in the world. This is what comes when you have no place to cry. I'm telling you it's an illness. She gives the baby her breast to suck, praying that her milk will come and this will show that she's in God's favor. The nipple cracks, she bites her lip. It's not important, I tell her. Minnie has enough milk. But I'm talking to a wall. To a brick in the road. To the wind. When you're dead, who listens? Tell me. Be honest with me. Isn't that just the same as being alive and talking to your children?

In Nehama's back room gas jets flickered, adding heat to the evening light that came through the window. "I don't believe that Lipski did it," she said, giving the cradle a push with her foot. Nathan had found it in the Lane and bought it with his card money. "I'm telling you, the boy is innocent."

"They caught him right there," Minnie said, wiping her forehead. Everyone was talking about it. The girl's name was Miriam Angel, like something from a play in the old Jewish theater. But she was murdered in a small East End room; it could have been any of theirs; the perpetrator was said to be Israel Lipski, her lodger. "He had the same poison on his lips as the girl."

"So you think the murderer poisons himself, too? Lipski was beaten up and pushed under the bed, just like he said." Nehama started up her sewing machine again. She was tired, and the baby was whimpering with the heat. The hot coals in Lazar's iron were just a thicker form of the air they were trying to breathe.

"No one should have lodgers. It isn't safe." There was nowhere to escape the heat of their small rooms. The theater had gone bankrupt, and even in the market every cabbage had a sickening smell, the juggler dropped his plates, the strong man was fat and broke a bench when he sat down to rest. The singing dwarf only cried bitter tears, and nobody cried with him.

"You want to be afraid? I'll tell you why," Nehama said. "Because a Jewish boy was found under the bed, he's going to be hanged. Any one of us could be him. Look at Nathan."

"I'm all right," he said. "Just put in that lining and don't talk so much." He had a bruise on his face. When he was walking home, a gentile called him Lipski and they got into a fight. Nathan's hand was cut, too.

"It's because there's no theater," Minnie said.

"What are you talking?" Nehama asked.

"If there was a theater then someone would be there the night of the murder," Minnie said. "Maybe the girl, maybe the lodger, or even the murderer. You think murderers don't like a good melodrama? There's nothing to do on a Saturday night."

"Or any other night," Nehama said irritably. The cradle was under the table, by her right foot. She sewed and she rocked the baby, who was named Gittel-Sarah. Everything had worked out; she had a husband, she had a child, she had a means to earn a living. So why couldn't she sleep at night?

Regent Street

Something as small as a gold cross on a chain could make all the difference in employment opportunities for a young woman.

Chesham House of Liberty's was a shop of many rooms and staircases and mirrors draped with artistic fabrics to give the impression of corridors where there were none. It had Oriental porcelain, bronzes, lacquerware, dolls, fans, handscreens, armor, inlaid cabinets, ivory, swords, Indian condiments, Arab sideboards, guava jelly, damask wallpaper, and in one small nook there was the Estate Agency department, managed by a rather large man. The two sections of Chesham House were separated by a shop that wouldn't sell to Mr. Liberty. A humped staircase over the store connected them, and a wire attached to a receiving box facilitated communication between the two sections. The Savoy Theatre purchased the costumes for *The Mikado* from Liberty's, and each was genuinely, authentically Japanese. You may depend upon it.

Emilia was sure that it was Miss Moffit's hair that made her the senior shopgirl in the basement. Her red hair worn loose in the Aesthetic style, her protruding upper lip, and that squint under her square eyebrows were all the rage. In her medieval shift, she could have stepped straight out of a Pre-Raphaelite painting. Miss Moffit was in charge of Curios, separated from the Eastern Bazaar by an archway.

Emilia sat on a stool, reading at the counter. It was a rainy day in September, and the wind rattled the basement window. The electric lights dimmed and brightened and dimmed to near darkness. Emilia glanced suspiciously at the ghost of the first wife, sitting on an unpacked case of clay horses from China.

"I'll light the candles," she called to Miss Moffit, putting her book down on an ornamental stand as two gentlemen came in, shaking out their umbrellas and leaving them in the corner. The taller of the gentlemen, an artist, had been in the shop before. The customers were always playwrights or painters or composers of operettas. Miss Moffit led him to her department and directed the other to Emilia.

"I believe that Mr. Zalkind would be best assisted by you, Miss Rosenberg," she said. That was Miss Moffit all over, choosing the better-looking gentleman for herself, leaving Emilia with the one that wore spectacles and his hair long.

The ghost of the first wife rose from her seat on the crate of clay horses and joined Emilia at the counter. "How may I help you?" Emilia asked.

"I wish to buy a present for my mother," he said. The ghost of the first Mrs. Rosenberg leaned her elbows on the counter beside the tall candle. She looked more solid in the candlelight, smiling fondly at the gentleman.

"Certainly," Emilia said with as much indifference as she could muster. "And what is the occasion?"

"Nothing in particular." He put a book on the counter. There were ink stains on his fingers. Emilia did not care for men that smelled of ink. She'd had enough of that in Minsk.

"What about a vase? We just had a new shipment."

"My mother has too many. I'd like to surprise her." He looked at Emilia with just a hint of appreciation. She deserved more, but after all, she was only a shopgirl.

In the Curios department Miss Moffit was showing her tall gentleman a bamboo writing desk. "What sort of thing does your mother fancy?" Emilia asked.

"A more pleasant son, I daresay. We had a disagreement." He paused, waiting for her to ask him about what, but a shopgirl doesn't have to pander to her betters' desire for her interest.

Emilia took a feather duster and busied herself with running it over the glass-fronted cabinets.

"My mother sees everything, even from the ladies' gallery in the synagogue, and she saw me go out rather earlier than I should." He looked at Emilia with the blank face of someone guarding himself. "I promised I'd go back."

"Will you?" she asked despite herself.

"I'd rather bring her a present later. What do you advise, Miss . . . ?"

"Miss Rosenberg. How about a fan?" She reached for an eighteenth-century fan, but the ghost of the first wife knocked another down. Emilia picked it up, turning the fan over and shrugging before she placed it on the counter. "This one would be most suitable," she said.

The silk fan was printed with a photograph of three solemn geisha girls. One had her hands over her ears, the second over her eyes, the third her mouth. Mr. Zalkind laughed. It was a pleasant laugh, and his face relaxed into an open smile.

"Hear no evil, see no evil, speak no evil," he said. "Well chosen." He thumbed the pages of the book on the marble counter. It was a Hebrew prayer book for the High Holy Days. The book was so old, it absorbed all the light from the candle flame.

"A person should not be dominated by ghosts," Emilia said, returning the gaze of the first Mrs. Rosenberg, who saw so very clearly in the darkness.

"How true." Mr. Zalkind leaned over the counter. "Perhaps you've read my column in *The Pall Mall Gazette* or my book? *The Longbow Mystery*."

"No, I'm sorry. I prefer *The Times*." The ghost threw up her hands. Well, what did she expect? Emilia was someone else now. A shopgirl. Did the first wife think that Emilia was so stupid as to have learned nothing from her trials? "Shall I wrap the fan for you?" she asked.

"Please. What's that over there?" He pointed to the ornamental stand.

"It's Emile Zola's new book. I just finished it."

"Did you study in France?" he asked. Surely he was cruel to tease a shopgirl. But his face looked serious, his voice was polite. "I can hear your accent, Miss Rosenberg. One shouldn't make any assumptions about what newcomers were in their home. I know that firsthand—my grandparents came from Russia."

"I'm from Minsk," she said. "Though my father was German. I had a tutor."

"Then we are countrymen of a sort. May I take you out for tea? We could discuss Zola's works."

The ghost of the first wife nudged her as if the dead are not bound by the conventions of the living. Emilia shook her off. "It wouldn't be right, sir."

"Because I'm a Jew? But I find myself rather more interested in gentile women, who are not afraid to exercise their intelligence."

"Is that so?"

"One must accept the truth, Miss Rosenberg, even when it's unpleasant. Jewish girls are spoiled and overbearing."

"Really. I haven't noticed."

"Why should you? It is from close experience that the truth is revealed. Then one can recognize it in a glance."

She ought to have told him right then that she was Jewish. The look on his face would have been priceless. But it was too amusing to finger the gold cross in the hollow of her throat, and watch uncertainty chase admiration across his face. Mr. Zalkind didn't smell of ink at all, but of a pleasant pipe tobacco.

"What did your family do in Minsk?" he asked.

"My father owned a factory. We were always outsiders there because he was German. After the factory burned down, I chose to come here because I would have been a foreigner in my father's homeland, too, and that would have been unbearable." The story came easily. Emilia had told it many times. Mr. Zalkind looked quite pleased with it.

"I'm terribly sorry, Miss Rosenberg. Are your parents with you?"

"I lost everyone, I'm afraid." She turned away as if overcome by grief. Miss Moffit's gentleman went upstairs to pay for the writing desk.

"It isn't easy to be both what you are and what you're not," Mr. Zalkind said, his voice gentle. "An evening out would do you good."

Emilia wondered how a man could be at once so perceptive and so very stupid. "That might be," she snapped, "but my mother would say that a girl who is too friendly with a man above her station may find herself in unpleasant circumstances."

"But this is surely not your natural element. Listen to me. I have another suggestion, one that is above reproach, I'm sure of it. My friends are having a soiree on Saturday. They are artists, and all their guests will be of interest to you. Aren't you entitled to an evening's release from your prison?" He pointed at the window with its iron bars and beyond it the gutter overflowing with drumming rain.

. "I don't know . . ."

"I'll ask Mrs. Abraham to arrange a carriage. Do come, Miss Rosenberg," he pressed.

"Perhaps, sir. I'll consider it. Here, take my book if you haven't read it. You can return it to me later."

"I will indeed and lend you one of mine." He bowed and took his leave, the book under his arm.

Miss Moffit came through the archway, pale as a sheet in the candlelight. "Oh, Miss Rosenberg," she whispered, "he is very handsome for a Jew."

Emilia watched him climb the stairs. "To each his own," she said. He had a good walk, his back straight, his step brisk, his umbrella left behind so that, although he'd be drenched, he'd have an excuse to return tomorrow.

The ghost of the first wife stood by the barred basement window, staring at the rain whipping through the gutter as if she would swim away on the wind to the sea if only she hadn't promised to look after a child that wasn't hers.

Berwick Street

Emilia sniffed her hands suspiciously, huddling in bed to keep warm. The wind came from the sea with the purpose of visiting the market in Berwick Street, but it had somehow misplaced itself in her room. Emilia sniffed the inside of her elbow. It was a never-ending battle to keep herself from smelling like she was born in Soho, the odors of the street seeping into her skin, the glances of the prostitutes teaching her to be hard. Emilia picked up the board that leaned against the wall by her bed and put it across her lap.

Dear Mother,

A Jewish man of good family can be introduced to the daughters of many fine Jewish families in the West End. Why then would he ever pay his respects to a Jewish shopgirl? He would not. That is the simple answer, I'm sure. If he prefers gentile girls, however, it is another matter. He thinks them more beautiful, perhaps, more intelligent or refined. What shall he do? A wellborn gentile girl would need some additional incentive to lower herself to marry a Jew. If he were very rich or very famous, it would be a possibility. If he is neither, he may think of lowering himself. As a gentile, a shopgirl is one step above; as a Jew he is one step below; and there they can meet.

The gentleman in question comes from a family of Russian Jews. Could anything amuse you more, Mother, than that he thinks I am a gentile? Perhaps it is all nothing, but it gives one pause to think of what life would be like as a gentile girl from dawn to dawn and not merely in a shop.

A wife is made in her husband's eyes, whether she intends it or not. Then why shouldn't it be to her advantage? I could be a gentile as easily as a Jew. Didn't Father always say that I was more of a *shiksa*?

Oh, Mother. I miss you.

Emilia blew her nose carefully, so as not to make it red. Then she crossed out the last line of the letter and just signed it as usual,

Yours ever,
Emilia.

The ghost of the first wife stood by the bed, looking at Emilia with the compassion of someone who remembers what it is to be twenty-one years old. Emilia closed her eyes to any such pity. She was not dying but merely suffering the ordinary fortune of every woman from the day that Eve was pushed out of her garden and realized that she must find a good address.

Fitzroy Square

The soiree was in Bloomsbury at the home of Mr. and Mrs. Abraham. If you went straight up from Soho you'd find yourself there, a short walk from University College, where Mr. Zalkind's brother studied medicine, in a neighborhood of plane trees with leaves of many fingers, shedding bark to get rid of the soot that suffocated other trees. The

Abrahams lived a few doors from Mr. Shaw, the playwright, in one of the old houses that weren't old enough to be venerable, merely run-down, attracting industries and art, both of which appreciated cheap tenancy. The square smelled of smoke and chemicals, the garden in the center was brown and matted, the houses losing pieces of stucco.

Inside the house, there were paintings on every surface, wicker furniture, Oriental pottery, and bowers of ferns, the host and his guests carrying themselves as if this was the most fashionable address and anyone who didn't know it was a Philistine. Mrs. Abraham was vastly pregnant but entirely without embarrassment as she waddled among the guests in her kimono. Emilia wore her hair loose, in the Aesthetic style, her gown more than a year out of date.

The dining room walls had been done as a mural during Mr. Abraham's Egyptian phase, and someone less cultured than Emilia might have felt entombed. But she was preoccupied only with the meat on her dinner plate as she sat between Miss Cohen the poetess and Mr. Moore the painter, a middle-aged gentleman with thin eyebrows that both slanted to the right as if blown that way by the wind while he stood on deck pondering the sea. He painted the animals of Borneo; his wife collected the sayings and customs of the people. Emilia poked at her dinner suspiciously. It looked rather pink, and she believed it had once belonged to a pig, though no one had actually used the word *ham*.

"The English are an old people. Like the Jews," Mr. Moore said. "Take our friend Mr. Zalkind. He has the best attributes of his race, but some of the less admirable characteristics are hardly to be seen in him. You might say that he's been tempered by the bracing British air."

At the moment a choking yellow fog was falling across the streets. "Very bracing," Emilia murmured, her shoulders sore with tension.

"His taste is not at all gauche, and he knows his opera. He'll make his mark in the world of letters, I daresay." Mr. Moore tapped his glass, and the maid poured more wine.

"I'm sure he'd be glad to know that his friends hold a high opinion of him." Emilia glanced around the table. Everyone was absorbed in conversation, silverware clinking, serving spoons digging in and out of platters, the maid mopping up a spill of wine. On the wall Egyptian ladies kneeled at the foot of a mummy.

"The ham is very nice," Mr. Moore said. "Rembrandt made a thing of beauty out of hanging meat. Perhaps I shall do a ham. There's nothing like a well-cured ham. You don't seem overly fond of it, Miss Rosenberg."

She shook her head. What did gentiles eat? Was it always pig? It must be so, and now at the very beginning of her career as a gentile, she was about to be dismissed for incompetence. "Well, you see, Mr. Moore . . ." She stammered and looked down at her plate, sure that waves of Soho odors wafted from her skin while Miss Cohen looked at her sympathetically. She knew. She could sense a fellow Jew. She was dressed in the very gown on the cover of *La Nouvelle Mode*.

"Are you a vegetarian, too?" Miss Cohen asked. "I don't eat any sort of animal, myself."

Emilia could have given her a kiss on each of her sallow cheeks. "Perhaps Mr. Moore could paint potatoes. Would you, sir?"

"Potatoes have a bad effect on the spirit," he said, pushing his into a heap at the far edge of his plate. "Deadly for an artist. When I was in Paris last month, I lunched with Degas and a friend of his. The man paints potato eaters, they say, and you never met a more erratic fellow. Mark my words, he will do someone a violence one day. I am a student of heads, Miss Cohen. And that man's head, well, I should not like a lady to see it. A criminal shape, I promise you."

Across from him Mrs. Moore was draped in flowing fabrics, everything she owned hanging loosely under it without benefit of a corset. She sat between Mr. Zalkind and his brother. "The men of Borneo have very nicely shaped heads," she said. "They are quite sane despite the fact that, as young men, they pierce their members with a bone and wear it there for the rest of their lives. What do you do, Miss Rosenberg?"

Emilia wiped her lips with the edge of her napkin. "Excuse me?"

Mr. Zalkind was looking at her with a concern that made her flinch. A man must admire you or else you're nothing in his eyes. "I don't think . . ." he began.

"I mean do you write or paint, dear?" Mrs. Moore interrupted. She wore kohl around her eyes like the ladies in the Egyptian mural.

"Paper-cuts," Emilia said, looking steadily at Mr. Zalkind as if she had not the smallest reason to be uncomfortable here, not a beetle of embarrassment crawled across her plate. He smiled and lifted his glass to her. "I make Oriental paper-cuts."

"How interesting. I do so enjoy these evenings with you young people," Mrs. Moore said. "And what is your opinion of the Jewish question?"

"We're all British here, that's my opinion," Mr. Zalkind interjected. "Only look at what we're eating."

"It may be the death of you," his brother said. Half the Jewish guests shifted uncomfortably; the others smiled smugly. Albert Zalkind hadn't eaten the ham. In fact there seemed to be a surprising number of vegetarians among the Jewish guests. "The ancient laws have a wisdom you underestimate. Pigs, for example, harbor many diseases."

Mr. Moore raised his eyebrows, glancing first at his wife and then at the Butlers, the other gentile couple at the table. What did he mean, now turning his eyebrows on Emilia? In the tomb painting on the wall, the Egyptian gentlemen were performing the rite of opening the mummy's mouth, though they looked as if they were attacking it with golden whips. It was too hard, being in society and not knowing what was polite. Not as a gentile and not even as a Jew.

Always ask a gentleman a question, her mother used to say, and remember that nothing is as believable as a grain of truth.

Emilia turned to Mr. Moore, her expression perplexed, her voice uncertain. "Would someone explain the Irish question? Being a foreigner at home, there were things I could never understand. And now I'm a foreigner twice removed. Are they not British, the Irishmen?"

Mr. Moore's face became grim. "Allow me to enlighten you, Miss Rosenberg," he began, and the whole company joined in to enlighten her until the pudding, Mr. Zalkind most eagerly of all. There is nothing more intelligent to a gentleman than a woman's interest in his thoughts.

When they moved to the parlor, Mr. Zalkind took her arm and seated her in a corner under a hanging of greenery, beside stands of ferns and vases of flowers. For himself he chose an awkward oak chair carved with Gothic creatures, pulling it close. His eyes were green-brown, his beard the color of sand. It was a very short beard, as if he couldn't make up his mind whether to please his grandfather and keep it or please his friends and take it away altogether. "I notice that you solicit the opinions of others but keep your own to yourself," he said. Beyond the cascade of greenery, Mrs. Abraham was showing her collection of pottery to the other guests. "What do you think of the Jewish question?"

Emilia smiled archly. A smile need not be affected by nausea. "See no evil, hear no evil, speak no evil," she said with the light tone she used to amuse her father's guests.

"Don't flirt with me, Miss Rosenberg. You needn't pick up the bad habits of Jewish girls because you are among them."

She bristled. She meant to tease him, but instead she picked a leaf and tore it to shreds. "Don't instruct me, sir. You are not my father."

"I was hoping for an answer from the girl that reads Emile Zola." He lit his pipe, his attention on tobacco and match as if they were the most important things in the world. "You must not lower yourself when you are among Jews."

"Very well. But you won't like it." Her voice was angry, she couldn't hide it. This person brought out the worst in her. He was her only chance, and he wouldn't allow her to take it. "My opinion is that anyone born on this island is British. Otherwise why come to it? The cold and the damp and the fog are not so very endearing as people here seem to think."

"But can a Jew be a citizen in a Christian country?" he asked insistently.

"Just give anyone a chance," she said. "Half a chance. That is all that anyone wants and deserves." She leaned toward a vase of flowers as if to smell them, her face hot. If only he would go away and leave her alone, no one would notice her crying.

"You see how pleasant it is to exchange opinions?" He signaled to the maid, who was pouring sherry. "Now I shall tell you that I disagree. When a nation is so generous as to allow foreigners freely onto its shores, then they ought to repay it by embracing its ways until they are indistinguishable from anyone else."

"Is that so?" she asked, abandoning the flowers. "Then why are so many of your friends Jews who are fascinated by the Jewish question?"

Mr. Zalkind tamped the tobacco in his pipe like gunpowder in a rifle. "Do you live near the shop in Regent Street?" he changed the subject.

"I live in Berwick Street," she said, too tired to think of a decent lie. Her feet still hurt from yesterday's shift. "Among the Frenchmen."

"And others," Mr. Zalkind said dryly, again the concern in his eyes.

"I can't say otherwise. It's a matter of principle." Her father's failings were always a matter of principle. "You live near here, I understand. And Bloomsbury is so dominated by the museum and the university that there is no room for an original idea. In Soho, a person is free to think, and beauty can truly be seen surrounded by ugliness." How much she wanted to be in her bed, the organ-grinder's music fading as she told the ghost of the first wife everything.

"An interesting point. I'll give it some thought and tell you my opinion of it, later." He smiled ruefully. "No doubt you will have a sharp answer, and that is the best kind."

She stifled a yawn. Her mother hadn't told her that one ought to work up to deception gradually, like walking after an illness. "I'm afraid that it's rather late for me, Mr. Zalkind."

Inside the carriage Mrs. Abraham had hired for her, she rested with her eyes closed, listening to the click-clack of the wheels over cobblestone, a sound that endured through candlelight and gas lamps and arc light and electric light, none of which could banish the fog.

Regent Street

Mr. Zalkind haunted the basement of Chesham House, examining fans, dolls, antimony metalware, and brass trays as if he wished to become a connoisseur of something. In October, he invited Emilia to the Adelphi Theatre and the Avenue. On Guy Fawkes Day, he invited her to a revival of *H.M.S. Pinafore*. In December they went to the Exeter Theatre, which had been rebuilt after the fire.

Every newspaper carried warnings about the danger of fires in the theater. The Lord Mayor of London sponsored a relief fund for theater fires. The Royal Adelphi advertised that it had numerous exits for efficient evacuation, quoting the vice president of the Fire Brigade Association that the time taken to empty the Adelphi was six minutes, less than any other theater with the exception of the Avenue.

Emilia couldn't escape conversations about fire; at work she flirted and argued with Mr. Zalkind; in her room in Berwick Street she thought of the fire in the Yiddish theater on the day her water broke. It was an imaginary fire, she said to the ghost of the first wife, it had nothing to do with the news of the day. Why did she have to think of it at all?

1888

Berwick Street

On January 19, the first anniversary of her daughter's birth, Emilia lay on her bed and stared at the ceiling, wondering if she was dead while the ghost of the first wife held her hand. But the day ended with the sun setting in its customary way, and the next morning Emilia got up from her bed as though nothing had happened.

Frying Pan Alley

So now you're chopped liver, too, Mrs. Rosenberg? Of course. One minute they hold on to you for dear life, the next you're nobody. Only the dead can understand what suffering is. So tell me something. If my grandchildren don't listen to a word I'm saying, then what am I doing here? I must be crazy. The room is colder than the grave. And there's nowhere to go. The taverns are for gentiles, the coffee houses only for men. On the street it's too cold to stand and talk. A year ago the women waited in line in Prince's Street, they laughed with their friends, no one thought of the snow falling on her shawl. Did she care if it was a cold winter? Not inside the theater. They were together, the women. She listens and she watches and her voice isn't choking her. But if there's no play? Then the women sit alone in their cold rooms. They sing old songs. Between you and me, I'm tired of it.

Nehama was holding the baby inside her shawl to keep her warm while she made herself a cup of tea. First she put the tea leaves in a strainer. Just one teaspoon, nothing more. Then she wet the leaves with hot water. In a cup, she put some milk and some sugar. Now she could pour water through the strainer. When the color was dark enough, she removed the strainer and topped up the cup.

On the mantelpiece there were four books. Two were from Mrs. Levy in payment for the maternity dress, one Mrs. Levy had read in the workshop, and Nehama had added *Oliver Twist,* too. She should have got something else. Melodrama it had plenty, but the orphan in the story wasn't at peace until he was returned to his real family. When she came to the end, Nehama wanted to throw the book at the wall. But a book you have to respect. It had cost her good money. And what else can you do when there's no theater? On Saturday nights, Nehama read aloud to her friends. In every word she heard Mrs. Levy's educated voice.

She took a sip of tea, thinking about a trunk that was sent to the post office in Soho. What was there in Soho? Brothels and French cookshops. She couldn't picture Mrs. Levy in either place. So who was real? Herself drinking a sweet cup of tea or a woman whose name no one could be certain of, running away to who knew what? If only she could stop thinking about it. This wasn't her business at all. No one had come back for the baby. That was what mattered. A year had gone by, surely she could stop being afraid. Gittel was sleeping, her head on Nehama's shoulder, her small hands on a breast.

Gittel-Sarah was named first for Nathan's mother, she should rest in peace, then for Nehama's old friend Sally. It was a break from custom; Russian and Polish Jews named their babies after deceased relatives, and Nehama didn't know if Sally was dead or alive.

She had another book open in front of her, but she couldn't read it. In the slack season there wasn't enough to do, and she found herself crying over her tea. God forbid anyone should see her like this. Now the baby was crying. "Sha, sha," Nehama said. She stifled her own tears and sang an old song to calm her child.

The Strand

When February came, Emilia was a new person. The wind had changed, her room was not so cold, spring was something a person could imagine now, even though the wind could turn again and spring could reveal itself in a cold fog. Emilia was alone with Jacob in box seats at the Adelphi Theatre. It was time; she couldn't wait any longer.

After the fourth act of *The Bells of Haslemere,* he was jubilant. "Did you notice the third villain?" he asked.

"Is it important?" She was wearing her second-best dress and new gloves to give her courage.

"It used to be that one unscrupulous villain was thrilling enough.

But now that there is revolving scenery and the audience expects fast-paced action, there has to be more villainy per square inch. This is the first melodrama with three villains." He was scribbling furiously in a notebook with a green cover. He used a pencil. Pen and ink were too cumbersome to carry about. "Acquisition of property is what drives the crime nowadays. No more love or revenge. Forgery and blackmail, there's your new villainy."

Emilia put her hand on his arm, and he stopped writing. "Mr. Zalkind," she said, "I don't think I can accompany you to the theater again. Please don't ask me."

"Miss Rosenberg! What's wrong—have I done something?" He shoved his notebook in his pocket. He always dressed meticulously, then bulged his pockets with pipe, tobacco, notebook, pencil, theater programs, a book, and string. God in heaven knew that a crisis of string might arrive any moment.

"No, really. I'm sorry. It's . . . It's the danger of a fire." She crumpled the program.

Her hand was trembling. He took it in his. "Of course. The fire in your father's factory. How could I forget? If it weren't for that, you'd be at home now. And what would my life be then?"

"Exactly what it ought to be in the normal course of events," she said shakily. The smell of beer and oranges drifted down from the gallery. In the box seats, gentlemen smoked cigars. Ladies fanned themselves with programs and stood up to see if anyone they knew was there.

"I disagree. My grandfather would say that God is the master of every event. I doubt it myself, but I do think that I've forgotten my duty. You must be introduced properly to my parents."

"It won't do, I'm afraid."

"It's exactly what will do, Miss Rosenberg."

She'd been preparing for this, lying awake at night with no one but ghosts to advise her. At last the moment had come, and the shaking in her hands and voice wasn't a sham. "You see, there was a gentleman a little older than yourself. He was in my father's employ," she said.

Mr. Zalkind's face was troubled. "And you were fond of him. Was he in the factory when it burned down?"

She nodded. "You're the first that I've told this. . . . It's been too painful to mention. I don't know if I can."

He pressed her hand. "There should be nothing hidden between us."

"It isn't enough that I'm . . ." She touched the gold cross on its light chain. "What would your parents say if they knew that this gentleman had been my husband? We had so little time together. Sometimes I wonder if it was a dream. But now you understand why it's been wrong of me to let myself enjoy your company."

He was silent; the noise from the gallery was horribly loud. She'd made a mistake, a terrible mistake. But what else could she do? It was her intention to have a wedding ring, which was generally accompanied by a wedding bed, and there had to be an explanation for what her husband would find.

So that was that. She took her hand from his, but he pulled it back, gently tugging at the glove, finger by finger, until it was off and in his pocket next to the pipe and string. He brought her bare hand to his lips. "It's not my parents' affair or anyone else's but ours." He kissed her fingers, he kissed her palm. "You ought to be my wife because I wish it, and if you like the idea, then we're in agreement, as husband and wife ought to be."

Anyone standing in a box seat would have seen her looking up at Mr. Zalkind, her hair hanging loose under a hat that matched her gown, and if the opera glasses were very good, someone might even have seen a hint of light on the cameo pinned to her gown. It was carved from lava stone, the goddess of youth feeding meat to an eagle. "It's a good idea," she said. "The best."

"All right, then." He put his arm around her waist, her head resting on his shoulder, one hand gloved and one bare as the lights above dimmed and torches were lit at the foot of the stage. Out of the frying pan and into the fire, the English would say.

Wigmore Street

Jacob introduced Emilia to his parents at the usual sort of awkward dinner, his face pale and his freckles standing out as if he were twelve and not twenty-five, grateful that Emilia had left her cross at home, wearing just her mother's cameo brooch. She was quizzed about her family, played the piano, recited in German, and correctly used three kinds of forks. She was not, however, wearing her best dress. That was reserved for tea with Mrs. Zalkind. The invitation came the very next week, and on Sunday afternoon, Emilia wore her new hat.

This season ladies' hats had a masculine line, softened only by a swash of ribbon, and dresses also had a hint of the masculine in high shoulders and lapels. Emilia's gowns from home were now two years out of date, and she'd had one made over. There was only a glimpse of the underskirt in front, but at the side her dark overskirt was pulled away to reveal a line of yellow brocade from waist to hip, giving the gown a slender shape despite the sizable bustle. Ladies still wore an abundance of cloth because they could afford to, and in Emilia's cracked mirror in Berwick Street, the gown was perfect.

The Zalkinds lived at the end of Wigmore Street, past the manufacturers of furniture sold to castles, in the corner near Harley Street and Cavendish Square, where Lord Nelson lived and Lord Byron was born a hundred years before. The Georgian house was square and sturdy, every room of equal size regardless of its function, the bedrooms too small, the dressing rooms cavernous, but it was a good address, chock-full of Pre-Raphaelite paintings. Bathrooms and gaslight had been added, and though the upper classes might consider such items marks of the nouveaux riches, Mrs. Zalkind could hold her head up in the lady's gallery of the synagogue. She looked to be in her mid-forties, statuesque, hair still dark with only a stray gray hair to be plucked, neck firm, a determined chin, a waterfall of speech that drowned out opposition. They were sitting in the parlor, crowded with piano and card table, armchairs, cabinets, doilies and vases, three different Persian carpets, one sort of wallpaper from floor to rail and another sort that went to the ceiling, but it hardly mattered as the wall was covered with paintings in gilt frames.

While Mrs. Zalkind poured tea, she explained that she kept a kosher home, not from religious belief but because it was more hygienic. She hoped that Miss Rosenberg would keep a kosher home, too, as Jacob had inherited her sensitive stomach. Mrs. Zalkind attended the synagogue because it was pleasant to sit among the ladies in the gallery and listen to the choir, as uplifting as the opera. Perhaps

Miss Rosenberg might come and see for herself. Would she like one lump of sugar or two? Miss Rosenberg ought to have more clotted cream with her scone. There was nothing like this in Russia.

Mrs. Zalkind counted many gentiles among her acquaintances. In fact she could count on her fingers the number of her Jewish friends, and all of them were of German origin. Jacob's father was a dear, but if he had been a German Jew, Mrs. Zalkind was certain that she would be president, and not just secretary, of the Society for the Protection of Hebrew Girls.

The German Jews were more aloof than the gentiles, if you asked her. They'd completely forgotten that, a hundred years ago, it was the Jews of Spanish origin who were terribly English, looking down on the German Jews as vulgar newcomers. Now they were neighbors in the West End and sat together on the boards of important charities and looked down their noses at the Russian Jews. They really ought to see that there were some Russian Jews who were just as English as the archbishop of Canterbury.

They were all British now. Loyal to the queen and worried about the East End. Such depravity. Nobody knew it better than she, who had lived there herself. Her sons were born in the East End, but you would see no sign of it in their demeanor now. They were British through and through, as she often told them. If one were not careful, civilization would soon be swamped by the moral plague bred in the East End. Soho was nearly as bad, and the Jews who lived there gave them all a bad name. Even her own father insisted on walking to that crude, noisy *shul* in Soho. He had not once attended the Central Synagogue despite the Roman pavement in front of the Holy Ark, as inspiring as anything you might find in a cathedral. Miss Rosenberg would surely agree if she saw it. More tea?

"Yes, if you please," Emilia said.

"I do wish my German were better," Mrs. Zalkind said as she poured tea from the silver pot. "I believe that I should find it easier if I did not speak the Jargon at all, for it only confuses me. It is most unfortunate that my father so loved the Yiddish theater. It was a corrupting influence and did him no good, I'm sure."

"Quite so," Emilia murmured, but Mrs. Zalkind had turned her head toward her father.

He was sitting in a corner of the parlor, reading a Yiddish newspaper. He wore slippers and an old wool cap, and on the wall above his head there was a large painting of Sir Lancelot and Guinevere. Every so often he would lower the newspaper just enough so that he could peer over the top and stare shyly at Emilia.

"If he would just take off that old cap," Mrs. Zalkind whispered. "Englishmen don't wear hats in the house." But that was how it was. An old man clung to his customs to keep him afloat in a sea of strangeness. His daughter strove to excise any difference from herself as she rose from the sea like Venus, taking her place in the English middle class.

Jacob's grandfather noisily turned the page of his newspaper. "Do you need something, *Tatteh?*" Mrs. Zalkind asked in Yiddish. "Are you warm enough? The damp gets into your bones. You coughed last night, I'm sure of it. At your age, you have no business walking from that *shul* of yours in the rain. Refusing to set foot in our synagogue when it would be so easy for you to go with us. I think you just want to spite me, *Tatteh.*"

"But I don't like it," he said, looking over the edge of the newspaper. "The rabbi makes a sermon in English. Did you hear such a thing? He wears a white robe like a priest. I hope my grandson isn't getting married in a church, God forbid. Then I'd have to sit *shivah* for him as if he was dead, and I might as well bury myself, then. Ask her, daughter."

"*Tatteh,* I told you before. Leave everything to me and stop worrying."

"Mrs. Zalkind?" Emilia said, keeping her face blank as if she didn't understand, glancing vaguely at the Yiddish newspaper, which surrounded the grandfather like the wall of the first wife's garden.

"My poor dear, you must think of me as your mother since you have none. There are so many things to talk about," Mrs. Zalkind said. "Baptism, for example."

"I beg your pardon," Emilia said.

"Such a thing could never occur in our family. Never. Do you understand me?" Mrs. Zalkind's eyes glittered with animosity as if her son had decided to marry a side of bacon, and though she'd like to indulge him, she might not be able to keep herself from frying it up instead.

Emilia carefully put down her teacup. She would have to keep a kosher household. "I hadn't thought—"

"No, you wouldn't," Mrs. Zalkind interrupted. "I do. And there shall be no church. It would be the end of my father, and I will not allow that."

"We were planning a quiet ceremony—" Emilia began to explain.

Mrs. Zalkind interrupted again, her voice quiet, clipped, and fierce. "There will be a rabbi. I have an acquaintance who was married to a gentile in the reform synagogue twenty years ago. I shall send the rabbi a letter of introduction."

"We were planning a civil ceremony at the registrar's office, but naturally I will follow Jacob's wishes," Emilia said. He would have nothing to do with rabbis and such. He often said so; and the more his mother would insist, the stronger his opinion would be. She was sure of it. There was no reason for her neck to itch so. She wouldn't scratch it, not if she had to dig her nails through the table.

The last time she'd seen a rabbi she'd been wearing this very dress. Before it was remade, the overskirt split at the knees, and she had looked past her folded hands at the gold brocade while explaining that she'd come on behalf of a friend. The question being so delicate, the friend was too embarrassed to see the rabbi herself. She was sitting in his study, the door open a crack because he wouldn't talk with a woman behind a closed door. It was in Minsk, the summer sun filtered by heavy curtains. She was warm in her dress, and the old rabbi's forehead was wet.

She lifted her eyes to see him scratching the corner of his chin. No *shaaleh* is too delicate for me, he said with a little smile. Women bring me their stained cloths to examine when they need to know if it's time to go to the ritual bath. What is it, my girl?

My friend is pregnant, she said.

And her husband could not come to me with the question? the rabbi asked. When she said there was no husband, he nodded as if everything was clear to him from this world to the next, though the light was dim in his study.

She's afraid to press the father of the baby, Emilia said, unable to meet the rabbi's eyes. She thinks—well, she thinks he can't marry her because she might be a *mamzer*. There. The terrible word was out.

It was a Sunday afternoon like this one, church bells ringing. Emilia expected the rabbi to look shocked, but he just pulled down a tall book from his shelves of many such volumes, dark on the outside, yellowed on the inside, as if nothing was new in life. He opened it, pointing a finger here and then there. A complex matter, he said. On the one hand, if a *mamzer* is a scholar, he ought to take precedence over a high priest that is ignorant. And yet there's no question that it is a defective status. A *mamzer* can marry only another person born of a prohibited union. And their children will also be forbidden for all time to legitimate Jews.

It's unfair, Emilia protested. The rabbi looked at her with great sadness. Cataracts were beginning to obscure the blue of his eyes, and he had to bend close to the book to read it.

It's the law, he said. One cannot change God's word, but maybe I can ease your friend's mind. What she did is shameful. She lost her virtue like a whore. But still, she's a mother's child—if she marries . . . Many things can be forgotten over a lifetime.

But not if she's a *mamzer*. Her father has often declared that she may not be his, Emilia said. Her manner was calm, hands quiet in her lap, as if she were not the one the rabbi had called a whore.

Ah, he said. Then your friend's father was living elsewhere in the year before she was born—not with her mother.

They lived together, Emilia said. And to show off her knowledge, she quoted her father, But as the Talmud says, one can always be sure of the infant's mother, however the father can be anyone at all.

The rabbi spoke angrily. That is meant in another context. Now you should understand why a girl is not to study the Talmud. It only confuses her and leads to immodesty. Listen to what I'm saying. Jewish law presumes that the husband is the father if he lives with the mother in the same house. And even if he was not living with her, if at any time he has called the child my daughter, or indicated his paternity in any way, such as paying for her education, he has no right to say she isn't his.

No right? Emilia asked, surprised at the anger in the rabbi's voice when she herself felt nothing but hope.

I'm telling you plain, such an action is despicable. Your friend is not a *mamzer*, and it's a great sin on the part of the father to lead her to think so. The rabbi then went on to explain more particulars of the law. So there is no reason for your friend to hesitate, he said. She should marry at once.

The rabbi stood up. His shoulders had shrunk in the last year, his caftan hung loosely, the silk sash tied several times around his waist to separate the purer upper half from the base lower regions of the body during prayer. This is how it is, my child, he said. It's been a long time since I visited your father's house. Do you think that maybe I should invite myself?

I'll be the one to send you an invitation, Emilia said, as soon as there is an occasion.

Good. I hope to recite the wedding blessings for you very soon. It's written that under the wedding canopy, every sin is erased just as if it was the Day of Atonement. You remember what I'm telling you.

It wasn't long afterward that Emilia found Mr. Levy. When she went to see him, she knew that in Jewish law the presumption of paternity, unlike in the case of a husband and wife, didn't apply to him. The mere fact of sexual relations was not enough; an unmarried woman must prove the paternity of her child through the father's admission that it was his. This she had learned from the rabbi, though at the time she'd been certain it was irrelevant until, to her astonishment, Mr. Levy admitted nothing. And so she discovered that all knowledge can be useful at some time or another, though it will not make you happy.

Later, on the boat that brought her to London, she dreamed about the Furies flying about with their snake hair. Sometimes they pecked out her father's eyes. Sometimes Mr. Levy's. Sometimes even the rabbi's. When she awoke, she saw only the ghost of the first Mrs. Rosenberg. But what business did the ghost have to cry as if Emilia were someone to pity? She had a first-class cabin and a trunkful of gowns in the latest fashion, which she knew how to wear.

Now she was in Wigmore Street, a different person, a gown made over in the new style. The grandfather took off his spectacles and folded up his newspaper. "I'm going out a little bit," he said in Yiddish as he stood up. He was a few inches shorter than Mrs. Zalkind.

"You're not going to Soho, Father?" He nodded, looking away. "If you must play cards, then let me send you in a cab. There's no reason for you to walk. It isn't *Shobbos*."

"I can walk." Her father's voice was stubborn though he was a man who wouldn't swat a fly, for it has a soul and even an animal soul deserves consideration. His face was round, his nose arched, his beard as yellow as fog.

"A mule." His daughter shook her head.

"So we're alike. Who would have thought?" He turned to Emilia. "Such a daughter. Aye-aye-aye. She'll make you a proper wife. In a kosher home. You understand?" In English he added, "Nice girl. Good girl," patting Emilia's cheek. How ridiculous that this should make her eyes wet.

Mrs. Zalkind put another scone on her plate, and cream slid down from a silver spoon.

Berwick Street

It was summer and the noise in the street was deafening, for who could stay inside those hot rooms? Two men and a woman had been thrown out of the Hound and Hare. The men were laughing as the woman beat at the window with her fists, the organ-grinder playing at double speed. Every day the street was louder, as if night would clutch its ears and go somewhere else. It was August, and newspaper vendors sold out their papers within an hour, calling "Murder most foul" and "Murderer identified." In the market Jews were buying fish for *Shobbos*. Who needs to be afraid here? they asked. But they kept their daughters close by them and studied every man as if he might be their enemy.

The ghost of the first wife was restless, looking at the package on the table, then the gowns laid out on the bed for packing, checking the inside of the wardrobe, inspecting the trunk.

"Do you think it should all go in?" Emilia asked. The engagement had lasted a respectable six months. She'd be married in three weeks.

The first wife turned toward her, lifting her hands as if to say, Why not?

"The new hat goes in and the gowns that have been made over. Maybe I ought to leave the others. No, you're right. The material is all first rate. I'll have the others made over, too." She unpinned the brooch from one of the gowns, putting it in the wardrobe before she packed the gown carefully between layers of muslin.

There was a small scroll painting from the Curios department on the wall beside the wardrobe. Emilia took it down and wrapped it in newspaper.

"Mrs. Zalkind has a very good dressmaker," she said. On the table was this month's issue of *La Nouvelle Mode*. "I want one just like Miss Cohen's, only with not so many ruffles and a little lower here and something in back." Emilia looked at herself in the cracked mirror.

On the table the package from Minsk was unwrapped, beside it a card from her mother, again cautiously signed as if it came from an old family servant. The front of the card was illustrated with two girls in frilly dresses, the bigger one holding the smaller one on her lap, a basket of flowers at their feet, and a sentimental verse in Russian. On the back her mother had written a note: Oh, the sorrows of mother and daughter separated by heaven's will, et cetera, followed by a few words about tears shed and hopes for the future and so on, finishing with "Each of your letters is more precious to me than gold even though they are so very short."

Emilia had replied with a quick thank-you for the present and good wishes, explaining that as she had much on her mind and much to do, there was no time to write more, and her mother should remember that Emilia was supposed to be an orphan. She had nothing else to say. It was the first Mrs. Rosenberg who'd come here from the other world.

Emilia shut the lid of the trunk. The present from Minsk was inside it: a box of scissors, paper, a small knife, inks, paint suitable for paper, stencils. Well, why not? All her friends did something, and Mrs. Abraham wanted a paper-cut. The cameo brooch she left in the wardrobe.

The ghost of the first wife climbed outside to sit on the roof, reaching up as if to draw smoke from chimneys that were cold.

Charlotte Street

At night Emilia slept in her room in Berwick Street; during the day she cleaned and painted the flat in Charlotte Street. Jacob had leased the first two floors of a house in Bloomsbury, his brother Albert already having the third. On either side were houses subdivided for rent to students and artists, who knocked on the door at all hours to borrow sugar, ink, scissors, pots, tea, cigarette papers, a shaving brush, and

Albert's cat, said to be the best rat catcher in Bloomsbury. Mr. Zalkind, who was a wholesaler of building supplies, sent in men to fix up the house so it wouldn't fall down around them. And while Emilia painted the walls and ceilings with designs she'd seen in Liberty's wallpaper books, the terrible murders in Whitechapel were making headlines all around the world.

She was painting the upstairs bedroom when the first body was discovered; then the second was found not far from where Jacob was born. August ended with terse headlines in *The Times*: "East End Murders." A letter to the editor of *The Pall Mall Gazette* deduced that the killer must be a broad-shouldered man with muscular hands and stunted thumbs, dark-complexioned, of foreign accent, middle height, wearing a flannel shirt, a silk handkerchief, dark gloves, and thin side-spring boots. Another letter, this one from a clairvoyant, said there was no doubt that the murderer was a blond American who sold organs to publishers of medical textbooks in New York. The editor of *The Times* wrote that the murderer was surely a tormented Russian Jew, perhaps a butcher, for an Englishman would never do anything so heinous.

Mrs. Zalkind had brought her maid and was cleaning the house from top to bottom, stocking it with sufficient pots and pans, silverware and dishes to separately serve meat and dairy, everyday meals and meals for Passover, so that everything would be kosher enough for even the grandfather. She came down from the upstairs bedroom, swathed in an apron, with an armful of dustcloths to shake out and a tattered game found in a closet, the Palace of Happiness. If a player landed on idleness, she was sent to the workhouse for the duration of the game. Behind Mrs. Zalkind, the maid was carrying a bucket of dirty water.

"You must remember. No shellfish," Mrs. Zalkind said as she entered the parlor, where Emilia was painting the ceiling. "Wait six hours after eating meat before you serve dairy. We are not lax like the Dutch. I hope you remembered to rinse the brisket before and after the salt."

Emilia dipped her small brush in the gold paint. From her perch on the ladder she could see into the dining room, where Albert was studying anatomy and Jacob writing his column. "I remembered," she said. "The brisket is in the oven."

At home it had always been the maid who *kashered* the meat, draining it of blood. Emilia liked doing it herself. There was something satisfying in flopping the brisket over on one side, then the other, covering it with chunks of salt, later rinsing it away and feeling the flesh smooth and polite, all sign of violence poured away.

Mrs. Zalkind glanced down at the newspapers spread on the floor to protect it from dripping paint, each headline more lurid than the one before. "Are you writing about Whitechapel, Jacob?" she called into the dining room. "You ought to say the Jews would never do such a thing."

He looked up, wiping his pen on a rag. The light in the dining room was green, filtered through a thin cloth hanging over the window until the curtains would be ready. "I'm writing about a lady's shop, Mother. My readers want entertaining, and they'll have it."

"Don't imagine that this has nothing to do with you, my son," Mrs. Zalkind said. "Soon those hoodlums will be marching through the West End again, smashing glass, turning over carriages, throwing bricks, plundering and ravishing. Mark my words. Ravishing, I say."

"My future wife is ravishing," Jacob said, smiling at Emilia on her ladder while his mother huffed at the ignorance of children, taking the dustcloths outside to shake them furiously.

Emilia was painting lilies on the ceiling because they couldn't afford very good wallpaper. Using the smallest brush for the dots in the petals as she leaned back on the ladder, she didn't give dinner a thought until the maid called in a small voice, "Miss! Miss! There's a bit of smoke coming from the stove."

The kitchen was as dark with oily smoke as if it were the Queen's Pipes furiously burning contraband. Emilia covered her face with an apron, opening doors and windows and pouring water on the pan, which made the smoke billow up, thick with failed gravy, and she coughed till tears streamed down her face, making a path in the streaks of soot on her cheeks.

Mrs. Zalkind found her sitting at the table in the kitchen, her head in her arms. Emilia didn't reply to her greeting. She couldn't bear to look up but stayed at the table, listening to the sound of a mop and water sloshing, a pan scraped, orders for the butcher and greengrocer. It was too humiliating. How did her mother stand it day after day?

"I'll never be able to do it," Emilia said without lifting her head.

"It isn't your fault that you can't cook," Mrs. Zalkind said briskly. "A girl should be taught from childhood so it comes as naturally as breathing. Gentile women have cooks and are completely dependent on them. How could you know anything? My poor son will just have to wait for you to learn, and if God above is good, then Jacob will not suffer greatly with his sensitive stomach. Wash your hands. Paint is not a wholesome spice. I brought you my cookbook, and I shall expect dinner from you today even if I eat it at midnight." Mrs. Zalkind seated herself at the table with the patience of Job's mother. "Do you have any carrots? Give me the knife, I'll chop. You go to the door. I see the butcher's boy is here with another brisket. Always buy from Greenberg's. His is the best kosher meat."

Frying Pan Alley

It was the first of September, a cool *Shobbos;* men who were so inclined went to the synagogue, and women sat on steps or stood in the alley, nursing and watching their children. It was the last Sabbath before the Jewish New Year, but Nehama wouldn't sit in the women's gallery of the synagogue. If she was there, she wouldn't understand what was being read from the Bible since there were no women's prayer leaders in the modern day to translate the *haftorah* into a language she knew.

Nehama and Minnie were sitting side by side on a bench pulled into the alley. The sky above was gray, and there was a warm, wet wind that lifted the fringe of their shawls. Minnie was darning socks, Nehama reading the *East London Gazette,* and Pious Pearl, who made them push over so she'd have room to sit down, was watching her boys. The women all wore red shawls, and the only difference among them was that Pious Pearl also had a wig and a kerchief over it, as if the double protection against sinfully inflaming a man's desire would counteract the effects of her drinking. Across from them and toward the school yard, there were other benches and other women standing and sitting, for on the Sabbath the alley could make room for everyone. They spoke in hushed voices, afraid of being overheard while the bigger girls jumped rope and the boys played hide-and-seek in their tattered suits from last year's donation by the school. The jump rope slapped the cobblestones as the girls sang:

First he bought me apples,
Then he bought me pears,
Then he gave me sixpence
To kiss him on the stairs . . .

"Don't go past the school yard," Pious Pearl called. "I'm warning you."

The babies played at their feet, hardly babies anymore. Libby was three, telling Gittel a story while she fed her dolly, which was made from rags. In her fingers she had a treasured raisin, and when her dolly was sated, she would eat it. Libby didn't like raisins, otherwise it would have disappeared into her own mouth.

"The murderer must have escaped from a lunatic asylum," Minnie said quietly. "Why else would he attack that poor woman—is there something to steal from a person like that? What does it say there?" She pointed at the newspaper with her darning needle.

"She was wearing a black straw bonnet," Nehama replied. At the end of the alley there were shadows made by the warm wind and the cool air turning into mist. "I used to know someone who had one just like it."

"No one in this street wears a straw bonnet." Minnie put down the half-darned sock and looked at Nehama. "It's nothing to do with us."

"Nothing?" Pious Pearl asked. "The gentiles are saying it was a Jew that did it. Haven't you heard them calling our men Lipski? I didn't want my husband to go to *shul* today; last week he was beaten up on his way home. But you know how pious he is. He thinks praying is almost as good as betting."

"I used to know someone who wore a wig like Pious Pearl's," Nehama said quietly. "What if they find her next, God forbid? You can stretch out your hand and touch the street where they found the body." The woman who'd been killed must have been feeling good that night. She had a piece of mirror in her pocket and she was wearing a new dress. It had been torn by the murderer when he slashed her body.

"Don't think of it," Minnie said. "Those streets are night and here it's day. You can't talk about them in the same breath."

"Boys! Get back here or I promise, I'll beat you black and blue,"

Pious Pearl called. "Better they should be afraid of me, who wants the best for them."

"Maybe she stole the dress." Minnie peered over Nehama's shoulder at the illustration in the newspaper.

"If things had turned out differently, she could have been anyone," Nehama said.

"No one I know," Minnie insisted.

The little girls were chanting the second verse of their jumping rhyme:

> I don't want your apples,
> I don't want your pears,
> I don't want your sixpence
> To kiss me on the stairs.
> Then he tears the leg of my drawers,
> And that's the last of all . . .

Nehama picked up Gittel and held her close. Her daughter's eyes had turned golden from their newborn indigo, but night had long arms that stretched darkness from corner to corner. It could eat any of them alive.

Great Portland Street

Two months before the High Holy Days, the congregation begins to prepare for its judgment in the court of heaven. First come the prophecies of rebuke, three of them, read on the Sabbaths leading up to *Tisha B'av*. On this day the temple was destroyed and God's name vanished from the Holy of Holies. The people mourn, the synagogues are draped in black. But after *Tisha B'av* the prophecies of consolation are chanted on seven Sabbaths, the last just before Rosh Hashanna, as the need for consolation is more than twice as great as the need for rebuke. Then the people in their exile, lonely and full of regret, arrive at the Days of Awe, when there is neither rebuke nor consolation but only the sum of one's deeds as a person comes before the throne in the court of heaven, wondering if the King will stretch out His golden scepter to say, You may stand before Me and live.

It was a short walk from the Zalkinds' house to the synagogue, Jacob and Emilia strolling behind the rest of the family in the stately pace of the Sabbath, his arm through hers like a gentleman. A religious man wouldn't do such a thing, and no wonder, for surely anyone could see the haze that surrounded them, caused by the meeting of cool morning air and the heat of exercise. She could feel the action of his hips throwing one leg forward then the other, and his lips were shaping not only words but breath that tasted—well, she wasn't quite sure of the taste, but it was there at the tip of her tongue. This wasn't intended by her, quite the opposite; on the way from Minsk to London, watching the sea sloshing against the porthole, she'd sworn off any such feelings. But while she'd been painting lilies and willow boughs, watching Jacob play chess with his brother or write in the notebook with the green cover, his scent had crept up the ladder like a skin of fragrant smoke that moved with her every move, a finger on her finger, a knee with her knee, a back over her back, and a taste in her mouth as if it kissed whenever she spoke.

It was a cool day with a warm, wet wind bringing a change, and the people who left their carriages and footmen in livery a block away from the synagogue (riding being forbidden on the Sabbath) walked in their own haze, one of greatness, the lord and the sir and the ladies in their jewels that would sparkle if there were sun but instead were muted by clouds that turned London into a city of olive skin, the hue of Portland stone favored by builders after the Great Fire.

The synagogue had been visited by the emperor of Brazil fifteen years ago and more recently by H.R.H. the Prince of Wales, who came for the wedding of a Rothschild. Today even Zaydeh would sit between his grandsons in the men's section. Only for such an occasion would he step foot in the synagogue with the twenty-five columns of Italian marble and the rabbi who was called "Minister" in the fashion of English Jews. A nice donation had been made to the building fund, and though it wasn't exactly an *aufruf,* the bridegroom's call to the Torah, for the bride wasn't Jewish, nevertheless Zaydeh would see his grandson go up and say the blessing for reciting verses from the Torah, and he himself was going to chant the *haftorah,* the reading from the prophets.

"It's all right, Emilia," Jacob said, as if she'd been protesting. "We don't have to stay long. After I go up to the Torah, I'll wait for you on the steps outside. The Moores are having a painter for lunch. One of the French group."

"What about Zaydeh?" Jacob's grandfather was walking on his own, hands behind his back, the only one in sight wearing a prayer shawl over a satin caftan.

"Right, right." They continued for a moment in silence, Emilia thinking about her gloves, how if only they could sit side by side in the synagogue, Jacob might pull one off and touch her naked hand, but she would be up in the ladies' gallery with Mrs. Zalkind. "We'll slip out after Zaydeh finishes the *haftorah,* then," Jacob said.

"How will I congratulate him from the ladies' gallery?" Emilia asked. "And if we don't stay until the end, then Zaydeh won't get any cake. Your mother disapproves of it. He should have cake on his day of honor. It's only fair."

"I'd do anything for him, Emilia. But this is just too embarrassing. It's an anachronism. Parading around with a parchment scroll dressed up in velvet and crowns. The Abrahams are calling me 'pious Yankel,' you know."

"Well, you're my Yankel, at any rate. That ought to be something."

Jacob grumbled, and Emilia leaned close to hear him, murmuring sympathy, her lips close to his cheek, inhaling his skin as if it were the smoke of tobacco sharp on her tongue. When they came to the steps of the synagogue, she was carrying her cloak over her arm, too warm to wear it another minute.

Zaydeh was waiting for them. "I have something for the *gitteh yokhelteh.*" The good gentile girl. It fit her as if she were born to it. "You see?"

He gave her a small Bible with a leather cover, translated into German. "But, Zaydeh, carrying?"

"Who says I carried something on *Shobbos*? It's not allowed. I was wearing it. If a woman can wear earrings, why not a man this?"

The first letter of each verse was illuminated, and above each chapter there were tiny illustrations inked in gold and red and green and indigo. He must have searched a hundred shops, two hundred barrows of old books to find it, and she stammered over her thanks while he smiled with shy gratification, taking Jacob's arm. They went in together, the first generation in his fur *shtrimel,* the third generation in his silk hat. Someone might say there was no language in common between the two of them, but such a person doesn't understand the longevity of the *mama-loshen.*

Upstairs in the ladies' gallery, Emilia sat with Mrs. Zalkind, holding the Bible she had once studied with her mother.

"The woman in the blue hat," Mrs. Zalkind whispered. "She's the president of the Society for the Protection of Hebrew Girls."

"You mean the woman with the plain, skinny face?" Emilia asked.

Mrs. Zalkind nodded. "The very one. She thinks rather well of herself. Her husband is a German Jew."

It was just the same as the synagogue in Minsk. A different tongue, the same talk. The ghost of the first wife was standing behind one of the Italian pillars while the velvet-clad Torah was paraded in its anachronistic manner, the gentlemen in their tall silk hats bowing low before it as they would before a king as Jacob went up to pronounce the blessing over it.

"For this commandment which I command you this day, it is not too difficult for you," the reader chanted in his honor. "Nor is it too far. It is not in heaven that you should say, Who shall go up for us to heaven, and bring it to us so that we may hear and do it. Nor is it beyond the sea that you should say, Who shall go over the sea for us and bring it to us so that we may hear and do it. The word is very close to you, in your mouth and in your heart that you may do it. See, I have set before you this day life and good, and death and evil."

There were other blessings and other verses, while the ghost of the first wife stood behind the pillar, a shadow within a shadow as light came and went through a tall, arched window. She waited for Zaydeh, watching the small man in his old-fashioned garb go up to the oak platform where the Torah rested from its labor.

The chanting of Torah and *haftorah* is directed by marks under the words. The marks of melody notation give the reader no choice; the words are drawn out or short, the voice rising or falling according to the notation; the reader is a vehicle; the words use him and not the other way around. A man can choose only the day he will chant, knowing the verses assigned to it. Zaydeh looked down at his grandson among the men and up to his daughter and her soon-to-be daughter-in-law in the ladies' gallery. He recited the blessings, and then he sang in his old voice like a windblown reed:

"You will be called a new name from the mouth of the Lord. . . . As the bridegroom rejoices over the bride, so will God rejoice over you. . . . And you will be called Sought Out, a city not forsaken . . ."

After the Sabbath, Emilia and Jacob were married in a civil ceremony at the Office of the Registrar.

Charlotte Street

In the *heim* Jacob's grandfather would have been called a man of the earth, someone uneducated, simple and crude. He played cards, took pleasure in food, and prayed the way a simple man prays, in between hearing the latest from his cronies in the *shul,* a room above a fruit store. From there to the house in Charlotte Street wasn't a long walk, and he came often to see how the children were coming along.

A week after the third murder in Whitechapel, Emilia was in the kitchen chopping parsley, her hands gold from painting the dining room with a border of autumn willow boughs. There was a kerchief around her head, her mother-in-law's cookbook propped open on the table. The chicken was in the pot, cut up and covered with water. The ginger, sweet herbs, and garlic were on a plate. She had only to add the parsley and pepper and a tablespoon of flour to thicken the stew. When it was finished, she was to garnish it with lemon, parsley, and boiled carrots.

"What are you cooking?" Jacob's grandfather asked, looking in the pot. He spoke Yiddish. Emilia answered in German, and so they understood each other as well as most people.

"Chicken stew, sir. The recipe is from Mrs. Zalkind's cookbook." She read the recipe again, adding a little garlic juice to it as she touched the page with her fingers. "What does 'garnish' mean?" she asked.

He shrugged. "Eating I do like an expert," he said. "The cooking is up to you."

The ghost of the first wife was standing at the window, gazing listlessly at the students who carried home satchels of bones to study. A costermonger was calling, "Rhubarb! Onions!"

The grandfather looked into the pot. "Maybe a garnish is a kind of spice," he said, keeping his eyes on the pot as if it was rude to stare at ghosts. "You have a guest?" he asked.

"Only you, Mr. Karpman," Emilia said, glancing at him sharply. Soon Jacob would be back from the newspaper office, Albert from his classes, and they would be hungry.

"I see," he said. And she was sure he saw nothing. On the table there was a jelly roll for the pudding. It was his favorite. Mrs. Zalkind believed that a man over sixty should not eat cake; Emilia was determined to master baking so that the grandfather could have some. She tried many times before she learned to get the heat just right.

"I'm worried for you," he said while she added the herbs and garlic, the ginger and parsley to the stew. "The things that are going on now. For me it's all right. Who's going to interfere with an old man? But you, a girl?"

Emilia didn't think about the murders at all. She was too busy mixing paint and learning to cook. You keep your mind on a thousand details, and you don't listen for the smashing of a window. She tasted the stew and added more salt. "What does it have to do with me? Those poor dead girls, they were . . ."

"I know what they were. But you have a Jewish husband."

"So? None of the girls were Jews."

"You have to hear what I'm telling you. When there's something to be afraid of, it comes to the Jews. Why did you bring this on yourself? Such a suffering isn't for you."

"You think I don't know anything about it, Mr. Karpman?" Her voice was quiet. Maybe it was even old.

The ghost of the first wife turned away from the window, looking for the door to the garden, but the house in Charlotte Street had no garden.

"All right," he said, sitting at the end of the table near the jelly roll. "But I'm not a mister. You should call me Zaydeh, like my grandsons."

Emilia cut him a slice of cake. "How is it, Zaydeh?" she asked, watching him closely as he took a bite. A look of pleasure spread over his face. It was enough. She was not her mother. There would be no burnt odors in her house. She hardly noticed when the ghost of the first wife left, walking up the stairs to the attic and through there to the cold roof, following the path of chimney pots east toward the docks.

Frying Pan Alley

On the Sabbath of Repentance, during the Days of Awe, another middle-aged woman had been killed. She was wearing her whole wardrobe on her back, a coat, a skirt, two bodices, two petticoats, striped woolen stockings, a neckerchief the same color as her stockings, red and white. Perhaps she was running away when the murderer caught her. He didn't know that she would have died anyway; she was very sick with tuberculosis and a disease of the brain.

Even Nathan was frightened enough to cover up his nervousness with chatter. "Business is falling off," he said, threading the needle of his sewing machine. The High Holy Days had come and gone. The slack season was over. In the front room the children were napping under a pile of new jackets.

"People still need coats," Lazar replied. "It's getting colder."

"One thing leads to another. If no one comes to the Lane to buy, then people lose jobs. They wear old coats, and the tailors have nothing to do."

The victim had lodged in Dorset Street; her name was Annie. Nehama knew the lodging house. It was large, more than a hundred people slept there. They had names like Polly, Annie. Maybe a Molly or a Sally.

Nehama pumped the treadle of her sewing machine. Of course her Sally, if she was still living in Dorset Street, would be much younger than the women who'd been killed, though she'd been on the game a long time. She might even be a madam by now. Nehama shook her head. Sally used to have a terrible cough. More likely she'd have ruined lungs like the dead woman, yet it was impossible to think of Sally as anything but the girl with thin puffs of hair, zestfully brushing a wig. And if she'd been walking in the wrong place? Nehama's foot trembled; her sewing machine slowed to a halting pace as she imagined the gutted body described in the newspaper.

The headlines read:

WHITECHAPEL TERRORIZED
MURDERER SIGHTED

POLICE INVESTIGATION
FULL DESCRIPTIVE REPORT

The latest murder had occurred in Hanbury Street near Brick Lane, where twenty months ago horses with black plumes had pulled hearses from the Yiddish theater after the night of the panic. More people had died that one night than in the months of the Whitechapel murderer's reign. But the world was mesmerized by him. It gave him names—Leather Apron, the Ripper. Who thought about a dozen and a half men and women and babies killed in one night by the fear of a few hundred of their neighbors and friends?

"I wrote another play," Lazar said. "It's better than the last one."

"It couldn't be worse," Nathan said.

Everyone knew it wasn't very good. The writers with talent left after the Yiddish theater closed, and the actors with them. But Lazar wrote the play, and he showed it to some tailors in the Friendly Society. The play was called *Malkeleh*, after the main character. It was performed in a tavern the way these things used to be done, in Black Lion Yard next to the dairy. The whole time cows were mooing, but the tavern was packed. As the old saying goes, when fear reaches the sky then it rains defiance.

"I wrote a song for the new play," Lazar said.

"You see?" Minnie said proudly. "My Lazar."

"Anyone can do it." Lazar turned over a jacket and thumped it with his iron. "You only need to know how. It goes like this. 'That drunk in the gutter, what does she sell? Who knows, but that street I know it well, the mud and the cold—'"

"That's an old song from home," Nehama interrupted. "How did you write it?"

"Ah, but the chorus is different. At home it was Warsawer Street. In my song it's Bell Lane. Listen how it rhymes. 'In Bell Lane I was born and there I fell with my cane.'"

Nehama laughed. Nothing could stop her from laughing till the tears came, not Nathan telling her to finish the jacket, not the headlines in the newspaper, not even the memory of herself sharing a bed with a young girl coughing. Nehama wiped her eyes. "If my grandmother was alive, she would come to see this play."

"Lucky for her that she's not," Nathan said.

But of course her grandmother would come just the same. All the grandmothers would, for their children had not succumbed to fear and they would enter the tavern, praising heaven in thankfulness.

Wait, Mrs. Rosenberg. Stay with me a minute. Why do you want to go back home? The theater is starting again. All right, Lazar isn't exactly a master. But soon you'll see what people will do. Listen to me. A voice can be mute for a month, a year, a generation. But it can't stay in the grave any longer than the memory of the dead. A feather of wind can lift it up to heaven. Such is the merit of Deborah the prophetess, Queen Esther, and our mother Sarah.

ACT II

Sing, barren one, you who have not given birth. Break into a song and cry aloud. . . . The children of the abandoned outnumber the children of the married wife. . . . Enlarge the place of your tent . . . Extend the size of your dwelling. . . . Do not hesitate. . . . Do not cringe . . . you will forget the shame of your youth, and the reproach of your widowhood you will remember no more. . . . With vast love I will bring you back.

—Isaiah 54:1–7

CHAPTER 5

In the Street

1898

Frying Pan Alley

The old theater in Prince's Street never reopened, but there were Yiddish plays in Vine Court Hall, sometimes in the Standard, and matinees in the Pavilion, a beautiful theater with seating for thousands. There was even talk of a regular season of Yiddish plays there. The old theater, which had seemed so grand years ago, sat only seven hundred. Well, God in heaven stays the same and everything else changes. Nehama had lost two back teeth, and a bigger theater was needed for the countless newcomers who arrived every month, squeezing themselves into the one square mile of London where Yiddish was still the mother tongue.

Now she had to decide what to do with the knotted handkerchiefs filled with coins and hidden under the loose board. The coins had accumulated slowly and surely, like the reading of books, a little bit here and a little bit there, over eleven years growing like a child, like their only daughter standing on a crate while Nehama pinned the hem of her new dress. Gittel's hair was dark and neatly braided, her eyes golden. She was singing quietly, it came as easily to her as breathing, and when she felt shy and didn't sing, she might as well be holding her breath, her face pale and still, her eyes fixed on a distant point, maybe even, God forbid, on the next world.

Nehama worried about her daughter. What mother doesn't? Gittel was just a child now, but in two years she'd be finished school and what then? A sewing machine wasn't for her. No—a person doesn't live like a pig in a sty so her daughter should live like that, too. There would have to be something better. That was why Nehama intended to have a shop. Then her daughter could study in peace and quiet in their rooms upstairs. She'd become a pupil-teacher and then a teacher and she'd live like a human being. If the prospect of life at a sewing machine or the counter of a pawnshop was too much for some people—Mrs. Levy, for example, or whatever her name really was—then Nehama would lift heaven off its hinges to make sure that *her* daughter wasn't driven to God knows what.

"A cobbler's daughter I am not, hammering nails I cannot," Gittel sang in a murmur, her eyes far away, as if she was dreaming of ruffles. "No, Mama, no—a cobbler I won't marry."

Nehama took out a pin from the hem and tucked it in again, making the dress a bit shorter. She had drawn and cut the pattern, copying the style from a magazine she saw at the library. Gittel's dress was almost the same as the one in *La Nouvelle Mode,* a little simpler in design but with more intricate stitching at the cuffs and waist, and if the fabric was cheap, her daughter didn't notice. For Passover, of course, there had to be something new. A dress and a pair of shoes— the shoes were to be a surprise, beautiful smooth leather, not nearly new but brand-new, hidden in the workshop behind the finished coats.

Nathan was using chalk on the wall. "Look, Nehameleh. If we get another machine, we could make four pounds a week over the year."

"Yes?" She stood up for a minute to look at the figures. "This is a lesson for you, Gittel. You see here—twenty-five coats a day. That's what your *tatteh* thinks. For that you need eight, maybe nine hands, and are they all going to be quick? You take the chalk, Gittel."

"Mama—I don't like doing sums."

"Am I asking if you like it? Get off the crate and take the chalk. Here. Fifteen coats a day makes thirty bob. Write it there. Now do the sum—you can do it." Nehama waited, hands on her hips, while Gittel slowly wrote the numbers on the wall. "Exactly right. You see what it is, Nathan? There's less profit than what we make now with two machines completely paid off."

"Number one. We could buy a machine outright with what you've put away." Nathan raised a second finger. "Number two. With me as boss there's twenty-five coats at least, I promise you."

Nehama shook her head. "What I put away is for my shop. It's going to be in the high road."

"You can dream anything you want, but a workshop we have and it only needs another machine." He crossed his arms and frowned as if they were at their sewing machines. But in the front room he wasn't the boss of her.

"I know every penny that I put away under the bed. God help you if I find a *groschen* missing." Nehama glared.

Gittel turned her head to look over her shoulder at her mother. An argument about sewing machines was much less interesting than the hem of a new dress. "Am I going to have a ruffle, Mama? You promised me. Even Shaindel's Pesach dress has a ruffle, and her family just came."

"And you promised me to study. No more books from the library until I see a good report." Nehama made her voice stern, yet how could she deny her daughter the new free library when she herself came to it every *Shobbos* like a thirsty man in a desert?

"I won't get my report until after Pesach, and I need a ruffle on my dress now," Gittel pleaded. "You made Libby's dress with two ruffles."

There you had it. What does a girl see? Not the complicated stitching, not the hours spent making the pattern just so. "Enough talking about dresses. You'll have what you have and that's all. Take this off and study."

"But everyone's jumping rope in the alley, and if I beat Libby, she's got to give me her new rope."

That's how it is with a daughter. She thinks you hold her life in your hands and all you have is water trickling away. "Such a bargain. All right. For a little while. Then you come home with some milk and you study." She'd barely buttoned the last button in the back of Gittel's everyday dress before her daughter tore herself away.

"A professor's daughter, I am not . . ." Gittel sang as she flew out the door. "But reading books, I can do. Yes, Mama, yes—a teacher I will marry . . ."

The last verse was Nehama's invention. You can never start too early giving your daughter the right ideas. "Don't think I'm forgetting," Nehama called after her. "If you want to go to the theater, you have to do your homework."

"We need another sewing machine," Nathan said. He tore a sheet of newspaper and stuffed it into the toe of his boot where it was cracked. "When Shmolnik has one in his pawnshop, I'll get a good price from him."

"Then you get a loan from him, too," Nehama said.

"That's crazy. We have the money. Why should we pay interest?"

"I don't know from 'we.' If it's you that's getting a machine, then it's you that's paying the interest."

"All right, all right." He pulled her toward him. "Then *we'll* go to the theater. I hear there's a new play in Vine Court Hall." He kissed her as if it were still *Shobbos*. When you have just one child, you don't get too tired for a nap without any sleep.

"Don't think you can get a new sewing machine that way," Nehama said, turning to get her shawl.

"All right." He jammed his foot back into his boot. "Do I like the new drama anyway? A play with Jewish kings, that was something. Now it's always peddlers. Nothing but peddlers."

"Never mind. I don't want to hear. I have things to do." She threw on her shawl, picked up a jug, and went outside.

There on the bench sat Mrs. Flacks, who wrote love letters in Yiddish. If ugliness were a trade, she'd be rich. The widow that lived in the cellar sat with her and Pious Pearl the beigel lady, who didn't look any older than she had ten years ago, though her foot was broken. Her husband, on his way to play cards, pressed a finger against one nostril and with the other blew into the mud of the street. And before he reached the end of the next house, he was a ghost, a white sheet of fog that muffled the clang of church bells. It was Sunday, and in the alley children played while their mothers talked. The boys were peeking through a cocoa tin with a hole at one end and a postcard pasted at the other. The girls jumped rope, singing:

> There come six Jews from Juda Spain
> In order for your daughter Jane.
> My daughter Jane is far too young
> To marry you, you Spanish Jew.

Farewell, farewell, I'll walk away,
And come again another day.
Come back, come back, you Spanish Jew,
And choose the fairest one of us.
The fairest one that I can see
Is Gittel Katzellen, so come to me . . .

As Gittel jumped in, the girls laughed and squealed, turning the rope faster and faster, the drizzle soaking their frayed dresses. Nehama waited another minute, watching her daughter, boots a size too big, black braids flying, eyes narrowed against the rain. She was concentrating on her feet, and no matter how fast the other girls turned the rope, she didn't miss a step. Nehama could still feel the weight on her right hip where she'd carried Gittel as a baby. A daughter doesn't know that she is always a part of her mother, the most vulnerable part jumping carelessly in the fog.

Minnie stood in the doorway, keeping an eye on her daughter, Libby. The two girls jumped together, and when Libby tripped, they both went out. "Girls!" Nehama called. "Here's the jug for milk. And remember, Libby. Make sure that Gittel gets the milk from the spotted cow. It has the fattest milk. Don't forget, I'm telling you."

"Did you see, Mama?" Gittel asked. "It was Libby what tripped, not me."

"I saw," Nehama said. "Just be careful with the milk. Go on, girls."

She slipped a slice of cake into the pocket of Gittel's pinny, watching the girls go off with their jugs, Libby running pell-mell, Gittel with her watchful, deliberate walk after she said, "Good-bye, Mama. Good-bye, Auntie Minnie," as if farewells must always be taken seriously.

"Don't do it, Nehama," Minnie was saying. She pushed back a strand of damp red hair.

"What are you talking?" There were gray strands in Minnie's hair, like tendrils of fog.

"Pious Pearl wants for you to get her new crutches."

"So? I didn't know that was a crime," Nehama said. A tile fell off the roof and broke at her feet. Sparrows rushed to steal the exposed hay.

"The crime is when she'll sell them for drink."

"Maybe she needs it more than the crutches."

Minnie rolled her eyes. "There's no talking to you."

"Talking you do plenty. Listening is something else." Nehama had a list in her pocket. Number one was Pious Pearl and her crutches. Number two was Pious Pearl's youngest, a boy with a stutter who should go to the Jews' Free School. And Mrs. Flacks, who'd arrived with her husband and children a month ago was number three. The husband had gone to America, and the middle daughter needed ointment for her eyes. Four through seven were other neighbors with other needs. None of them was deserving. The lady visitor who came from the Jewish Board of Guardians to inspect their moral hygiene said so. But Nehama knew what it was to be undeserving. If you listened to the *yetzer-hara,* the evil inclination, the instinct for survival, you could hear it gasping for a breath of air among the flames of this world. Nehama drew her shawl over her head and stepped out into the fog and the rain.

Black Lion Yard

There were no secrets among the Jews of the East End. How could there be when they lived in each other's armpits? No, the problem was that everyone was a tailor, and when it came to a secret, he considered himself a bespoke master who could elaborate a few rumors into a whole suit. Concerning Gittel's first mother, people said that she was a lady. A grieving widow. Everyone agreed on that, and Gittel had heard it herself from Mama. A lady what was well spoken, well read, and well mannered. Quality. Then she ran away, and there were any number of stories about why and where. But it was the whispering that Gittel noticed most, and when Mama and Aunt Minnie whispered, she heard pieces of sentences, parts of questions, like What can a person do on her own? and Remember what goes on in Dorset Street. Then just as she thought she'd hear the whole story for once, Mama would say, *Shhh,* little pitchers have big ears, we'll talk later.

So out of the cabbage leaves of many conversations, Gittel sewed the mixed-up coat of her life. Mama told her that no one knew anything and that *loshen hora,* malicious gossip, was the worst sin, so Gittel should just keep her own counsel, but a person couldn't help wondering about her own mother who'd left her. Maybe she cried too much. Yes, she had been a crybaby, a homely, howling baby, and her mother took one look and said, This child belongs here, and off she went.

Carrying her pitcher, Gittel walked straight ahead, moving neither to right nor to left, and the grown men carrying racks of shirts back from the rag market in Petticoat Lane walked around her, muttering until she gave them a peculiar look with her golden eyes. *Thpoo, thpoo, thpoo,* they spat, averting the evil eye.

"Do you think as there's a place for cows in heaven?" Gittel asked. The streets were more cheerful on Sundays. Everyone was hooking it: the Jews by working and the gentiles by going to market while the bells in the foundry chimed a tune.

Libby shook her head. "Don't be an idiot. Whatever do you want to ask something like that for? Come on, Gittel." She was a year older than Gittel, and whatever she didn't know, her older brother told her. He was out in the world, fourteen and apprenticed to a book-binder.

Somewhere the spring air wafted the odor of green shoots, but here it was kippers and barreled cucumber, and a good smell it was, almost as good as the eating of it. At the corner, a boy was buying toffee from a stand. He wore the thick corduroy suit given out by the Jews' Free School.

Gittel wiggled a loose molar. "The men have to study Torah all day in heaven, poor sods. But Pious Pearl, when she dies, she'll be having schnapps from morning till night."

"Don't say 'sod.' It ain't nice." Libby swerved to avoid the muck falling from an open window above. "When you go to heaven, you'll have to sit at your real mother's table."

"I won't," Gittel said. "I'm sitting with Mama." Heaven, Gittel imagined, was a kind of coffee house where men placed bets and, because they were dead, also studied Torah. But among the women there would be singing. All the grandmothers were sure to want to learn the new songs from Gittel, for after being dead so long, they would be tired of the old ones.

"You don't have a choice," Libby said. "It's written in the Book of Life." She meant the book in which God wrote a person's fate on the Jewish New Year. Libby thought that heaven was something like a wedding banquet and the Book of Life was its seating plan. "You have to sit with your real mother and your real grandmother and not your bubbie that you were named after," she said.

"Then I'm blessed if I'll die. So there." Gittel stood between the old stone posts at the top of the steps where Old Montague Street met Black Lion Yard.

"Make room! Make room!" a man in an overall was shouting as he herded cows down the steps toward the dairy.

Gittel leaned against the post of the old gate, listening to the music of Sunday, the bells and the moos, the talk of men going to prayers and placing bets and women going to buy an ounce of tea or take a shirt to the pawnshop. The cows clattered past a jewelry shop with fish knives and wedding rings in the window, hoofs churning up the mud under the sign that said, "Best and cheapest funerals."

"My other mother," Gittel whispered to Libby, "is a baroness. And when she comes, she'll make us both princesses."

At the wooden gate of Jones the Cowkeeper, a sign in Hebrew letters said, *Frish fun di coo.* Fresh from the cow. Inside the byre a milkmaid, with ashes on her kerchief and a smear of manure on her apron, took the jugs. "So girls, what's doing?" she asked in Yiddish. "Are you ready for Passover? A new ribbon for the *seder,* maybe. Or even a new dress—yes?"

"I have a new dress," Libby said. "With ruffles on the collar. Her mother made it. She's having the same one."

"We're sisters," Gittel added. If she could have two mothers and an auntie that was no blood relation but had nursed her, then why not a sister? Gittel craved a sister. She craved any number of relations, but they all seemed to be in the *heim* or dead or unknown.

The milkmaid looked at one, then the other. Libby's round shoulders and Gittel's skinny ones in her pinny. Libby's untidy red hair, a mischievous grin as she hopped on one foot. Gittel's smooth braids, her square chin, her stillness. "Of course, who could miss it? I look at you and I see her. Like a mirror. Well, girls, the boss is coming to tell me to stop talking and start selling. What will you have? A wedding ring, maybe. Or a pair of candlesticks." The girls shook their heads. "Oh. Could be you want some milk? Lucky for you that we have plenty."

"From the speckled cow," Gittel said, peering around the milkmaid as she handed over her tuppence. There were thirty cows in the stalls and plenty of flies for each of them. The milkmaid dropped the coppers into her pocket and headed to the back, where a dim figure was shoveling manure onto a pallet for sale to Kew Gardens.

Libby waved away the flies. "What happens if your real mother comes to take you away?" she asked.

Gittel hadn't considered this. Crowns and gowns, yes, but not leaving her mama and her *tatteh*—her father. "What do you mean?"

"You're not going to be a princess and that in Frying Pan Alley."

"Then I won't be one."

Libby looked at Gittel with the force of her twelve years. "Your real mother can do as she pleases with you."

The milkmaid was returning with their jugs. Gittel held herself carefully. "Libby Feffer," she said, "you're a liar and you jump rope like a cow."

"She'll just haul you off to wherever she is, mark my words," Libby replied, though she didn't say where because she was a good friend.

Gittel kicked a stone down the yard. She could kick a stone and not spill a drop of milk from her jug.

In the Lane, no doubt Pious Pearl the beigel lady was saying to Mrs. Flacks, "Let me tell you, a lady she was for sure. But she run out of money, and in London, God doesn't send manna down from heaven, only fog. So what did she do? Well, I'm telling only you. A lady doesn't have hands for a sewing machine, am I right? She does what any abbess may do in Dorset Street."

So what? Gittel had heard it a hundred times. She'd just think about the shoes Mama had promised her for Passover. In those she would jump to the moon.

Petticoat Lane

The Jewish Board of Guardians funded asylums for the aged, the deaf, the orphaned, the infirm, and the insane, a soup kitchen, schools, evening classes, a workingmen's club where neither drink nor gambling was allowed (and hence few members), a boys' club with military uniforms (very popular), a girls' club (also very popular) run by a wealthy spinster who was in love with a rich, but unfortunately married, Spanish Jew, lunch programs, boots and school uniforms for children, sanitary inspection and building projects (which promised a reasonable profit to investors). The board's most popular program was its capital loans. A few pounds could set up a newcomer in business—a very small one, to be sure, but one that made him self-sufficient. It was, after all, a Jewish precept that the highest form of charity is to provide someone with the means of earning his own living. It is also a Jewish precept that when a beggar asks for charity, it is a duty to provide it without scrutinizing his merit, but this precept was cast aside with other old-fashioned and superstitious rituals.

The trustees of the board were Jewish gentlemen of wealth and peerage like Baron de Rothschild and Lord Montagu. The donors were middle-class Anglo-Jews whose hearts went out to the oppressed in Russia and recoiled from them in East London. Oppression, close up, was rather rank, and there was concern that English gentiles might not be able to distinguish so well Jews of one type from Jews of another. Hence the board's open-passage program, which offered tickets, immediately on request, back home. Or to America. Or at the very least out of London. There were five million residents of the County of London; one hundred thousand were Jews. Enormously visible. The Jewish question was debated in Parliament. What that was, exactly, it was hard to say. But it made the Anglo-Jews anxious. After all, it had been only seven hundred years since the Jews were expelled from England and seven since they'd been driven out of Moscow. The need was great, the money never enough, the newcomers vastly outnumbering the established community that was attempting to help and subdue them.

The office of the Jewish Board of Guardians was in Petticoat Lane, the interview room looking down on stalls of secondhand goods. Along three walls there was a strip of greasy dirt behind the heads of newcomers who sat on benches, arguing and chattering and speaking in Yiddish undertones. The women nursed babies, the men studied racing forms, they all read the newspaper, ate peanuts and dropped the shells on the floor. Some of them wondered if they'd made a mistake. It was true that in the *heim*, to be a Jew was much worse. You could easily die of it. But on the other hand, Jews had their own towns and the *goyim* were the guests there. Until you left, you didn't know what it meant to be the stranger.

A little pale around the edges from the smell of newcomers who had no water to wash and sweated fear, a gentleman sat at his shining desk under the portrait of the queen. He had two grown sons, one a doctor, the other an author. The gentleman wasn't young anymore, and he had volunteered for the thankless task of these Sunday interviews. No one seemed to appreciate the fact that it took him away from his own business. The trustees wanted to know why he used up the month's budget in the first three weeks; the newcomers that were turned away heckled him. All this Nehama had heard during her previous visits to the office. Not that the gentleman spoke to her about any of it. He was speaking to his secretary as if the newcomers, like servants, had no ears or at the very least no intelligence to understand what they heard.

The gentleman's name was Mr. Zalkind, and he was a man of olive complexion with a silver mustache that made his skin seem as dark and smooth as that of the builders of the pyramids. He'd spent the fall in Egypt, avoiding the November fog that burned the lungs with sulfur. But the spring fog, if not quite as poisonous, had driven a yellowish tinge into the hollows under his eyes.

"When did I last see you, Mrs. Katzellen?" he asked. Beside his desk there was a tea trolley with a plate of biscuits, a cup, and a Wedgwood teapot. The gentleman's secretary poured tea while he pulled a report from one of the piles on his desk.

"I don't wish to bother you, sir." She spoke in a loud London voice so he could hear her above the din of street noise coming through the window behind him. "I come about something what's important."

"And what might that be?" he asked, drinking his tea. There was a small ink stain on one of his white cuffs. When she had her shop, she wouldn't sell cuffs; a gentleman did not buy in Whitechapel Road.

"A good boy, sir. Very clever and that," she said.

"Then his parents ought to come in."

"They only speak the *mama-loshen,* so they sent me." She would have shirtwaists in her shop; skirts and blouses were the new fashion, and a girl earning a wage could buy two, maybe three, even four shirtwaists for one skirt.

"And you are what relation to them, Mrs. Katzellen?"

"A cousin, sir." She would do alterations, make over old dresses into something new and stylish. And she'd sell books. There should be a place where working girls could buy books and not be embarrassed. A book that was a person's own made her someone.

"I believe you came about a cousin last week, too," the gentleman said. "Tell me—are you related to every Polish Jew in Whitechapel?"

"My little *cousin* should go to the Jews' Free School. And he'll need boots, Mr. Zalkind, sir. He wore his shoes clean through trying to sell lemons alongside them Irish boys. How's he to have a chance when he stutters like Moses our Teacher?"

"You must realize the fact that there are only so many places," he said. "On registration day, the child's mother may line up—"

"She's lame. She can't," Nehama interrupted.

"I'm afraid there are no exceptions," he said.

"And this is something else. She has want of proper crutches. The ones as she got don't fit. They're too short. She walks like a hunchback."

He peered at her over his spectacles. "Mrs. Katzellen, this is not a village square where you can haggle like a fishwife." Through the window behind him, she could see the new warehouse coming up, another half-demolished. There was no work crew on a Sunday, so people pilfered wood and bricks; guards were chasing them.

"Am I someone to argue with you, sir? My cousin—she only wants crutches so she can get around to sell beigels, sir. It's not for charity, sir, but her business."

"I see." Mr. Zalkind picked up some papers and looked them over. "There's a waiting list for the clinic, but I shall put her under the general fund. Her name and address, please." While Nehama answered, the gentleman wrote in his ledger, then turned to his secretary. "Get her a ticket for the hospital."

"I have another cousin, sir."

"How surprising, Mrs. Katzellen." He rubbed his forehead. "And this cousin?"

"Poor Mrs. Flacks. Her middle daughter can't see, her eyes is that runny. Oozing, sir."

"What shall I do with you, Mrs. Katzellen—ought I to ban you from this office altogether?" He wore a lounge coat with slits in each side seam. It had a casual look, but Nehama was not misled. This was the latest style. A gentleman who wore it thought of how he appeared to others.

"You know, sir, if I might say so. Everyone speaks well of you."

"Really," Mr. Zalkind said, casting a glance at the people waiting on the benches. "I did not suppose any of them were thinking of me at all."

"Charity is a great virtue," she said emphatically. "It will stand you in good stead when the Holy One, blessed be, writes our names in the Book of Life and the Book of Death. You don't look so very well, sir. The weather disagreeing with you?"

"The damp disagrees with everyone." Mr. Zalkind rearranged his papers in even piles.

"As it is written, Open your mouth for the poor and plead the cause of the needy. It was a Jewish mother who said so. The mother of a king, Mr. Zalkind. In the Book of Proverbs."

"I'm familiar with it," he said dryly.

"A girl with oozing eyes is very needy. To save a child's sight, can there be a better *mitzvah*? It won't be forgotten. And then before you look around, she'll be working herself and earning a living."

"Well." Mr. Zalkind passed his hand over his tired eyes. "I should not wish this girl's disease of the eye to infect others. It would burden the office needlessly." He wrote something in his notes.

"And the school for the older boy?" she asked.

"Yes, yes." He frowned and shut his record book. "But do not tell me of any more cousins." He waved for the next petitioner. "I don't wish to see you anytime soon."

Very good. She'd come in with the rest of her list after Passover. Soon, soon she'd be a shopkeeper, and everything for her neighbors would have to be done now because in the first year of the shop she'd be working night and day. She could just see the sign above the door, *Davka Bicher un Kleider,* and underneath, in smaller English letters, "Necessarily Books and Blouses."

Whitechapel Road

As Gittel popped through the narrow end of Black Lion Yard, she craned her neck to see if she could find her father among the Jewish tailors gossiping in clumps as they did every Sunday between the Yard and Great Garden Street. The men stood in the fine drizzle, a crowd of them in caps and wool jackets, hands shoved into pockets or cupping matches, her father standing over there on a step to light his cigarette in the shelter of a doorway.

No one could pull a tooth like Papa. Some fathers used string and a doorknob. Some just waited till the tooth dropped out of its own accord. But with a quick flick of his finger, her *tatteh* could present her with the tooth that just a second before had been hanging by a tough string, its underside sharp against the tip of her tongue. When she was small, he'd tell her that he was collecting the teeth for a display in the British Museum, paying her in toffee or monkey-nuts. Now she went along with the game for the pleasure of it.

He was talking to Mr. Berman, who wholesaled slop coats. You could always tell one of his jackets. The lining hung down like a collapsed womb from a woman who'd died in labor. Her father made nice jackets.

"This is a sight." Papa clapped a hand to his cheek. "I believe it's Sarah Bernhardt, the famous Hebrew actress. Might I have your autograph?"

"Anytime you want, *Tatteh.*" She leaned her head against his shoulder, feeling the rasp of the yellow-checked jacket that he'd been wearing as long as she could remember, smelling of sewing machine oil and cheap cigarettes, now damp with rain.

"The resemblance is uncanny," he said in Yiddish, stroking her head, "but I see it's only my beautiful daughter."

Gittel stood proudly. "I have a loose tooth that I might be willing to sell."

"Mm. Then you came to the right dentist. I'll have it out. Give your jug of milk to Libby to hold. That's right. Open up. I see. I see. Whoops. Here we go. Ah, a good one for the collection. What will you have for it?"

She probed the hole with her tongue. "I don't have many left to come out. I'll want at least a crown for it," she said, and grinned.

"What—five bob? No, that's too dear. I can get a dozen teeth for half a crown. Fine teeth. No, you can have a farthing."

"Ask for monkey-nuts," Libby whispered to Gittel, returning the jug of milk.

"Tuppence," Gittel said, serious now. This was real bargaining. "And monkey-nuts for me and Libby."

"Done!" Her *tatteh* slipped a piece of toffee into her hand as he shook it. "I have a little business here. Then I'll get your apple." He turned to Mr. Berman. "What do you think this would fetch?" he asked, taking something glittery from his pocket. A chain, Gittel saw. A delicate braid of gold. Something her other mother might wear. If only she could have it.

"A few months' hard labor," Mr. Berman replied. "Where did that come from?"

"The gutter near Dorset Street," Papa said.

Maybe her other mother had actually worn it. The chain might have been a gift from one of the gentlemen that liked to go slumming in Dorset Street. She could picture it, her mother with the chain as golden as her hair, the gentleman in his tall hat, the gutter running with blood, for in Dorset Street there was such violence. Her cheeks were hot with the thought of it.

"I picked it up in front of the coffee house where your brother makes book. I always put my bets with him," Papa said. "Someone was coshed and rolled and this was missed, I'd guess."

"If it were me, I'd just give it to my missus," Mr. Berman said.

"What's a chain with nothing on it? No, I'll sell it and get my Nehama a nice bit of cloth for a holiday blouse. She's always making do with cabbage leaves of leftover stuff. And Passover's coming. She should have something new."

"I think Mama would rather have that," Gittel said softly. It didn't matter how quiet she was. Papa could always hear her.

"You think so?" he asked, looking down. She nodded. "Then it's my lucky day. What a bargain—a tooth and a chain, too. Maybe my horse will place. Who knows?"

Gittel walked home with her father, and he let her hold the chain for Mama in the pocket of her pinny. She must always remember that her other mother was a lady. She spoke German and French, and she taught Mama to read English with the very book, *Pride and Prejudice*, that lay under Gittel's pillow.

Petticoat Lane

In every Jewish room the evening before Passover, Father or Uncle carried a candle and a feather, searching for the last few crumbs of bread. The children followed the candles, peering into dark corners, only the oldest of them realizing that their mothers had hidden a few crumbs here and there for them to find and add to the pile that would be burned on bon-fires in the morning. Every room had been cleaned, every rag of cloth-ing washed, every mattress aired and turned. It took weeks, and if there wasn't so much excitement, the women would have dropped from exhaustion. When the leavened burned up in the fire, so did everything heavy in their hearts and they were ready for the festival of freedom.

In the *heim* people had the same tradition of searching for crumbs, but here there was a whole evening of festivity called Chametz Battel Night, for Jews always take something from their surroundings to add to their customs and in London it was the excitement of the street. On other days, they got a teaspoon of jam, a pinch of tea, an ounce of sugar. But tonight they spent money without a conscience. It was a *mitzvah,* a virtue, to make the festival great. They needed *motzos* and tea and sugar and meat and carrots and onions, maybe a kettle, a spoon, a frying pan. It was all piled high right here in the Lane. And between the stalls offering all the foods that were needed for Passover, there was every sort of entertainment, juggling, fire-eaters, contortion-ists, and ordinary men chasing each other with squirters and feather ticklers. Even the grandmothers walked here and there, watching it all. But who could they tell? Who could they warn? Once you're dead, you shout but only heaven hears you.

"MOTZOS FRESH FOR YOM-TOV!"

"SEE THE FIRE-EATER! SEE THE SWORD-SWALLOWER! BOTH FOR A PENNY!"

"*SHAINK* A POOR LAME BEGGAR A COPPER FER PESACH!"

In a far corner of the Lane the two families, Nehama's and Min-nie's, were together in the dusk. They stood in front of a makeshift stage, gazing longingly at the other end of the Lane, where the fire-eater was fighting with the sword-swallower. All except for Lazar, who was rapt. It was his play up there.

"How many acts are there?" Nehama asked. She had one hand on Gittel's shoulder to keep her from running off with Libby. The two girls were whispering and counting their pennies as they eyed a stall of paste jewelry. Maybe there was enough for a small shining brooch. Libby could wear it one day, Gittel the next.

"One act," Lazar said. "Who has time to write anything longer in the busy season?"

"He means the actors wouldn't give him more than an hour," Minnie said to Nehama. It was a play in the new style. The actors spoke like ordinary people, like anyone right here in the Lane. There wasn't a single rhyme. No dancing interlude. No Roman guards. No camels. No Bengal fire. They even had the script onstage because Lazar had just finished the play this morning.

It was about a father and son, peddlers who wanted to leave London because there was too much competition. They were discussing where they should go. They'd been arguing about it for twenty minutes, and it seemed that they would continue to argue for the entire act.

"As full of *dreck* as real life," Nathan said. He was wearing his favorite and only jacket, with the yellow checks. He refused any other. This one suited him exactly.

"That's real art," Lazar replied, tipping his bowler hat. Minnie was proud of it, no wool cap for her husband, who attended the free lectures on art at the library. Nehama went to the lectures on economics.

"For such a demand you'll have more than enough plays," Nehama said. She liked the yellow jacket. All the others Nathan might have worn were in the coins knotted in handkerchiefs and stored under the loose board. Torchlight glinted on her husband's face as he turned to wink at her.

"No, Nehameleh. You're completely wrong. Who wouldn't want to see something like this? You watch it and you feel like your life is very long," he said.

Onstage, the father finally rose from his bench. He banged a fist on the rough table, looked defiantly at Lazar, and broke into song. "What does he think he's doing?" Lazar asked.

Nehama and Minnie clapped. The thin crowd started to swell. The actor told a funny story and everyone laughed. Sometimes it happened like this. Yiddish actors weren't yet convinced of the new style. They were used to making up their own lines when they got bored.

"Stop it!" Lazar shouted. He jumped onto the stage. The audience clapped harder. This was good fun. This was Chametz Battel Night.

"You're not paying me enough to speak these lines," the actor said, shaking the script at Lazar.

"You suppose anyone else would pay you more?" he asked. "You're not even any good as a presser, never mind."

"And you think you're a Jewish Shakespeare? Better you should press paper with a hot iron than put a pencil on it."

"A favor I did you. Giving you my best part where everyone could see you."

"Better my grandmother should see me at my funeral," the actor said, picking up the small table, which he'd brought from home, and stomping off the stage. The son shrugged and followed with the bench. The stage was empty, the crowd parted, some drawn by the smell of chocolate at the stall of sweets, some to the escape artist tied in ropes and hanging from a lamppost, others to the vendors of cooked meat.

"KIDNEY PIE CERTIFIED KOSHER BY THE CHIEF RABBI!"

"BRISKET! REAL KOSHER! NO PISS IN IT!"

"Very good," Nathan said. "A wonderful play."

"But it's not over." Lazar dug his hands into his pockets as he glared at the naked little stage.

"Now you can go," Nehama said to Gittel. "Here, take my shawl. It's getting cold. And don't come back too soon. I have a lot to get for Pesach, still."

"All right, Mama. All right."

Nehama put the red shawl around her daughter's shoulders, murmuring warnings and instructions and scratching Gittel's back in that one spot midway between her shoulder blades where it itched whenever she got excited.

It was just then that Nathan saw Mr. Shmolnik, the pawnbroker, across the way and said that he needed to have a word with him about getting a third sewing machine as he'd heard that Shmolnik had gotten one in very cheap. So why did it have to be that minute—who knows? It was a night for buying. A night for selling. Maybe Nathan thought he'd get a deal and tomorrow Passover was coming; it would be days till Mr. Shmolnik's shop would open again, and tonight money burned to change hands.

The Lane was slick with wet muck, all the dropped bits of festivity tramped underfoot. When Nathan slipped and hit the ground with a thud, he got up and made such a face that everyone laughed as he slapped his hat back on his head. He waved at Mr. Shmolnik and called to him to stop. A cart with nuns from the convent was passing by. They looked happy to be outside; they were chattering and pointing and laughing. The cart was painted with lilies for Easter, the horses in straw hats laden with flowers. But why should they go down to Whitechapel Road through the Lane tonight of all nights?

There was a noise. Of course there was a noise. There was lots of noise, all kinds of noise. But something startled one of the horses. Maybe it was the stall of chocolates that fell over when the men chasing each other with squirters crashed into it. Or maybe it was the juggler who dropped his plates on purpose to startle his audience. As Nathan stepped back to get out of the way of the nervous horse, he slipped again. He was flat on the ground, the driver struggling with the reins. A man jumped from the cart, a priest, and the nuns were screaming. Nehama blinked, then the horses were rearing and Nathan's arm was sticking out from between the wheels of the cart.

Lazar was saying something she couldn't hear. Minnie had her by the arm and Lazar gripped her shoulders as the horses were taken out of their harness and tied to posts. Nehama was holding on to her basket. Everything for Passover was there. How can you have a holiday without what you need for it?

She waited for Nathan to jump up and run back to her with a joke. But he was just lying there, a crumple of yellow jacket. *"Tatteh!"* Gittel was crying. When he wouldn't answer, she threw herself at him. Nehama stood by, saying nothing, holding on to the basket with everything she needed for Passover except the one that mattered most.

Whitechapel Road

The sages wrote that it is the duty of every man to bring joy to his household with nuts and new garments on the festival, and wine to cheer the telling of the Passover story. Gittel knew that in every Jewish room in the East End, there was a table with a white cloth, a pair of candlesticks, a *seder* plate with a burnt egg, a shank bone, greens, bitter herbs, and sweet apples mixed with crushed nuts and wine. In the center of the table was the best cup for Elijah the prophet, who would invisibly travel from home to home, taking a drop of wine from each to share the joy of freedom.

But what did Gittel care about holidays? Papa was unconscious.

His head was banged up and no one could tell how badly. On the outside it didn't look terrible. There was a bruise above his right ear but no blood.

Sister Marion, who was in charge, stood by Sister Frances, the shorter of the two, stout and ruddy. She spoke like a Cockney, Sister Marion like a shopkeeper's beady-eyed and self-important wife. They were taller than Mama, the white wimple made them more imposing, but she faced the nurses with their clean sturdy hands and immaculate aprons bleached and boiled by fallen women and orphaned girls who had no festival of freedom, holding Gittel's trembling hand. The nurses didn't want Gittel to stay.

"Don't say a word, my daughter," Nehama murmured in Yiddish. "Leave it to me." They stood next to Papa's bed. There was a row of such beds. In each of them a man was maybe dying and maybe living.

"Girls don't belong here," Sister Marion said. "The men are exposed when the dressings is changed. You people think you can do whatever you please. But rules is just the same for them as think they're above such things. She has to go."

"Then who's allowed?" Mama asked in the polite tone she used for lady visitors who came from the Jewish Board of Guardians to inspect their rooms.

"His wife, of course," Sister Marion said. "And other married female relations. A sister, for example."

"Oh, that's all right then," Mama informed her. "This is my husband's littlest sister what's married." The nurses glanced at each other. Gittel was blushing. "Yes, don't you know? Jews marry their children off dreadful young."

"Disgusting," Sister Frances said. The head nurse wiped her nose as if something were stinking more than the men's wounds. But Gittel stayed.

They spent Passover in the hospital. Mama pushed two chairs together for Gittel to sleep on, which wasn't any worse than how many a lodger or cousin slept. Aunt Minnie and Uncle Lazar brought food. No one could eat, but the point was not to eat, only to have it so that they were reminded of the existence of food. They talked fast, as if any pause would be a door for death to enter, but Gittel heard them only now and again. Something about Uncle Lazar's play, he'd write another act, it would be about this or that, you see that Nathan's color is better, a little rest, that's all. Aunt Minnie was taking things out of a basket, finding a place for them on the small bedside table, on the plate that she pushed into Mama's hand, on the cloth she put over Gittel's lap.

Uncle Lazar had lost his hat, the bowler hat that made him somebody. It fell off when he was lifting Papa into the nuns' cart so they could take him to the hospital. He hoped that Papa would appreciate what he'd sacrificed. Only for such a friend, a brother, would he give up that hat. Look at this odd wool thing he had on his head. Could you call it a hat? It belonged on an old man, an *alter-kacker,* never mind.

So they went on, the talk hurting Gittel's ears until she thought she would bleed if anyone said another word. But at last they were ready to leave. Aunt Minnie swept up the crumbs and wrapped the uneaten food in newspaper. Uncle Lazar put his hand on Nathan's head, murmured a blessing, then turned away, embarrassed.

"Let me take Gittel home," Aunt Minnie said. "She shouldn't get sick. Look at her eyes, she's so tired she's ready to fall."

"I'm staying here," Gittel said. There was mud on her dress and a spot of dried blood where she'd cut her knee, throwing herself on the ground over her father.

"Come with me. A child needs sleep." Aunt Minnie was pinning her hat to her hair, the hatpin as long as a sword in the moonlight.

"You should go," Mama murmured, her eyes far away. She was touching the gold chain that Papa had given her to wear for Passover. There ought to be something hanging from the chain, a locket, a jewel set in gold, but Mama said she liked the chain just the way it was.

Gittel folded her hands in her lap as if she were in school. "I'm staying," she said. A person had to sit still with her hands folded. That was the rule.

"It's all right. Go on," Mama told the others.

The ward was bright with moonlight while men moaned in their dreams. Some of the moans were in Yiddish, some in English, one was in Chinese, and several in no language at all. There were two rows of beds, each with a small nightstand. Beside one was the wicker frame used to hold the canvas that wrapped a patient for hot air treatments.

"What happens after someone dies, Mama?" Gittel asked quietly. She had to be quiet. When someone cries, people run away. It was her crying over her *tatteh* that had driven him into unconsciousness.

"People sit *shivah*. They mourn and then they get up." Her mother's voice was quiet, too. The night nurse was walking between the rows of beds. Her white habit made her look like a ghost, but her shoes clump-clumped on the linoleum. It was the day nurse who washed the floor with carbolic acid.

"I mean the person that's dead. If his body is in the ground, how does he turn the pages of the Torah when he's studying in heaven?"

"Do I care?" Mama asked. "That's God's problem. Me, I want my family to use their hands to make a living and clap when there's a good show at the theater."

"What if there's nothing, Mama?" The biggest boy in her class said that after you die, worms eat the body and that's all. Papa was lying in the bed, a thin line under the sheet on his way to nothing. His face was without expression, the crease in his forehead made by the bandage. If only it was worry about finishing an order or concentration on the last line of a joke. "Do you think there's nothing after a person dies?"

Her mother looked from the bed to Gittel, pushing her chair closer to Gittel's before saying in a confidential tone, "I'm telling you, what you hear now, you'll hear then."

"I hear Papa breathing," Gittel said. His breathing was slow and shallow though there wasn't anything wrong with his lungs or his heart, the physician had said. "But, Mama, I smell something."

"What—is it blood?" Mama stood up as if to pull back the sheet, looking around for the nurse, who had gone back to her station.

"No. It smells like trees."

With a sigh, her mother sat down again, taking Gittel's hand in hers. "What kind of tree?"

"A linden tree when it buds." Mama's fingers were long and elegant. If they weren't rough, they could be a lady's. But a lady wouldn't touch a dead body, and Mama would wash Papa if it came to that.

"If it's a linden, then it's the tree in the courtyard of my mother's house, may she rest in peace. Is there anything else?"

"Roses. I smell roses," Gittel said without any wonder that she might smell spring in Poland or summer in Russia, for when this world comes close to the other, it seems stranger that they're separated than that they can touch.

"We didn't have any. But my father's customers did. They all had rosebushes in their gardens."

There was a sound from the bed. Papa was smacking his lips as if they were dry. Mama poured water from the pitcher on his nightstand and held the cup to his lips. He drank like a man so old he could be in the museum. "How will we wake *Tatteh*?"

"We just have to wait," Mama said. The man in the next bed groaned as he turned over. "Is there another choice?"

"You could tell me a joke," Gittel said, looking away from Mama's mournful face.

"I'm no good at telling jokes. But it's all right. God laughs plenty."

"Please, Mama. Just one." The smell of carbolic acid mixed with roses and lindens and something else—yes, it was the smell of a stream filled with trout. The ward was a night garden, and if her *tatteh* only knew it he would realize that this world wasn't such a bad place to return to.

"All right. Just one," Mama said, kissing Gittel's forehead. "And then you go to sleep. I don't want a sick child on top of everything else."

So Mama told one joke and then another. Every single joke of Papa's, all the bad jokes, the terrible puns, the stories about the angel of death and the priests and the converts and the two brothers, one rich and one poor, all of them she told while Papa was unconscious. Before dawn, in the darkness between the moon and the sun, when you couldn't even see the gold chain on Mama's neck but just touch it as you leaned against her, she was hoarse and she was still telling jokes. She said, "And then the convert sprinkled a little water on the boiling beef and he said, Holy, Holy, Holy, now you are a fish." She said, "You mean you're not Moisheh from Minsk?" She met Gittel's eyes with a promise, and she said, "You without me is like a door without a handle."

So the first sound that came from Papa was a faint laugh. Gittel jumped up to embrace her father, and Papa laughed again before he looked down and discovered the bandage on his arm where his right hand should have been.

Frying Pan Alley

The front room was just as Nehama had left it. The iron stove was shining. It had taken her a day to get it ready for Passover. The curtain hung in front of the bed, sewn in a patchwork of remnants so that when she lay with Nathan her eyes fell on pieces of their life together. The loose board under the bed was still loose, and under it were the handkerchiefs knotted around silver and copper coins. The Passover dishes were piled on the dresser, the blue glass vase was on the mantel and beside it the program from a children's evening at the school with Gittel's name in the chorus. Nathan's newspaper was still on the table, Gittel's homework, Nehama's book from the library: *The Woman Who Did*.

"Minnie! Come down!" she shouted.

There was a clatter on the stairs, the door flung open. "My God, Nehama. What is it?"

"Did you move a sewing machine?"

Gittel was in school, Nehama had just come from the hospital. It was Hol Hamoed, the middle four days of Passover, when work is permitted. In the street someone was calling, "*Motzos!* If you didn't get enough on Chametz Battel Night, now's your chance! Half price, slightly burnt!" The barrow rattled over cobblestones, the voice grew fainter.

"What are you talking?" Minnie asked. "Why would I do such a thing? Is there a reason to *shlep* sewing machines here and there?"

"Then it's gone, Minnie. There's only one in the workshop."

"That's impossible. Let me have a look."

"You think I'm blind all of a sudden?"

"Maybe just a little crazy. It happens. With Nathan in the hospital . . ." While she was talking, Minnie walked into the back room, Nehama following, the book still in her hand. It was easy to see the workshop with a single sweep of the eyes. The mantel for the gaslight, the pressing table, the soot on the window and the paper over the crack, the rough table where in the busy season four people worked, and now only one sewing machine. "Joe's bag is missing, too." Minnie pointed to the bench. A black-and-red-striped bag should have been under it. The bag belonged to Joe, the lodger, who'd been training on the sewing machine and sleeping on a bench in the workshop for the last month. He was a *landsmann* from Plotsk. He knew Nehama's next older sister or at least her husband, the one that smelled like onions, or so he'd said.

"You think he stole it—I don't believe it." Nehama dropped her book on the table and sat down, her hands over her eyes.

"It has to be the lodger," Minnie said.

"Tell me, Minnie. Just one thing. How could I forget? A person claims to be a *landsmann*. You offer your trust and then . . . Now you see what happens. You see it with your own eyes."

Minnie was sitting on the bench beside her, a hand on her shoulder. "It's not a watch he put in his pocket. A sewing machine? The whole street would be looking."

"A cholera on him." Nehama put her fist against her mouth. How easily a life could come undone in just a few days. If only she'd sleep. Maybe then she'd wake up to everything as it was before Passover.

"He had to go somewhere with it," Minnie said. "A new lodger with a sewing machine won't be hard to find. I want to see a man with such *chutzpah* in his face and then I'm going to scratch it out."

"All right," Nehama said. Of course the missing sewing machine was the better one. Nathan had bought it after she had the miscarriage. "You go, Minnie. You tell me if you find out something."

"By myself? Don't be foolish. Come on. Let's go now. Everything can be fixed."

"I can't do it, Minnie. Not again. How many times do you think a person can start from nothing? From less than nothing, from beneath the grave."

"You're smarter now." Minnie was taking her by the hand and leading her to the other room. "Here, put on your shawl. It's raining again. If only I was a fish, I'd be ecstatic. When you have your shop—"

"What are you talking? Without the sewing machine, we're going to be lucky if we don't starve to death."

"Cakes and blouses, am I right?" Minnie asked.

"Books," Nehama muttered. But she was shrugging into her coat, the shawl over her head. "Books and blouses."

"Who wants books? A good cake, a honey cake or a butter cake—that's something I can make. Should we be partners, Nehama? I'll want a striped blouse. A shopkeeper should have a striped blouse. Do you think pink or blue?"

Nehama shook her head, but she couldn't help smiling a little. Minnie was arguing with her about the sign over the shop and the color of the awning, and before she could look around, they were out in the street among the barrows and stalls dripping with rain.

They went around the alley and to all the small streets that made up the Lane; the rain was gray and the houses leaned over them as they went from door to door. No one saw anything. It was Passover; on the last two evenings everyone had been inside at the *seder* while the moon was full and the streets as bright as by day. Did you see something? No, No, No, and then Yes. Mrs. Flacks's youngest child, when she opened the door for Elijah the prophet to come in and drink his drop of wine, she'd seen something. What did she see? they asked, everyone excited. It was Elijah, she told them. Did he have a sewing machine? That was too funny—Elijah wasn't a tailor, he was a prophet with a long white beard and sweets for children and maybe Mrs. Katzellen had a farthing for her to buy a peppermint as she'd seen the holy Elijah.

Pious Pearl was holding an umbrella over her beigels at the corner of Sandys Row and Frying Pan Alley outside a shop that sold uniforms from the Crimean War and weapons from the wars of Napoleon, everything rusty and moth-eaten. The owner of the shop, twice as wide as her doorway, was standing outside looking for customers in the drizzle. Beside her was the hot-chestnut seller who, ten years ago, had seen a man fleeing on the night of the murders. It was a corner for seeing things. It was a corner for listening.

"Chestnuts, all 'ot!"

"Knives and sitthers to grind!"

"Special edition, 'orrible railway accident!"

"Did you maybe see our lodger?" Nehama asked Pious Pearl. Her voice didn't belong to her. How could it sound so calm when she was strangling?

"Joe with the striped bag?" Pious Pearl asked. She didn't have to think for a minute. "I saw him on the first night of Pesach." She'd been a bit tipsy from her four glasses of wine and the vodka both before and after, but it was no one else. They'd had a little conversation. The lodger said that Nehama had asked him, as a favor, to pawn the sewing machine for her rent while Nathan was in hospital. "It's not true?" she asked Nehama.

"Not a word."

"Maybe he took it to Shmolnik's. Have a dozen beigels, Nehama. No, I don't want a penny. Take it or I'll curse you till you're sorry you ever saw me. Here."

"Keep it," Nehama said. "Curses I have plenty."

Minnie took her arm as they turned down toward the high road. The rain was soaking through her shawl, and she needed a drink. She wished she was Pious Pearl. She needed to be the kind of person who could drink and not throw it up before she got drunk.

Whitechapel Road

The pawnshop was long and narrow. At the very back the pendulum of a grandfather clock swung gracefully back and forth in its glass casing, though the hands on the face of the clock never moved from thirteen minutes past one. Behind the counter, the walls were lined with shelves from floor to ceiling, on every shelf tattered goods with tickets hanging on string. Mr. Shmolnik had two men working for him. There was no slack season in this trade, and several women were waiting to pawn their husbands' Sunday boots, their sheets, a clock, a wedding ring, a beer stein.

"I'm sorry to hear about your husband." Mr. Shmolnik wasn't a brown man with a knot for a nose anymore. He had a gray beard and a gray face under it. Only his eyebrows were still dark. He'd never found a third wife, but somehow he'd managed, and with God's mercy, his children had grown up. "How is he, Mrs. Katzellen?"

Nehama wanted to kill him; it was the good inclination that was telling her to rid the world of a man that caused decent husbands to fall in the mud and nearly die, sacrificing a right hand, the hand that made a living, the hand that made love. But the evil inclination, the savage instinct, the instinct for self-preservation has more sense. It forced her to think of herself, her family, the shop that would give her daughter a future better than the street. "Awake, thank God," she said, her voice cracking.

"A terrible thing. I'll never forget the sight of him falling under the cart." Mr. Shmolnik turned his head as someone came in through the connecting door from the coffee house. Nehama could see the men playing cards, reading the racing pages. The bookie was consulting with Mr. Shmolnik; someone must have won for a change. They whispered, they nodded—what was this to her?

"He was going to talk to you about a sewing machine," Minnie said as the door to the coffee house closed again. She had her hand on Nehama's arm, holding it close to her side as if she thought her friend might fly apart. "He heard you got one cheap."

"I know the machine you mean." Behind him one of the countermen was taking something off a shelf. A miracle—the woman with the mole on her cheek was redeeming a suit. So the lost could be found again after all. "A beauty, if I may say so," Mr. Shmolnik went on. "And a bargain. But now it's gone. They go very quickly in the busy season. I give good terms. And why not? It's a virtue, one person to help another."

"So tell me. Did you happen to get another such cheap sewing machine this week?" Minnie asked.

"I did," he said. "I can give you very good terms if you're interested. I have it in back with a few other things."

"Well, as it happens we lost such a sewing machine," Nehama said. She leaned on the counter, her elbows on the oilcloth that covered it.

"Is that so?"

"Yes, our lodger took it off with him. On the first night of Passover. I'm sure you were at the *seder,* a pious man like you." She spit out *pious* as if it were a bit of worm. But Mr. Shmolnik did not get upset. He knew where he stood with God.

"Let me tell you, it was some surprise when my youngest opened the door for Elijah the prophet and there stood a man with a sewing machine. I told him, It's Passover, I don't do business. But if he wanted to leave it inside the door, should I stop him? One sewing machine looks very much like another. Who can tell if it was yours?"

"The lodger, his name was Joe. He talked very slow, like he was dreaming. He had a striped bag, red and black."

"You know, I think that was the man. I paid for the sewing machine yesterday and he had a train to catch."

"So you'll give it back."

"Mrs. Katzellen, I paid for it. How can I give it back to you?"

"What business is it of yours to buy stolen merchandise? Are you a fence like that Mr. White down the street?"

"A fence—that's crazy, if you don't mind my saying. But a copper, I'm not either. Is it my business to ask questions about the merchandise? Fortune goes up, it goes down. People need money. So a man comes and sells me his sewing machine. It's black. It has a needle. Now you say it's yours. What should I think?"

"It's my livelihood you're stealing, Mr. Shmolnik. What does the Torah say about that?"

"Look. Just give me what I paid for it. That's all I'm asking you for. A profit I wouldn't make from you." He took some tobacco from one pocket and paper from the other and began rolling a cigarette.

"But it's ours, how can I buy our own sewing machine?"

"Look, Mrs. Katzellen. If it's charity you want, then say so. It's a great virtue to help the poor. You want *tzedakah*? Then hold out your hand. I'll give what I can. As the law says, you should never turn someone away, but God forbid you should make yourself into another beggar. You understand me?"

She waited for her strength to rise up, for the *yetzer-hara* to save her. But she could barely stand. If Minnie hadn't been holding her up, she'd have fallen. How could Nathan come home and find his workshop dismantled, the good sewing machine stolen like his other hand?

"Your bloody charity, I don't want. How much for the machine?" she asked. Yesterday she had a shop, at least it was nearly a shop, with the sign so vivid in her mind that she could measure it with a tailor's tape. Now she had nothing. Only a hidden stash of coins flying into Shmolnik's till. "Just don't say a word to anyone. God forbid Nathan should hear about it."

"Then let me go to the back and check what I paid." Mr. Shmolnik told one of his men to take the next customer, a woman in a battered hat, holding a clock and a braid of hair.

Nehama stood to one side with Minnie and waited. The door blew open and closed, the rain came in, the floor was tracked with mud, the women brought their tattered treasures and left with the rent money in pocket. Nehama sang under her breath, "The wind, the wind, the raging wind . . ."

She knew the story of the song because her sisters had told her about it. When Grandma Nehama traveled by boat to get married, she was accompanied by her aunt, who frightened her from Warsaw to Plotsk. You see that girl. A lovely complexion, am I right? Consumptive. Pale skin, red cheeks. She'll be dead in six months. Why aren't you eating, where does it hurt? Your stomach. Aah, well. I knew a woman in Warsaw, she had a stomachache just like that and in a week her belly stuck out like a balloon. People thought she was pregnant and she wasn't married, her family was mortified. She had cancer. The ulcers, how they stank. In a year she was dead. And so it went on through all the diseases and disasters known to humankind. The boat rocked and she said that a storm was coming just like the one she'd heard about last spring that drowned everyone on board. A middle-aged couple were heard arguing and she said that her neighbors had argued just like that and in the middle of the night the husband ran away, deserting the wife and leaving her an *aguna,* neither married nor unmarried, and she killed herself. The other passengers nodded knowingly, adding their own two *kopecks.* So you're going to get married? *Mazel-tov.* Never met the groom, of course it could be all right. I remember hearing . . . You can be sure it was nothing good they heard. Grandma Nehama became so nervous she thought she would faint, until she was befriended by a *badhan,* a wedding jester going to visit his brother. As the aunt started going on about another tragedy, he broke into song. It was a sad song, the kind that makes the mother of the bride cry, about the wind and the streets and the gloomy shadows. But whenever Grandma Nehama glanced at him while he was singing, he made such faces that she laughed, and the other passengers shook their heads. She said to the *badhan,* Stop making me laugh. People think I'm crazy. He answered, Is that right? Well, you shouldn't be surprised. That's how people are. They look at an elephant's foot and they think it's a tree trunk. Only God in heaven sees everything. Don't forget what I'm telling you today. So after the wedding when she held the sad baby, her stepdaughter, she sang this song to remind herself of what the wedding jester had told her. While she sang, her breasts began to give milk and the baby came to know that she had a mother again.

Nehama had never been able to nurse her baby. She'd forgotten about it after Gittel was weaned, but now she realized that it was a sign.

The end of the story was coming. If she had no life to offer her daughter, she'd lose her to the street.

The Jews' Free School

From the school to Dorset Street was just a five-minute walk, but it could have been over the sea. Here was the world of shops and synagogues and the rooms of tailors in the Lane, and there the doss-houses where criminals slept after their jobs were done. The two kinds of streets were right next to each other, like the world of the living and the world of the dead, but you couldn't cross over from one to the other. It was unthinkable.

The girls marched to their classroom from their entrance in Frying Pan Alley, fifteen hundred of them. On the other side, the Bell Lane side, two thousand boys filed in, stamping with the new boots handed out by the Jews' Free School at Passover. When the first bell rang, the girls put on their white pinafores, the boys their blue smock shirts. The sound of "God Save the Queen" rose above the squeal of chickens in the slaughterhouse on Bell Lane.

It was the largest elementary school in Britain, and the headmaster for nearly sixty years was Mr. Moses Angel, whose single aim was to remake his students in a respectable image. Even the queen's minister of education sought his advice. He was no relation to Miss Miriam Angel, the girl who'd been murdered the year that Gittel was born, though he came from the East End, too. Everyone knew that his father was Mr. Angel of Vinegar Yard, now long deceased, who in his day had been known as Money Moses. This Mr. Angel was transported to Tasmania for fencing stolen gold while the future headmaster was left behind and raised by someone else. Never once in his years at the school had Mr. Angel flogged a child. His students were more afraid of him than if he did.

Mr. Angel was eighty years old now, but he still checked every clock in the school and visited each classroom in turn. "Good morning, Miss Lipshitz," he said to Gittel's teacher. In the dim light he looked as if he'd live forever.

Miss Lipshitz was red with awe as she faced the headmaster. "Good morning, sir. What do you say, children?"

The girls rose and stood beside their desks again. "Good morning, Mr. Angel," they said.

Leaning on his cane, he mounted the platform at the front of the class and turned to face them. "What have your girls been learning?" he asked.

Miss Lipshitz wore her hair in a knot at the back of her head; perched on top was a navy blue bow that matched the blue of her skirt. Miss Lipshitz was seventeen, and Gittel wanted to be just like her. "We've been doing verses, Mr. Angel," she said.

"Good. I should like to hear something."

"Verse thirteen," Miss Lipshitz said. "Remember your *h*'s, girls."

Folding hands over their midriffs, the girls began to recite as if they were jumping rope, some dashing on to the second line while others like Gittel were still doddling on the first, gazing at the bust of Wordsworth on Miss Lipshitz's desk:

> I wandered lonely as a cloud
> That floats on high o'er vales and hills,
> When all at once I saw a crowd,
> A host, of golden daffodils;
> Beside the lake, beneath the trees,
> Fluttering and dancing in the breeze . . .

Of course it made no sense at all. Clouds weren't lonely. How could they be when they always gathered in gray masses, following as closely as the cows climbing down the steps of Old Montague Street? And a crowd of daffodils? You had only to use your eyes to see they came singly in pots or gathered in paper by flower sellers in Piccadilly. Papa said that Wordsworth would never have succeeded in the Yiddish theater.

That was his low taste. Miss Lipshitz said that music halls and theaters in the East End were low, especially ones in Yiddish. Theaters in the West End were not low, they had plays by Shakespeare. The best students from every class were going to see *Hamlet*. Gittel's deskmate, Clara, was one of the chosen. Gittel was not.

"Well done," Mr. Angel said.

Their teacher beamed as Mr. Angel seated himself at her desk, putting his cane across it. On the wall behind him was the blackboard and to either side of it a portrait of the queen at her coronation, a portrait of Baron de Rothschild, the school's benefactor, and a map of the world, largely colored pink to indicate the Empire. "I want to tell you girls a little story," Mr. Angel said, lifting his voice above the one-man band banging cymbals in the alley. "Just yesterday a boy was brought to me for discipline because he threatened his teacher with a knife. That is a vulgar thing to do and most un-English. I will not have my students become hoodlums in Dorset Street."

Gittel's first mother would be as nicely spoken as Miss Lipshitz. Gittel tried to correct her own pronunciation so that on the day she met the other mother—who would be a teacher, if not a baroness—Gittel wouldn't put her to shame.

"I expect you girls to lead your elders to English ways of feeling. You must begin right and go on as you begin. Speak well, and that means you must not speak the Jargon, you know I mean Yiddish, not even with your parents. Poland came with them to London. It's here on the streets." Mr. Angel waved at the flies that came through the windows from the barrels of smoked fish outside. "And it will defile you if you allow it."

Did her other mother's street smell like fish? Gittel wondered. Or would she be disgusted?

"Your teachers make every effort to wipe away all evidence of foreign proclivities, but you must all help them," he said. "Only by being English in thought and deed can you defeat anti-Semitism. Remember that all Jews are judged by your behavior, not only those of Whitechapel."

Maybe her other mother wasn't Jewish at all. Libby said she was, but how could she be sure?

"Love and honor the flag." Mr. Angel turned toward the map behind the teacher's desk, tapping it with a pointer. "Then you shall take a deserving part in this great Empire."

Gittel gazed at the Union Jack drooping in the corner. Yes, her other mother was English, and she'd be disgusted by Gittel and her low taste. She ought to stop speaking Yiddish altogether, as the headmaster said. But then she wouldn't be able to go with her father to the theater. Ever since he'd woken up crippled, he'd stopped telling jokes. Gittel was sure that if she'd only take him to a play in the Pavilion, he would feel like himself again. And when he started telling jokes in Yiddish, what was she supposed to do? She had to laugh. Otherwise he might suspect that she didn't think he was the same anymore.

Mr. Angel was aiming the pointer at her. "And what is your name, child?" he asked.

Gittel could see that Miss Lipshitz was dismayed. She'd have called on Clara, who often had her name written on the blackboard at the end of the week under the caption "Best Pupil."

"Answer the headmaster," Miss Lipshitz said.

Gittel rose from her chair, hands behind her back. "Gittel Katzellen, sir," she said.

"And what progress has Gittel made?" he asked Miss Lipshitz.

Gittel couldn't bear to meet Miss Lipshitz's eyes. "A quiet girl. Modest."

"Good, good," Mr. Angel said. "And?"

"And, well." The teacher paused. There wasn't much else to say. "A lovely voice, Gittel has. Would you sing something for Mr. Angel?"

She didn't like to sing in public. Her throat tightened when people looked at her. "I'm don't think I . . ." Her voice was barely audible.

"You know 'Rule Britannia.' Now one, two, three . . ." Miss Lipshitz counted while the headmaster waited. Gittel loved her teacher, even if it was unrequited, and for love a person can do anything. Poets said so, and they had busts made of them.

Gittel closed her eyes, then opened them, focusing on the bust of Wordsworth as she began to sing, squeaking along as she imagined that she was the baroness. Clara would know it. They often played that Clara was Lady Montagu and Gittel was Baroness Rothschild. But today Gittel was imagining that she was her other mother and the name was an English name: Baroness Englander. Yes.

Outside hawkers were calling: Fish fresh for *Shobbos*! Jackets like new! Chairs to repair!

Whitechapel Road

In the hospital ward, a nurse stripped Nathan's bed and carried away the linen while he got ready to go. A sack with his nightclothes was on the bedside table, written instructions from the doctor, the morphine and syringes. Nehama held out the new jacket. She'd got it in the Lane, a navy blue jacket with double brass buttons and one of the sleeves sewed up at the end.

"What's this?" he asked as he awkwardly pushed his right arm into the sleeve. His neck was stringy like an old horse's, and his hair, though still black, was thinner on top. It made his forehead high, and before the accident he'd have said, Thank God, now someone might mistake me for an intelligent man.

"I sewed it up to make it more comfortable for you," Nehama said. His eyes were the same dark brown, almost the color of charcoal.

"You think my hand is going to fall out the end?" He smiled at the joke, his new bitter smile, his voice low and sharp. His voice was new, and so was his walk, a shuffle and a hobble instead of the old light step, his eyes wandering restlessly, avoiding Nehama's gaze as she picked up the sack.

"We shouldn't lose the rest of the busy season," she said as they left the hospital. "I could be best. Really, it was always a waste for me to do the plain sewing. Minnie can do it now. I know what you're thinking—she has more thumbs than fingers—but if it doesn't work out, then she can go back to being the general hand."

"And what will I do?" Nathan asked.

"You'll get better. Let's take the streetcar. You'll be too tired to walk after lying in bed for so long."

"I'm as good as I'm going to be, Nehameleh. Which is to say, not much."

Around them the throng pushed and shifted, the boot makers, the drunks, the match girls scarred by phosphorus, the whores and the boys selling lemons, the beggars, the gentlemen on their way to warehouses, the wives buying bread and the mothers drinking gin. The horn and trombone band marched beside the roar of horses and wheels, the streetcars striped green and red or blue and orange. There was no fog today. The sky was clear and cool. So why was she sweating while the bell foundry tolled its bells?

"You can help Gittel with her homework," Nehama said as they stepped up into the streetcar. "God only knows that she needs someone to watch her. Her report wasn't so good. I want her to be a pupil-teacher, Nathan. That's a life for someone. She has a head on her shoulders, but she won't use it right unless someones makes her do it. Believe me, I know how it is. I was just the same."

Nathan was looking out the window, his eyes raised not to the hills from where God's help would come, according to some, but to the chimneys and the factory smoke thickening across the sky. "If I died, at least you'd have a payout from the Friendly Society."

"Don't talk like that," Nehama said.

"I'm only telling you the truth." Nathan's hand rested on his knee, trembling as he jiggled his leg up and down. "When is it time for another shot? The medicine is wearing off."

It had been his light step that kept her safe. It had been his eyes on her thigh, making something beautiful of a scar. Now the moon was rising, cutting into the darkness that was enveloping her, a dark scythe cutting the dark sky. And she herself was the moon.

CHAPTER 6

Today as Then

1899

Charlotte Street

It was the end of the fin de siècle, the last year of the yellow decade. People said that not to be new in these days was to be nothing. Shops for women had sprung up, and in them electric lights beamed. There were bicycles with pneumatic tires that women could ride on their own, even miles into the countryside, where rest houses catered to them. There was *The Yellow Book* with its new fiction of slums and syphilis and women who had affairs and some who had babies without the benefit of marriage. Everyone spoke of bourgeois decadence, intellectual bankruptcy, and the abyss of freedom. Despair was fashionable; so were ghost stories and detective fiction, but a living had to be made just as in the days of old, and Jacob Zalkind's books sold well. Emilia often shopped at Liberty's. When she wasn't shopping, cooking, at the ladies' club, or doing good works, she made paper-cuts. They hung in her friends' homes; a few of them had even been sold. The ghost of the first wife was just a childhood memory, and Emilia didn't think of her, not even when the garden was planted behind the house.

She was dressing for the theater in an off-the-shoulder gown cut low enough to distract the eye from her waist. She wasn't sure when to tell Jacob her news. Harriet Abraham said that the best time was before dinner so one wouldn't eat with a knotted stomach. But Emilia's father had thrown the soup, so the story went.

Jacob was concentrating on his tie, his head above Emilia's in the small mirror they shared. "Mr. Edwards wants me to rewrite the new book. He says it doesn't come alive. Well, it's just words, isn't it? He gives me an advance of five shillings a page, and if there's three hundred words on a page, that comes to a fifth of a penny per word. I don't think he ought to expect me to create living beings at that rate."

"You're not God." Emilia gathered her hair and twisted it at the nape of her neck, but she couldn't hold the pins. They kept dropping, pins all over the dressing table, around the jewelry case, and on top of the silver hairbrush. Outside their window the organ-grinder was playing "Ta-Ra-Ra-Boom-De-Ay."

"How can I concentrate on my work with that?" Jacob asked. Oh, all he cared about was his book and here her pins were driving her mad. She could just cry. "The noise is worse upstairs," he said. Now that Albert was in Harley Street, Jacob had his study on the third floor.

There. Emilia dropped her hair. Let it hang loose. "We could put you somewhere else, I suppose."

"And do what with my study?" Jacob asked.

"It could be a nursery. What do you think of that?" Her earrings wouldn't go into the holes in her ears. The posts were suddenly too thick. Oh, she had to tell him or she'd never finish dressing. "I'm going to have a baby."

He pulled a chair next to hers and sat down heavily. "Dear God in heaven. Really?" At least there was no soup to throw. "I didn't think we ever would. It was all right, you understand me, Emilia. But now . . . This changes everything." He took her hands in his. "How are you feeling?"

"Well enough." A little faintness didn't signify.

His face was serious, more serious than at any friend's where he argued about politics or even at dinner with his mother when he argued about religion. "Do you think—will it be a girl or a boy?"

"Harriet says a boy. She hung a needle from a thread and dangled it over me."

Jacob stood up again, looking into the mirror. "If it's a boy, there's a bit of a thing, you see." He pulled on the tie. There was ink on his fingers. He was particular about his clothes but never minded the ink.

"What thing?" Emilia gazed at her part of the mirror as if there were nothing more engrossing than her earrings. Everything was golden, Jacob's short beard, her hair, the earrings.

"A father expects his son to look like him. Of course we are English, we are all English now." He glanced down at her and away. "My son will be English. But, well. It's like this, Emilia. Do you know what a *bris* is?"

"Is it another sort of brisket, Jacob? Or a calf's-foot jelly?"

"No. It's not anything to do with food," he said as if he hadn't heard the sarcasm in her voice.

"Oh, I see. A custom then."

"Yes. Well. You know I don't look exactly the same as other Englishmen. That are not Jewish, I mean. For example, I wouldn't look like your father did. Gentile men are different. Of course you wouldn't ever have seen . . . Well, I—in certain parts. It's the covenant . . ."

"Yes, Jacob?"

"A man's private . . . Never mind. My mother will tell you everything."

"Jacob." She shook her head. "You must be very nervous to forget. I've been to a *bris* before. Indeed, with you standing beside me looking rather pale." All men paled when the baby's tiny foreskin was removed. The girls looked on curiously. The mother of the baby cried in the next room. "Why think of it now? Wait till there's a baby."

He didn't smile. His tie was dangling on either side of his high collar, his hands in his pockets searching out something to occupy them. "It is absolutely necessary if I have a son."

"All right, Jacob." She stared into the mirror, meeting only her own eyes. If she looked at him, he might see too much.

"Thank you, Emilia. You are a jewel among wives. Then I shall ask Mother to send a letter of introduction to the rabbi."

"What are you talking about?" She picked up her gloves and her fan.

"You'll have to convert, naturally."

"Convert to what?" Her cloak was draped over a stool. It had a high ruffled collar, copied from the cover of *La Nouvelle Mode*.

"Judaism. I'm sure it's not terribly hard for a woman. You wouldn't have to pray or anything."

"Jacob! I'm not doing anything of the sort. Whatever can you be on about?"

"But my son can't have a *bris* unless you are Jewish. It goes through the mother's line. If you aren't Jewish, then he isn't."

"Your feelings for me have changed." That was a man for you. He'd been happy enough with her as a gentile.

"No, Emilia. Don't say that. I love you more than ever. But my son . . ."

"And this is my child. Don't you ever forget it's mine." Now she was expected to turn around and become a Jew again.

"Then I'll ask you," he said, taking her hands. "If you love me, then love my son for being like me."

"I'm not saying no, Jacob. But to come out with this after all these years . . ." And just being a Jew wasn't good enough either—her husband wanted a converted Jew, a gentile made kosher, a bit of bacon with ritual water sprinkled on it.

"No woman could be as sympathetic to her husband as you, Emilia." He kissed her, and his kisses, at least, hadn't changed at all, so she opened her mouth softly for another.

There was a story her mother used to tell about Samson and Delilah. Remember, she'd say: Delilah tried to find out the secret of his strength many times. First, she asked him how he could be tied up and made helpless. He replied that if he was bound with seven fresh tendons, he would be as weak as an ordinary man. So she tied him up and called out, "Samson, the Philistines are upon you!" Then the Philistines rushed out from her room, where they were hiding, and Samson pulled the tendons apart. After that Delilah accused him of lying to her, so he said that if he was bound with new ropes he'd be as weak as anyone. At the next opportunity, she tied him up with new ropes and called out, "Samson, the Philistines are upon you!" The Philistines rushed out from her room, where they were hiding, and Samson tore off the ropes like thread. She accused him of lying again and begged for his secret. This time, the third time, he told her that he could be tied up if his hair was woven into a loom and pegged there. He was getting closer to the truth, but when she called out, "Samson, the Philistines are upon you!" he was as strong as ever. Yet she didn't give up. Every day she asked him about the secret of his strength until his soul was ready for death and he admitted that if his hair was cut, his strength would leave him and he would be like an ordinary man.

Do you realize, Emilia's mother used to ask, that Samson was awake when he was tied up the first three times? Why did he let her do it? And then he went to sleep just like that after telling his secret. You have to wonder whether he just wished to give up his burden. A man with such strength has a cannon on his back and when he's piqued, he brings the house down on top of himself. After Samson is captured, there's no more mention of Delilah. But if you ask me, the money she received from the Philistines allowed her to buy a little house with a vineyard and settle down quietly far from the cannons.

Petticoat Lane

The new year began with the ram's horn announcing the Jewish year of 5650. It was early September, the weather mild as the busy season approached for everyone but Nathan. After the accident, he'd tried to use the sewing machine with his left hand and not only botched the jacket but nearly injured his hand. He frightened himself as much as Nehama, and never tried it again. Often he forgot what he was saying in the middle of a sentence. He didn't play cards, and he wouldn't go to the theater. Sometimes he slept for days; sometimes he couldn't sleep and lay on his back all night, moaning from the pain of his missing hand. The only jokes he told were so bitter that no one laughed. When his sick benefits from the Friendly Society were used up, Nehama was able to get some sewing here and there, but she had to sell the gold chain, and the stash of coins under her bed was slowly shrinking to make up rent. One day there would be nothing, and what then? So as the ram's horn sounded the new year, she decided that something had to change. While neighbor was asking forgiveness of neighbor, she made Nathan as presentable as she could and dragged him to the office of the Jewish Board of Guardians.

She waited with other newcomers sitting on the benches, reading the racing pages and eating apples. Babies cried, mothers nursed as they discussed *The Slaughterer,* the new play in the Yiddish theater. It was about a girl forced into marrying a rich man who made her live in the same house as his mistress and her two children. The script was supposedly adapted from a Yiddish play written in New York, but that couldn't be true. They all knew who was meant by the slaughterer, and Mr. Berman was threatening to sue. Nathan leaned against the wall, too restless to sit. He wore the dark blue jacket with the sewed-up sleeve. Double-breasted it was, with brass buttons. His beard was neat; Nehama had trimmed it herself that morning. Then she'd rolled his cigarettes and put them in his pocket.

"Mr. Katzellen," the secretary called.

Nehama took Nathan's arm and walked him to the interview chairs. He sat down like an old man, his back curved, his mouth slack as if he'd had a stroke, not lost a hand. Where was he, her Nathan? That was what she wanted to know. This person beside her was someone else, an embarrassment. "Good morning, sir," she said to Mr. Zalkind, sitting behind his shining desk piled with overflowing files. His secretary was pouring tea from the Wedgwood teapot. Through the window she could see the warehouse that had been going up before Nathan's accident last year. Trucks stood in front of it, men with rolled-up sleeves unloading the goods. All the best things in the world came from the river and were stored in the East End until they could be transported to places that deserved them.

"Both Mr. and Mrs. Katzellen. To what do I owe this honor?" Mr. Zalkind smiled under his gray mustache.

"*Sholom aleichem,*" Nathan said vaguely. His eyes wandered to the portrait of the queen on the wall behind Mr. Zalkind's desk, then to the window, with its view of secondhand stalls and trucks.

"We come about a loan, sir." Nehama ignored her husband as she unfolded the paper on which she'd written the figures.

"What is the purpose of the loan?" Mr. Zalkind asked, looking not at her but at Nathan, who was taking out a cigarette and lighting the match with one hand.

"Excuse me, Mr. Zalkind," she said. He turned his attention to her. She'd copied the figures so carefully onto a sheet of new paper. "You see it all laid out here. We're to have a shop. Here's how much is wanted for stock, how much for rent. This is what we has, and here's the loan we want."

Mr. Zalkind nodded. "Yes, it's all quite clear." But even so, he wouldn't speak to her, who knew what was what, turning again to Nathan. "Mr. Katzellen, do you have any experience in shopkeeping?"

"A shop? I'm a tailor," he said. "What do I know from shopkeeping? My hand hurts and I need medicine."

"I see. Were you crippled in an accident? Yes, well, it happens too often, I'm afraid." Mr. Zalkind motioned to his secretary. "I can give you a ticket for the infirmary."

"Tickets we don't want," Nehama snapped. "Only a loan and a shop." She jabbed the paper with her finger.

"I'm sorry for your troubles, Mrs. Katzellen, but women are not eligible for capital loans." Mr. Zalkind's face was full of pity. She wanted to smack him, and Nathan even harder. He was getting up to go as if this was all finished.

"Listen to me, Mr. Zalkind. The shop's for my husband that he might work. A man that works knows he's alive." Her heart didn't beat this way when she came here on behalf of her neighbors. "My husband will sign the loan. Won't you, Nathan?"

He shrugged and nodded. "Why not? With my left hand I can make an X. You have something that wants an X, sir? I'll make you a row of X's."

"It isn't necessary," Mr. Zalkind said. "If you wish, I can give you a month's receipt for medication."

"Tell him, Nathan." She turned to her husband. "Do you need two hands to keep a shop? Only a pleasant manner so people like to come in. Who else tells a joke like you, Nathan?"

"You want a joke?" he asked, his eyes empty, his voice flat as he put out his cigarette and took another from his pocket. "I'm a tailor with one hand. Did you ever hear such a good joke, sir?"

"Perhaps I could find your wife a situation," Mr. Zalkind offered kindly enough. Oh yes, his kindness would stand him in good stead in the next world, but in this one it gave her nothing. "In a nursery looking after children. I will vouch for her myself."

"Living in the lady's house, am I right?" Nehama asked. "Then what's to be done with my own child? And my husband, who can't roll a cigarette?" Her voice quivered with the effort of keeping it down so the whole room shouldn't hear her pleading.

"There's an asylum for orphans and there is an asylum for the infirm," Mr. Zalkind said. "One should apply to charity when it's warranted."

Everyone was looking at her. Oh yes, there was a charity for everything. But even the deserving poor were not so deserving as to warrant having their own business kept to themselves. Nathan's face was red as he stuffed his unlit cigarette back into his pocket.

"Thank you, sir," she said. "I'll die before I see my husband and my child put away." Outside in front of the warehouse, a crate burst, and hats were blowing down the street, rolled felt hats in the new styles, trilby hats, homburgs, even fedoras. The foreman was shouting orders, but the hats blew away and his men chased them with no result except their own appearance of foolishness.

Mortimer Street

When the founders of the first ladies' club lobbied municipal authorities for public lavatories, the authorities had been implacable. What did they care that a woman who shopped all day had no relief until she returned home? So the ladies had built their own resting place, and now there were clubs for every sort of woman: the Writers' Club (editors allowed by invitation only), the Pioneer Club (where women wore tailcoats), the Empress Club (decorated with the Union Jack), the Women's University Club, the Tea and Shopping Club, the Ladies' County, the Ladies' Army, and the Ladies' International Club (opened by the sister of Miss Cohen the poetess after she made a fortune in Kettledrum Tea Rooms).

If Emilia left her in-laws' house and walked down their street past the square where Lord Byron was born, she came right to the Muse Club, a three-story mansion decorated with murals painted by members. Like the other clubs, the Muse was in the vicinity of the best shops and theaters. It had a dining room, tearooms, reading rooms, a lecture room, and bedrooms for suburban ladies with business in the city. It was an old club, founded in 1872 by the wives of artists who uneasily agreed that if women must have lunch then it was, at least, in a club dedicated to their muse. Men were allowed to dinner on Thursday evenings only.

The reading room was decorated with draped silks and a fretwork arch hired from Liberty's. The arch was set over a table, framing the mural of Urania the Heavenly, muse of astronomy, her head surrounded by stars, a celestial globe in her hand. She wore a flowing blue robe that might have come straight from Liberty's if the ancients had been fortunate enough to have the shopping conveniences of London.

"What I would give to have a whole day to shop," Harriet was saying. She and Emilia sat at a round walnut table piled with art pieces made or collected by members of the club for a charity auction. Emilia had donated a paper-cut. "I do admit. It's the one thing I miss by not having a wet nurse. I can't be away from home for more than a few hours." Harriet was as plump and unselfconscious as ever.

"I'm going to wear the new gown to the auction." Emilia's parcels had been sent over from Liberty's. "Wait till you see it, Harriet. The gown is burnt umber; it has no waist and falls from the shoulders. There's a robe over it with velvet trim. I won't wear a corset with it."

"Nor should you. A Liberty's dress is never worn with a corset; it's just too bourgeois." Harriet's waist had passed into oblivion with her third pregnancy. "What shall I do with this?" She picked up a lacquered ashtray.

"It looks perfectly fine. Just wrap it."

"But it's so common."

"Oh, then pair it with that thing." Emilia pointed to an unidentifiable objet d'art. "I want some tea." Each reading room had a console wired to bells in the scullery. Emilia pressed the button; two rings meant tea. Three meant scones with it.

"How is Jacob taking your news?" Harriet asked after the maid wheeled in the tea trolley.

"He's very happy." Emilia cut a length of ribbon. "Look at this! Another nail broken. My fingers are so ugly." She spread out her hands. "I shall have to wear gloves with my gown and I have none to suit. White gloves won't do, Harriet. They won't do at all."

"It's all right. I've got yellow gloves. I have to go home to nurse the baby and I'll bring the gloves back with me before you're finished dressing. Don't cry."

"I'm not." Emilia blew her nose into the handkerchief Harriet gave her. "Jacob doesn't want a gentile wife anymore."

"He what?" Harriet paused.

"I mean he wishes me to convert." Emilia tied the ribbon around a framed photograph.

"Oh, I see." Harriet put cream and sugar in her tea, stirring with a silver spoon. "Is it difficult?"

"Not according to Jacob. But I don't wish to do it." Emilia took up the photograph.

"Why not? It's just a ceremony."

"Just! I won't be myself anymore." The picture was in soft focus, a mother in a loose white robe, looking back at her daughter. The mother's face was slightly blurred.

"So? You'll be more like me. Except that you keep kosher. Thank goodness no one is making me talk to a rabbi. I'm sure that I should fail miserably. But not you, Emilia. You're *di gitteh yokhelta*."

"Don't tease. I won't have it." The girl in the photograph was playing the piano, her hands above the keys. "I've been dreaming about the baby."

"Of course you have. And I assure you that it will have all its fingers and toes and none extra." Harriet smiled. "I had those dreams through every one of my pregnancies."

"It isn't that sort of dream," Emilia said. "I'm nursing. Upstairs in the synagogue."

"And?"

"People are pointing at me."

"Oh, I have just that sort of dream, too. Only I'm not even sitting in the ladies' gallery but down among the men. That's the sort of dream you'll have after the conversion." She laughed.

Harriet had many dreams that she just had to tell Emilia, each one stranger than the one before it. So there was no need for Emilia to say anything more about herself. Certainly not that the dream wasn't about this baby. It was the other one. And while she was nursing it, she was looking down in horror, saying, But this can't be my baby. This is a Jewish child and I am a gentile. Her mother was sitting beside her in the ladies' gallery. She was old.

"There. We're all done and the table is lovely," Harriet said. "I'd better go back and nurse the baby if I'm to be here in time for the auction. Are you staying?"

"I might as well. Go on. I'll finish my tea," Emilia said.

The reading room was quiet; a sign on the door said, "No admittance until 5:00." There was only the sound of the piano from the next room, the murmur of voices, the occasional laugh. It had been a long time since Emilia had touched the piano in the parlor at home. Their Bloomsbury friends liked to talk and talk, and there was no call for music, thank God, though Emilia could do it as well as her mother.

When guests came, her mother always used to play the piano. It was expected. The top of the piano was draped with a fringed scarf, and on it there were silver candlesticks on either side of a vase of flowers. The candlesticks were ornate and heavy and would make good weapons if someone needed one, more effective, Emilia thought, than charm, but it would be better still to sell them and use the money to pay for a fast horse. A gas lamp hung above the piano, but her mother would light the tall candles anyway, then seat herself gracefully, her skirt spread out over the piano bench. She always began by singing Psalm 137.

Father would say, What a voice, my wife has missed her profession. She ought to have been in the opera. Emilia always wondered why it didn't make her mother stop. He would stand by her while she played, leaning on the piano, disdain crawling down. Her mother's hands would stumble, but she'd carry on. Even after she developed pain in her hands so that she couldn't do the paper-cutting anymore, she still managed to play the accompaniment for this one song.

The first wife did not like to play the piano. She didn't do it well, at least so Father said, and no doubt after a few years in his house this was entirely true. But he expected her to play when they had guests; it was a wife's duty, and she bore him no daughters to be the mistress of the house and take care of him in old age. All she gave him were sons, and sons had to be educated and set up in business; they were a constant worry. She was a disappointment to him from the day of their wedding canopy, a squirrel not a wife, scurrying out into the garden. He hated the garden. What business did she have there?

The first Mrs. Rosenberg used to stand in the garden when it rained. She'd stand under the tree as if begging for lightning to cut them both down. Finally she'd caught her death there. She got drenched and died of pneumonia. Among her things was a book of psalms, a ribbon marking the place of her favorite one. Emilia's mother had kept it, and she used to sing Psalm 137, looking up at her husband with an odd little smile as she seated herself gracefully, spreading her skirts over the piano bench.

In the reading room of the Muse Club in Mortimer Street, Emilia's hands went to her belly without her knowing it. She was singing so softly that someone watching would have thought she was talking to herself:

By the rivers of Babylon, there we sat down,
Yes, and there we wept when we remembered Zion. . . .
Our captors required of us a song
Our tormentors asked us to amuse them saying,
Sing us one of the songs of Zion.
How shall we sing the Lord's song in a strange land?
If I forget thee, O Jerusalem, may my right hand wither.

Brick Lane

Mr. Berman stood by the entrance to his warehouse, watching the men unload cloth from a horse-drawn truck. In the same block of Brick Lane were a wig maker, a bookseller, a chemist, a glass cutter, an upholsterer, a woolens merchant, a matchmaker, a manufacturer of artificial teeth, and Schevzik's Russian Vapour Baths. The road was wide, and over it the sky hung like the green awning of a well-to-do shop.

Mr. Berman was known as a kind man who gave his illegitimate sons work. Nehama could see them inside the warehouse, packing boxes for shipping. His wife had to serve them tea in the afternoon because her husband was so kind. If her hand shook and she dropped a lump of sugar, did Mr. Berman slap her? Not on your life. He only stopped her from taking a bath. It wasn't his business that she smelled so high, the women in synagogue wouldn't sit near her. Sugar costs money, you know.

"C'gar lights, 'ere y'ar, sir; 'apenny a box." A man in a cap so large he seemed to have no eyes took a couple of farthings from Mr. Berman.

Nehama waited for him to light his cigar and take a slow puff. "Mr. Berman?" she reminded him.

"Sorry, missus. All I've got is trousers." No one ever said what became of Mr. Berman's illegitimate daughters.

"So let it be trousers."

"It isn't for you," Mr. Berman said. "I give trousers to *yokheltas*." That was the custom. Gentile women sewed trousers.

"Who are you to say what's for me?" Nehama asked.

He turned to the man struggling under a bolt of cheap wool. "If you drop that in the gutter, my boy," he said, "you'll pay through the nose for it."

"So do me a favor," Nehama said. "For Nathan's sake. He always placed his bets with your brother." She stepped aside for the man now balancing the bolt of wool on his head. A cart rocked on the uneven cobblestones, a bale of newspapers fell off the back. The man winced as it struck his shin.

"Then let me tell you what's what." Mr. Berman took a knife from his pocket and began to trim his nails, round and pink, each of his strong fingers scrubbed clean with a brush. "It's umbrellas you should make. Don't pay much, but that's what Jewish widows do."

"I'm not a widow," she said.

"As good as one," he answered, pressing her hand as if he could touch her for free because he was used to dealing with people that needed something from him.

"We're starting up the workshop again," she said.

"You didn't sell Nathan's machines?" He tipped back his hat. Underneath, he was bald and freckled.

"We can take up orders the same as we did."

"So, so. . . . Why don't you go to Nathan's wholesaler? Your husband never did the slop I make."

She'd gone to Nathan's wholesaler last year. It hadn't occurred to her that he wouldn't deal with her. Another woman, maybe, but her? It was crazy. She had two sewing machines and she was as good as, no, better than some self-proclaimed tailor who'd been a rabbi in the *heim*. She'd learned to sew from the time she could walk. Cloth jumped from her fingers into the shape of a sleeve, a collar, a back, a lapel just by her looking at it. But the wholesaler wasn't impressed. A woman was a plain sewer, a man a best, he said. Nathan, he should only live to be a hundred and twenty, was crippled, it shouldn't happen to a dog. Thank God the Jewish Board of Guardians ran a soup kitchen, he said. Nehama had thanked the wholesaler for his generosity and assured him that if he had any worry about his place in the world to come, he need not, for surely there was a special hell reserved for him.

"He didn't offer me a good rate," she said. He wouldn't even look at what she'd brought to show him as samples of her work. A woman her age could pick up dog dung, "pure," as they called it, collected to sell for tanning skins. That was what he advised her. She was too old to go on the game even to save her family. Only *dreck* and Berman—those were her choices.

"Well, then. We'll see what I can do for you. Come inside," he said.

Mr. Berman emptied his pockets, lining up the contents on a stack of cloth. First a bottle of milk. Then a long knife. A couple of nicely rolled fags. A packet of tobacco. A gold coin. A sheet of paper. "Dovidel!" he called to a boy with thin hair, cutting cloth on a large table at the other end of the warehouse. "That's to be finished, I don't care if you work all night." Mr. Berman pointed his knife at Nehama. "I can read you like a book, Mrs. Katzellen. I can read anyone. That's why I'm here and your husband is sitting at home. But never mind. I've got an order of coats for someone else. I'll let you take it." He sawed at the string around the tobacco. Though he nicked his finger, he took no notice. "A shilling a coat, I'll give you."

He usually paid half again as much. "Very good," she said.

"Any coats not to my satisfaction and I dock you."

She nodded. With her as best and Minnie as plain sewer, she'd make just enough to cover the week's rent. They would all eat as long as there was no sickness. As long as the wholesaler didn't withhold an order one week. As long as—there were any number of contingencies. She would go mad thinking of them. She might go mad not thinking of them.

She walked back along Brick Lane, following behind Berman's boy and his cart full of cut pieces of the cheapest and sloppiest jackets. She paid no attention to the match girls' factory, where girls with phossy jaw, their jawbones visible through decayed flesh, were coming out to get their gin as the whistle signaled the end of the day. She didn't feel the warm wind that made women roll up their sleeves and hike up their skirts while children ran down to the Tower to play along the river. She didn't see the sweatbaths and the sign that read, "Wednesday Evening for Ladies." Where she walked it was the color of fog and the only thing visible was her fear.

She was at the end of it. Why did God put human beings on the earth only to torture them with misery? Her husband barely moved from his bed, and she could provide nothing for her daughter, who in time would run away. How could it be otherwise when Gittel had two mothers, both of them the kind of person who runs away from an undesirable fate? Nehama could just imagine what lay in wait for her daughter, a wolf watching the girl who jumped rope, her face still and determined, the sudden smile with the gap, a grown-up eyetooth not yet descended. "Dear God in heaven, help me," she prayed. "I can't make a life for my daughter."

No one answered. That was to be expected. Does God speak to tailors? Maybe to a custom tailor in the West End, but not to a seamstress of slop in Brick Lane, walking through the dirt churned up by a cart. But a prayer didn't cost a penny, and what else could she do even after she'd given up praying so many years ago? Nehama walked in a fog, not hearing the wheels of a streetcar, the dog tearing skin from a piece of meat, the gulls wheeling above, the factory whistle. The street was silent, for she walked in a fog, and in that silence it was possible to hear the voice of her dreams.

Don't feel so sorry for yourself. A child with a living mother is blessed by God. Are you listening to me? I've had enough talking to the walls. I'm tired of it, let me tell you. You think it's so ay-ay-ay sitting around in this world? Don't you recognize me? I talked and I talked until I'm blue in the face. Believe me, even eternity can be a long time.

"Is that you, Grandmother?" Nehama whispered. "Then why are you here?" An answer could come in a dream, a way to save her husband and her daughter.

Look out for your daughter. That's what I came to say.

"That's it? For this I could stay awake." Nehama shook her head. "Maybe someone should take Gittel from me. I don't deserve her. I don't have what to give her. You remember the story of King Solomon. He knew the real mother, and to her went the baby. She wouldn't let anything happen to it."

My granddaughter. What makes you so sure that it was the woman who bore the living baby that spoke? The other one, she knew what it was to suffer. She held the stillborn child and cried till her eyes were raw. Wouldn't she be the first to say, "No. Better the baby should live"? You listen to me, Nehameleh. What was done can be undone.

"Then help me, Grandmother. I pray to you. Intercede for me with the Holy One above."

And Nehama believed that her grandmother would. Against all logic, she came into the house in Frying Pan Alley, thinking that even if she was now fully awake, in the front room she would find Nathan whole again.

When she saw him lying in bed, the wounded arm flung over his face, she cried out, "I have no grandmother. She's no relation to me at all."

And her step-grandmother wondered why God in heaven had chosen the darkest of her grandchildren, the most obstinate, the loneliest to hear her. Even in the next world, it's possible to have a broken heart.

Charlotte Street

The garden was nothing like the one in Minsk—the bushes were rhododendrons not roses, the tree was a plane tree and had no fruit, the wrought-iron fence was not a brick wall, and no ghosts walked in it, for in London vagrants were swept up by the police—but Emilia liked to work at the table by the window on the third floor, looking out on the garden. She stored her inks, brushes, stencils, and paper on shelves to her right, and there she also kept the German Bible from Zaydeh to study the illustrations for inspiration when she was tired of cutting.

"Emilia, I want your help with something." Jacob's desk was behind her in the shadows under the slanted ceiling, lit by a tall lamp with a glass shade.

"What is it?" She was working on a paper-cut of Samson and Delilah, painting the figures in the center of a delicate frame of flowers and trees.

"Pictures for my column. I have to choose one." He had a sheaf of photographs in his hand. His voice was excited, his eyes uncertain.

"Let me see." She had to smile at the sight of him in his shirt-sleeves, as if writing was too hot an exercise to keep his jacket on, small pieces of paper torn from his notebook stuck in his waistcoat pockets, ready to hand when he needed them, his golden beard freshly trimmed so she could glimpse his chin beneath as he scratched it. "What are you writing about?"

"The street where I was born. It's gone now, torn down with the clearances." Today there was more brown than green in his eyes. He looked at her with a question, but what it was she couldn't guess as he put the photograph on the table. "It was rather like this one." Emilia glanced at the bedraggled square with the beigel lady sitting on a crate, a tin pail of zinc embers on the ground warming her feet.

"Was it?" she asked. The picture wasn't any worse than something you'd see in the newspaper. But her husband's hand on it, his ink-stained hand, worried her. He'd taken off his spectacles and put them in his pocket. There was nothing between his eyes and hers.

"You see this school? That's where I went." He put down a picture of the Jews' Free School rising high on three sides, in the center six double rows of little girls stretching as far as the eye could see. She peered at the faces as if looking for something familiar.

"You had classes with the girls?"

"No, but I used to chase them through the girls' door in Frying Pan Alley. The old headmaster had me in his office more than a few times. He died last year, you know. I'm going to speak at the *yahrzeit* memorial." He pushed aside her paint palette, the brush, and the rag to make room for the rest of the pictures. Small boys exercised in knickers and clean collars, front legs bent, arms held out straight as if pushing away the wretched air. Girls in a cookery class, each with a mixing bowl. A smiling costermonger, his donkey baring his teeth, too. Nice pictures, oh, so very nice. But they did not belong in her house, on her table.

"Jacob! Look at what you're doing to my paper-cut." A drop of paint splashed onto Delilah, a bit of yellow in the eye like a sty. Emilia put it all away on a shelf. "How can you just come here and throw aside what I'm doing?"

"It's just a paper-cut. I'm talking to you about my work."

"Fine. We shall talk about it." Now there were just the photographs on her table, pictures of the East End taken with a large-format box camera, every detail clear. But only this child was hers, the one making the flutter like a brush of wings under her hand. "Your mother will be embarrassed by this. She won't like her friends to see it."

"My mother is always embarrassed by me. Thank God in heaven she has a physician for a son in Harley Street. Which of the photographs do you think I should use?"

"I'm not a publisher. What do I know?" She pushed the pictures away in a rough pile, making room for her brush and her palette again, noisily searching through the tray of scissors and knives for just the one to make an adjustment to her paper-cut.

Jacob was looking at her quizzically, like Samson suspecting that Delilah has an unhealthy interest in the secret of his strength. "When are you going to see the rabbi?"

"I've an appointment with him after Sukkoth," Emilia said, but she couldn't make herself smile. It was a frightening thing, the obstinacy of her mouth, as if she wasn't the *gitteh yokhelta* at all. Just because there was a burning in her chest and she was thinking that it was too early in her pregnancy to have heartburn, something she shouldn't know at all. Not when to expect the itchy nipples, the kicking, the pressing of a crown. "Why this sudden preoccupation with your history?" she asked. "You used to say it wasn't worth remembering."

"Now I think it is."

"Well, it's old. The Jewish question is old and tired." In the fin de siècle there was nothing worse than something old.

"Honesty is a great virtue, Emilia. I appreciate it." He returned to his desk. There he stood, bending a little under the slanted ceiling as he picked up his notebook and shoved it into a folder with the photographs. "I'll work at the *Gazette* office. You might think about calling in your dressmaker. That dress is too tight," he said. "You're getting fat." His steps were quick on the stairs, the same haste she used to hear on the steps of the shop in Regent Street.

Samson had a penchant for gentile girls. His parents asked him, Can't you find a girl among your own people that you have to go and take a wife from the uncircumcised Philistines? He said, I like the Philistine girl. Get her for me. This wasn't Delilah but his first wife. Her father's wedding guests threatened to set fire to her and her father's household if she didn't help them win a bet that Samson had put them up to. Later the Philistines set fire to her anyway after Samson, being angry about something, destroyed their grain, vineyards, and olive trees. Maybe when Delilah was offered a bribe to find out the secret of Samson's strength, she remembered the fate of the first wife and took matters into her own hands.

Frying Pan Alley

"Get my medicine," Nathan called out. He was lying on his back, eyes closed.

"You can't have it," Nehama said as she showed Berman's boy where to pile the pieces of cut cloth in the back room. He held out his hand for a penny and she gave it to him, or else the next order might be accidentally dropped in the mud. Then she took a dark bottle from the dresser and poured the contents out the window. If a man doesn't look at what his wife is doing, why should he have a choice in the matter?

"I want it now, Nehama. My hand is killing me."

"There isn't any. I just spilled it into the gutter."

She took Nathan's shirt off the hook and sat on a stool next to the table, attacking the stitches on the sewed-up sleeve. If she couldn't undo the accident, then at least she could rip out stitches and sew something else.

"Are you crazy? I need my medicine." The sun was struggling through the dusty window, making faint shadows on the wall.

"The doctor said you had all that's good for you. Get out of bed."

Nathan rolled over to face her. "I'm not well. I need sleep."

"You've had enough sleep to last the rest of your life. What about the newspaper? God alone knows how many horses have won since you looked at a racing page."

"What do I care?"

"I'm fixing your shirt. Next I'll do the jacket. It was a mistake sewing up the sleeve. You have an arm if not a hand there." She threw the shirt on the bed. "And with your legs, there's nothing wrong. Don't wave your stump at me. There's more stumps in the next world than I know what to do with already. Them as is Rothschilds may lie in bed. Get your bleeding arse up. The boy brought an order from Berman."

"I don't want slop here." He glanced back at the workshop, but from where he lay on the bed he couldn't see anything.

"So what about me? Rent has to be paid and I want your help."

"What are you talking—can I do something now?"

"You can read to me, Nathan." Her breath came quickly; this was a man she didn't know, swinging his legs over the side of the bed, but he was sitting up, and in his eyes she saw something of the old Nathan that she'd missed like her own heart.

"A book doesn't pay rent," he said.

"You read and I'll forget that I'm making slop for half what every-one else gets."

"You shouldn't speak to Berman. You know what he's like." He put the shirt on over his long underwear with the hole near the collarbone, leaving it open because he couldn't manage the buttons with one hand and she wasn't moving an inch to help.

"Next time you talk to him, then," Nehama said. "Come on."

He followed her into the back room, his voice angry. "Well, maybe I should."

"Maybes I don't want to hear. Do it or don't bang me on the head with complaints." She put the library book on the worktable in front of him. *Our Mutual Friend.*

"I don't read English so good," he said.

"Good enough for me." Before she put her foot to the treadle of the sewing machine, she stood for a minute next to the table, looking at Nathan. "It's too hot," she said, hiking up her skirt and rolling down her stockings ever so slowly. She did it to wake him up, though only God in heaven knew what kind of husband she had now. It was ridiculous, a middle-aged woman doing this, but she couldn't stop, her hands belonged to someone else, pushing down her stockings just so, for the good inclination is a harsher master than the wiliest *yetzer-hara,* and Nathan's gaze was alert.

"My old scar is fading," she said matter-of-factly, sitting beside him on the bench, her bare foot on the treadle of the sewing machine.

"I can still see it," he said, and whether it was the old Nathan that was speaking or the new Nathan, she wasn't sure.

"Start here." She pointed to the page where she'd left off on *Shobbos,* and he began reading in a halting voice.

"Has a dead man any use for money? Is it possible for a dead man to have money? What world does a dead man belong to? T'other world. What world does money belong to? This world." Nathan looked at her uncertainly.

"Go on," she said. Later she would hire Lazar for pressing and Minnie to do the plain sewing, but now there were just the two of them, herself and Nathan, her back to the pressing table, her eyes on her husband's as dark as charcoal. "Don't stop."

CHAPTER 7

Master of All

1899

Charlotte Street

A person might wish to live in Bloomsbury, Mrs. Zalkind said at every opportunity, though why someone might is a mystery one must accept, as God offers many mysteries in life and an ordinary person cannot comprehend them. Nonetheless, if a person wishes to live in Bloomsbury, then there are many good streets. She had made a list of them and inspected the houses. In fact, following her advice, Mr. Abraham, the renowned Jewish artist, had moved his family next to the house of a famous dead poetess. Well, not exactly beside it, for the street of the poetess had decayed as had all the streets where the literary luminaries of twenty-five years ago lived; one must keep abreast of change, and the Abrahams, on Mrs. Zalkind's advice, had found a house in the square next to the dead poetess. But Mrs. Zalkind's own children were deaf to her.

A woman in her fifties ought to be *shepping naches,* reaping pride from her descendants. But Mrs. Zalkind couldn't hold her head up in the ladies' gallery of the synagogue. Not when her firstborn son lived in a pink street! As secretary of the Society for the Protection of Hebrew Girls, she had a duty to study the color code of Booth's London Street Map. One must trouble oneself with the unfortunate, and there were many gradations of poverty: the dark blue streets of the starving poor, the light blue of the merely hungry poor, the pink of bricklayers and carpenters, even to the red of struggling shopkeepers, but there was only one color for the better classes. Yellow. One must live in a yellow street. Mrs. Zalkind's only consolation had been her son's proximity to the playwright Mr. Shaw, but he had left his home in Fitzroy Square last year.

Jacob's family came for dinner during Sukkoth, the festival of the autumn harvest. All over the East End, small huts were made of boards and roofed with green branches, open to the sky in memory of the dwellings that the Israelites put up and took down in their wanderings through the desert. The *sukkah* was decorated with fruit, paper chains, leaves, lanterns, and chestnuts, and there the Jews of the East End ate cake and drank schnapps. Weren't they commanded to rejoice? Each night they invited their ancestors into the *sukkah,* newcomers like themselves. Abraham. Joseph. Moses.

Special prayers were recited in the synagogue, and on the seventh day, Hoshana Rabbah, the grandmothers came. Living women were not permitted to stand among the men, but the dead came to add their prayers. A person's fate, sealed on the Day of Atonement, was yet subject to one last appeal on this day. Seven times the men circled the synagogue, shaking the branches and the fragrant *esrog,* the fruit of the tree of splendor. Save us, save us. They beat the ground with willows and when three stars were visible in the sky, the grandmothers looked up to the Court of Heaven. What was written was then sealed and the books closed.

On Hoshana Rabbah, while the heavens were still open, Jacob's family came for dinner. Zaydeh wore his holiday clothes, a satin caftan and fur hat, like a figure of ancient days, mortifying his English daughter and son-in-law. Holidays exist, however, so that mortification, insult, and loneliness may have their moment, and the house in Charlotte Street was ready with wine, meat, and cake.

"Come in, Zaydeh," Emilia said, ever the good *yokhelta*. He held a *lulav* and *esrog*.

"Would you take it to the kitchen?" he asked Emilia. "A *lulav* shouldn't dry out, God forbid. The steam from cooking will keep the branches moist." Emilia motioned to the maid, who took it from Zaydeh.

They were all standing about the parlor, furnished with everything that would be most fashionable in a year or so, the long and lean lamps casting deep shadows, the leaded window painted with oak leaves, a collection of cloudy glass bubbled and streaked as if it came from ancient Rome, the wallpaper with its overgrown thistles, the posters for this season at the Royal Adelphi, which happened to be a season of dramas like *The Drink* and *Two Little Vagabonds*.

It was fashionable, and that was all. But the autumnal light and the painting of the empty road overtook Mr. Zalkind, who hugged his son like a Jew on the holiday of rejoicing, forgetting that an Englishman ought to shake a hand or offer a cigarette. He quickly retired to the fireplace—there was still a fireplace and most fortunately a mantelpiece to lean one's elbow on—and he fumbled for his pipe. There he could stand back as usual, thinking of his business and the Board of Guardians and the sad people he saw every Sunday. He wore a lounge coat with slits in the side seams; it was the latest style. His mustache was not gray but silver.

Albert's young wife was a Spanish Jew, her family distinguished. "My dear sister," she said, taking Emilia's hands in hers. Judith was dressed modestly. Of course, if you knew clothes, you would immediately see that the gown was, in fact, very dear. "Your poor nails. I don't care what anyone says, a woman in a certain condition has nerves and ought to take care of them. Are you feeling quite well, Emilia?"

"Just a little tired. If you'll excuse me, I might check on dinner." But there was no escaping to the kitchen, for Mrs. Zalkind was taking her arm.

"It's most confusing," she said to Emilia, walking with her to the dining room. "Everyone knows how showy the Spanish Jews are," she whispered, "but look at that gown of Judith's. It is absolutely plain. I hope that you are not insulted, my dear. She ought to have worn something a little nicer. I don't entirely trust her. A person ought to be what she is; then one knows what to think of her. It's most disturbing, though naturally I shall love her as a daughter. Something smells appetizing. Did you try that new recipe for brisket?" Mrs. Zalkind sailed into the dining room; Emilia followed like a dinghy behind a battleship. "Ah, you have one of those Art Nouveau things with the droopy flowers. I don't feel it necessary to be current with every small decoration myself, but everyone to his own. After you are converted, Emilia, you will be even more my daughter. Though it's such an awful word.

One converts rubles to pounds. I prefer guineas. The better shops price everything in guineas."

"Please, Mother. You're to sit there beside Jacob," Emilia said, pointing to the place card and seating herself on Jacob's other side. She took a deep breath and resumed smiling. The maid was serving soup.

"Have you thought of a name for the baby?" Albert asked.

"A good British name. Not something from the *heim*," Mrs. Zalkind said. The table had been expanded with two leaves to accommodate Jacob's family. Even the linen had been monogrammed by Mrs. Zalkind. Emilia was hemmed in by the last letter of the alphabet. *Z, Z*, everywhere *Z*, as if the world snored.

"If I had a son, I'd name him after Albert," Judith said. Emilia had placed her behind the centerpiece, an iridescent blue vase filled with flowers. Judith stretched her neck to peer over them. "That's the tradition among Spanish Jews."

"God forbid. And bring down the evil eye?" Mrs. Zalkind asked.

"You have to think of the sound of a name." Jacob tapped the table with his spoon. "Jacob—one, two. There's a hesitation in it. A strong name has one syllable. John. James. Paul." He tapped the table: one; one; one.

Only Zaydeh didn't have an opinion. At his end of the table, he was saying the blessing over the bread he'd taken from the silver basket. On the wall behind his head were framed photographs of Zalkinds and their relatives.

"You must have another servant," Mrs. Zalkind said. "Beating carpets in your condition, it's outrageous. Don't think I haven't been talking to Annie. I know everything. Now listen to me. The orphanage in Norwood has excellent girls, trained for domestic service."

Emilia flinched. "I don't want another servant. I manage fine." Her daughter would be twelve now, old enough to go into service.

"But it's a *mitzvah* to bring a Jewish girl into a Jewish home. God knows what would happen to her otherwise, a maid among the *yoks*?"

In the orphanage there'd be a twelve-year-old girl who didn't know that her mother lived in Charlotte Street. Such a girl could have any name and any face; who would recognize her? "I don't want a stranger in my house. Not now," Emilia said. It was hard to swallow, her stomach begged to be filled with something.

"Who's talking about a stranger? Only another servant. There's nothing better than a young girl you can train yourself. She'll do for you very well."

"I shall do much better if you stop meddling, Mother Zalkind." Her mother-in-law's face reddened and Jacob's eyes flashed, but she had to eat something or she'd faint. The smell of cooked meat made her too warm. She wanted a sweet taste, and a woman in her condition shouldn't have to wait for the pudding. "Excuse me," she muttered as she rose from the table. "I have to see to dinner."

There was a large window in the kitchen, and a door into the garden, but the pantry was a small room off the kitchen with no windows, just shelves of dishes and jams and pickles and scented sugar, flour, bread, a sink, a stool. The pudding for meat meals was on the right side, for dairy meals on the left. The jubilee cake was on the right, made with cherry jelly and claret, decorated with confectioners' sugar sifted over a doily, adapted for a meat meal by using a dozen egg whites instead of butter.

Emilia made do with the pound cake on the dairy side of the pantry. A pound of flour, a pound of butter, a pound of raisins, and each slice was worth a pound of flesh on one's hips. It would require ever so many pounds for her to withstand the onslaught of Zalkinds.

"I have something for you," Zaydeh said, peeking into the pantry.

Emilia quickly pushed her plate onto a shelf. "I didn't have any meat," she said defensively. "I can have dairy cake."

"Is it good?" He took something from his pocket, wrapped in thin paper. "Here, for you."

"What is it, Zaydeh?" Emilia asked, standing up so that he could sit on the stool.

"The stem of the *esrog*. You see the withered blossom still attached to it. Smell it—just like the fruit, it smells. A funny thing, I'm telling you. The *esrog* is the fruit of the Tree of Knowledge. For a taste of it, Eve was punished with the pain of childbirth. But that was then and this is now. Everything changes in life. You put that under your pillow when it's time. For a safe delivery. An easy one."

"Thank you," Emilia said. She must have been looking unwell, for Zaydeh was pushing her onto the stool, putting a cup of cold tea into her hands. The real odor of the *esrog* wasn't strong enough to cover the remembered odor of childbirth, which she could forget as long as she was busy ordering wallpaper or cooking for twelve or choosing just the right earrings for her gown or even eating pound cake.

"I want to name my child myself," she said. But how could he realize that there was another child, and she didn't know its name?

"All right, all right. Who else?" he asked, for how can a mother not know her child's name? "But today you need to shake the *lulav*."

"I—what?"

"It's a *mitzvah*." A virtue, a commandment, a religious obligation. "For a woman, too. It's Sukkoth, the season of our joy."

"Sukkoth," she repeated.

"You see? You say it just like my wife, *alleva sholom*. Come with me and I'll show you how to shake the *lulav*. You hear what I'm saying? It's Hoshana Rabbah. There's still a chance. The Court of Heaven is ready to make a different decree." He was picking up the *esrog* and the branches of the *lulav*.

"Thank you, Zaydeh, but the family is waiting for me. Another time."

"Next year, who knows if I'll be alive to teach you. You do it like this. The branches are people. You hold them together, all the different kinds with the *esrog*. This one, the date palm, it has no smell, but so what? It brings forth fruit and the taste means learning. This is the kind of person that learns but doesn't do good acts. Like me when I was a young man studying in my father-in-law's house while he did business. You smell the myrtle? A beautiful smell, but taste? Nothing. A person that performs good acts but has no learning. Like my daughter, may God bless her always. And the *esrog*"—he held up the citron fruit—"is fragrant and edible. My wife, *alleva sholom,* made a wonderful jelly from it. A person who has learning and also acts."

"The willow has no fragrance and it doesn't produce fruit," Emilia said.

"Very good. You're learning already—a willow you're not. For the willow is a person who doesn't learn and doesn't do good. But even such a person isn't abandoned. You hold all the branches with the *esrog* and shake them in the six directions, like this . . ."

"But, Zaydeh, what does it mean?"

"Just shake the *lulav*. It's a *mitzvah*." Below his fur *shtrimel,* his eyebrows were white, but his eyes were Jacob's eyes, the same greenish brown, the color of a turtle's shell. "Come. Do it with me. You think because this is just one thing it doesn't count? It's not so. Listen to me. What you do here is also done there. You know what I mean. In the other world. A spark here is a fire there, like the fire that spoke to our teacher Moses. Such a fire sang the Tree of Life into being, my good girl. Take the branches from me."

As she reached for them, in the garden in Minsk the ghost of the first wife climbed high in the apple tree and higher still into the clouds to see the gate where the heavens were opening for a last plea, a final meeting with God.

Frying Pan Alley

All through the Lane, there was the sound of hammers as men took down the boards and branches that made up the decorated shelters of joy. The festival of Sukkoth was ended, the season of yellow fog beginning. Gittel was turning a rope by herself and jumping while she waited for Libby. She was humming as she jumped, her voice part of the music of the street, the hammers and the streetcar, the organ-grinder and the smoked-fish vendor rolling his barrels to the corner. Libby was tying her braids together with a yellow ribbon. It was a spelling prize, and she tied it slowly so everyone would see.

"Aren't you finished yet?" Clara asked, holding her doll as she always did. There were five girls and they needed another to make two even sides. They were going to play Please I've Come to Work a Trade.

"Just about."

The sky burned orange as the sun lowered itself into a bath of smoke and fog, spreading dusk from house to house. "What's your trade?" Libby and her side chanted.

"P.H.," Gittel answered, pretending to pick hops.

"Picking hops!" Libby shouted and chased the girls down the alley toward the school yard till they saw the sparks from the forge in Bell Lane where horses were shod. The girls shrieked and ran fast between the barrels of smoked fish and behind the toffee stand, but Libby ran faster and, with a wallop on their backs, said, "You guess now!"

Libby's side huddled against the railing of an "aree," the little square by the basement door where the rats had a conference and someone was finding a bit of privacy; sounds of moaning drifted upward.

Libby's side left the aree. "We have come to work a trade."

Nearby, the boys were playing hide-and-seek. One of them leaned against a lamppost and counted while his friends hid. "Ready or not," Herman shouted, making a dash for it, only to slip on some rotten cabbage leaf. The girls laughed as he got to his feet, hitching up his trousers. "Laugh at this," he said, pushing Libby into the muck.

"Who do you think you are, then?" She shoved him back.

At one end of the alley, men were coming back from praying at the Dutch synagogue in Sandys Row. At the other end they were coming from the Plotsker Congregation. "Clear off home," one of the Dutch Jews said.

"Piss up your leg and play with the steam," Herman answered. "Hi! Hi! A dolly!" He grabbed Clara's doll, tossing it end over end, its bare bottom showing. The dress flew up, a bit of pink peeking out of the muck in the gutter. Clara was crying as she picked it up.

"Your mother's got a bloke," Gittel said, giving Herman the look that made adults blow away the evil eye. But Herman was a London child. He stood his ground.

"She don't. You're a liar. A liar with a cripple for a dad."

"I'll call him. See if I don't."

"Too good, you are. You wouldn't dare to fetch a stone from Dorset Street."

"Maybe I would," Gittel said.

"Let's see you." Herman put his hands in his trousers and took out a shining half crown. "Give you this if you do."

"Where'd you nick that from, Herman?" Libby asked.

Everyone was looking at the silver coin. "I wouldn't go to Dorset Street on a bet," Clara said. "My mother would kill me." All their mothers would kill them. Dorset Street was the exemplar of evil, the birthplace of ogres, the darkest mystery that children could imagine. They talked about it all the time.

"She could go," Herman said. "Her real mother's an abbess in Dorset Street, isn't she?"

Clara put her arm through Gittel's. She shouted something at Herman, and Libby shouted, and even Sheindel shouted, though she didn't understand a word of English.

"You're a double liar," Gittel cried. "My father will tear your arm off if you don't leave me alone!" But Herman was running off with the other boys and she knew that her father wasn't going to do anything.

Night was falling on the street as mothers called from windows and doorways, "Come in. I mean it. This minute or I'll give you what for." One by one they went in, Clara, Sheindel, even Libby. But Gittel stayed outside, jumping rope. Above her head was the needle of night, beneath her feet cobblestones and the fog creeping over her boots. She could jump to one hundred without breathing hard. Then to two hundred. But at two hundred and ten, the rope burned her hands and the sweat was pouring off her and Mama was in the alley, as real as anything, taking her by the arm and hauling her inside, away from the darkness.

The Other Charlotte Street

It is common in London for a street to change its name several times along its length, and any number of entirely different streets can have the same name. A letter to someone living in a street, for example, like Frying Pan Alley would bear the address: Frying Pan Alley, Sandys Row, Whitechapel Road, London—to ensure that it was going to the right alley and not another one with the same name in a different snake's nest of twisting, crooked lanes. It was said that only criminals and the drivers of hansom cabs truly knew the streets of London.

Just a few minutes west of Emilia's house, there was another Charlotte Street, one block from Great Portland, where the synagogue was situated. Great Portland was a yellow street, as yellow as the sun. Naturally the minister of the synagogue had a house in the same street, one that would not cause him to be ashamed to greet prominent members of the Jewish community who came to the synagogue on important occasions like the consecration of twenty-five columns of Italian marble. But his assistant could not afford a house in Great Portland. He lived on the next street over, a red street, among the shopkeepers and clerks of the other Charlotte Street.

Emilia ought to have been calm as she stepped out of the cab, realizing that life was not going to change with this appointment. It was, like her pregnancy, merely making her more. The good *yokhelta*. Jacob would thank her all of her days for presenting him with a Jewish son. Keeping kosher was nothing compared with it. So there was no reason for her itchy neck, none at all. And if she scratched until there was blood under her nails, it was only an old habit and everyone knows how tenacious such habits are.

The rabbi's house was next to a cookshop, and the smell of fried pork sausages followed Emilia up the stairs. He was not called Rabbi Nussbaum, as the English Jews did not like the word *rabbi*.

"The Reverend Mr. Nussbaum will see you now," the maid said as she opened the door to the study.

Mr. Nussbaum was an average man in every respect, height, weight, features, everything except his mouth. It was wide and mobile and lived three lives for every word it spoke. He wore no spectacles, though they would have improved his appearance, at least giving him a scholarly air and hiding the flicker of annoyance in his dark eyes. A minister's assistant has many tiresome duties.

Like a gentleman, he took Emilia's hand. A rabbi in the *heim* would never touch a strange woman. Nor did he look like a rabbi, with his frock coat and his study furnished like a sitting room with armchairs and a Persian rug. His desk was piled with correspondence, not yellowing volumes of religious commentary. And on the wall there was a portrait, not of Moses but of the Zionist Theodor Herzl. It was not even a painting but a cheap print, the kind that came with New Year's cards. A real rabbi would not have the painting of a person at all; it was tantamount to a graven image.

"Good morning, Mrs. Zalkind." He directed her to a comfortable armchair with a crocheted doily on it to protect it from hair oils. A gentleman, yes, but one that couldn't quite afford to be fashionable. His frock coat, with an outside pocket on the left breast, was three years out of date. His wife no doubt still wore puffed sleeves. Emilia's sleeves were tight from shoulder to wrist. She wore a blouse and bolero and a skirt that flared around her ankles; her hat was so covered with feathers that the brim was indiscernible. But Mr. Nussbaum did not even glance at the hat; a man of no taste. Neither a real rabbi nor a real gentleman.

"Let me tell you something, Mrs. Zalkind," he said without any of the small courtesies that grease social intercourse. "In ancient Rome there were millions of converts to Judaism, but the first Christian emperor made conversion to Judaism a capital crime. Very wise. You can be certain that your converts are quite sincere when their heads might be cut off for it. Now you take Spain—"

"I am not interested in Spain," Emilia said.

Mr. Nussbaum took no notice. He did not even have a beard. Was there a real rabbi without a beard? "Hundreds of thousands of Spanish Jews were forced to become Christians, but one might question the religious fervor of someone who converts to save his neck. To this day, their descendants are called New Christians and are considered . . . *trayf*, we shall say. They are not kosher. They simply cannot be trusted. I should like to trust you, Mrs. Zalkind. Tell me. Why do you wish to convert to Judaism?"

"I'm going to have a child."

"So? There are many gentiles that have children without ever converting." She did not like his smile. It was too full of humor.

"It is a known fact that gentiles do not have Jewish children, and my husband wishes to have a Jewish child."

"Well, in that case he should have a Jewish wife. Who will my sister marry if all the Jewish men take *yokheltas* to wed? Intermarriage is the greatest problem of our time, Mrs. Zalkind. Should I encourage it?"

"It is a fait accompli, sir, and I have a duty to my husband." She nodded at the maid, who was discreetly placing a tea tray on the low table next to Emilia.

"Keeping a Jewish home is far too much trouble. Ask my wife. She'll tell you. For a lady—well, you might have to hire another servant. Religion doesn't come cheaply. Perhaps your husband ought to reconsider. Two sets of dishes for milk, meat, then another two sets for Passover." Mr. Nussbaum cleared his throat. "And there's the fifth set— if your husband should fancy a pork sausage, so as not to mess up the nice arrangement, you understand."

"I have kept kosher since my marriage," Emilia said coldly. The special frying pan and the blue plate used for Jacob's bacon and eggs were kept in a bread box in the pantry. "My mother-in-law showed me everything."

He leaned toward her. "Did she tell you that you may not ride in a carriage to call on your friend on Saturday?" he asked. "So inconvenient. And in the summer, when the days are long, you would not go to the theater on a Saturday evening, for the Sabbath ends at sundown. It would be very dull, don't you think?"

"Jacob doesn't do that," Emilia said, stirring two lumps of sugar in her tea. But even a third would not make this interview more palatable. "It isn't fair to ask it of me."

"But he is a Jew already. Perhaps not a very good Jew, yet an authentic one nonetheless," Mr. Nussbaum replied. "And whenever he does go to the theater on a Saturday evening, he is aware that he ought not. He eats pork with his fellow Englishmen and knows that he ought not and they might. It is a most unpleasant state. But presumably one that he enjoys. He shall not be pleased when you convert and require him to go to synagogue."

"My mother-in-law would be most unhappy if we could not shop on Saturday," Emilia said.

"It is an interesting fact that the Jewish family of a convert is often the most inconvenienced. It's a bad business all around. My recommendation to you, Mrs. Zalkind, is that you remain a gentile." The smell of sausages was drifting up from the cookshop downstairs. She could hear the squeal of a streetcar's wheels as it turned the corner.

"I should prefer it, but my husband doesn't. And I love him as much as myself. That comes from the Bible, you know."

"Yes, and so does something about turning the other cheek."

"Does it?" The cheek business was in the New Testament, she was sure of it. Something among the Marks or Johns or Apostles or suchlike. Mr. Nussbaum was looking at her intently. This was a test; he expected her to reveal her true inclinations as if she were Delilah, ready to deliver Samson to the uncircumcised Philistines. But she could not be Delilah, however much the minister might wish it, for she hadn't the proper education.

"My father was an atheist," she said. "He absolutely forbade any discussion of religion and only allowed my mother to read the Old Testament with me because he believed it to be of historical interest."

"Ah. An enlightened man. So you are willing to be *shomer Shob-*

bos?" He paused as if confused by her nod, not quite realizing that he hadn't translated the Hebrew phrase for "Sabbath observant."

Emilia cast her eyes around his study, looking for a subject to distract him. There was a collection of oil lamps in a glass cabinet, photographs of sand and ruined walls hung above it. "You are interested in Palestine, sir?"

"Who wouldn't be?" He stood up and came around his desk, striding to the wall of photographs. "Here. Do you see this Roman column?" He pointed to the one fallen on its side. "If you look closely, you'll see the Crusaders' cross cut into the marble. This is our Holy Land. And yours, of course."

"My father put a great emphasis on history." She finished off her cup of tea. "But I don't care for it, myself."

"There is no escaping it if you become a Jew," he said. "I shall give you a book to read. Come again in two weeks, and we'll see what you have to say about it."

He returned to his desk and rang for the maid, who led Emilia to the door. A *mezuzah* was nailed to the doorpost, an ancient prayer written by a scribe on parchment rolled up inside the casing. The outside of the casing was engraved with the letter *shin* for *Shaddai,* the Almighty, which allowed just enough light to shine on the special holy letters inside to entrap any demons lurking about.

Charlotte Street

Every year the Torah is read in the synagogue; every year Moses dies and the world is created again. It is all brand-new, God sees that everything is good, and then evil comes upon the world. There are those who say that evil is born when God's judgment is not sufficiently tempered by mercy, but in any event on the Sabbath that Noah built an ark and God sent a flood to cover the generation of evil and all the earth, Emilia was polishing silver. It is also said that if you hear someone saying, Look, the Messiah has arrived, and you are in the middle of polishing silver, you ought to finish what you're doing.

"Annie! Don't you hear the knocker?" she called to the maid. Of course there was no answer. Annie was upstairs, nursing a toothache. Emilia went to the door herself and took in the post. There were letters for Jacob, a magazine for herself, a letter from Minsk, and behind the postman, the ghost of the first Mrs. Rosenberg. The first wife made herself at home, beginning with the kitchen, where she looked into the pots on the stove before seating herself at the table covered with silverware, the polish and cloth just where Emilia had left them.

"Not you!" Emilia bolted the door to the garden. "What do you want?" She threw the post onto the table, picking up a silver knife as if with it she could attack the angel of death. "Is something going to happen to my baby?"

The ghost of the first wife shook her head as Emilia sat down, staring angrily.

"After all this time. I don't believe it. You wouldn't come here now."

But the first wife was right there, standing in light so strong that in the dining room the painted willow boughs fluttered in a breeze.

"Well, you might as well go because I have no business with you." Emilia slit the envelope from Minsk with slow dignity, the silver knife throwing luminescent balls at the wall. She took out the letter and smoothed it flat. The ink was blotted here and there in her mother's manner, the words uneven as if she'd had a headache and was writing in bed. The ghost of the first wife read over her shoulder.

Dear Emilia,

Something wasn't right in your last letter. Are you well? Your husband? Here all is as usual. We go from day to day and I wait for your letters.

When you are very young, every day seems endless. After a while you learn to think of tomorrow and the days fly away, then it's years, and when you reach my age, the decades slide by before you know it. Sometimes a person can forget what time she's in and think if she walked into a certain kitchen, she would see a girl, her head bent over a book . . .

Emilia folded up the letter and put it in her apron pocket. Such letters ought to be read in private, where no one, not even the dead, could see her face. In the street a student artist was bargaining with a streetwalker; would she pose for him? A bob an hour he couldn't afford, but he'd split the proceeds of the painting with her. The French colony had moved up from Soho, the prostitutes and the gambling clubs following. Emilia could hear the same street sounds she'd heard in Soho years ago, even the organ-grinder playing "The Marseillaise." But this time her breasts were filling with milk instead of emptying.

"Emilia!" Jacob called as he opened the front door.

"Hello, dear," she said, leaving the ghost of the first wife to do whatever she liked in the kitchen. But the first Mrs. Rosenberg followed behind. The dead never realize when they aren't wanted.

Jacob smelled of herring and schnapps as he kissed her. "Look who I brought home with me."

"*Gut Shobbos,*" Zaydeh said, the deepest pleasure in his face, for what can be more satisfying than celebrating the holy Sabbath with your grandson? "*Sholom aleichem.*" He nodded at the ghost of the first wife.

"Do you see something, Zaydeh?" Emilia asked.

"What does a man of my age see?" He was the same age as her father, the same height too. "By me, seventy-eight is already an *alter-kacker.*" Old shit. That was Zaydeh with his coarse peddler's talk.

"Come into the dining room and sit down. Will you have some cake?" Emilia asked.

"After a walk, tea and cake is always good."

Zaydeh was soon seated in the dining room, and the tea served. Emilia watched carefully. Something as small as tea could determine a person's future. Zaydeh took his in the old way, with lemon in a glass, but Jacob poured milk into his teacup like any Englishman.

"Zaydeh looks a little like my father," Emilia said, cutting the cake.

"Does he? A bigger slice for me if you please." So Jacob still liked cake, but it didn't signify; in that respect he already took after his grandfather.

"My father wasn't a tall man, either," Emilia said, though in all her memories, her father stood above her.

"You don't have to be afraid to speak plain with me," Zaydeh said. "An oak tree, I'm not. A cabbage, maybe."

The ghost of the first wife laughed. She didn't make any sound but clapped her hands to her knees and shook her head as if she needed a good laugh, any excuse would do.

"As it happens, my wife, *alleva sholom,* she made a cabbage soup like no one else." For a moment Zaydeh looked directly at the ghost of the first wife, pointing to one of the framed photographs on the wall. "You heard from her, maybe?"

The ghost of the first wife put a hand on his shoulder and shook her head.

"I never liked that picture," Jacob said. "It doesn't look like my grandmother at all. It's much too serious."

In the days when the photograph was taken, you had to hold still for a whole minute while the shutter of the camera waited for the light to slowly form the image on the silver-salted plate. The woman in the picture wasn't smiling, but she had clear eyes; it was remarkable how clearly she looked at them.

Zaydeh said quietly, "She shouldn't be serious? She married a scholar and had great honor from it and then what did she have? A peddler."

"I didn't know you were a scholar in the *heim*," Emilia said.

"Neither did I. Why didn't you tell me?" Jacob asked, his hand in his pocket as if to find something of comfort there. A notebook to write down a thought or a pipe to smoke. But writing and smoking are forbidden on the Sabbath.

Zaydeh smiled at the ghost of the first wife. She would understand that the old and the dead are pleased when they can still offer a surprise. "You never know the end of a book till you read the whole thing," Zaydeh said. "I wanted to translate the Bible into Yiddish, but a peddler has time only for calling out, Needles! Thread! Combs! One thing, I managed. *Eishes Hayil*. 'A Woman of Valor.' A husband recites it to his wife on *Shobbos* after the candles are lit."

Jacob dug into his cake, avoiding Zaydeh's gaze. "My father doesn't," he said. It was one thing to sit anonymously beside your grandfather while he prays, quite another to stand up and recite biblical verses at the dinner table.

"I don't want Jacob to do it either," Emilia said, putting a hand on Jacob's arm. "I should be embarrassed." He gave her a grateful glance, and if only someone would have told her the new rules of their marriage and the penalty for breaking them, she could have decided whether his gratitude was sufficient.

"You listen to me, children." Zaydeh looked from one to the other.

"You know who wrote *Eishes Hayil?* The mother of the wise King Solomon. She was the wife of David, whose great-grandmother was Ruth the convert. She was a good *yokhelta,* too, and from her comes the Messiah."

The ghost of the first wife crossed her arms. There it was—Ruth or Delilah, which would it be?

"I'll fetch more tea," Emilia said. When you can't make up your mind, that is always a good thing to do.

Her father used to recite "A Woman of Valor" with a mocking smile. Sometimes he asked if the heroine of the verse had charmed Russian officers into sparing her family. He made it sound like a sin. Every Sabbath her mother used to take a double dose of the Lady's Health Tonic made of water and alcohol laced with opium. While her father recited *Eishes Hayil,* her mother's eyes would glaze over.

A woman of valor, who can find? Her worth is above rubies. The heart of her husband safely trusts in her. She does him good and not evil all the days of her life. She is like merchant ships bringing food from afar. She considers a field and buys it. She makes strong her arms. To the needy she stretches out her hand. She is not afraid of snow for her household, they are clothed in scarlet. Strength and dignity are her clothing, she laughs at the time to come. Give her the fruit of her hands and let her deeds praise her at the gates.

Whitechapel Road

There were twenty-seven thousand crystals in the gaslit chandelier of the Jerusalem Music Palace. Though the children were sitting in the cheapest seats high up in the gallery, they knew that these were the very best seats—why, you could practically touch the rainbow prism of crystals from this peak, this Mount Sinai where even God might take the evening off to watch the act. Gittel sat on her rolled-up coat. She'd come with Libby and her brother, Sammy, and his friend. Not that he was in the habit of going around with children but, as Libby had discovered, her brother wasn't giving his entire wage packet to his mother, having lied about his wages, and the price for his deceit was that he must take his sister and her best friend to the music hall.

The audience was shouting, "Marie! Our Marie!" And out she skipped, the famous Marie, one of them really, the daughter of a flower maker and a seamstress, wearing her girl's short dress covered with a pinny, though she must be nearing thirty, and there was a burst of laughter as she put her hands together to sing the song she'd done for the Vigilant Committee, the "Ballad of Isabelle," a song as proper as any poet laureate's poem. However, such gestures as accompanied Marie's rendition of "Go into the garden, Isabelle" were never seen by any morality committee, and the audience downed its pot of beer and howled for more.

From Gittel's high seat, the hand and leg motions of "wet dripping roses" looked silly, even if Sammy was laughing so hard he was choking and his friend punched his shoulder. She had a nice voice, that Marie, but if it was a very good voice, she wouldn't want any gestures. Still, there was an orchestra with strings and brass and a drum, and Gittel couldn't stay away from any music even if it meant another talking-to by Mama, who would say, Tell me one thing—just one thing I'm asking—who is looking after you when you go off to the music hall? A girl alone? She's a bone to starving dogs. An ounce of sense she doesn't have. Better she should give herself up to the asylum for the feeble-minded. Look at me, daughter mine, am I lying to you?

That would come later. For now, Gittel closed her eyes to listen to the music. Libby was going to do her hair for the concert at school. The girls' choir was performing songs from *The Mikado,* and the teacher had asked Gittel to be Yum-Yum as her hair was perfect for the song "Braid the Raven Hair." But Gittel was too shy to sing alone, her throat closed up, and she stayed in the chorus. Only here, high in the balcony of the Jerusalem Palace, could she dream her dreams of flowers that fell from every side as she sang on a stage like this one.

The Strand

For the opening of his new play, Jacob rented a box and invited certain of his friends, who still met regularly to assure each other that they were artists and not Jews, though these days beigels and smoked fish were finding their way back onto luncheon menus. The set was made by one of them, and every muddy cobblestone, every soot-covered brick was painted with a mixture of love and shame.

"In memory of Mr. Moses Angel, headmaster of the Jews' Free School" was written at the top of the program. And then, "A new drama by the creator of the famous Bow mysteries," and below that, in an arc of bold letters, *Angel of the Ghetto.* Emilia scratched the back of her neck, listening to the curious chatter of the sculptor and his socialist brother to her right, an editor and a cartoonist behind them. A Jewish play? It won't run more than a night. I disagree. It's the fin de siècle, my friend. Have you seen the cigarette case made from the hanged murderer's skin?

"It's only expected to run for a week," Jacob was saying to Solomon Abraham. "It was put together rather quickly. I couldn't think how to start it, so I stole the beginning from *The Beggar of Odessa.*"

"When did you see a Yiddish play?"

"Ages ago. I went with my grandfather to the old Yiddish theater. It wasn't as bad as you might think."

The ghost of the first wife, who loved a play in any language, stood at the front of the box, looking around at the half-full theater, the critics with their notebooks, the empty royal box, the gallery where a couple of soldiers and a handful of working men and women were eating their supper. The Adelphi was one of the theaters from a time before electric lights, and the gas lamps cast deep blue shadows across the curtains rising on a dark street, a flickering lamp, a street sign.

"It's only one play. Even if the critics don't like it, Jacob is still a successful author. Don't be nervous," Harriet whispered to Emilia.

"I'm not." Emilia stared at the familiar street sign, Whitechapel Road, and there a shop that looked like Mr. Shmolnik's. The last sound she'd heard in the East End was the brass balls ringing over the pawnshop door.

Onstage the lamp cast no light into the corner where a solitary figure was picking through rubbish. It seemed impossible for the Jewish actor who'd changed his name to perform Shakespeare to be this bent man, speaking as if he'd just come from a Polish *shtetl,* somewhere near Warsaw perhaps, on a riverbank where the willows dipped into the water and he studied God's law from dawn until dusk.

A Jew actually playing a Jew; it was entirely novel. The audience clapped.

While the ragpicker dug through the rubbish heap for whatever small thing he could sell to keep his soul in this earth, daylight came and the lamplighter snuffed the flame. Then the alley filled with barrows, and all the East End types appeared. The beggar, the cripple, the bookie, the unworldly man, the beigel lady, the costermonger, the pawnbroker, the match girl, the mother of eight, with their funny way of speaking and their quaint customs, each of them someone Emilia recognized though she shouldn't and told herself she didn't.

At night the ragpicker slumped into sleep in the doorway of a warehouse and a copper picked him up for vagrancy. He was thrown into the sullen grayness of the workhouse, there set to work breaking rocks. At the end of the day, his quota wasn't filled and he was made to stay another night and given another day of breaking rocks till he should learn industriousness. At the long table of hopeless men, he prayed his foreign prayer and blessed the bread that was given him, and when darkness fell he was released into the fog of Whitechapel Road. End of Act I. The curtain fell.

The audience thundered with applause. There were shouts of "Bravo!" from the gallery. The critics were writing furiously.

"Tomorrow the house will be full," Solomon Abraham said. He had painted the backdrop.

"A Jewish mother never lets go." Jacob lit his pipe. "One might as well make a blessing out of it."

Emilia smiled; she could always smile, even if her face was frozen. As Jacob turned to speak to a theater critic from *The Times,* Harriet asked what she thought of Miss Cohen's outfit, waving her opera glasses at the Cohen sisters in the box across from theirs. And Emilia answered as if she really cared that Miss Cohen wore a low-cut gown, which would save her on the cost of it but a woman over thirty doesn't have the neck for décolletage and Miss Cohen was no exception. Then they asked the men to get them something to drink, and Emilia wondered if her mother's Lady's Health Tonic had as little flavor as the greenish beverage in her glass.

In the second act, the ragpicker became an old clothes man, using a loan from the Mutual Friends' Society to buy a barrow and pay for a route. Mist was blowing across the stage when an old woman came down from the poorest of the houses, its windows covered over with paper. Emilia recognized the house. Of course it wasn't a real house, just a façade painted by Jacob's friend. But he must have known it, too, the one with the ruined chimney and the peaked gable next to the washhouse in Goulston Street.

The old woman was putting her bundle of rags in the barrow, and when the old clothes man offered her a penny for it, she refused. He insisted, she refused again, running back into the house as if she was afraid. And soon the reason became clear to everyone. Something in the barrow was crying, and as the old clothes man unfolded the rags, he found a baby.

The audience sighed with satisfaction. Every good story has an orphan in it. Handkerchiefs were pulled out, eyes riveted to the stage.

This baby was a boy, and the old clothes man, whose name was Mr. Angel, made a cradle out of an orange crate, calling the child Moses, for he'd found the baby in a barrow in the fog, which was close enough to a basket floating in a river. End of Act II.

The applause was satisfactory, the critics lit up cigars. The sculptor left Jacob's box to go backstage and look at his set, the socialist brother read the racing pages of the newspaper, the cartoonist and the editor went to eavesdrop on the gossip in other boxes.

"A Jewish penny dreadful. How clever," Harriet said. "Everyone will love it."

Her husband, Solomon, wore his jacket open, the paisley waistcoat rounding across his stomach. "The boy will have a good accent, if you ask me," he said. "Every hero in a play, even if he's born in a sewer, has a good accent and gets discovered by rich relations."

"Just wait and see," Jacob said, drawing on his pipe and slowly blowing out the smoke. "In the new drama there are more poor relations than rich ones."

"Then the old man will take the baby to an orphanage?" Emilia asked, her throat very dry. "Like the Jewish asylum in Norwood."

It was Nehama who'd told her about the orphanage. They were in Goulston Street, walking by the house with the ruined chimney and the peaked gable. Nehama carried the bundle of laundry on her head. Emilia was looking at the nest in the chimney, wondering if the birds would come back to it after their winter sojourn in Egypt. There were carolers singing, and the Salvation Army Band was marching through Whitechapel Road.

The socialist brother looked up from his racing pages. "A chimney sweep, they always want small children for that. Are you going for a social commentary at last, Jacob? Then let me shake your hand."

Jacob laughed as he fixed the loose tobacco in his pipe, arguing with the socialist until the others returned. The editor had good news. He'd heard the manager of the Adelphi saying to the *Times* critic that the run of the play would be extended for another week.

"You should consider a novel," the editor said. "This is new. Very new."

"I could," Jacob said. "I've got reams of notes."

"Then you must. The only ones writing about the ghetto have been reformers. There's nothing like this. Jews as Jews. My God, Jacob, you could spend a lifetime on the East End."

"One day there is already a lifetime." Emilia yawned. The ghost of the first wife was shaking her head, but it was too late. Jacob's smile faded. He turned away, speaking in a low voice to his friends, the smoke of pipe and cigars rising like the business of factories.

She would have to order a pair of yellow gloves tomorrow and stop borrowing Harriet's. In fact she would get half a dozen colors. That was all she'd think about and not dare to meet the first wife's gaze while the conductor led the orchestra in the overture to Act III.

Onstage, young Moses called the old clothes man Father as he rode on top of the barrow, scrutinizing all that he surveyed. He was a born mimic and the audience laughed as he became the bookie making bets, or Mrs. Teitelbaum, who sold corsets and had a house of her own in a square, two rooms it was, one up and one down, and stairs they had, just like a squire's, no one should cast an evil eye on their good fortune, God forbid.

Naturally the boy wanted to leave school and work with his father. But the father wished him to study. An English scholar he should be, not a Rabbi Ragpicker. The son was stubborn. The father shouted, "As it is written, 'Hear, O my son, what I am telling you and your years will be many.'" And the son, just as angry, grabbed his father's barrow and called out, "Ol' proverbs. On'y a penny. Have a heart, guv. Won't do you no 'arm to take one of my proverbs. Fresh from yesterday they are."

That evening, Mr. Angel went to see the headmaster of the Jews' Free School, who stroked his chin and nodded and then came out with a proposal. There was a wealthy Jewish couple without children who were looking to adopt a boy. Moses would be well educated and have his choice of going into the family business or a profession if he preferred. Mr. Angel shook his head. This wasn't what he came for. He wished only advice on how to make his recalcitrant son study. How could a person give up his child, his only child? But the headmaster was persuasive. He knew these streets. It would be all too easy for a clever boy to go the wrong way. Didn't the father already see it happening? A person must wish the best for his child. What did he have? An old barrow.

Above, on the platform made by the Jewish artist to represent an attic room, a cradle rocked as if it rode in a storm-whipped river. Mr. Angel bowed his head, and the audience watched him age in an instant, his heart broken. They didn't see the ghost of the first wife on the stage, forgetting that this was just a play, looking up at Emilia with a face full of tragedy, kneeling beside the cradle.

But Emilia saw a man that was relieved to be rid of the burden of a child. A person should never forget the true facts of the world.

The curtain fell and rose again on the next scene. The boy had become a fashionable young man, returning to the streets of his child-hood with a bemused look on his face. Where he remembered a narrow passageway through a warren of alleys, there was now a model block of flats. But the Lane hadn't changed. All the types were still there, the beggar, the bookie, the beigel lady, Mrs. Teitelbaum with her corsets hanging on a pole, measuring one of them against the back of a buyer. The Jews' Free School stood as always, with its front to Bell Lane and its back to Frying Pan Alley, where the children were buying toffee from the stand at the corner. Moses hesitated for a moment, then ran like a boy through a door and upstairs to a forlorn attic room, where his father, alone and sick, cried out with joy to see his son again. They sat and talked, the moon rose above the stage, darkness fell, the sun came up, and the father said that he was proud. Only one thing he asked of his son. That he shouldn't forget the children surrounded by bookies and pimps eager to teach them a trade. "Remember the first Moses," his father said. "Remember Moses our teacher." And he died in his son's arms.

The audience cried buckets of tears. There were even a couple of sniffs from the critics' box. Emilia clapped with them, not knowing what it was she applauded as she thought about her half brothers. The older one was Gabriel, the younger Samael. Those were her father's sons, of course. The other half brother, the one that was the miller's son, found his father fallen among the flour sacks after his heart gave out. Mama didn't know what became of this half brother. He grew up, wasn't that enough? But surely he had a name. Everyone deserves a name.

When the curtain rose on the next scene, Moses Angel was the white-haired headmaster of the Jews' Free School. He sat at the teacher's desk, under the map of the Empire and the portrait of the queen, telling the boys about his father. "This is how I came to be here. May his memory always be for a blessing," he said to the boys in their rows of double desks. The spotlight on the old headmaster dimmed.

One by one, the boys stood up to face the audience, putting on their bowlers and homburgs and tall hats, and it became apparent that they had become men. Then the first of them said, "Whenever people called him the angel of the ghetto, the headmaster would say that he was nothing more than a messenger of his father's. As it is written in the Book of Proverbs: My son, don't forget what I've taught you here."

The audience rose to its feet, and the thunderous applause shook the roof. Emilia whispered to Jacob that she must leave as she was dreadfully tired, but that he should stay among his friends and enjoy his moment. No one else would notice the ghost of the first wife on the dark platform, tearing apart a cradle made from an orange crate. Only the dead can afford to create a spectacle.

The Jews' Free School

Ever since her twelfth birthday, Gittel had known that her first mother couldn't be a baroness or a princess. No—she must be a singer, like Gittel, but she wasn't shy and her voice never squeaked. One day Gittel would be sitting in the theater or a music hall and the crowd would hush as a beautiful lady came onstage. She would begin to sing, and then, as she looked over the audience, their eyes would meet, and for the first time in the illustrious singer's career, her voice would falter as she recognized her daughter. And she would open her arms wordlessly as flowers poured onto the stage.

The girls' choir was rehearsing in the Great Hall, still so new that it smelled of fresh pine. The material for the costumes had been donated by the trustees and made up into kimonos by the girls' mothers. Gittel's was blue with roses on it. How lovely the blue velvet ribbon would be with it.

"Girls, girls! Louder, please. I wish the birds to hear you through the new roof," Miss Halpern said. "Our Yum-Yum is feeling poorly today, so you must come forward and sing her part, Gittel."

"I don't know it, Miss Halpern." Gittel had been careful to pronounce the *h* in her teacher's name, so why was Miss Halpern frowning? She was older than Mama, her hair as gray as the fishmonger's donkey, her blouse dark and her skirt dark and only a string of pearls for adornment.

"But I heard you myself," Miss Halpern said. "I was coming from the drill hall."

"Oh, but . . ." Gittel had come early for the rehearsal, and before anyone else arrived she'd sung every part on her own, standing in the light that came through the stained glass. "I don't know it," she said, scratching the back of her neck.

"Are you telling me a falsehood?"

"No, Miss Halpern. I swear I'm not."

"Come on, then. 'The sun whose rays are all ablaze . . .' Let me hear you, please."

Gittel stepped forward. Miss Halpern was waiting, the girls were all watching her, and she was wearing the nicest kimono of all, for Mama knew how to sew and it was just like something you might see on a real stage, but Gittel was now a fish, maybe a whitefish or worse, a carp, with its pouty lips opening and closing while the fishwife scooped it out of the water for someone's *Shobbos,* and not a word could Gittel sing for she couldn't breathe any more than the poor carp, dizzy in the terrible air.

Miss Halpern tapped her pointer on the podium. "I'm most disappointed, Gittel. I don't expect defiance from my girls, but we'll say no more of it. Just step off the stage. If you can't be truthful, then you'll not be in the choir. Clara, please come forward."

Gittel stumbled off the platform and ran to the cloakroom, where no one could see her among the girls' coats, her face puffy, her nose running, the beautiful kimono crushed as she kneeled on it. She didn't mean to lie. She really didn't. If her other mother was a famous singer, then no wonder she left Gittel behind, seeing that she'd grow up to be a liar. But perhaps it was as Pious Pearl said. Her first mother was a madam in Dorset Street, and the teacher had to find out, oh yes, though she might wear a blue kimono with pink roses, there was no hiding what was underneath, was there?

Charlotte Street

Emilia pushed the window a crack to let in the cool wet air. She had to be nimble when people were awake, remembering what she'd said and guessing what she ought to do, but in the night she could just sit, looking at the streetlamps and the shadows of vagrants huddled over grates. Someone with a tray strapped to his chest was selling coffee to nightwalkers. The wind was coming in from the sea as she watched the moon.

"Emilia—what are you doing?" Jacob asked sleepily.

She didn't want to talk to anybody or explain herself. She wished only to watch the moon hanging like fruit on the corner of a chimney. Tomorrow she would finish the sketch for a paper-cut. "Shh. Nothing, I just want some air."

He sat up, the moon bright enough to cast his shadow on the wall. "Should I fetch you some warm milk?"

"I hate milk. Just go back to sleep, Jacob." She would make a paper-cut of the London moon and send it to her mother.

Jacob lit the lamp. "You were asleep when I came home from the theater." On the chest of drawers there was a clock; behind it shadows were cast by the moon. He reached over to the bedside table and found his spectacles and his pipe. "What woke you up?"

"The baby was kicking." She looked at the clock. It was three in the morning. The clock was mounted in a bronze casting of Lady Time, her arms raised above her head. There in her hands rested the timepiece. One might wonder if her arms didn't get tired.

"Is that a postcard from Minsk you have there?" Jacob asked. "You're never yourself when you hear from that old servant of your family's. Those Russians are too morose."

"She's Polish. And anyway I'm drawing the moon." There was a pencil and a sheet of paper on her lap, a book for a desk. In the picture the moon was hooked on to the side of a ruined chimney, but it was only the start of a paper-cut. She wasn't thinking of anything else, not of the house with the peaked gable in Goulston Street.

"Put it away and come to bed."

"In a minute." Emilia was drawing a house, its windows covered over with paper. There she'd once stood, pushed aside by the carolers while Nehama cursed as her bundle of laundry fell. I want to ask you something, Emilia had said. What would you do if you remarried and it turned out that your new husband didn't want your child?

The Jews have an orphan asylum in Norwood, Nehama had said as she lifted the bundle from the street. The matron names the babies. There has to be someplace for children to go if they don't have a mother. But even if I was dead, I would come back from the other world to look out for my child. You think anyone could stop me?

"I have a meeting tomorrow," Jacob was complaining. "How can I sleep with you sitting there like that?" He wore pajamas, blue silk pajamas, for he was a modern man. The moon slid behind a bank of clouds. There was nothing more to do tonight. Emilia left her drawing on the window seat.

"My father didn't want a child," she said. She was fair like Jacob. Their heads were golden on their smooth pillows.

"Then he was a fool."

"Do you think so?" When she used to read aloud in the workroom, she'd hear the rhythm of sewing while Nathan and Nehama, their dark heads almost touching, bent over their dark sewing machines. They must be there still, Nehama singing and Nathan working at breakneck speed until the order was done. The baby in the orange crate, its head covered with a dark fuzz, would be there no longer.

"The child is mine—that is British law."

"Take it out if you like." She pulled up her nightgown so that he could see her bare legs and her bulging navel. She took his hand and held it over her belly. In the street a woman was offering the vagrants a cut rate on her services. "Come on, Jacob. Take the baby and bring it with you to the Reading Room."

"I can feel something," he said.

"It's your imagination." She dropped her nightgown. In the Jews' orphan asylum, there would be a girl with dark hair, neatly braided, in a row of other girls learning how to mend and scrub and peel potatoes so they could make their way without anyone in the world. "This baby goes where I go."

"Not without me. Even reformers admit that Jewish fathers are stuck on their families. And God knows the reports are damning enough. They have no love of Jews, I daresay."

"Then why make your wife one?" Her voice was light, as if she weren't wondering if the girl with braided hair looked like her at all.

"Exactly because she is the mother of my child." Jacob kissed her, and her mouth was suddenly hungry for kisses. A woman after her fifth month doesn't get enough of them, and kisses can swallow disruptive thoughts. "The beautiful mother of my child," Jacob said.

A convert immerses herself in the ritual bath, naked before a witness who ensures that even the ends of her hair are covered by the water that changes her from flour into dough. Of course if you are dough already, it will only make you soggy like paste, the thin sort of paste used to put up theater posters.

Jacob turned out the lamp, and there were no more shadows as he covered her with kisses like the water of a *mikva*.

The Other Charlotte Street

The last new thing of the fin de siècle began when the London fog was at its thickest, yellow sulfur burning the lungs like hellfires. The British had annexed territories with gold and diamonds, and the Boers retaliated by laying siege to British towns in South Africa. The *Daily Mail* had a correspondent in Ladysmith, reporting the whiz of shells and the shrill of guns, and it was thrilling, this last new thing of the fin de siècle, when war came right into one's sitting room.

Steam billowed through the cookshop window, carrying its odor of pork and cabbage up into the minister's study, mingling with the smell of wood burning in the fireplace. Mr. Nussbaum was sitting behind his desk and put down the *Daily Mail* just as Emilia arrived for her appointment. There was talk of forming a Jewish Lads' Brigade.

Zaydeh was with her, dressed like a workman, in an old wool cap and a jacket stuck together in a sweatshop with more soap than thread. He wished to see for himself whether the Reverend Mr. Nussbaum was kosher enough to make his grandson's wife a Jew.

"Good morning, Mr. Nussbaum," Emilia said. "This is my husband's grandfather, Mr. Karpman. He's so kind as to keep me company today."

"Please sit down, sir," Mr. Nussbaum said to Zaydeh, pointing to the armchair opposite Emilia's. There was no humor this morning in Mr. Nussbaum's mobile face. "I'm so very pleased that you came today, sir. My father used to quote your treatise on the laws concerning malicious speech."

"Me? No. It must have been someone else," Zaydeh said quietly. He sat down, taking a Yiddish newspaper from his jacket pocket, unfolding it and smoothing it down, then engrossing himself in it as if he weren't listening to every word, weighing and balancing and forming his judgments.

"Let us review a woman's *mitzvos*," Mr. Nussbaum said. He closed the scrapbook of clippings on his desk. A photograph of bayoneted men slipped out and floated to the floor. "You are not obligated by any of the time-bound commandments like formal prayer." Zaydeh was nodding. "A woman's first duty is to her children, though she has many other obligations. Charity, for instance."

"Charity she knows," Zaydeh said over his newspaper. "Doesn't she get for me the best herring?"

"I'm sure of that, sir," Mr. Nussbaum said, his eyebrows working themselves up and down as if to discover the wisdom that must be hidden in Zaydeh's words. After all, he'd written a treatise.

"Don't let me disturb you. Please." Zaydeh waved his hand.

"Then let us consider the three commandments that are particular to women. Sabbath candles, the dough offering, and *niddah*."

Emilia grimaced but said only, "Oh."

"Then your mother-in-law has explained it to you?" Even through the closed window they could hear the sound of a parade. It was not the parade of a Torah scroll dancing to a new synagogue but pipes and drums and marching men on their way to a ship.

"Yes, she tells me everything," Emilia said. Zaydeh lowered his newspaper. "Everything," she repeated. Hadn't her mother-in-law told her about *niddah* before she got married? Surely she must have. Along with salting meat so that there was no blood in it and how many hours to wait until dairy could be served. She answered Zaydeh's look with a shrug.

"I'm surprised your mother-in-law spoke of it. These days women among the better classes ignore this virtue, even though reformers say that the children of poor Polish Jews are born healthy because of it. However, in such private matters, one may not know everything. Please go on."

"Is this really necessary?" Emilia asked.

"I'm sorry to embarrass you with a delicate matter, but I have to be sure that you know what a Jewish wife should. Don't be shy—a rabbi deals with everything."

Zaydeh rustled his newspaper and turned the page, even moving his lips to show that he was paying no attention to this. Outside the drums were beating time to "God Save the Queen."

"Very well," Emilia said, keeping her eyes on the collection of ancient oil lamps in the cabinet to the right of the desk. "A husband must not touch his wife during her time of month and for a week afterward or until her cloths are completely clean. Then she goes to the ritual bath and makes herself ready. I hope you're satisfied now."

Emilia's mother used to say that the laws of *niddah* were a gift to a woman with a disagreeable husband. Her days of impurity often extended from one month to the next.

"Very good, Mrs. Zalkind. Let us then repeat the blessing a woman says at that time, for you will say it in the *mikva* when you are immersed in the water for your conversion. Repeat after me." Mr. Nussbaum said the Hebrew words, and she repeated them.

A convert is said to be the daughter of Abraham and Sarah our ancestors, not her own mother and father, and better so. A person with no past is a person unburdened. So why would she notice that she was saying the blessing with the Minsker pronunciation?

"That isn't bad," Mr. Nussbaum said. "Let me just correct you a little. Listen to me and try again."

"No, no. I like the way she says it." Zaydeh put down his newspaper, looking at Emilia pensively. "She reminds me of my wife of blessed memory. A *samach* and a *shin* were the same letters to her. She was a Litvack, and she made a blessing like one. Very refined. She made gefilte fish with pepper."

The Jews of Minsk spoke the northeastern dialect of Yiddish like the Litvacks.

"Me—I'm a plain sort of person from a *shtetl* near Krakow," Zaydeh said. "I like sweet fish. I'm a simple man. I don't know any *kintzn*." Tricks. Stunts. A *kintz-macher* was a juggler.

"I should hardly say that," Mr. Nussbaum said, his face alight as torches passed the window, darkening again as fog engulfed it. "A scholar is a juggler of words."

"That may be. But I'm just a peddler. The streets where a child plays have more influence," Zaydeh replied. "Here in London, Jews speak Yiddish with a Polish pronunciation. Even when my daughter blesses Sabbath candles, she sounds like a Jew from the middle of Poland, not like me or even her mother, she should rest in peace."

"That's rather interesting." Mr. Nussbaum uncapped his silver fountain pen and made a note.

Emilia wished that she could disappear as easily as the ghost of the first wife.

"And now I see that God is good and sent me a girl for my grandson who says a blessing just like my wife of blessed memory. Where did such an accent come from? Such is the mystery of the Holy One, for the girl is a gentile."

"It's my Russian accent," Emilia said.

A person can miss a hundred small things because what he believes makes him blind and deaf. But there they are in his mind just the same, waiting for him to open his eyes. Zaydeh's eyes were angry. If Samson had a grandfather, he would look just like this as Delilah tried to hide the shorn locks behind her back. An old man's eyes can have a lot to say.

"It's another funny thing," he continued. "My daughter and son-in-law have two dressing rooms but only one bedroom."

"Is that so?" Mr. Nussbaum asked gently, for it appeared that the old man's mind was wandering. A leather blotter protected his mahogany desk from splotches of ink and scratches. Everyone's life should have a leather blotter.

"My daughter is like a date palm," Zaydeh said. "The taste of many good acts is in her house, and whatever she does, she taught my grandson's wife. Anything else, she doesn't mention."

Emilia was picturing her mother-in-law's bedroom with its one large canopied bed. A woman who observed the laws of *niddah* would have two beds, sleeping apart from her husband during her time of separation. Therefore Mrs. Zalkind didn't practice *niddah,* so how did Emilia know about it? She met Zaydeh's smart old eyes with her own smart glance, keeping her hands tightly folded in her lap so that she wouldn't scratch the fiery rash on her neck.

Her own mother was an *esrog,* the fruit of the Tree of Splendor, which had been mashed into jelly and consumed. But not Emilia.

"What do I know? I'm a willow branch," she said. A willow has no taste or fragrance, neither learning nor good deeds, but it can take root anywhere, like a weed. The world was full of gardens; there was no end to them. One must only go on and not turn to look at the angels with their flaming swords blocking the way back.

It was November, just before Guy Fawkes Day, and fog slithered through every crevice.

ACT III

With closed eyes
The sea sounds closer
With feverish fingers
You feel the jaunty rhyme.

The golden peacock
You know from its flight
And a longing is lovelier
When she's from away.

Tiredness is exhaustion
At the threshold of home,
On your knees you feel keener
The greatness of God.

The master of all things is great
Today as then
Not in the thundering sky
But when he sobs in the street.

Favored is the one
Who can hear the weeping
And as for you,
Listening is your fate.

For when such a tear
Falls on your soul
Wounded and wondrous
It blooms in a song.

—Itzik Manger

CHAPTER 8

Who Can Hear

NOVEMBER 5, 1899

Frying Pan Alley

Here they could meet on a night of fire and fog, the two mothers, the one we remember and the one we forget. Here they could stand, a breath away from each other, for it was a night of masks and tricks. Darkness was falling, and in the darkness the grandmothers would be visible, the alley making space for them as the costermongers left with their donkeys and barrows, jackets and corsets came down from where they hung, oilcloth was rolled away, boys ran off after counting their coppers to see if there was enough for a ticket to the music hall. In the last light, a few people called their wares, voices growing faint.

"Buy any sandbag? Buy a window bag?"

"Wild rabbits! Kosher rabbits if you like!"

In the afternoon of Guy Fawkes Day, Nathan was working in the back room. It had taken him a month to learn to use the sewing machine again, a month of thumps, curses, rattling and ripping sounds coming from the workshop while he made himself over. Now wool flowed slow and dark from his sewing machine, like cows climbing down the steps to the dairy in Black Lion Yard. Nehama was in her place across from him at the sewing machine, working on a dress ruffled with scraps at neckline and hem. Lazar was pressing the last jackets while Minnie turned over the rough edges of seams to sew them flat, from time to time banging Nehama with her elbow as she turned over a jacket. The wind rattled the windowpane and the gas jets flickered.

"Is it ready, Mama—is it?" Gittel called as she came in, throwing her schoolbooks on the small table in the front room.

"Almost," Nehama said. It was a dress for Gittel's guy that she'd made out of straw, using a turnip for the head.

Nathan was yawning. All night he sold coffee to nightwalkers, a tray strapped to his chest. When he came home, he'd lift the loose board and, holding it up with his foot, put the night's earnings away. He'd sleep for a couple of hours, then slowly, slowly work the sewing machine, doing the plainest work. And between the dark of the morning and the dark of the afternoon, there would be fog and rain.

"Where are you going tonight?" Nehama asked him. Through the door to the other room, she could see Gittel buttering a slice of bread.

"The usual places," Nathan said.

"He means Dorset Street again." Nehama turned her head toward Minnie. "Do you believe it?" Her life had become a tale of two streets, the good one and the bad one, here and there, and God must be laughing, such a joke.

"It's close by," Nathan said, "and I have to go where people are awake." His walk had changed again. When he strapped the tray to his chest and went into the alley calling, "Coffee hot! Hardly any chicory," his pace was brisk, and he made jokes about giving change with the missing hand, risking himself night after night to make a life possible for his family when all she could think was that time was going backward.

"So who says you have to sell coffee at night?" she asked. "Show me where it's written." The needle of her sewing machine bit into the dress. It was made from scraps of three different fabrics: green, red, yellow.

"A man has to work for his family. Am I right?" Nathan appealed to Lazar, who was sweating as he pressed the hot iron, steam hissing. "Nehama's going to have a shop."

"Do I need it if I'm a widow?" God's joke was that she hadn't been able to save Nathan; instead he'd done it himself, believing that he was saving her hopes, feeling himself to be a man again in the very place that was her torment. Every night she dreamed about Dorset Street, waking up and wondering where she was. "You don't know what kind of people you're dealing with," she said.

"Of course I know. I see them every day. Unless you think I'm blind as well as crippled, Nehameleh."

"Argue with a wall," she said, frilling the fabric that made the ruffle as she stitched it over the neckline. The dress she'd worn in Dorset Street had been made of a cheap, stiff fabric like this. The longer she wore it, the stiffer it got. When she used to take it off, there would be a red mark across her chest.

"That's it for me." Minnie put away her needle and thread. "I'm going upstairs to prepare supper. When Nathan goes out, I can use the machine. All right?"

"That's fine," Nehama said. She could feel exactly where the mark was. An irritation, a scratch.

Nathan went into the front room, and she followed while he poured himself a cup of cold tea. "Here's the dress. It's all finished," she said, hardly looking at her daughter as she put a hand on Nathan's good arm. "Promise me you won't go there." She was sore in places that shouldn't be sore in a middle-aged married woman whose husband was gentle and slow with her.

"How can I promise? We need the money. Unless you found a way to grow some. Give me a pot of mud and I'll put a penny in it. Then tonight I'll dig up a sovereign." He winked at Gittel.

"The dress doesn't fit." Gittel was kneeling over the guy, trying to put it on him.

"A straw man fits into any dress." Nehama pushed some straw in here and out there, tying up the dress behind. "There. Done." The kettle was boiling. Nehama stood up and took it off the stove. She put milk in the cup, poured the water through a sieve of tea, added two spoons of sugar. She needed a very sweet tea. The guy and the dress would burn on the bonfire. May all such dresses be burned to ash.

"I want more bread," Nathan said.

"Bread you want?" She buttered a thick slice for him, the good dark rye from Grodzinski's bakery, and slapped the plate on the table. "God forbid a wife denies her husband anything. Should I stop you walking in the streets at night? A widow with two sewing machines has plenty of suitors."

"And a dowry under the bed, too. Listen to me." He smiled his old smile and for a minute she could imagine that nothing had changed.

"If there's trouble in the street, I go inside and have a pint. Mrs. Dawes from next door likes to drink at the Horn and Plenty, and I have a little talk with her."

"But she doesn't have a choice. Her granddaughter sings for her supper and the old woman keeps an eye on her." Nehama picked up the broom to sweep the floor, remembering how else a broomstick might be used.

"How much does she get singing?" Gittel asked.

The twigs of the broom went scritch-scratch across the floor. "Are you still here? You're supposed to be out the door already." Her daughter, in a plain dark school dress, braids looped with a ribbon, was tying a rope to the crate. "Take an apple. You shouldn't be hungry." She slipped it into her daughter's pocket, and Gittel waved as she left, pulling the crate behind her.

"I saw a good location for the shop," Nathan said. "Lazar came with me. Am I right?"

"Beautiful!" Lazar called from the back room. "A jewel of a shop."

"It's right on the high road and already divided in two sections. One for you and the other for me, Nehameleh. You can preside like a queen over the women. But I was thinking to have a coffee house like Shmolnik's."

"For gambling?" She would let him sell coffee one more night. Then tomorrow she would break his tray.

"A workingmen's club."

"In part of a shop?" She could tell him that she accidentally stepped on it. And she accidentally cut the straps that bound it to his chest. "The Board of Guardians has such a nice place for their workingmen's club. Who's going to come to us?"

"You need to ask, Nehameleh? I'm surprised. In my club men can play cards and have a pint. Then they'll enjoy reading a newspaper, maybe even a few books in the *mama-loshen*. Not to sell, just to read there."

He held the bread in his good hand, forgotten while he went on about tables and chairs as if in half a shop you could have the furnishings of a mansion. What could she do? She made herself nod because her husband's eyes were full of life. "You see what a trade I'm making out of selling coffee," he said. "May God in heaven bless the night-walkers in Dorset Street and make them very thirsty."

"Amen," she said, lighting candles as the room darkened. Gaslight was only for the workshop. In here she watched the candle flames like torchlights at the foot of a stage. If it were *Shobbos,* she would be reading *Esther Waters,* forgetting herself in the drama of the book. But as it was a weekday in the busy season, she would go upstairs to see Minnie and then she would sew cheap jackets until midnight, imagining every shadow that is cast in a street of riotous despair.

Charlotte Street

In the West End, too, kindling was laid for the bonfires and floats were given the final touches for the parade. An erudite symposium on the Guy Fawkes conspiracy was being hosted by the university, and there was to be a masked ball in the museum. But though it was late in the day, Emilia was still sitting in bed, wearing her silk dressing gown while the ghost of the first wife sat beside her among the magazines and newspapers. The latest issue of *Ladies* had articles on winter colors, a charity tea held by the Duchess of York, crystallized party decorations, the women's suffrage calendar, the annual report of the Women's Trade Union Association, and a recipe for German chocolate cake. Emilia thought that Zaydeh would enjoy it if he was ever willing to eat with her again, now that he knew she was not the good gentile but the bad Jewess. On her bed tray there was a letter from the shop in Regent Street regarding the sale of a paper-cut, a bill from Liberty's, a catalog, and a postcard from Minsk. Beside the bed, a tea trolley was laden with cakes and sandwiches for, as the physician had noted, her condition hadn't affected her appetite, thank God. He said she was suffering from irritability due to neurasthenia, a weakening of the nervous system brought about by pregnancy, and she was to be humored.

Jacob didn't seem to understand the prescription. "Put down the magazine and get dressed," he ordered. There would be no symposium or masked ball for them. They were to attend the memorial evening for the old headmaster of the Jews' Free School. Jacob would speak; funds would be raised for the school.

"As soon as I'm finished." Emilia picked up the Liberty's catalog.

The wallpaper in the bedroom was too bright. It ought to be replaced with something in modern, muted colors, and she would do it if she was sure that she wasn't going to be thrown out of the house.

Jacob glanced at his pocket watch. He was in evening dress, his fingers scrubbed clean of ink. "I have to be on the platform with the other speakers by seven-thirty." The affair was to be held in the new wing of the school, with its entrance in Middlesex Street, where the rag market had been held since Shakespeare's time. Hence the street had been called Petticoat Lane from that day to this. If the present queen found the word *petticoat* too indelicate, well, she had never learned how to squeeze bedbugs with a click of her fingernails.

"Oh, Jacob. No Jewish function begins sooner than half an hour after it's called for."

"Always late, Jews are?"

"Well"—she cut out the recipe for chocolate cake as if she'd be staying long enough to bake it—"facts are facts."

He pulled up a chair and sat down, lighting his pipe. What could be more civilized than a brier pipe? Fine-grained and flawless, made from the root burl of a heath tree growing on a hillside in Italy. Someone had to ride up the hill on a mule to cut out the root for this pipe. "Would it nauseate you if I smoked?"

"Not at all." She liked the smell of his tobacco. It was the smell of the third floor, where he wrote and she cut scenes out of paper. But that was then and this was now. There was always a new now. One must make accommodations. The ghost of the first wife was reading the postcard from Minsk.

"Whenever you get one of those postcards, you mope for days afterward," Jacob said, his tone friendly enough.

"I do not." What was he getting at, looking at her through the smoke of his pipe?

"You do. I think you miss your life there."

"Hardly at all, Jacob." There was a pain in the center of her chest, a blunt stabbing at the juncture of her ribs.

"By the way"—he flicked a bit of ash off his lapel—"Mr. Nussbaum told me that you canceled your appointment this week."

So that was it. Now he could begin. The accusation, the recrimination. Zaydeh told me that you're not a gentile girl at all. You tricked me into marrying you.

"I'm not feeling well," she said, just as her mother would have. "Didn't you see the physician leaving my room?"

"You look well enough to me. Except when it comes to getting ready for this evening."

"Well, it's mean of you, Jacob. To ask me to go out to the East End when I'm pregnant and sensitive to odors."

"I wonder if there isn't another odor that's bothering you."

"What do you mean?"

"Well, let's look at the facts together. One—you didn't want a girl from Norwood."

"We can't afford it. I told your mother so." Through the heavy curtains, she could see flashes of light and hear firecrackers explode. Dusk was passing into night.

"I'm not so sure. Would you have the same objection if it wasn't a Jewish orphanage? Wait—I'm not finished. Second, you didn't think much of the article I wrote about the street where I was born."

"Jacob, what are you talking about? I never even read the article."

"That's just what I'm saying. Third—my new play. We've been married for eleven years. Do you think I don't know what it means when you start scratching your neck?"

She picked up a plate from the tea trolley and put it on her breakfast tray. What she put on the plate didn't matter. It was white—a slice of cake or a sandwich or even a piece of cheese, it gave her a moment to think. "I'm sorry, Jacob, but I don't think it the best example of the new drama. Your mother didn't like it either."

"I wish you did like it, but that's neither here nor there. You canceled your appointment with Mr. Nussbaum this week. My son isn't going to have a *bris,* is he?" He crossed his legs as if to protect the snipped evidence, the crux of the matter, for if a wife doesn't want a man's son to look like him, then what does she think of her husband?

"No *bris?*" she repeated. So Jacob didn't know. Zaydeh hadn't told him that she was Jewish.

"Everything was all very well when I was an author of detective fiction and all that, but now it's too much for you, though you won't come right out and say it. You might just as well, Emilia." His face was furrowed as if he had a killing toothache.

"You think I harbor some hidden feelings toward—what?"

"Shall I spell it out? Right, then. You don't like Jews."

"Jacob! That's ridiculous." It was impossible. He thought she was an anti-Semite. The ghost of the first wife looked up from the postcard as if she might try to catch Jacob's eye, but he was gazing past them, his eyes on a painting of a white villa, a maiden, a flock of sheep.

"There's nothing much to distinguish me from any other gentleman, is there? I'm a quasi-Jew, we'll say."

"And your grandfather—you can't doubt my affection for him." She was blinking as if there were suddenly too much light and the sun hurt her eyes.

"One little Jew, an old man at that, anyone could be fond of him. But the East End is rather more overwhelming."

"Certainly, and it's not a matter of race. Admit it, Jacob, the poor aren't partial to baths."

"If that were all, then why did you leave my play early? I saw your pained face. No, Emilia. When we come to this evening and the odor of the streets, I want to know whether you don't mean the smell of Jews."

"I can't believe you'd say such a thing." She threw off the bedcovers, magazines and letters sliding to the floor. "Just you wait and I'll be dressed in five minutes. It's the ideal evening for a memorial. Bonfires and lit-up tar barrels, perfect for starting a fire, as if there aren't enough fires in the East End already and people stampeding at just the thought of it. And thieves in the crowd, I don't know if they're Jews or not, but no doubt ready to trip someone and bang her on the head for a wedding ring. The smell of the slaughterhouse is very nice, to be sure, and the flies . . ."

She stalked into the dressing room, her heart beating hard at the unraveling of her world. A button flew off her dressing gown as she yanked it off.

"Don't bother, Emilia." Jacob leaned against the doorframe. If this was a religious household, there would be a *mezuzah* there, and the letter *shin* would trap any demons. But as it was, the doorpost was bare and Jacob turned on his heel, calling back, "Stay in bed. I don't care."

She listened to his footsteps descending, the slam of the front door. It wasn't fair. He had it all wrong, and in the end it was just as if he had it right. "Well, what do you think now?" she asked the first wife. "I told you the minute I came back from the other Charlotte Street."

She sat down at her dressing table, head in her hands. Someone who could fit in anywhere and please everyone surely could find a way to pull herself together like a new outfit when the styles have changed. It wasn't only her life that depended on it but her child's. A feather in a hat, a change of overskirt.

Petticoat Lane

All through the Lane, men held torches made from sticks and sacking soaked in paraffin, waiting for the signal to set them alight. Three hundred years ago on November 5, a plot to blow up Parliament had been foiled, the traitor Guy Fawkes was caught, and the free land saved. Well, it was saved for the Protestants at any rate. This was a Catholic plot, and effigies of the pope used to be burned on Guy Fawkes Day. But that was then and this was now. Everyone celebrated, wearing masks and old clothes as if they, too, were guys about to be cast into a great fire that turned anger into revelry and sorrows into warmth and light. Here the girls were coating doorknobs with treacle, there some boys were stuffing drainpipes with paper and setting them alight. A tin can full of ashes was hung over a doorway. Windows were daubed with paint. Who could see? Who could know? The year was winding toward its end; it was the time for mischief and tricks, for burning effigies, for parades and firecrackers, for children begging pennies and shouting:

> Remember, remember
> The fifth of November
> Is gunpowder treason and plot.
> I see no reason
> Why gunpowder treason
> Should ever be forgot.

On this night of fire, there was nothing so delicious as a potato baked in a tin can or a slice of sponge cake made with oatmeal and treacle, except maybe the toffee apple Gittel was biting into. The girls were standing on either side of their guy, which was stuffed with straw and slumped against a wall, its head a painted turnip bowed like a drunk's. The guy wore a man's hat and the three-colored ruffled dress that Mama had made for it out of "cabbage," the leftover pieces from tailoring work.

"A guy ought to wear trousers," Libby said.

"Not mine." Gittel had a plan. When the guy was burned in the bonfire, it would be a sacrifice, just like when Abel in the Bible put a sheep on the fire. Then she'd ask God for a favor. In case God didn't speak English, He'd get the idea from the dress and He'd make Gittel's teacher forgive her and let her back into the school concert. Then she wouldn't have to tell her parents that she'd been cut from the choir. Did that count as two prayers? If she had only one, maybe she ought to pray for money. Mama wouldn't let her take a job after school, not even to help out in their own workshop. She had to study, though she didn't know what for as she'd have to turn to sewing anyway once she left school. Her first mother would let her take a job. As an opera singer if nothing else.

"The guy has no legs," Libby complained, spreading the guy's dress over the sides of the cart.

"What a *mitzvah*, then, to give a penny for him," Gittel replied.

"Penny for the guy!" they called, holding out a hat.

In the Lane the torches burst into flame, one after another, like the bonfires on the hills of the Holy Land announcing the arrival of a festival. The first float was pulled by the Samsons, a dozen Jewish boxers in suspenders and open shirts. The guy rising eight feet above the float had a fat head and an ornate hat and glittering chains: he might be the pope or poor Guy Fawkes; he could be the commander of the ascending German navy or even the editor of the *East London Observer,* who believed there were altogether too many Jews in London, but certainly he was the enemy and eminently ugly. Facing him on the float, standing higher still, ten feet high, fifteen feet, as high as the black sky, was the tailor's guy with a needle for a spear, seven-league boots, and a cigar in his mouth. Behind the float marched the tailors, swinging rattles made of spools tied together. Then came the boot makers, who sweated harder than the tailors in basement factories, shouting curses at the traitor Guy Fawkes. Behind them young women arm in arm flirted with the young men who were climbing poles, the better to see the parade. Last the cigar makers swaggered, throwing fancy firecrackers that exploded above the crowd, threatening to alight on some roof and start another great fire, while the children ran and screamed, breathing in gunpowder and ash as they called, "Penny for a guy!"

The parade was making its way down to Whitechapel Road, where it would pass the Salvation Army Mission and turn up Brick Lane, returning to the Jews' Free School. In the school yard the guys would be burned on a pyre, both of them: the guy of the master and the guy of the slave, and the people would shout for joy at their destruction.

"Mama's worried," Gittel said. She had to shout so Libby could hear her, though she didn't like to shout. It made her feel undressed. From stalls parked on either side of the road, hawkers were calling, "Eels jellied!" "Firecrackers fresh!" "Red apples. No worms, guaranteed!"

"They all do. When I'm a mother, I'll worry, too. Next year, I'm putting my hair up." Libby was fourteen and working as a general hand in their workshop.

"It's my *tatteh* she's worried for. Because he's in the streets at night. We need the money, and Mama doesn't want me leaving school."

"You won't be thirteen till January. You're still too young, Gittel. You can't do nothing." Libby stepped over some muck. Several boys pulling a red wagon shouted at the girls to move over. Their faces were cut, their noses flattened by fistfights. Libby pulled Gittel into the doorway of Shmolnik's pawnshop. Inside, little Morrie Cohen stared at them as he waited for his mother to finish her business. He had a crush on Libby. She stuck her tongue out at him, and he waved the pair of sticks he was pretending were guns.

"I'm not too young to add up the accounts on the wall," Gittel said. "We need *Tatteh*'s coffee money to get through the slack season, but he's begging to get his head bashed in. He's got only one hand to defend himself."

The girls were silent. "It'll be all right." Libby took Gittel's hand. They stood in the doorway watching firecrackers smash the sky with light.

"Mama don't have to worry, I've got all my eyes about me," Gittel said at last.

"Sure you do." Libby held Gittel's hand tighter as a drunk in a mask bumped against their cart.

"I heard them talking about Jinny. I heard Mama say as she sings for her supper in Dorset Street. That's what I'll do. And then *Tatteh* won't have to sell coffee at night." What did she care for school concerts? Her destiny was somewhere else. It was impossible to avoid.

"Singing in pubs is for *yokheltas*." Gentile girls. "It's dodgy. And you hate singing in front of people."

"My other mother could do it," Gittel said. "She sings in the Savoy Theatre."

"What a lot of rubbish. You listen to me, Gittel Katzellen. You're too big for pretending."

"What do you mean?" Gittel asked, knotting the end of the rope that pulled the guy in its cart. But how could she fool herself—didn't she know the truth in her heart? She felt it in her bones. She heard it in the air, calling louder than the voices of the dead.

Libby didn't look unkind as she started to say something, then just shook her head. "Aunt Nehama would never let you sing in a pub."

Gittel stuck out her chin. "You watch me, Libby." It was there, the answer was there, hidden in Dorset Street, creeping along the gutter at the heels of dangerous men.

"Where do you think you're going?" Libby hurried to catch up with Gittel, turning a corner both darker and louder.

Frying Pan Alley

Minnie and Lazar's room upstairs looked much the same as it had many years ago. It was two steps from bed to table, where you could lean over and open the door, and the table was still made of crates and boards, but Minnie's pride and joy was a real wardrobe with a door and a mirror. All right, the mirror was cracked, but Minnie could see all of herself in it, not like the little piece of glass she'd been using before, stretching herself one way and then the other to see her hair, her collar, her waist. One day a cameo brooch fell out of the wardrobe, just like that, and Minnie always wore it to *shul* on the holy days; it made her the equal of any woman in a feathered hat.

"I got a letter today," Nehama said.

"From one of your sisters?" Minnie opened the window and threw a pile of fish bones onto the roof of the backyard shack that housed a tinsmith, his family, and his workshop. Then she wiped the bowl with a rag so it could be used for the potatoes. Her apron might be stained, but her hair was combed and curled and pinned in some ornate style she'd seen in an advertisement for Pears soap.

"It's from Shayna-Pearl." Nehama had letters from one or another of her sisters at the New Year and Passover and whenever there was a birth or a death.

"Remind me. Which one is she?"

"The teacher." Usually letters came from Nehama's oldest sister. Sometimes one of the others. Even Bronya had written her eventually, though every so often she made a reference to earrings that could never be replaced and who can imagine the things that one sister could do to another.

"You just had a letter from her."

"No—you're thinking of Bronya. I mean my middle sister with the bad temper."

"I thought she didn't speak to you."

"That's it exactly," Nehama said. "This is the first I heard from her."

"What does she say?"

"She saw a play, and it reminded her of me."

"After twenty-five years?" Minnie asked, peeling an onion. When she was finished, she'd fry the fish and cook the potatoes and onions downstairs. They'd all eat together, her family and Nehama's. "You'd think a teacher would have a better memory. What was the play about?"

"I don't know. She didn't say. Only that the play reminded her of me and when she came home she cried. I don't remember Shayna-Pearl crying over anything. Yelling, yes. That she did plenty. Slamming doors, fine. But she says in the letter that she cried and she had to write to tell me a story."

"It gets better and better," Minnie said. "So she finally finds her tongue and she wants to tell you stories. What does she say?"

"It's about my grandmother. My step-grandmother, I should say."

"It must be something to make your sister write to you after all this time," Minnie said.

"Let me tell you, and then you can be the judge." Nehama picked up a potato and began to peel it. She needed something in her hands.

"So? I'm listening," Minnie said.

"Grandma Nehama had a miscarriage."

"A lot of women have miscarriages. I had one between Sammy and Libby." Minnie sliced the onions like a juggler, fast fast fast, the knife invisible. The tireder she was, the faster her knife went, cutting her distress into paper-thin slices—she'd add a little salt, a little pepper, fry it in oil, and eat it as something good.

"That's what I mean. Why did my sister have to write me about it now? Anyway, Grandma Nehama had a late miscarriage. It was her last child, and she was the same age as I am now. The midwife didn't want her to see the baby, but she insisted on looking, and she saw that the baby was deformed. Afterward she told everyone it was better this way, because at her age taking care of such a child wouldn't be easy and the child's life would be a misery."

"And you never heard this from your sisters?"

"Never. Shayna-Pearl said in her letter that she overheard our grandmother talking about it to her closest friend. It was a Thursday after the women finished singing and were eating cake. Everyone was eating cake. Only Grandma Nehama was in the other room with her friend, putting on the dough to rise for making *challah* for *Shobbos*. No one noticed my middle sister, who'd found the raisins and was hiding behind a barrel eating them all. Shayna-Pearl never told anyone because she thought she'd get it for eating the raisins."

"So that was all? Just about the miscarriage," Minnie said.

"Wait, I'm not finished. Grandma Nehama told her friend that after the miscarriage a neighbor came into the house in a panic because her son was *khapped,* taken for the draft. Grandma Nehama was holding the babies, my two oldest sisters, but it didn't ease the pain she felt over the one she'd lost. The thought of another child being taken cut her like a sword. It made her crazy. So she picked up the hatchet to defend herself and her family and her neighbor's family from any more misery. After she came home she was horrified at what she'd done. Cutting off a couple of toes from a child's foot isn't cooking dumplings. But in the end it turned out all right. The boy wasn't drafted; he lived and everyone was thankful."

"That's it?" Minnie asked.

"Now that's it," Nehama said. "My sister sends her best wishes, we should all be healthy, and to tell Gittel that she should become a teacher like her auntie."

"Very nice," Minnie said.

"Maybe. My grandmother used to say that as long as you can preserve life, there's hope. But I'm telling you, Minnie, that hope doesn't cure the cholera."

"I'd like a new blouse myself," Minnie said. "You can't wear hope to the synagogue. When you work like a pig all week, then at least if you have a nice blouse for *Shobbos,* you feel like a human being."

"Listen to me. I'm trying to tell you something. It's a sign, Nathan going to Dorset Street." Nehama looked at Minnie, and her friend looked at her. She knew what Nehama was talking about. A person can't get through the busy season year after year without telling somebody her secrets. "I'm thinking one thing. Like mother, like daughter."

Minnie looked at her hesitantly. "I don't know if I should say this, but you can't change a nature. Wait a minute, Nehama. Think on it. That Mrs. Levy, well, she was an educated person. Why wouldn't Gittel take after her?"

"If only," Nehama said. "From your lips to God's ear. But I'm telling you, Minnie, and only you, that there is nothing more bitter than praying that your child isn't truly yours."

"Come on. I'm ready. Let's go downstairs and I'll cook supper," Minnie said, giving the plate of fish to Nehama and carrying the bowl of potatoes and onions herself.

There was one thing that Nehama didn't tell Minnie. Who could say why? She meant to, and then she was walking down the narrow staircase, holding a plate in one hand, a candle in the other, watching her step that she shouldn't fall on the broken riser, for dusk had given way to night and the sound of firecrackers could startle someone.

Her sister had said that she'd remembered the end of the story only when she was writing the letter. After Grandma Nehama covered the *challah* dough with a cloth, she'd wiped her hands. Then she turned to her friend and said, Every pain in life makes a scar. The scar thickens and it becomes a snake around your neck. It's up to you if the snake chokes you or if it looks into the night and tells you what it sees. Then you can know what's there in the darkness.

Charlotte Street

Emilia wandered through the house in her dressing gown, remembering the first time she invited her mother-in-law for tea, wearing a made-over gown that had seemed so elegant at the time and was now the maid's Sunday best. She was restless and needed to walk about. Here was the parlor with its Liberty's paper of lilies and thistles, and the ceiling she'd painted in the days before they could afford wallpaper from Liberty's. And here the dining room where Jacob used to play chess with his brother, and the same old walnut table, scratched by the cat who was locked out once and snuck in to pee in protest on the blue Persian rug. The painted willow boughs still shook in an imaginary wind, and only the door was new, filled with stained glass. But in the kitchen no smoke billowed, no brisket burned, there was only the maid cleaning ashes from the stove as Emilia climbed up the narrow back stairs to the attic.

The third floor looked just like Pompeii, preserved in the midst of activity when the inhabitants were overcome by flowing lava. Jacob's desk was strewn with papers, the title page of his new play on top: "Shmuel in America, or The Melting Pot." Emilia could smell his tobacco, she could see him turn his head with an abstracted air, awareness coming into his eyes as he looked at her, leaning forward to ask what she would imagine when she heard the title. She'd immediately said *cholent,* the slow-cooking Sabbath stew cooked with whatever came to hand—beans, meat, bones, fat, potatoes—the house redolent from a mixture more delectable than any humble part of it. Exactly, Jacob had said, coming around his desk to kiss her with more enthusiasm than finesse because his mind was still on the play.

There was time. She could run down and dress, send for a carriage, and be at the school before it was Jacob's turn to speak. She'd wear the amber-colored gown from Liberty's and the bracelet Jacob had given her for her birthday. He would look at her with the same admiring glance she'd seen in his eyes when she was a shopgirl reading Emile Zola, sitting on a tall stool in a basement, electric lights shimmering on Chinese porcelain. Why should anything in the Lane disturb her—did it have a thing to do with her? She wouldn't remember the sound of street vendors calling, "Hot chestnuts!" "Rabbit 'air skins!" She wouldn't take notice of the smell of fried fish that was the smell of childbirth.

A wave of nausea came over her. That was what Jacob would see, his face drawn with suspicion as he read the worst motives into her distress. She'd better sit at her worktable and consider the garden in darkness, doused in a dismal autumn rain. Pinned to her cutting board was the sketch for a paper-cut commissioned by the salon in Regent Street. She leaned her chin on her cupped hands. The smell of paint. The smell of ink. Think for a minute, calm herself. That was what she must do.

She'd been over and over this for days. There had been too many mistakes. The rabbi would surely realize, if not from the last meeting then from the next, that she was Jewish. Yet if she didn't go back to see him, Jacob would continue to think she was an anti-Semite and he would hate her. She'd end in telling him the truth. And then he would hate her just the same, since he'd never liked Jewish girls and she'd made him think she was something else. Oh, she'd rather he hated her for the lie than the truth, though she couldn't stand the look on his face when he'd left the house and her tears were falling on the paper-cut, ruining it.

He could leave her and take her child. The law gave him custody. That she couldn't allow. Instead she must pack her trunk, for she was now a woman in her thirties, not a girl dependent on her mother. Everything would be different this time.

Downstairs in the dressing room, Emilia inspected her jewelry box. It was made of exotic wood, decorated with a geometric mosaic, the contrasting hue and grain of the wood creating something marvelous even out of disease, for the best pieces were green oak, colored and shaped by an attack of fungus. It was a gift from Mrs. Zalkind, her own favorite box, with two removable trays lined in velvet.

The ghost of the first wife sat on the dressing table, her face livelier than Emilia's as she looked at the necklace in the top tray, a gold necklace with rubies and pearl drops that had come with the box from Mrs. Zalkind. How much would it fetch? Probably more than the bracelet from Jacob, set with a sapphire and four rose-cut diamonds. The bracelet was thicker, but the gold in the necklace was higher quality.

Pearls didn't go for so very much, but she had a string of dark green, almost black pearls, and that would fetch more than white. She'd have to sell it all, and even so it wouldn't do for long. The jewelry of an author's wife is not anywhere near so large in quantity and value as the jewelry that may be provided by a man who owns a brick factory. How long could she support her child?

The ghost of the first wife shook her head as she put the postcard from Minsk on the dressing table, tapping it with her finger. Maybe there was a message in it, something known only to the next world, a note of consolation or, better yet, the winner of a horse race, a long shot that would set her up with her baby in a villa on a warm hillside where she'd never miss the damp of London or the people who lived in it.

The postcard was the usual sort of thing, a warning to watch her step, a sigh over the distance between them, a prayer for her health. It helped as much in her present situation as giving medicine to a corpse. No offense to the first wife, who was impatiently turning over the post-card.

It was illustrated with a picture of Hannah in the temple, her lips moving as she prayed for God to give her a child. Standing over her was the angry high priest, accusing her of mumbling in a drunken stupor. How easy it was, even for a high priest, to misconstrue what the eyes perceive when he'd never watched anyone pray privately before but knew plenty of drunkards.

Outside in the street, revelers shouted and set off firecrackers. Someone was singing:

> Of friendship I have heard much talk
> But you'll find that in the end,
> If you're distressed at any time,
> Then money is your friend.

At the sound of the song, the ghost of the first wife looked up, startled, ran first to the window and then out the door of the dressing room and down the stairs. Her footsteps made no noise—who would expect them to? She was gone, and Emilia was alone. That was the message.

Dorset Street

It was one thing to be reckless where Yiddish signs were visible in the torchlight, quite another to turn off Bell Lane into the forbidden street, the sky smoky and scorched above Itchy Park, where vagrants slept. Fog made the end of the street a million miles away, a sea between continents, a wall between this world and the next. There were blind streetlamps, broken glass underfoot. Figures gaunt and grotesque loomed in the fog like guys with painted turnip heads, picking cigarette butts out of the gutter. Lady guys with eyes cut out of masks wore dark dresses that turned red in the window light of a pub. If only Libby would insist that they had to go home, Gittel would, but Libby was unnaturally quiet, her red braids shivering against her back.

Humming under her breath, Gittel pulled the crate with her sacrificial guy in its three-colored dress. The wind was cold, but Gittel's cheeks were warm, as warm as when people whispered in the dark evenings, starting a story but never finishing it, glancing at the children and leaving off in the middle of naphtha lamps exploding with paraffin vapor and the bright colors of gin palaces and hideous corners where the Ripper had lurked. And here she was, walking by the striped awning that sheltered a wax figure and the hawker advertising the wonders inside. "Wax figures! Only a penny a view. Each one figured exactly like one of them poor ladies mutilated most horribly. Move along, my dears, unless you have a penny. Don't block the gentleman's view."

The fortune-teller's house was next. "Madam Fortune," the sign said, in case someone could read, and if not there was a picture of a crystal ball. Maybe she ought to stop there and find out just where she ought to go. Her teachers at school warned children about spiritualists and mediums and other fakery. God used to talk to people in the Bible, and when He'd had enough of people, He sent angels, but that was only because there wasn't any science. Now there was the telephone in the post office, but it wouldn't do you much good if the other party had no telephone. You might as well communicate with the dead.

Unless, of course, the other party was your first mother. Gittel would know her in an instant; it would be like looking at her own face in a mirror. Her other mother would be worn out, down at heel, all hope abandoned until she heard her lost daughter sing. How she would weep to hear the voice she never knew could be so sweet, but it was all too late. Much too late. Her eyes would grow large as she saw the coins that Gittel would pile into Mama's lap, glittering gold and silver, saving one—all right, maybe two or three—for the mother that bore her. Gittel wasn't scared, not really—wasn't God answering her prayer right now, the real prayer to find things out once and for all? It was just that her legs felt terribly weak and Libby was holding her hand so tight it hurt.

"Where are you going?" Libby whispered.

"Right here," Gittel said, pointing to the first open door she saw.

One of the slumming gentlemen was talking to a pretty girl with hair cut short as if she'd just been released from the workhouse. She wore a dress almost as ruffled as the guy's. Gittel wished for a dress like that. Very grown-up, it was. But the girl's arms were bare, and even Gittel's shawl was getting damp and clammy and cold against her back.

Charlotte Street

The wallpaper in Emilia's bedroom was an old Morris paper, a trellis pattern handprinted with climbing roses that reminded her of the garden in Minsk. It was one of the things she disliked about this house. She was back in bed, making a list of the house's flaws. So far she had fifteen items, including the shape of the roof (too pointed), the number of fireplaces (too few), and the back door (sticky). A quiet back door was indispensable. How else was a trunk to be removed without comment?

"Excuse me, missus," the maid said. "Mr. Zalkind's grandfather is come to see you."

"Tell him that I'm still indisposed." But she could hear his slow step on the stairs and the sound of his labored breath. "Zaydeh!" she said as he came in. "It's a sin to be in a woman's bedroom."

"Is this a bedroom? I don't believe it. A bedroom is where a person sleeps at night, not where she sits around all day with magazines and trays. This is a sitting room, am I right? I know I'm very old. Too old maybe to see exactly right, but this is how it looks to me." With a slight groan, he sat down in the chair beside the bed, though keeping his eyes away from Emilia. In honor of Jacob's speech, he wore a new wool cap.

"So what do you have to say?" Her face was defiant.

"I'm going to tell you the truth. I was very angry." He shook his finger. So what was that? It was nothing. Just an old, knobbly finger.

"I don't need anyone's blessing." In the street ragamuffins were calling, "Penny for a guy!" Emilia added another item to her list. This was no longer a good address. "I'll take care of things myself."

"Ah, you're smarter than me. I asked the Holy One what I should do, but He didn't answer. All right, I'm not Moses our teacher. Why should He talk to me? Still, an old man has to do something, even if he isn't strong and for sure he isn't wise. So this is what I say to myself. An old man mishears half of everything." With his little finger, he scratched the inside of his ear. "But one thing I know. Everyone's at the school. The whole family except you. And for a man, there's only his wife."

Emilia put away her list. The page was full. Her trunk would soon be packed and she was ready. "My father hated my mother like no one else," she said.

Zaydeh didn't look shocked. On the contrary, he was nodding as if he knew it all long. "Because she mattered the most, so you see what I mean. The wife is everything. Come with me in the carriage."

Emilia shook her head. "Jacob hates me now, too. This isn't your problem, Zaydeh. Have some tea and cake, please. There's jelly roll." She pointed to the tea trolley, and he cut himself a slice as if they were sitting in the kitchen on any other day and he never knew or cared that she was living on false papers, so to speak.

"This I like. You made it, *mine gitteh*?"

"I'm not your good one anymore," Emilia said.

"What are you talking?"

"Everyone likes to pretend something. Even you, Zaydeh. A man of the earth—what a lot of nonsense. No one I know is as clever as you."

"Absolutely, you're wrong. It's only the word I didn't say that changed. Before, it was my good *yokhelta*." Gentile girl. "Now it's my good *yiddina*." Jewish woman. "You see. *Mine gitteh* . . . what?" He showed her his empty hands. "It's written that there's one Torah in the letters of the Bible and another one in the space between the letters. So. A person can be very angry. But *nu*. What did I tell you? Until you finish the whole book you don't know what you're reading. Jacob's child will be a Jew. In a good hour, I say."

It didn't make her afraid. The tears in her eyes and the quickness of her breathing weren't fear at all. She just didn't know what her child would be. It would all depend on where she found herself. "Everyone knows Jacob's your favorite," she said with a little smile, certain that she had enough charm left to divert an old man for a few minutes.

"He's my favorite because he's not my daughter's, she should live to be a hundred and twenty, please God. She favors Albert. He's just like her husband. And with Jacob she was always nervous because he looks a little like me. Much finer, I should say. But something, there is. When I was young, I even argued like Jacob. All right." He pushed aside his plate. "So you're going to come with me."

"I told you I'm too ill."

"Is that right?" He put the glass teacup laced with silver back on the trolley. "I can't force you. Of course, if you're not there, God in heaven only knows what I might say to your Jacob. An old man. You know, his mind wanders and his tongue with it." Now he looked at her with a straightforward gaze, letting her see the backside of his anger, the tail flicking at her. He would tell everything, and then there would be endless questions. Her mother-in-law jubilant, Jacob furious. To sell a box of jewelry, to buy train tickets, to make arrangements, a person needs to be unnoticed.

"It's a miracle, Zaydeh. I'm feeling much better. If you go downstairs, I'll dress. Please send Annie up to help me."

She wouldn't think about where she was going. She was not dizzy and she wouldn't faint on the threshold like her mother, for she knew that tomorrow, yes, tomorrow, she would go to Shmolnik's herself to sell her jewelry. She'd be on the train before night. A person was always on her own. Anything else was delusion.

Outside in the darkness, the carriage stood in front of the house. The horses' breath blew at the light of streetlamps, the driver taking a nip of something in a bottle. Children were calling, "Penny for a guy," and men carried torches. From behind the carriage, the ghost of the first wife came strolling toward the streetlamp as if she were out for a Sabbath promenade, but if she thought that Emilia would greet her with open arms, then she was mistaken. A person, even a ghost, can't come and go without so much as a by-your-leave. The grief at such partings becomes tiresome.

There was someone else accompanying the first wife, a woman rather older but just as dead. In the fashion of religious women fifty years ago, she wore a bib and apron, the bib embroidered in green and gold, and a turban covered her hair. She wasn't wearing a cloak. Why should she—do the dead feel cold? Emilia drew her fur collar closer around her neck.

"*Sholom aleichem,*" Zaydeh said to the first wife. "And to your friend, too."

"*Aleichem sholom,*" the other woman said, as if the dead could speak just like ordinary people. And so they can when the time is right. "Your wife is famous up there."

"My wife? You know her."

"Not personally. But everyone heard how she taught Deborah the prophetess to sing 'A Woman of Valor' in the *mama-loshen.* Come on. There isn't much time. We have to go."

"You're not here to take him," Emilia said. The carriage might soon carry her into the fog, but she was still here in front of the house. And at least on this night the house was hers and she was the possessor of its keys. "I won't allow it." She put her arm through Zaydeh's as if she had no intention of forgetting him the minute she stepped on the boat. Zaydeh tried to disentangle himself, but she held on tighter. "I won't allow it, I'm telling you. There's no use in your even trying."

The old woman laughed. "Don't worry so much. I'm here for your sake, my girl. Let's get into the carriage. I have something to say to you." She turned to the first wife. "But, Mrs. Rosenberg, you please hurry."

Emilia let herself be led into the carriage, bewildered by all the comings and goings in this world and the next, which she couldn't seem to understand or govern, as the ghost of the first wife left her again, waving good-bye and walking away into the night.

Frying Pan Alley

In the front room, there was a blue vase on the mantelpiece and beside it a school picture. The dresser stood next to the table; on the dresser were the dishes and, on the top shelf, books. It had begun with two volumes of fairy tales received in return for making a maternity dress, and now there were fifteen books, each one protected by a quilted cover that Nehama had sewn from scraps. The used-book sellers were impatient with her because she thumbed through every page to make sure they were all there. Just buy already, it's a good price, they'd say. Are you a librarian?

In her shop, she'd let a person look from beginning to end and not stand like a copper over a vagrant. That would be if she had a shop, which she wouldn't, for she was sure that her husband would be coshed in Dorset Street. The sages taught that the *yetzer-hara,* the instinct for survival, arises when a person is born, but the *yetzer-hatov,* the selfless impulse, develops only with maturity. If its growth was stunted, then the *yetzer-hara* grew large to compensate, and Nehama herself could testify to its success in acquiring a certain expertise.

Firecrackers were exploding just as they had on her wedding night while she crept from her bed and stood before the dark window, crying because she loved her husband and couldn't tell whether he smelled of tobacco or sweat or anything at all. Sparks flew up above the rows of chimney pots now as then. The children were outside, enjoying the fireworks, while Minnie and Lazar, she and Nathan ate their supper, fortifying themselves for their night of work. The front room must smell of fish and onions tonight, but for Nehama there was just the sensation of grease and the taste of salt; the slippery texture of fish and onion were the same to her tongue.

"What do you think of the war?" Lazar asked, his round cheeks puffing as he chewed a good-size bit of potato and onion.

"My grandmother cut off a boy's toes to keep him from the draft," Nehama said. "At least he lived to have children."

"But that was the czar. We were slaves then. Can we let the Boers shell our towns? No." He slapped the table. "Here free men should fight."

"Are you going to fight with your pressing iron?" Minnie laughed.

"Don't laugh," Nathan said. "His iron is heavy enough to clobber someone. Just don't drop it on your foot, Lazar."

"I got the *Daily Mail,*" he said. "They have a reporter right there. You think a sweatshop is anything? Listen to this."

But before Lazar could read, there was a knock at the door, and when it opened, Mrs. Cohen from down the alley stood in the door-way with her boy Morrie holding a stick of wood over his shoulder like a soldier's rifle. She had a simple, square body covered by a coat too threadbare for even the pawnshop. Her cheeks were chapped from the fall wind, her nose wet as she wiped it with the back of her hand.

"Good evening, good evening," she said. "*Sholom aleichem.* Don't get up, Mrs. Katzellen. I'm just here for a minute. No, please. Not even a cup of tea."

"Do you want me to turn over your coat?" Nehama asked. Last year she'd made over a *Shobbos* dress for Mrs. Cohen, creating a waist for her with darts and tucks. "I'm too busy, now. But in the slack season . . ."

"I need to tell you something," Mrs. Cohen said. "I was at Shmol-nik's . . ."

Right away Nehama knew that something was wrong. It had to be if it involved Shmolnik. "What does he want from me?" Nehama said.

"Him? Nothing. It's nothing to do with Shmolnik."

"Then what?"

"I'm trying to tell you. Morrie was waiting for me and looking out-side at the parade."

"And?" Minnie asked. She went to the stove, her wooden spoon dripping melted chicken fat as she put another serving of potatoes onto her plate.

"He heard your girls talking. Tell them, Morrie."

The boy looked down at his scuffed boots. His face was dirty, his ears stuck out under his cap. Everyone knew that the glazier paid him a penny to break windows when the trade was slack. "They said as they was going to Dorset Street."

"What?" Nehama asked. She couldn't have heard right. A person's nightmare doesn't suddenly turn into a supper of fried fish and the snotty-nosed neighbor boy, who has a crush on Libby, speaking of doom in the half-Yiddish, half-Cockney English of the alley.

"Something about singing like Jinny what used to live with her grandma next door," the boy said. "Does Jinny sing? That's not what I heard."

"Shh." His mother cuffed his ear.

"That's ridiculous," Minnie snapped, pouring fresh tea into Nehama's cup and pushing it into her hands. "I shouldn't say it, but everyone knows your Morrie makes up stories."

"Is it true, Morrie?" his mother asked him. "If you're lying, tell me now and I won't say anything. Otherwise I'll use that good stick for your backside, don't think I won't."

"I heard what I heard," he muttered, his face so sullen that no one could think he was lying.

"The girls went to the Jews' Free School," Minnie said, taking her shawl. "They said they'd be burning the guy on the bonfire there. I'll run out and fetch them."

Lazar was still holding the *Daily Mail,* opened to the photograph of ruined houses in Ladysmith. "I'm sure the girls are fine," he said uncertainly.

"Stay here in case they come home," Nehama said, hardly seeing as Mrs. Cohen and her son left. How could she see when she was dreaming the worst of dreams? "I'm going to look for them in Dorset Street."

"You think Gittel is really singing in some public house?" Nathan asked, already standing up and shrugging on his jacket. "Our Gittel what's so shy?"

"It's my fault. Don't you remember? I said that Jinny sings for her supper. I shouldn't have mentioned her name. Not even in a round-about way. A girl that does what she does." Nehama threw her shawl over her head.

"So maybe Gittel misunderstood and it gave her an idea. Then the important thing is to find her."

"Where are you going?" she asked him.

"If she's in Dorset Street, God forbid, I'll bring her home. I'll be all right, Nehameleh. People there know me."

And she knew them. God forbid he should see it and realize what she'd been. "In the damp, you'll catch your death. Do I need to nurse you back to health in the middle of the busy season?"

"Don't look so scared. You think I can't do it? You think I can't take care of my daughter and my wife?" His voice was sharp, the bitterness returning.

"Of course not. But shouldn't I think about your health? All right, if you don't care, then I won't say anything. Come on. Let's go. Better the last mile together. Am I right?"

Her mind was running on ahead of her, down the alley, past the school, up Bell Lane, where there was a small wooden sign in Yiddish between the kosher butcher and the German blacksmith's. When she came to the sign, she would turn back into what she'd been. She must—so that everything she knew could guide her. Nathan would only have to take one look and he would hate her, but all that mattered was that she get her daughter out of a room as bright as a gold tooth biting down. Then she would atone for being the selfish mother in the court of King Solomon and she would offer her own heart to pay off her outstanding debts.

CHAPTER 9

The Song

NOVEMBER 5, 1899

The Horn and Plenty

The door was open, the gas jets making a cave warm and light, only five steps down. Gittel stood at the bottom of the stairs, cold air at her back, Libby's fingers gripping her arm. The smell of beer and sausages made her stomach peculiar, and she suddenly didn't want to know which of the slack-jawed women standing at the bar might be her mother. But it didn't matter what she wanted, only where she belonged. The pub was bright with lion glass lamps, colored posters of music hall singers winked in the gas jets, and on the wall was a bill for the new melodrama at the Victorian, set in India. Women stood at the counter, talking and dipping a finger into glasses of gin for their babies to suck on.

"An' is she no better?"

"Nor won't be till she's gone."

"A great expense the burying is. Our Davey lay dead on the table six days till we found the money for him."

"It wants doing respectable. With mutes and plumes and that."

Gittel listened to the accordion, the hiss of taps, the click of conversation, the clang of a metal ring tied to a rope and flung against a hook on the back wall. Ringing the Bull, the game was called. In Roman times the hook had been a horn. On one side of the pub was a map of London 1807, at the far end a door marked in black paint, PRI-

VAT. If only she could just take one step inside, she'd be all right. She'd sing and bring the money home so her *tatteh* wouldn't have to sell coffee and be coshed and rolled in the street even if she had to come back here to stand with her first mother somewhere at the bar. But her feet wouldn't move, and Libby was whispering that she wasn't going to catch it on Gittel's account and she'd go herself in a minute. Help me, Gittel prayed, and her prayer was answered in the way that prayers can be in the days of science, with the voice of a neighbor rather than an angel, for there are immigration laws to prevent the sudden arrival of strangers sent by God incognito to a dusty tent.

"Over here." It was Mrs. Dawes from next door standing there at the counter, the frills of her cap rising like petals, and beside her was Jinny, with her yellow hair and a lacy bodice not quite covering her chest. Gittel made her way to Mrs. Dawes, trying not to be dazzled by the green walls and the three-tone posters, the stripes of Jinny's dress and the peacock feather eyeing her from a glass behind the barman, who kept order with a butcher's mallet.

Mrs. Dawes had two living grandchildren, one that lodged with her and Jinny, who rented a bed by the night in Dorset Street. Jinny's nickname was Star to rhyme with *car*. Her dress was striped like a streetcar, and men rode her, people said. Gittel wasn't certain what was meant, though it made her skin hot, as if her teacher were telling her to get the yardstick and hold her hands out for discipline while the whole class looked at her.

"Hello, Libby. Hello, Gittel. Are you sleeping on your feet, then?"

Gittel blinked. "Hello, Star," she said, putting her hands in her pockets.

"A rum guy, that is," Mrs. Dawes said. "Looks more of a dolly-mop than our Guy Fawkes."

"It were her mother made the guy's dress," Libby said in an angry voice. "And we ought to go now, Gittel, and throw it in the fire. Remember?"

"Right. Off with you girls," Mrs. Dawes said. "Your mother don't want a pot of beer, and there's nothing for you two in the Horn and Plenty."

Gittel put her hand on the old woman's arm. "I want to earn some money. Can you tell me who I ought to talk to so I can sing like Star?"

She hated the sound of her nervous, squeaky voice. No pennies could come from that.

"A good girl, that is," Mrs. Dawes said. "Thinking on your mum. That's as it ought to be. But our Jinny don't sing, she—well, she sews trousers. Don't you, Jinny?"

"Oh, yes. Trousers. You can take a quid out of a good pair of trousers, you can."

"I could do that. Mama taught me to sew," Gittel said quickly. Not one of the women looking at her curiously was familiar. Her other mother wasn't here, and she couldn't go to the next pub and the next. Her legs wouldn't hold her up. Maybe God meant her to wait, after all, and appear on the stage with a bouquet of flowers and help out now by sewing so that she could rip out any mistakes. "Could you get me some trousers, Star?"

"You see the Squire over there, Gittel. Him as is sitting at the little table near the back door." Gittel nodded. She'd noticed the watch fob on his vest, and how he was knitting like a sailor. "The Squire gets me any number of trousers, he does," Star said. "For a little girl like you, he'd have a good price. Ten quid, I'd say."

Six months' rent—a fortune. But Mrs. Dawes was shaking her head, the frills on her cap fluttering like Mr. Wordsworth's daffodils. "I don't hold with little girls having any truck with trousers. You'd best wait till you're thirteen, like our Jinny did." She reached down and ran her fingers along Gittel's face as if she could steal away some of the softness for her own. "But you can sing a little song for the Squire and I believe as he'll give you a few pennies to take home to your mum, and enough left over to stand us one."

Dorset Street

Nehama was forty-one years old now, and the street didn't look much different from when she was seventeen. Smoke from the bonfires crept up to the roofs and hung among the chimney pots, listening to what went on behind the gaping doorways. Shadows moved in holes where doors had been stolen off hinges. There still wasn't more than a single streetlamp. Over there the waxworks was new and the fortune-teller's sign, though the Horn and Plenty was where it had always been.

She couldn't remember much about the first time a man lay on her for money. She knew that she didn't want to understand what was expected of her, but that was no impediment. She was led behind a door marked PRIVAT in black paint. The room had a tiny window, the man a vague shape, as if the fog were as much inside as outside. The Squire came to the room afterward and laughed at her for trying to cover herself while he picked up the money. But England was a free country, he said, and as soon as she'd paid off her debts she could go on her way.

She didn't remember where she slept or if she slept, only that she came out of a stupor after some days, stiff and sore as she stood at the counter in the Horn and Plenty with a pencil and a Christian tract. On the back she added up her debts, glancing now and then at the map of London. Someone beside her was eating winkles with loud lip smackings, and Nehama believed that she herself would never eat again. Always it came back to the dress.

You couldn't profitably go on the game—or the turf as they called it then—without a dress that caught the eye. The Squire had provided the fancy dress, and his niece followed Nehama wherever she went to make sure that she didn't sell or pawn it. Her earnings, even with what she could pick from a man's pocket, were never enough to buy herself out.

The first time she ran away, it had been raining. She made her way to the train station through alleys and passageways only she knew, certain that she'd lost Lizzie, the Squire's niece. At the station, the dress got drenched while she bought a ticket for Brighton and stood waiting for the train. There they found her. The Squire looked like a country gentleman in his vest and watch fob, and no one stopped him when she called for help.

After the beating, she couldn't stand for a week, and the lost earnings were added to her debt.

Later she would say to Minnie that there are two kinds of criminals: those that lie and those that steal. She would be sitting on Minnie's bed at the time, wearing a borrowed brown dress, in her hand a needle and thread as she fixed the badly mended shawl. Minnie sat at the table, basting hems. Forgers and fences and pimps are liars; thieves and prostitutes steal. She had already proven what kind she was when she snuck into her sister's room, taking her earrings to sell for a boat ticket, and in her opinion, liars were smarter.

She always remembered that when the Squire knocked her off her feet with his walking stick, she felt gravel digging into her cheek as she watched Lizzie standing under the station clock, her head turned away and water dripping from her hat, so wasn't it strange that she could never remember exactly how the dress itself looked? She'd dream it was red and then that it was green, that the sleeves were wide or narrow, that the skirt had five flounces or that it was plain in front with a short train hanging from the bustle.

After Gittel asked for a dress for the guy, Nehama looked at what she'd made and was sure that it was a copy of the very one she couldn't remember before, and Heaven would forgive her as soon as it was burned on the fire. Only now it seemed that the gown was a sign that her sin was to be passed on to her daughter.

Nehama would, like the woman that came before King Solomon the Wise, gladly have given up her daughter rather than see her split in two on Dorset Street.

Under a striped awning, someone called, "Wax figures! See the Ripper's victims! Only a penny! Come in, guv. You never seen nothing so fine in the British Museum." A gentleman was inspecting the wax woman laid out on a plank under the awning, her internal organs artfully shaped and colored, a pamphlet (only tuppence) with diagrams of the mutilations proving the accuracy of the model, and further wonders just inside the door. Across the road, someone was waiting under a sign swinging precariously from one bolt.

Of course Nehama knew it was a ghost. Anyone who used her eyes could see that. A cow isn't the same as meat on the table, nor a ghost a human being. A kosher cow—there was no question of that face, but why should it be standing in Dorset Street staring at her?

"I'm looking for my daughter," Nehama said, catching her breath. "For you, I don't have time unless you're here to tell me where she is."

"Who are you talking to?" Nathan asked.

"A ghost from the *heim*. You see her earrings—just what my father's customers wore to *shul* on *Shobbos*."

"No, I don't see anything but the Horn and Plenty." Nathan followed her gaze.

"Excuse me," Nehama said, pushing past, but the ghost wouldn't let her by. There was a hand on her arm, and although most people will tell you that a ghost is transparent and one can merely walk through, Nehama was stuck.

Nathan was whistling her grandmother's lullaby, looking curiously from Nehama to the space where the ghost stood. That was the power of a ghost, to make people stop in their tracks and forget why they were there.

"What do you want from me?" Nehama asked.

"I know what's going on. Your grandmother told me. All she cares for is your well-being."

"Then let me go, already." If she stood in one spot much longer, someone would knock her down to steal her boots, and while she was lying there like a corpse, her daughter would be alone among the vultures.

"She didn't deserve what you said."

"It's none of your business." In the street, children with bruised faces were throwing stones against a wall. "I have a daughter, my only child. I have to get her."

"And what about the next time she goes looking for something? You'd better listen to me." The door to the Horn and Plenty swung open and closed on the sound of an accordion. The wind was rising. "A child in the court of King Solomon has questions to ask. Who will tell her how to find an answer if not you?"

"You mean my Gittel." The wind was calling.

"It isn't easy to have two mothers."

"I had six—my mother and all my sisters."

"At least you knew them." The wind pulled at their shawls in the darkness.

"But not my grandmother, and she started everything."

"Just so." The wind pushed the sign back and forth, swinging on one bolt. "What's she to think? That you're like my sons, who don't remember me? I'm telling you, it's as if someone never lived at all. God in heaven, how can we bear it?"

"Just let me go, I'm begging you." Nehama felt the grip on her arm loosen. "You can tell her I'm sorry. Tell her it's all right. I know about the baby."

There was only the door. And the wind opening it.

The Horn and Plenty

"Give us a little song, then," the Squire said, puffing on a fourpenny cigar. His face hung in fat pouches, like that of a rich man's dog. Behind his head was a poster of Lottie Collins kicking up her heels, "Ta-Ra-Ra-Boom-De-Ay" printed across the petticoat.

Gittel stood on his table. The air was heavy with beer and smoke, yellow as fog. On the Squire's left was the man with the accordion, on his right a onetime soldier whose bare arms were tattooed. Gittel's eyes darted from her boots to the arms. Jews didn't have tattoos. The table shook as someone stumbled against it on his way to the front for another pot. The accordion squealed. She crossed her arms over her chest.

"Never mind the row. I'm listening." The Squire nodded encouragingly.

The table was sticky and her feet itched. If she were at home, Mama would take off her shoes and socks to rub her feet with a piece of cotton as if she were polishing shoes and making them shiny and lovely.

"Sing 'Hearts of Oak.' I heard you do that one," Mrs. Dawes urged.

Gittel had sung it in the spring concert, but she was all done with concerts now, wasn't she? Her mouth clamped shut as if she was afraid of swallowing the rancid smoke from the Squire's cigar.

A man with a fresh scar on his cheek held out a pot of ale. "Pretty chavy. Come and have a tiddley." As he put the rim of the cup to her lips, she took a sip. The foam was so nice, she was startled by the bitterness, and he laughed as she spat into his hand. The beer on his fingers smelled like old hay in a privy.

She looked down at her boots, black and stiff and heavy like every girl's, the toes scuffed, the laces frayed, and next to her boots the Squire's knitting wool trailing silver. A famous singer would have soft slippers that would make no sound as she walked onstage during the overture. She'd sing in a voice without fear that carried to the cheapest seats at the top of the gallery, through the roof and to the moon. And while she sang, it wouldn't matter who was listening.

"You're having us on, Mrs. Dawes," the scarred man said. "This girl's a mute as sure as I'm alive. Look at them pleading eyes. Here you are, dearie." He gave her a penny and another sip of ale. Something brown floated in the glass. If only her stomach would stop tipping bile into her throat she might be able to sing on her own, but she was afraid she'd throw up in a minute.

"Give us a song," Mrs. Dawes said in a low voice, pinching Gittel's arm.

The Squire smelled of cod-liver oil and mustard plasters, an old man odor, a sick man smell, and his hand on her leg made her feel cold. Gittel would pray for nothing, now, let anyone have the guy in his dress to burn if only she were home.

"Stow kidding, Granny. You had your joke. So off you goes," the Squire said, patting Gittel's knee under the hem of her dress. She shuffled her itchy feet.

Mrs. Dawes leaned her head close to Gittel's. "Throwing away money like dirt in the street," she whispered, "is for them as has it. Open your mouth, my girl."

Gittel stared at the door marked PRIVAT. Whoever painted that door didn't know how to spell. Keeping her eyes on the uneven black letters, she clasped her hands behind her back as if for recitation. This was her theater and the sticky table, her stage. She took a deep breath so she could sing loud enough to cover the sound of Libby crying. Her eyes on the door she was facing, Gittel imagined the *e* that she would add to the end of the word *Private* as she began to sing in a quavering voice:

> Of friendship I have heard much talk
> But you'll find that in the end,
> If you're distressed at any time,
> Then money is your friend.

The Squire tapped the table in time to the beat of Gittel's heart, smiling as he reached into his pocket to put a half crown into Mrs. Dawes's cup. Coppers were landing on the table or on the floor, Jinny gathering them up while Mrs. Dawes carried her cup around the pub. Gittel held out her dress like a bowl, and coins fell into it.

If you are sick and like to die,
And for the doctor send,
To him you must advance a fee,
Then money is your friend.

In and around the odor of wet beer and the scent of dried sweat, Gittel could smell linden trees in bloom, rosebushes and a fast-flowing stream. As the Guy Fawkes parade wound its way through Whitechapel, the worlds were very close. As it is written, blessed is God, life of all the worlds.

Whitechapel Road

On the day that Emilia had run away from the East End, there was fog and cold and darkness. It was still night though the sun would rise in an hour. She'd walked down to Whitechapel Road in her cloak and a shawl over it, one of the ubiquitous red shawls that Jewish women wore in the East End, so that she didn't look out of place, a woman hurrying in the darkness, perhaps to a pawnshop. And that was where she'd gone. To Shmolnik's pawnshop. There she'd begged him to take her books and give her some money for them. This he'd done, and the money had hired her a hansom cab to Soho, paying her rent until her milk dried up. She hadn't even known that her breasts were leaking milk but imagined that the rain was soaking her to the skin. She'd walked in her stocking feet, forgetting to wear boots, and when she arrived at the pawnshop, her stockings were in shreds, her feet stinking of muck. She went to Soho, newspapers tied around her feet with string.

This time she rode in a carriage much finer than a hansom cab, having four wheels and two horses. Everything was the same and different, the carriage slowed by the changeless ragged crowd, the posters pasted to walls still promoting the latest Yiddish melodrama but in lurid colors, the street-drawn bus painted with advertisements for Nestlé's milk and Cameo cigarettes. Beside her sat the ghost of the old woman, Zaydeh opposite. He was dozing, the new plaid cap over his eyes, his head down on his chest, breathing slowly while the carriage inched forward. The street was jammed with carts and carriages and walkers on foot shouting and singing, children running, girls with long braids flicking in and out of the fog, and one of them could be her daughter.

"Is it so terrible to hear your husband give a speech?" the old woman asked.

"No, it's quite painless," Emilia said, feeling her will separate from her like a soul that slips away into the irretrievable darkness.

"I have something here." The old woman looked at Emilia, her eyes full of suggestion. The next world delights in leaving hints. Emilia shrugged. "It's yours, no?" The old woman opened her hand. In it was the cameo brooch, but Emilia didn't reach for it. She wasn't sure what she might touch if she reached for the hand of a strange ghost.

"That's my mother's. Where did you find it?"

"In a room over there." The old woman gestured up the Lane. "You know how it is. Everything is sold down from street to street until it ends up in the river and then it comes back up again. It's a fine cameo."

"You keep it. Or sell it. Whatever you like."

"Are you sure? It's very nice to wear on *Shobbos*." The ghost held the cameo against the green-and-gold bib above her apron. Perhaps it was only the ghost of a cameo.

"It's from Paris."

"You don't say." The old woman looked at her with feigned astonishment. "I thought it came from Minsk."

Zaydeh snored. But it didn't matter if he was awake or asleep. It was all the same to her now. "My mother told me about it just once. The trunk was packed and we were sitting on the steps of our house. She began with the story I heard a hundred times."

The old woman was nodding as if she'd heard it, too, and even in the next world, where stories are repeated from the days of creation, they said enough is enough.

"I didn't need to hear it again. How all was well until her first husband died. He was a miller, and during the Polish rebellion he provided boots and coats; my mother and the baker's wife carried the stuff to the rebels hiding in the woods. But this time she told me that one of the Polish officers fell in love with her. After he escaped, he sent her the cameo from Paris. It was outrageous, a gentile officer, a member of the gentry, falling in love with a Jewish wife."

"Still, a gift isn't a sin. Your mother would want you to have it."

Emilia shook her head. Didn't they know anything in the next world? "He found her again in Minsk a few years after she remarried. I was about three then. She was very angry with my father because he made her leave her son from her first marriage behind though he expected her to look after his two from his first wife. You met her."

"Mrs. Rosenberg, you mean. Yes—we have some people in common."

The carriage slowed as the parade came down the Lane into Whitechapel Road. The tailor's guy teetered in the float, then straightened up as someone tightened the ropes. "I can remember him. It's my earliest memory, a visitor with a large blond mustache waxed shiny. You see, my mother had an affair with this officer. He wanted her to run away with him, but she wouldn't leave me behind. In after years she broke down inch by inch."

The old woman looked at the cameo, a profile of the goddess of youth feeding meat to the eagle Zeus. "Don't blame yourself."

"Why would I?" Emilia asked in a huff. After all, guilt, like grief, was no one else's business. "She told me about it when I got into trouble because she wanted me to know that we were alike. They say that the apple doesn't fall far from the tree, but a person isn't a piece of fruit. Right?"

The old woman smiled. The turban she wore was gold, and it shimmered as they passed through the light of a streetlamp. "Does a fruit have eyes to see? Of course someone might say that a person who can see the dead and not the living might as well be an apple."

"What's that supposed to mean?" Emilia asked. How like the dead. They wouldn't call a spoon a spoon, but an implement for carrying God's will between the worlds.

The ghost of the old woman looked out at the street as if watching for someone in the parade. Maybe one of the girls flirting with the young tailors. "I was a second wife, too. Just like your mother. When I got married, there was a baby."

"Yours?" The old woman still held the cameo in her half-closed fist.

"First she was someone else's, then she was mine. I loved my stepdaughter so much I nearly fainted, but she was sickly. After she grew up, she told her children that I saved her life. I nursed her, and my milk ran like cream—it was a miracle."

"How did you have any milk?"

"A good question. I'm telling you the miracle was that she held on to life until I got pregnant and had milk to give her. Then she got strong from it. But that isn't how she told the story. What she said was that if you love your baby, then milk runs like cream."

"You see? A person shouldn't listen to old stories." But the ghost of the old woman didn't take the hint and continued with no sense of tact at all.

"My youngest grandchild grew up and had a baby but no milk. From my story, she was filled with guilt and I've never forgiven myself."

Emilia crossed her arms. With grief one must be firm. "Jacob always says the teller of a story means one thing by it, the listener hears something else. It can't be helped."

"Not a stupid man, your husband." The old woman wiped her eyes. Someone might be surprised that the dead can cry, but aren't all tears those of the Shekhina, the divine presence weeping with us in our exile?

"Here," Emilia said, handing over her handkerchief. She'd swear that she heard the old woman blow her nose.

"A lot of girls in that crowd. I hope their mothers are watching out for them."

"Not likely." The street seemed to be filled with twelve-year-old girls in too-short coats, braids dampened by rain. "They're hard in these streets."

The old woman followed her gaze. "Do you think your daughter is one of those, pulling the cart with the guy in it?"

"I wouldn't know. If I thought she was that close, I couldn't bear it." Her daughter might be in Norwood, she might not. A person has to live with the things she doesn't know. "Listen. Put the cameo back where you took it. I have other jewelry."

"Then why are you so ready to sell it off as if you have nothing? Your mother sent you a postcard." The old woman took something from the pocket of her apron and pushed it into Emilia's hand. Then she opened the carriage door and stepped out. Zaydeh woke up as the door slammed shut.

Mine gitteh?" he asked, his eyes bleary and a little confused from sleep.

"I'm here," she said, leaning forward. "I'm here with you, Zaydeh."

His eyes cleared, and he kissed her cheek like a daughter's.

The band that followed the parade was playing "God Save the Queen," and the carriage began to move again. On the cacophony of instruments playing a beat behind and a beat in front, each with its own time signature, Emilia's will slipped back to her.

In the street the old woman took the cloth of gold from her head and threw it into the sky. There it drifted like feathers around the moon and the stars.

The Horn and Plenty

Tradition says that in the beginning there was only God. Then came the *tzim-tzum*. The Holy One withdrew to make space for creation, though it left Him lonely and it left us lonely, separated from each other. The feminine aspect of God didn't go, but stayed with us in our exile, and She, the divine presence among living beings, is called the Shekhina. She sings and cries and comforts us with her broken wing as she is also limited by the world of imperfect stuff. For instance, a faded sign swinging on one rusted bolt.

"Listen to me," Nehama said. "If there's any kind of trouble, let me talk."

"Better you should leave it to me. This isn't the Jewish Board of Guardians; no one's giving out crutches for Pious Pearl."

"I know what there is to be afraid of," she said.

He stopped to look at her. What he saw, she had no time to think about.

The door in the blind street opened, and whoever took a step passed through it into a warmth that hadn't changed in twenty-five years, though the long trestle tables were gone. Instead there were three-legged stools and round tables, and on the walls, between the posters of music hall stars, there were framed advertisements in red and silver, "Fine Old Glenlivet" and "Dunville's V & R Old Irish Whiskey." The map of London on the left wall was still behind cracked glass, and the men tossing an iron ring missed the hook as often as not. The talk among them was the same as it had always been.

"Got me a piece of iron bedstead. A hook for cutting and a thicker end for coshing. You want something like that. Cut old Neddy's ear right off, I did."

"It's the knack, not the gear, mate. Sent that bloke from the Old Nichol to the infirmary with naught but a bit of bottle. His scalp come right off."

Behind the counter stood the barman, jaw like a horse's, arms as thin and hard as iron rods, wearing a buttoned vest and rolled-up sleeves, a checked neckerchief knotted inside his collar. Just like the barmaid of twenty-five years ago, he filled glasses with a friendliness that could turn mean in an instant, and he kept order with a butcher's mallet.

"It's our little Jew," he called to Nathan. "You're getting an early start tonight. What'll it be, then?"

"A short drop of something," Nathan said, holding on to Nehama's arm with his one good hand. Near the counter stood women with their children, and among them was no one that Nehama could still recognize.

"Better learn English, mate." The barman laughed.

"Too bad I'm born a foreigner," Nathan said, "but I lives with the handicap, don't I?" and he winked as he took the glass in the crook of his right elbow, leaving the left hand free to put some coins on the counter and take Nehama's arm again.

He was pushing his way deftly between the men playing draughts and drinking at the round tables as if he was the one that knew this place instead of her. "Careful," he whispered in Yiddish. "One or two hands doesn't matter. A man that starts up something here ends his day in the infirmary, and if he's a Jew, then in the morgue."

"I know where I am, better than you think." She looked to left and right, scanning the tables. She couldn't see over the heads of men playing Ringing the Bull, but she knew what was there as surely as if she wore a crown of snakes that could see in the night. The darts flew back. Someone chanted, "Guy, guy, guy, Stick him up on high, Hang him on a lamppost, And leave him there to die."

"You hear, Nathan?"

"Tomorrow you'll forget everything," he said.

She shook her head. "Hell doesn't have an end."

"You're mistaken, Nehameleh. Hell, I know. Here it's much brighter, though I have to admit it stinks the same. Never mind. Just remember, where you go, I go."

The pub was long and narrow, the distance from front to back just as far as she remembered. The smoke was thicker than the fog outside, and in the very back of the pub, farthest from the entrance that blew open and closed, the smoke was thickest of all. The Squire's table was there in its place next to the door marked PRIVAT. She could hear a voice singing, and she was afraid. It sounded like Sally; soon she'd hear her own younger voice joining in.

The Squire had got old but even dead would not be old enough; her heart beat just as hard as if he could still stand her in front of a mirror. Beside him stood a shaggy man with an accordion, and on the other side a man wearing a soldier's cap was drinking ale at his table. The Squire had a fourpenny cigar stuck in his mouth; in his hands flashed knitting needles trailing silver wool across the table. The flaming gas jets burned while she saw Minnie's daughter huddled against the back door, and standing on the table her own daughter singing:

> My cap is froze unto my head
> My heart is like a lump of lead
> Oh let me in, the soldier cried
> It's a cold haily night of rain.

Gittel was truly hers, and hell was laughing as the Squire put down his knitting to stroke her leg. And if Nathan weren't there to say "Careful!" in her ear and hold on to her arm, Nehama would have thrown herself at the Squire, who was not a hasty man but conducted beatings with a thoroughness that was occasionally overzealous.

She looked up at Gittel. Her girl looked down, a wobbly smile on her face as their eyes met. She was holding the hem of her skirt to make a bowl for the coins. Her neck was as red as if it had been painted. How it must itch.

Clapping her hands to keep them from shaking, Nehama began to sing, too.

> Your dad and mum are fast asleep,
> Which makes me under your window creep,

The doors and windows they do creak.
    I dare not let you in, oh.
Oh let me in, the soldier cried,
And blest the cold night of rain.

She needed to get closer to her daughter, even if it meant that she pushed past the man with the tattooed arms and the tattered uniform and stood next to the Squire, his shoulder brushing her hips. His mouth was old and fallen in, his forehead marked with liver spots. She remembered the smell of the grease he'd used to keep his lips and hands from getting chapped, and it made her as sick as if she could smell it now.

"Give us another song," the Squire said. His face was old, but in his boot he would have a knife.

Nehama reached her arms up to catch Gittel by the waist and swing her down. Money clattered to the ground.

"Mama—you let the coins fall! I'm not finished."

"You have school tomorrow," Nehama said, as if calling Gittel in from jumping rope in the alley. "You had your fun. Now it's home with you and not any cheek."

"Wait," the Squire said, putting his hand on Nehama's arm. "I know you."

"And me, sir." Nathan put his glass of gin in front of the Squire. "You know me. I sell coffee, though I'm sure you have no want of that, do you? This is my wife," he said, maneuvering himself between Nehama and the Squire. "No doubt you seen her with me. A seamstress, she is. Done nothing but sew since she were two. Maybe your friend here could stand to have his uniform repaired. Anytime, sir. Anytime."

Gittel was picking up the coins. Nehama took the money from her and laid it on the table. "Stand you a pot, mister, for putting up with my naughty girl." Her voice was choked; she'd have liked to shove his knitting needles through his throat.

"Get me a drop of Glenlivet," the Squire said to the man dressed like a soldier. "It's a windy night. I want something warm." The accordionist struck up. What he played made the Squire grimace, for he was drunk enough to hear the dead that were singing.

A person can lose her sense of smell when the force of her life asserts itself against the evil strangling it, and the strength of her life can be such that it draws out even the voice of the dead. Nehama could hear her grandmother singing; if she looked back she'd have seen her wearing a cameo brooch, but Nehama didn't turn around. Instead she held her daughter's hand, humming as her grandmother sang:

> The house is in shadow, the street is in gloom,
> Wild burns the fire with a crackling song
> In the wind, the wind, the fervent wind
> It can't be seen, yet it can be known.

Nehama pushed her daughter before her through the crowd. And though her shoulders twitched, expecting a hand to pull her back any minute, she didn't look to see what had happened to the guy in its fancy dress. If she did, she might turn to salt like Lot's wife, who looked back at Sodom burning with God's wrath.

"What about the guy, Mama? I need it for the bonfire."

"From you, not a word or you won't sit for a week," Nehama said in a low voice. Lot's wife had daughters too. They were sacrificed to protect the lives of strangers. A mother that saw that wouldn't mind becoming salt. But Nehama, she was black pepper.

The Jews' Free School

The windows of the Great Hall were filled with leaded lights and, above the platform, stained glass bore the arms of Lord Rothschild, who had provided funds for the new wing. It fronted on Petticoat Lane, and the speakers had to shout above the noise of horses clomping and wheels grinding on the wooden paving outside while the one-man band made his own Guy Fawkes concert with drum, cymbals, and harmonica. There had been a tour of the new wing, with its scientific laboratory and drill hall, the ladies nodding in approval while they held scented handkerchiefs to block the smell of chickens from the slaughterhouse, which generously shared well-fed flies with the school. One of them buzzed around the portrait of Mr. Angel, set on an easel to the left of the podium.

During the tribute this evening, the portrait would be presented to

the school by Mr. Abraham, who had painted Mr. Angel as Moses carrying the Ten Commandments on Mount Sinai. One of the trustees had
thought it irreverent, and there'd been talk of his withdrawing his
financial support. Much discussion had ensued among the Bloomsbury
artists, but in the end Harriet had persuaded her husband that integrity
and money might be reconciled, and so he'd painted the trustee's face onto
the figure of Aaron, the brother of Moses. The painting was then titled
In Each Generation, and the trustees unanimously agreed that nothing
could be more fitting. The trustees, the new headmaster, and the speaking guests sat in a row on the other side of the podium. The men wore
tailcoats, the headmistress of the girls' department a high-necked gown.
Jacob's pocket bulged where he'd stuck his pipe.

He was at the podium, his eyes on Emilia in the front row between
Harriet and Mrs. Zalkind. "Ladies and Gentlemen, I have little to offer
in comparison with my friend's painting," he began, "but I hope that
you will humor me with your attention for a few minutes and that,
despite the unimpressiveness of my speech, you will honor the memory
of Mr. Angel with a generous contribution to the school later this
evening."

The trustees clapped, the audience following their lead while Mrs.
Zalkind nodded with pride. Emilia kept her mind on the smell of fresh
wood from the ceiling made of varnished Oregon pine, and disre-
garded the other odors that floated through the Great Hall. Her
mother's postcard was tucked between the pages of her program.

"Mr. Angel had two fathers, but I intend to speak of my two mothers. I'm not referring here to my father's wife, though she is certainly
worthy of any number of accolades and speeches, as my brother and I
could not hope for a better mother. But I mean my two mother
tongues. English and Yiddish."

One of the trustees raised his eyebrows and glanced sideways at the
younger Rothschild brother, who abhorred Yiddish. This was not a
good choice of subject. English Jews were edgy, sitting as they did on a
spiked fence between their Englishness and their Jewishness, wanting
to prove one and too often reminded of the other, whether by their
own hearts or by the distrust of the English-English. So they sat on the
fence and pretended it was an upholstered armchair, never minding
that such furniture might be made in Soho by foreigners.

Jacob was looking at Emilia, who sat uncomfortably on her own spiked fence. She was still his wife and always liked to be good at what she did. She wouldn't think of the school, the street where it abided, the vendor outside the door calling, "Herring! Schmaltz herring!" She was making her face full of encouragement and attention. But Jacob didn't smile.

"Mr. Angel of blessed memory sought to drive Poland from his students and to make them English through and through. Many of you might count me one of his successes, but I am here to tell you that I am one of his failures." The new headmaster coughed. "Where else than here, among you, my friends, should I confess that, despite my entire loyalty to this, the country of my birth and my grandfather's refuge, I sometimes have un-English yearnings?"

There was an uneasy shifting in the audience. Harriet was whispering that she was afraid Jacob's speech would diminish the funds obtained for the school, and Mrs. Zalkind was protesting that she had no un-English feelings whatsoever.

"A man may believe himself to be one thing, but in the course of life he will realize that he is two or even three or more, and the confusing jangle will not be separated into convenient pieces, some to bury and others to place on view. He can only hope that those he holds in esteem and affection will not be repelled. The truth is that I do weep," Jacob said, his eyes searching hers. "My heart might just as well be the old Yiddish theater, and it's no use in panicking, for if it is closed down, it will only rise up with a larger need to express itself."

Emilia took her mother's postcard out of the program. The illustration was a print of a theater bill. "Hannah's Prayer," it said in Yiddish, "A New Drama." She fanned herself with the postcard, not knowing what Jacob would see in her eyes, knowing only that she was looking back at him.

"I'm telling you now," he said quietly, as if he were talking just to her. "Speak up!" the last row called out. "I'm telling you," he repeated louder, "that out of this cacophony of feeling, this jargon of ideas, a man may find new thoughts rising up in great profusion. As it is written"—he paused, managing a grin for his grandfather, who was wide awake under his fine new plaid cap— "'The Lord hath put a new song into my mouth' and 'Let them be ashamed and abashed that seek after my soul to sweep it away.' And 'Let them be appalled by reason of their shame that say unto me: aha, aha.'"

The new headmaster rose to his feet, leading the audience in applause as he strode to the podium though Jacob shook his head, his speech not yet finished. But they all clapped loudly in gladness that their discomfort was brought to an end, and the next speaker had many well-known vignettes, both humorous and poignant, to tell of Mr. Angel's life. Jacob left his chair empty on the platform and went down into the audience, where everyone seemed to prefer him.

His mother moved over to make room for him next to Emilia. "It was an interesting speech," Emilia whispered. "I'd have liked to hear the end of it."

"You're certain?" he asked.

"Oh, yes. I'd like to know if a person seems to be one thing and then turns out to be rather more, whether you think such a person ought to be forgiven."

"There could be no doubt in my mind," Jacob said, as if he imagined that the person in question were himself. "What are you holding?"

"Look. It's a postcard from Minsk."

"Oh yes. From your Mrs. Plater." He smiled at the Jewishness of gentile servants known to keep kosher and teach the children of the family Hebrew blessings and even, in this case, send postcards to a foreign land with pictures from the Yiddish theater.

"Hannah invented prayer," Emilia whispered, applauding with the rest of the audience as the more satisfactory speaker took his seat. "She was so sure that she was right, she challenged God."

"Who told you that?" Jacob asked.

"Shh. They're introducing another speaker." Emilia put the postcard back in her program.

Hannah was one of two wives. The other wife had many children and teased Hannah till she wept because she had none. She prayed for a son and she had a son, but in her bargaining with God, she had promised to bring the baby to the temple after he was weaned; there he'd be brought up to become a priest. So her son went to the temple, grew up to be the prophet Samuel, who crowned the king of Israel. The only thing that would keep a mother's heart from breaking would be to forget her baby, Emilia thought, but every year when Hannah's family came to the temple with their sacrifice, she would bring a little robe that she'd made for her firstborn. She had five more children after Samuel, three sons and two daughters, and Emilia wondered how she could attend to them with a heart that was breaking over and over while she sewed.

It was written that Hannah's prayer was furious. She hurled words at God, threatening to feign adultery so that she would undergo the ordeal of waters, after which, as the Bible promised, she would be cleansed and conceive. So it was written in the Talmud, Emilia's mother had said while they sat at the kitchen table.

It was very strange that a text written by men could so describe the fury of a woman's prayers. And even though she didn't have the righteousness of Hannah, Emilia threw one of her own at heaven.

Bell Lane

Just up the street was the blacksmith's forge, and people in masks were jostling each other as the remnant of the parade wound down toward the school. In the middle of the lane, someone in a long gray cloak and a crown of cut tin was lighting a bunch of firecrackers. There were bells ringing and shouts of "Hang him up high" and "Remember, remember," but there was no cart rattling behind Gittel with a guy in a three-colored dress. Sparks flew over the Jews' Free School, and she had nothing to throw into the bonfire.

"I want my guy," Gittel said.

"Be happy that you still have a behind to warm in front of the fire," her mother answered.

Gittel walked quickly, keeping step with her. "I had a quid of coppers in my dress."

"Consider it charity," Mama snapped.

"I was taught that a person should always give charity at the end of a journey. It's a good custom," Papa said. He was walking behind them, holding on to Libby.

Gittel glanced back at him suspiciously. He was whistling something from *Angel of the Ghetto*. Everyone knew the song. Her teacher even had the girls sing it in school. It was about Jewish mothers. There were too many songs about Jewish mothers. Papa ought to whistle something from *The Witch,* featuring an orphan and a wicked step-mother who had a grip just like Mama's.

"I'm telling you before God," Mama said, "that if you ever do something like this again, I will make you sorry you were born."

"I'm already sorry," Gittel muttered. It was all for nothing. The guy lost, the sickness in her stomach, the punishment sure to be waiting for her. "Good money, I made. It wasn't yours to throw away."

"And you think you could just walk out of the pub, your pockets full of coins, and no one would bother you?"

Mama was looking at her like she was an idiot. But she wasn't. And she didn't care who knew it. "You don't understand," she said, the words bursting out of her. "You don't understand, Mama. I can't sing in the school concert. Miss Halpern kicked me out of the choir. She called me a liar. It's because of my mother, isn't it? She lives in Dorset Street and I must be just like her. But I made up for it. I was going to bring home money so that Papa didn't have to work at night and get coshed."

"Oh God." Mama covered her mouth with her hand.

"But nothing's come of it now." Firecrackers split the sky with light, and in the street, the king in the crown of tin struck a match to light another string of them. "I couldn't sing in school but I sang there. I did it for Papa and you made nothing of it. So you can give me any punishment. It doesn't matter now."

"Gittel. My Gittel. I have to tell you something. Listen to me." Her mother's voice pierced the sound of firecrackers, the drums, the calls for jellied eels. "I knew a girl once that even stole something from her sisters because she wanted to run away from home. Her own sisters. I know you won't repeat a word I'm telling you," Mama said.

There was something different in her tone; it made Gittel pay as much attention as if she were overhearing Mama and Aunt Minnie whispering when they thought she was asleep. "All right," she said. "Go on."

"Well, I was the girl, the one that ran away from home with her sisters' things. You think someone should be punished? I got into terrible trouble."

It was hard to imagine, but it must have been true. Mama looked so shamefaced. And Gittel knew that this was her chance to find out things she'd only half heard in whispers, so she asked, "Why?"

"Why doesn't matter, only that I could have died. If it wasn't for Aunt Minnie, I wouldn't be here. I'm telling you, Gittel, I prayed that you wouldn't take after me. You deserve better. It's all I want in life."

Mama's voice was breaking and yet Gittel had to keep asking. Someone had to tell her at last, no matter what came after. "But what about *her*?"

Mama stopped in front of the wooden sign advertising Yiddish letters written home for a penny. She looked at the sign as if the answer were there. But still she was holding Gittel's hand. "You mean Mrs. Levy. Is it so important?" Mama paused, biting her lip. Then she nodded. "All right. I don't know where she is, exactly, except that she went to the West End. One thing I can promise you, not Dorset Street."

"Are you sure?" Gittel asked. So it wasn't there she belonged, it really wasn't at all, but then she could belong anywhere, and London was so very big, though just a few feet away *Tatteh* was waiting for them, the double row of buttons on his jacket catching the light as four big men rolled barrels of fire toward the school yard.

"Of course I'm sure," Mama said. "If she lived five blocks over, do you think she could keep herself from coming to have a look at you?"

Next to the wooden sign, a woman was selling treacle cakes. She wore a black hat and plush jacket, and though her boots were down-at-heel, her golden earrings flickered in the torchlight. And maybe she was someone's mother, too. "Not for me," Gittel said. "I cried so dreadful much, and I was ugly."

"What are you talking?" Mama asked as if it was the most absurd thing she'd ever heard. "You think I wouldn't come to find you, my Gittel-Sarah? If someone tried to hurt you, I would kill him. I would lie down in the gutter and let anyone walk on my back to keep you safe, my daughter. Even from the next world, you can't lose me. I promise you."

Mama's hand was tight in hers as if she really would never let go, and Gittel knew that she would have to be the one to pull herself away someday, but not yet, and so she glanced at her scuffed boots and then at Mama, and she asked, though Mama was sad, because she couldn't help herself, "Did she look like me, Mama?" It was a terrible question, but wasn't this a night of such questions?

"No, she was fair," Mama said as if they were talking about anything at all. "Maybe you take after him, Mr. Levy, or someone else in the family. This is just between us. Your *tatteh* shouldn't hear you and feel bad."

So there were two fathers—of course, though she'd never thought of it—and two mothers and at least six aunts and many grandmothers that she'd never meet, but the air smelled of fried fish, it was the smell of home. "I sang, Mama. I sang in front of everyone." She searched her mother's eyes for a hint of pride.

"I heard," Mama said, kissing the top of her head, and that was almost enough. She could imagine herself singing onstage, her parents in the front row with Aunt Minnie and Uncle Lazar and Libby and Sammy, the audience clapping like thunder. Above in the box seat, the velvet curtain was drawn and someone was sitting there. Maybe more than one person, listening behind the curtain.

Tatteh was still whistling the song from *Angel of the Ghetto*:

> *A thousand years I floated*
> *Between here and there*
> *And she comes with me everywhere,*
> *When the wind tears the roof from my house*
> *I hear my mother's speech.*

Gittel held on to Mama's hand, her cheeks wet from night and fog. Such moments between mothers and daughters are over quickly. Aunt Minnie was running down the street, calling them. And that was how it would always be in eternity, for those in the next world remember everything for us.

Frying Pan Alley

As the crowd threw the eight-foot guy with the glittering chains down from the float, the pillar of fire opened to meet it, the heat driving back autumn. All along the alley it was a summer night, women pushing shawls down to their shoulders, men taking off caps to wipe their faces. The tailor's guy in his seven-league boots was lowered with ropes. His spear of a needle made from wood and painted silver was flung on top. On the sea wind, sparks rose up to heaven, where for a moment, at the touch of His creation, God might not be lonely.

The girls watched, leaning against the school fence, Minnie between them, her red hair hanging loose on her red shawl, everything made of fire tonight. Nehama was standing between the barrels of smoked salmon, her back to the slippery brick wall as she talked with Nathan, the streetlamp beating feebly at the fog.

Her husband had seen her singing in the Horn and Plenty as if it were the most natural place for her to be. Does such a person know from *Shobbos*? Does such a person know from making love in the afternoon? No, she's a nightwalker. A person who buys coffee, someone whose children run away from her womb.

"Gittel went to Dorset Street because she thought Mrs. Levy was there," she said.

"What—did she want to find her there?" Nathan stood close to her, speaking into her ear so she could hear him above the roaring fire.

"I don't know. She had the idea that Mrs. Levy was no good and somehow Gittel would make up for it." She rubbed her hands as if she were cold, though the fire made the street like summer.

"*Gotteniu*. We have to talk to her. Explain to her that she can be anything she wants. Isn't she your daughter?"

"Let her be better than me." Nehama shivered. Was her shawl made of such a thin wool? "I'm not what I want."

"You think I am? 'One-Hand Nathan'—it doesn't have a good ring." He took her hand in his as if he wasn't afraid to touch her. But he didn't know, he couldn't know, and she was unable to stand the pressure of his hand.

"How can I let you go there another night, Nathan? It's killing me. A shop isn't worth it. Believe me, I know. I was in Dorset Street before."

"I could tell." He didn't let go of her hand, though she tried to pull away.

"It's where I got the scar. It always reminds me."

"Then it's going to remind me, too. How lucky we are that you knew what to do."

"Luck isn't exactly what I'd call it."

"Mmm. Not for you, I'm saying, only for me and Gittel."

"That's what you think?"

"It's exactly what I think. Who knows what counts? Only God in heaven. Maybe that's why I sell coffee in Dorset Street. To go with my wife one night."

"Listen to me, Nathan. I'm trying to tell you, but it isn't easy. You don't know . . ."

The crowd was cheering as the tailor's guy broke apart in the bonfire. The brightness of the fire made the darkness even darker. There were teachers and students and neighbors standing around the bonfire, some wearing masks and others the night. No one could tell who they really were.

"What's to know? I see you, Nehameleh, and I'm here with you. God in heaven should only have my luck." But she pulled her hand out of his.

"I want too much. From that comes every mistake I made." The *yetzer-hara,* the evil inclination, had given her desires stronger than a fire. When she was young, she'd wished for a house as big as the moon, and a child for every room where she lay with her husband, for every sigh of pleasure a book bound in fine leather, and on the wall a plaque commemorating her great deeds.

"And every good thing, too," Nathan said. He rubbed the back of her neck where it always knotted. He'd learned to do it just as well with his left hand. She couldn't help but sigh with pleasure.

So let the good inclination use her desire to get a shop with used books and cheap blouses, a room above, where she would lie with Nathan on the Sabbath, and there would be no great deeds, only necessary ones. Sparks flew over the fence and hissed on the damp cobblestones. She lifted her gaze to him, his eyes darker than darkness.

"We were married on Guy Fawkes Day," he said. "You remember the firecrackers?"

"God forbid I should forget," she said.

They stood together, both of them bearing scars, and they saw what they saw while the night clothed them in dignity. For the time being, the children were safe, and in the darkness the fire was blooming as the tears of the grandmothers fell on the souls of those who could hear their weeping.

On the other side of the fence, Emilia stood with Jacob, watching the effigies burn. They'd come outside with the rest of the audience to join the many people masked and cloaked, defying darkness with flashes of fire. The air was hot and smelled of smoked fish as Emilia held on to Jacob's arm, her bracelet glinting in the firelight.

"Do you remember my cameo, Jacob? I was wearing it when you introduced me to your parents."

"Yes, of course. I was looking for the gold cross you always wore." He patted his pockets for matches and tobacco. "Whatever happened to it?"

"Your freckles stood out against your cheeks, you were so pale." Someone walked by carrying a torch. In the fire the tailor's guy was melting into remnants of straw and cloth.

"I was rather nervous. I'd have been much more nervous if I'd thought that someday I might look under my wife's bed to find a slipper and instead see a train schedule." Jacob fumbled with his pipe, dropping his tobacco first and then his match. He shrugged and put the pipe back in his pocket. "Are you leaving me?"

His face was just a shape in the darkness. His hands, if he would take hers in them, would have the familiar warmth of a favorite pair of gloves. "Sometimes you act like you might prefer it," she said, pulling away.

"Because you're offended by Jews? You and a few million other Londoners. I was naïve to think any different, but just the same I don't see how I can do without you."

"There's a lot you don't see." She looked at him with such dangerous sincerity that he went after his pipe, ready to give it another go so that he could do something he was sure of. "I want to tell you about the cameo," she said.

"You're thinking about leaving me and you want to talk about some old piece of jewelry?" he asked. "There's only one explanation. You murdered someone for it. Ah, you should have told me before. I'd have made notes and written a play about it instead of the ghetto story and not upset you." He held his pipe as steadily as he could, cupping the match in the wind.

"I'm serious. Then you'll see what I mean. It's about the woman that gave me the cameo." Emilia looked over the fence. If her daughter was there among the East End Jews, she wouldn't know her name or her face, and if she met her, she'd be dismayed by the unsavory odor, the bad teeth, the Cockney accent overlaid by the school's grammar teachers. "This woman I'm telling you about. She came from a Jewish village in Poland. A *shtetl*."

"Is that right?" Jacob asked, looking at her sharply. Newspapers blew over the fence and into the dying fire, feeding the last few sparks. He would be angry, and whether he'd ever stop being angry and how long it would take she couldn't guess, but if she threw herself again into the sea of streets, she might lose another child. Someone was calling "Fried fish!" The smell mingled with the smell of Jacob's pipe tobacco, and she didn't faint because the memory of her daughter demanded something else. So instead she would tell a story.

"This woman used to say to me, It's better to open a door yourself than have it smashed open. What use is a broken door afterward? She knew what she was talking about. At one time she was strong enough and clever enough to play the piano for the Russian officers who had blown up her husband's mill . . ."

Her hands were bare. She hadn't thought to put on gloves and her hands were cold though at home she had a dozen pairs.

"That was my mother," Emilia continued. She wasn't going to sell off her life as if she had nothing.

On this side of the fence, the ghost of the first wife nodded.

In the alley among the women with red shawls, and in the school yard among the last few revelers who watched the crackling fire kiss the night, the grandmothers walked back and forth. It was for this that they had risen up from their graveyards in Minsk or Pinsk or London, to be with their children in the night, in the wind that rages, in the fog swept in from the sea, and in the singing fire. If you listen to them speak, then you hear the voice of Her, the presence of God, who is with us in our exile.

In the darkness of the alley they stood, the two mothers, facing each other in the smoke of night, their prayers rising through the sliver of sky between rooftops. As it is written: The sins of the parents last unto the third or fourth generation, but the merit of those who love will go on to the thousandth.

Amen. Selah.

ACKNOWLEDGMENTS

I want to thank Alexis Gargagliano, my editor at Scribner, for her perspicacity, her adroit and delicate suggestions, her enthusiasm. I would also like to thank Susan Moldow, the publisher of Scribner, for her ongoing interest in my work, and Louise Dennys, the publisher of Knopf Canada, for her confidence in me. I am grateful to my wonderful agent, Helen Heller, for her feedback while the manuscript was in its early drafts; her honesty and insight were invaluable. My thanks also go to my two amazing daughters, who came along during the writing of this book, thus irrevocably changing both me and the story I wrote. Many other people have generously supported my work, and I want all of them to know how much I appreciate it. Finally, and most of all, I want to thank my husband, Allan, who cheered me on through every draft.

About the Author

Lilian Nattel is the author of *The River Midnight,* which was published to international acclaim and won the Martin and Beatrice Fischer Jewish Book Award. She lives in Toronto with her husband and two daughters.